Praise for Scottsboro

'Ellen Feldman has shaped the 1931 trial into a taut, haunting legal thriller . . . *Scottsboro* is a pleasure to read, even if the history makes one wince. Impressively, Feldman has cast a non-fiction story that dragged on for years as a suspenseful page-turner. Those who don't recall the resolution of these notorious cases are fortunate. If you want to know what happened to the Scottsboro boys, read the book'

Lionel Shriver, *Daily Telegraph*

'An astute history . . . clear-sighted . . . There were real innocents: African American young men who lost years of their lives, their health and hope. It is for them, and the bitter lessons they taught everyone who touched the case, that Feldman's book has been written and should be read'

Independent

'A riveting drama . . . inspired and inspiring . . . Ruby is a gem of a character, and belongs with the best of William Faulkner's, or Alice Walker's, women'

San Francisco Chronicle

'Feldman re-animates the drama in a novel that is based on archival records, court records, and first-person accounts but that succeeds overwhelmingly as a work of imagination . . . distilled with great subtlety and wit, into a story worth retelling and remembering'

Boston Globe

'A keen sense of drama . . . What emerges is a raw sense of alienation and collision'

Publishers' Weekly

'A page-turner . . . Feldman has a talent for reimagining history [and] methodic[illegible] erritory of the Jim [illegible]

Book List

SCOTTSBORO

Ellen Feldman is the author of five novels,
including *Scottsboro*, which was shortlisted for the
Orange Prize for Fiction, and most recently *The Unwitting*.
She lives in New York City with her husband.

Also by Ellen Feldman

The Unwitting

Next to Love

The Boy Who Loved Anne Frank

Lucy

ELLEN FELDMAN

SCOTTSBORO

With an introduction by Jayne Anne Phillips

PICADOR CLASSIC

First published 2008 by W. W. Norton & Company, New York

First published in Great Britain 2008 by Picador

First published in paperback 2008 by Picador

This Picador Classic edition first published 2015 by Picador
an imprint of Pan Macmillan, a division of Macmillan Publishers Limited
Pan Macmillan, 20 New Wharf Road, London N1 9RR
Basingstoke and Oxford
Associated companies throughout the world
www.panmacmillan.com

ISBN 978-1-4472-7534-3

Interview with Hollace Ransdall by Mary Frederickson, November 6, 1974 (G-50), in the Southern Oral History Program Collection (#4007), Southern Historical Collection, Wilson Library, University of North Carolina at Chapel Hill. Reprinted with premission.

1 3 5 7 9 8 6 4 2

A CIP catalogue record for this book is available from the British Library.

Printed and bound by CPI Group (UK) Ltd, Croydon, CR0 4YY

Introduction

Ruby Bates . . . told me she had been driven into prostitution when she was thirteen . . . working in a textile mill for a pittance. When she asked for a raise, the boss told her to make it up by going with the workers . . . Here was an illiterate white girl, all of whose training had been clouded by the myths of white supremacy, who, in the struggle for the lives of these nine innocent boys, had come to see the role she was being forced to play. As a murderer. She turned against her oppressors . . . I shall never forget her.

— Studs Terkel, *Hard Times: An Oral History of the Great Depression*

On History's Train

Novels based on history are a special form of imaginative transformation. History gives us the facts, but literature often tells us the story. Human beings are creatures of narrative; we connect across the chasm of time, class, race, and gender through the imperatives of empathy. The "voice" of the successful novel or fictional character tells a form of truth unbound by prejudice, fashion, or political persuasion. Fiction cannot petition the reader, or ask for sympathy, or require continued attention. The created world of the novel must simply feel as "real" as the sensory world we all experience, and communicate an authority the reader trusts, for every reader's response is individually alive. Reader and writer collaborate in the mysterious creation of empathy: the sense of understanding, even vicariously experiencing, the thoughts, point of view, and personal history of an "other." No proselytizing, propaganda, or dry recitation of fact can evoke the reader's "willful suspension of disbelief." Empathy blurs the boundaries between the self and the other; connections and sympathies created by means of language remain deeply intimate. The self is not challenged, but invited. No decision is required. The reader may enter the narrative immediately or engage as slowly and completely as a swimmer traveling the shifting flow of a private river.

Ellen Feldman's carefully researched *Scottsboro* hews closely to the facts of a case familiar to anyone with a passing knowledge of American history, yet her novel moves inside the place and time almost magically. Feldman's Ruby Bates, a sometime mill worker, speaks directly to the reader: "I knew there was lint in my hair. Other folks knew it too . . . but I wasn't thinking about none of that on the way back from Chattanooga. Lookout Mountain was coming into sight yonder, and the train was slowing down, and some of the boys started funning around . . . jumping from car to car, and swinging off to run alongside the train and flip back up on the car behind . . . just to show they could. That was how it started." Mischief, showing off, but these were poor white boys, and poor black boys, and two "white trash" girls riding a freight train on the sly. To be black was very nearly a crime; to be poor was to be dispensable, useless, trapped. Feldman's amazing skill with voice achieves a form of time travel: the reader is there. "Later I'd get so I could tell the story real good . . . in Harlem, New York, and Washington, D.C., and all over . . . a white foot come down on a black hand. And folks would holler back, Yes, and You tell it sister, and Free the Scottsboro boys." Ruby Bates' sensory perceptions and witness are inarguable; Ellen Feldman makes her *Scottsboro* an urgent, illumined, necessary book.

The Scottsboro case has been the subject of numerous non-fiction accounts, including superb award-winning books by Dan T. Carter and James Goodman. It has been a film and a musical, and the origin of lawsuits. It stands firm in America's beleaguered racial history as a travesty the law could not undo. We think of Scottsboro as a 1930s miscarriage of Southern justice, a litmus test of Depression-era racism, sexism, anti-Semitism, and bigotry, but mill towns and racism, and young girls "in direct contact from the cradle with the institution of prostitution as a side-line necessary to make . . . meager wages . . . pay the rent and buy the groceries," (Hollace Ransdall, in her 1931 report to the ACLU) were not limited to the South. All over the world, today as then, Ransdall's comment on thirties-era Huntsville, Alabama, holds true. "Promiscuity," she wrote, "means little where economic oppression is great." Female experience in the deep South, with its history of slavery and Jim Crow, its myth of "the flower of (white) Southern womanhood" was a combustible mix long before Scottsboro. Protection and privilege for women had to do with class, but all women were beaten, raped, and humiliated if the men who controlled their fates cared to engage in behaviors considered a masculine birthright.

Poverty can erase privilege altogether, in any historical era – yet the Scottsboro case is inextricably bound up with the hobo trains of the thirties, a time when poor whites and blacks rode the trains from camp to camp. Particularly risk-oriented or self-demeaning white girls, girls who had nothing to lose, wore overalls over their dresses and committed to mobile homelessness and happenstance. They picked their protectors and engaged in trading sexual favors for food or liquor or community; perhaps they saw a glint of temporary romance in the shadowy freight cars. Life would use up these girls quickly, and aimless movement seemed preferable to standing still in their mother's shanty houses. Feldman's *Scottsboro*, unlike any other account of the case, uses the depth and breadth of fiction to bring the women of Scottsboro alive. Here are the two girls who cried rape because they feared being arrested as prostitutes or vagrants: the conniving Victoria Price, with her arrest record and time served in the workhouse for adultery, and the compliant Ruby Bates, who first followed Victoria's orders and backed up the lie, then recanted and found supporters who showed her worlds unseen in the North – worlds in which she was only a visitor.

Victoria and Ruby, whose characters are based on the words,

images, and historical records of real persons, find a foil and goad in Feldman's invented Alice Whittier. Women with room to breathe can think for themselves: Alice's upper-class background and small trust fund allow her to follow her intelligence and intuition into progressive circles. Her thoughts and perceptions are based on the work of respected leftist journalists Hollis Ransdall, who wrote for the ACLU, and Mary Heaton Vorse, who wrote for the *New Republic*. But Alice is younger, less accomplished at the start of *Scottsboro*, and finding her ambitious way by writing for a fictitious Communist newspaper called the *New Order*. "In those days," Alice explains, "the party . . . was a serious moral alternative, some said the only moral alternative, for anyone with a mind and a conscience." Captains of industry like Ford, Rockefeller, and Mellon became titans on the backs of workers who couldn't feed their families. Unemployed Americans wanted jobs and the protections of labor unions. The leaders of the International Labor Defense (ILD) saw revolution in formerly feudal Russia as a promise of what might take place in a desperate USA; progressives argued over how to simply hasten that desperation. Others worked to benefit the common man through political organization. Conservatives saw these "agitators" as foreign-born intellectuals (Jewish Communists) or rabble-rousers (Italian anarchists).

If the Scottsboro Boys were sacrificial lambs, their lawyer, Samuel Leibowitz, was the tireless shepherd who stayed the slaughter. Leibowitz, who immigrated to the US at four from Romania, went to Cornell and entered the law because it was one of the few professions open to Jews. He was a mainstream Democrat with no history of interest in class-based crimes, but the ILD and the American Communist Party valued his record over his politics. By 1931, Leibowitz had defended seventy-eight clients accused of first-degree murder; he'd achieved seventy-seven acquittals, one hung jury, and no convictions. He worked tirelessly for four years without pay on the Scottsboro defense, and was hated so venomously in the South that four National Guard troops were assigned to protect him. Another hundred and fifty were retained to defend him against lynch mobs. Haywood Patterson, most feared of the Scottsboro defendants, the one anointed "the leader" by white Southerners incensed by his rage and unbowed attitude, said of Leibowitz, "I love him more than life itself."

Ellen Feldman's invented Alice Whittier lives and observes the Scottsboro case from within; she observes Samuel Leibowitz, the Scottsboro Boys and their families, the obsequious NAACP lawyers, Theodore Drieser, Eleanor Roosevelt, and so many others. *Scottsboro* skillfully telescopes time; decades unspool before us, measured and illumined by a woman living history as it happens. Educated, upper class, and female, Alice doesn't fit into any group completely, but her ambition, common sense, and probing intelligence lead her to recognize Ruby Bates' story as the natural preface to the Scottsboro travesty. Alice, like everyone involved in the Scottsboro Boys' defense, makes her name on the passions and publicity of the case. She begins a meteoric rise as a journalist by winning over her source; she takes Ruby's arm, flatters and cajoles her to get the truth, aware that class privilege ensures her own sexual freedom while poverty and bigotry have sealed Ruby's fate from birth. No one will ever quite believe Ruby; she will never quite believe herself. Feldman wisely opens *Scottsboro* with Ruby's voice: "Happy wasn't nothing usually gave me the time of day. Some folks said happy wasn't nothing I had a right to, on account of between being good and having a good time, I didn't see no contest." Though the Left fashions Ruby into a temporary heroine, Ruby is a realist with few illusions: "It was white against colored, like it always is . . . nothing brings white folks together . . . faster than a colored boy, a piece of rope, and a tree." Ruby, a gun in her ribs, intimidated by a white posse, hesitates in the lie of rape, but rationalizes that no one will believe her anyway, if she doesn't go along: "Folks wouldn't take my word against Victoria's anyhow not when Victoria was so smart and such a good talker, and I was the girl with the tongue the cat always got."

Scottsboro unfurled publicly between 1931 and about 1943, when various of the Scottsboro victims, nine black youths ranging in age from thirteen to nineteen when they were falsely accused of rape, began to receive paroles from governors pressured by the obvious facts of the case. They did not recover their lives. They could not live with any self-determination in the South. Some left in violation of their paroles and were returned to prison; some escaped and surfaced later in Northern cities.

It took seven decades for American justice to finally recognize and confess to blind prejudice and murderous bigotry. Alabama Governor Robert Bentley, on April 19, 2013, signed legislation officially pardoning and exonerating all nine men. Barack Obama began his second term as President of the United States in January of that year. Twenty-four years earlier, almost to the day, on January 23, 1989, the last surviving Scottsboro Boy, Clarence Norris, had died. Sam Leibowitz died in 1978 at eighty-four. The defender of the Scottsboro Boys did not live to see the case resolved, but the tragedy of Scottsboro was not his. It belongs to the nine defendants who remained defendants all their lives, unable to outdistance the crucial miscarriage of justice that defined them. Sacrifice is seldom voluntary, but the suffering of these nine, if we conceive of time as a seismograph, moved the needle. They exposed the truth at the cost of their freedom, their dignity, and their lives.

Let us go back to the beginning, with *Scottsboro*; we owe them that, all these vanished lives. Let us repay with our attention some small part of the debt on which their nation defaulted. Nine young black men, on March 25, 1931, catch a freight train between Chattanooga, Tennessee and Huntsville, Alabama. Their only "crime" is in riding the wrong train, on the wrong day. Seven white youths try to throw them off, onto the unyielding ground along the tracks. There's a scuffle, and they throw off the whites, all but one, whom Haywood Patterson pulls back onto the train. Nine young black men, together, resist and win a small, temporary victory. Most of them don't know each other.

Olen Montgomery is seventeen.

Clarence Norris is nineteen.

Haywood Patterson is eighteen.

Ozie Powell, Willie Roberson, and Charlie Weems, are sixteen.

Eugene Williams is thirteen.

Andy Wright is nineteen; his brother, Roy Wright, is thirteen.

Now they are all brothers, linked in life, remembered beyond death. They are on the train, and the train is speeding up. Chattanooga recedes "in the green haze of hickories and sweet gums," and the future barrels toward them.

JAYNE ANNE PHILLIPS

SCOTTSBORO

A Novel

FOR EMMA SWEENEY

I was scared before, but it wasn't nothing to how I felt now. I knew if a white woman accused a black man of rape, he was as good as dead.

—Clarence Norris, 1979

Who ever heard of raping a prostitute?

—Langston Hughes, 1931

Is justice going to be bought and sold in Alabama with Jew money from New York?

—Wade Wright, summing up for the state
in Alabama v. Patterson, 1933

PROLOGUE

That is how the Scottsboro case began . . . with a white foot on my black hand.

—*Haywood Patterson, 1950*

March 25, 1931,
an Alabama Great Southern freight train

I was happy that afternoon. Happy wasn't nothing usually gave me the time of day. Some folks said happy wasn't nothing I had a right to, on account of between being good and having a good time, I didn't see no contest. But I was happy in the freight car with the green haze of hickories and sweet gums chugging past, and the sun trickling down, and Victoria setting alongside.

Victoria had a mean streak a mile wide, I'd be lying if I said different, but back when I first went into the mill, she was the only one who treated me halfway neighborly. She learned me how to spin, and to mind myself around them machines that could take off a finger before you knew it, and to keep a distance from the bosses who were fast with their hands when you weren't looking. Victoria been around the block. She even learned me how to fix up for hoboing. The day before I recollect being happy, when me and her left for

Chattanooga, we each of us put on three dresses apiece, and a coat on top, and a pair of men's overalls atop the coat. The dresses and the coats were for keeping out the cold, and cushioning our bottoms too, on account of you never knew what you were going to end up setting on in a freight car. The overalls were for staying out of trouble, on account of all them men on the train. Lest we felt like getting up to some trouble, and then wasn't no law said we got to keep them overalls in place.

We had a heap of chance for trouble on the train that day. It was full up with boys, white and nigger both. Some of the whites tried to get friendly, and most times me and Victoria wouldn't say no to a piece of fun and maybe two bits in the bargain, but that day we didn't pay them no mind. Chattanooga, where we went yesterday and were coming back from today, wasn't near the high cotton Victoria reckoned, and when we got home, Huntsville wasn't likely to be no better than it was one day back, but just for a while we were in between, and in between was all right with me. No telling what could happen in between.

The sunshine was thin as the watered milk the company store doles out, but if me and Victoria hunched down in the gondola next to the low sides of the open car, we could squeeze a little heat out of it. The sky hung over us clean as new-scrubbed wash, and the air coming down from the mountains was near sweet enough to chase the lint out of my hair. Wasn't nothing else could do that. I knew, on account of I never stopped trying. I brushed till my arm was likely to fall off, and washed with store-bought shampoo, when I could get my hands on some, but no matter how much brushing and washing I did, I stood about as much chance of getting the lint out of my hair as a dog stands shaking off fleas. Even by then, when more than likely the bosses said sorry no work today, and me and Victoria had to turn 'round and go home without stepping foot in the mill, I knew there was lint in my hair. Other folks knew it too.

But I wasn't thinking none about that on the way back from Chattanooga. Lookout Mountain was coming in sight yonder, and the train was slowing down, and some of the boys started funning around. They were jumping from car to car, and swinging off to run alongside the train and flip back up on the car behind, and whooping and hollering like it was Christmas, Fourth of July, and daddy's-come-home all rolled into one. Then some of the niggers started swinging down the side of the tanker and hanging on just to show they could. That was how it started. Later, I'd get so I could tell the story real good. I'd stand up in front of a crowd, colored and white folk both, all mixed up together, in Harlem, New York, and Washington, D.C., and all over, and tell them that was how it started. A white foot come down on a black hand. And folks would holler back, Yes, and You tell it sister, and Free the Scottsboro boys.

But that come later. On the train that day, the niggers were hanging off the side of the tanker when Carolina Slim, the boy from the hobo jungle the night before, come over the top of it. His real name was Orville Gilley, but he said his railroading moniker was Carolina Slim, and he wasn't just no hobo neither. He was a hobo poet. That was the way he talked. He came dancing over the top of the car, waving his arms in circles, playacting like he was going to fall. Or maybe he wasn't playacting, on account of the next thing I saw, Carolina Slim's foot come down on the hand of one of the colored boys hanging over the side. Could've been an accident, could've been on purpose. I don't like to say.

The colored boy didn't say nothing neither, and Carolina Slim just kept going. But when he got to the end of the tanker, he turned 'round and come back again. This time it wasn't no accident.

"The next time you want by," the colored boy yelled over the wind, "just tell me you want by, and I let you by."

"Nigger," Carolina Slim hollered back, "I don't ask you when I want by. What you doing on this train anyway? This is a white man's train."

They went back and forth with words for a spell, then just as sure as boys got to do, they went from word fighting to fistfighting. They were swinging and punching and kicking like nobody's business. It was a regular free-for-all, and I couldn't make out who was whupping who, but I knew one thing for positive. It was white against colored. You couldn't miss that. It was white against colored, like it always is. You can live right in among them, like I done all my life; you could play with them when you were little, like I used to; you could jazz them, and I reckon I jazzed more than my share, not even counting Shug; but when somebody draws the line, you better get on the right side, the white side, on account of you better believe the niggers are going to get on their own side.

After a spell, the white boys started throwing rocks, but by then the coloreds were whupping them all the same, maybe on account of there were ten or twelve niggers and only six or seven whites, or maybe on account of the niggers had color hate on their side, on their side and in their murderous hearts. I don't have nothing against coloreds. Wouldn't have took up with Shug if I did. But they're different from white folk, closer to animals, or at least children. It ain't their fault. Reckon they just can't help themselves, whether it's stealing or fighting or jazzing. Folks say they really can't help themselves when it come to jazzing, specially jazzing a white woman. I don't know about that, on account of I come up against plenty of niggers who never tried to jazz me, but it's what folks say, so it must be true. I reckon the coloreds who didn't try to jazz me were just scared.

The white boys were going off the train by then. Some were getting throwed and some were jumping, but they were going one after the other, hollering and threatening and cussing. We'll get you, you nigger bastards, they yelled as they hit the ground and rolled away from the wheels.

Only one white boy was left by then, Carolina Slim, and three niggers were trying to throw him off too. He was screaming and cursing and begging, and he didn't look like Carolina Slim the hobo poet no more, just a scared white boy named Orville Gilley. I didn't blame him none for that. The train was going so fast anybody falling off would break their neck for positive.

The niggers were still hanging him over the side, and he was kicking and hollering like hell was opening up under him when two of the coloreds pushed in among the others, grabbed him, and hauled him back up on the top of the tanker. When they let go, he fell on all fours, panting and heaving like a sick dog. The colored boys didn't pay him no mind, not even the two that pulled him back. They just turned and walked away. That was when I saw their faces. One of them was the boy Orville stepped on, first going one way, then coming back the other. There ain't no accounting for folks. In that nigger's place, I would have let them throw Orville off the train, didn't matter how fast it was going.

Things quieted down some then. The niggers drifted off, and Orville hunkered down at the other end of the car, and me and Victoria went back to trying to wring some heat out of the sun and watching the Alabama spring go by. A sign went with it, but I didn't make it out in time. I asked Victoria what it said.

"Scottsboro," she told me.

I didn't mind none missing that. I never heard of nothing happening in Scottsboro. It wasn't Chattanooga, and Chattanooga wasn't much to write home about neither. It wasn't even big as Huntsville, and Huntsville was going to be bad enough once me and Victoria got back. Just thinking about it sucked all the happy out of me.

I felt the train slowing down and pulled myself up to look over the side. I couldn't see no depot, no buildings, nothing but fields coming on to spring. There was a town yonder, but it was a long distance away.

The cars creaked and clanked to a stop. Victoria was standing up now too, saying what kind of a place was this to stop a train. Then we saw them. Must have been forty or fifty men, every able-bodied white man within shouting distance, and some not so able-bodied. Every one of them was toting something. Some had shotguns, and some had sticks and clubs, and one old buzzard in overalls and a suit coat had a pitchfork.

"Come on," Victoria said and started pushing me over the side of the gondola. "Keep down. Don't let them see you."

I reckoned there wasn't no way I could keep out of sight with Victoria shoving me over the side and down the ladder, but I dropped to the ground and tried to hide there. Victoria hit the dirt a second later, grabbed me, and started in to run. We were going away from the men with their guns and sticks and pitchfork, but I couldn't keep from looking back over my shoulder. Some were still coming on, but others were swinging up into the cars, hooting and hollering and carrying on.

"You take that one, Deems. Me and Vanders going in here."

"We gonna find them niggers."

"We gonna find them, and then we gonna find a tree."

"We'll teach 'em to mess with white boys."

Then, like in a big tent with the preacher up front and the whole church following, came the cry.

"Hallelujah!"

Then again.

"Hallelujah, I got me one!"

And before the amens could start in, "Whew-ee, make that two!"

That's when I reckoned me and Victoria were saved. Nothing brings white folks together, no matter if they're nose-in-the-air church ladies, fresh-with-their-hands mill bosses, or plain old linthead trash, faster than a colored boy, a piece of rope, and a tree. Only one time in my life I saw it, but once is all you need to know that.

Victoria was still drugging me along, but all of a sudden she stopped. I saw why. More men were coming at us from the other direction. They were toting guns and sticks too.

"Quick!" Victoria yanked me around and started to run back the other way, but it was too late. The second bunch of men was already around us. They crowded in so close I could smell the barn and the sweat and the sour rotting-teeth breath.

One with red rheumy eyes and a long nose that needed a good wiping poked me in the arm with his shotgun. "Well, I'll be damned. It's a gal. A gal in boy's overalls."

"They both gals," another one shouted. He was younger, and a good-looker, unless you took note of his eyes. One was blue as a robin's egg, the other was all cloudy. The cloudy one kept rolling off yonder. "They didn't say there was no gals on the train." He was squealing, and jumping up and down, and holding himself.

A man with a brown hat pulled low down on his face so all you could see was a nose like an ax and a big tobacco-stained mustache hanging under it reached out and laid a big hand on the good-looker's shoulder. "Now, calm down, Billy. Ain't nothing to go getting yourself worked up over. You seen gals before. Even in overalls." His voice was real quiet and low, like when you're trying to hush a baby.

He turned to me and Victoria. "You girls on that train?" he asked in that same voice. It was all warm milk and lullaby, but something underneath made the hair on the back of my neck stand up. I kept my eyes down and my mouth closed. I reckoned Victoria would know what to say. But the next thing I knew Victoria was on the ground. She went down kind of soft and loose-kneed, the way she did sometimes when she was funning, but this time I couldn't figure if she was fooling or for real. I didn't know if I was supposed to go down too, but one thing I did know for positive. I wasn't going to be the one left standing with the old man poking his gun into me, and the boy jumping up and down and holding himself, and the rest of them pushing in so tight I couldn't hardly breathe. I went down on my knees and bent over Victoria. The smell of barnyard boots was worse down there, but the sour breath wasn't as bad. The man with the kindly voice that scared me all the same was saying step back and give her air.

Victoria opened one eye a slit, then closed it again real fast. I leaned in close and put my ear next to her mouth.

"You tell it like I tell it," she whispered.

I felt the man's thick fingers on my arm pulling me up. His touch wasn't near as easy as his voice, and I already knew his voice was a lie.

"Give your friend some air." He let go of my arm and pushed his hat back on his head. His eyes were pale gray, glinted with white, like a rock in a creek bed that's been dry all summer.

"You gals on that train?" he asked again.

Victoria said to tell it like she told it, but I didn't know how she was fixing to tell it. Cat got your tongue, folks were always saying to me, like they're so smart and I ain't, but this time the cat really did have my tongue.

I looked past the man. The posse was pushing and kicking and shotgun-shoving the coloreds off the railroad cars. One short skinny boy was leaning on a cane and limping so bad he couldn't hardly walk. I knew that limp. The boy had bad blood, real bad. What the docs call syphilis. The man with the pitchfork held on to the tines and swung the handle end. The cane went out from under the boy. The boy went down.

"The man asked you a question, sister," a voice behind me said.

"You on the train with them niggers?" someone shouted.

"Take it easy, boys," the man with the glinting eyes said. "This ain't no possum you're running up a tree. These gals may be hoboes, but they're white women hoboes, and in Jackson County we treat a white woman proper."

He hunched down on his haunches next to Victoria. Her eyelids opened and closed a few times.

"You okay, ma'am?" he asked, and scared as I was, I near had to laugh. Nobody excepting colored folk ever called me and Victoria ma'am, and not even them most times.

Victoria opened her eyes and looked around. "Where am I?" she asked in a soft whispery voice I never did hear her use before.

"She don't even know where she is."

"Can you beat that?"

"You think you can set up now?" the man asked, but he didn't wait for no answer. He just pulled her up so she was setting. "You're in Paint Rock, and there ain't nothing to be scared of. All I want to know is if you two gals were on that train."

"We was," Victoria said.

"Now we're getting somewhere." He stood and pulled Victoria up till she was standing too. "Now I got one more question, ma'am, and it ain't a hard one to figure. Did them niggers on the train interfere with you?"

I knew what he meant by interfere, but I didn't figure the rest of what he was saying. Me and Victoria didn't have nothing to do with them coloreds on the train. And he couldn't know about that chippy house the last time we went to Chattanooga, or Victoria's nigger day outside the factory neither. If he did, he wouldn't be calling her ma'am.

"Course they did," the man with the shotgun said. "They niggers, ain't they? They see it, they gotta have it."

"I ain't asking you, Horace, I'm asking the lady."

I couldn't believe my own ears. Ma'am was nice, but lady was something Sunday special.

"Did them niggers interfere with you?" the man asked again.

Victoria licked her bee-sting lips. She looked the man right in the eye. I waited on her. She was good at making up stories. Practical jokes too, like the time she sneaked hot pepper into her snuffbox to stop Annie McGinney dipping into it when Victoria wasn't looking. Annie near to died with coughing and hiccupping and spitting up. But even Victoria wouldn't tell a lie about this. She knew what it meant for the niggers.

Victoria's tongue went over her lips again. Her eyes slid to me, then away.

"Them niggers raped me. They held a knife to my throat and raped me and my friend both."

A murmur, almost like in church when the preacher says something good, and the amens, and the hallelujahs, and the glory-glory-bless-the-Lords ring out, rose around us.

"I kicked, and I screamed, and I fought, but they was too many of them. Six raped me and the rest raped my friend. They held me down, and they had a knife, and they just kept raping and raping and raping."

I still didn't believe my own ears. Victoria knew. She knew good as me, better maybe, what would happen.

The man turned his hard white eyes on me. "That true, ma'am? Did those niggers rape you and your friend?"

I tried to look at the man, but his eyes cut me like broken glass. I gazed yonder where they were tying the colored boys together with a rope, one after the other in a long line, with their hands behind their backs.

The man leaned down and put his face in front of mine. "You just look at me, missy, and don't pay no heed to them niggers. Now, it's a easy question. All you gotta say is yes or no. Did them niggers rape you like they done to your friend?"

You tell it like I tell it, Victoria whispered, but if I told it like Victoria, them boys were good as dead. Maybe right now, maybe in a couple of weeks, maybe swinging from a tree, maybe in the electric chair, one way or another they'd be dead. Only maybe they wouldn't. Maybe they would just go to jail. Maybe Victoria knew that. That was why she made up the story. Between me and her going to jail for riding the rails, and crossing state lines with men ain't our kin, and vagrancy, and a bunch of niggers going, I didn't see no contest.

"I'm still waiting, sister."

Besides, they were only niggers. Probably used to jail. Probably spent half their lives in jail and didn't mind it none. Probably liked it. Lots of niggers did. Only way they got a roof over their heads and a decent meal, folks said. But it would be different for me. It would be worse for me than Victoria even, on account of Victoria already laid out a sentence for adultering with Jack Tiller, but I never was in jail.

And I wasn't fixing to start now just to save a bunch of niggers I never laid eyes on before a couple of hours back.

"Cat got her tongue."

"Else she's a nigger-lover."

"Yeah, that's it. Had to rape the one, but the other didn't put up no fight."

"Put her in the truck with the niggers."

"Best place for a nigger-lover is in jail with the niggers."

"Gal like that's worse than a nigger."

The colored boy who lost his cane was having trouble getting himself into the truck. Another boy started to help him. A man swung a shotgun. The butt caught the boy who was trying to help in the small of his back. His body jackknifed. I didn't know a body could bend that way.

"Now, I'm going to ask you one more time, sister, and this time I expect a answer."

Victoria was staring the words at me. You tell it like I tell it. The gun was poking in my ribs. Folks wouldn't take my word against Victoria's anyhow, not when Victoria was so smart and such a good talker, and I was the girl with the tongue the cat always got.

"I'm still waiting," the man said.

Victoria stared knives at me.

"Yes or no?" the man asked.

"Yes," I answered.

Book One

So the Scottsboro case came up . . . that's the most exciting time of my life! I was happy. I stepped into a red hot situation.

—Hollace Ransdall, American Civil Liberties Union investigator, 1974

Even after all these years, the injustice still stuns. Innocent boys sentenced to die, not for a crime they did not commit, but for a crime that never occurred. Lives splintered as casually as wood being hacked for kindling. Young manhood ground to ashes. But there is another side to the story, and that is not the destruction of the boys, but the making of so many other men and women. Sometimes when I read familiar names in the newspaper or see on television a face made faintly unfamiliar by time, I cannot help thinking how well the helpers and the hangers-on did. How did Clarence Norris put it? "For lots of folks, us boys was nothing more than rungs on a ladder."

We did not set out to exploit. The lawyers, and the Communist Party members, and the reporters, and the do-gooders wanted only to help, and we did help. But we also managed to appropriate the story for our own ends. In the long history of white highway robbery, Scottsboro was just one more holdup of black America.

The odd thing is that when the report first came over the wire that afternoon, I did not think the story was news. I don't mean I was not incensed by it. I was twenty-six and had outrage to spare. I had it the way some women have a matrimonial hankering or a maternal instinct. But in 1931, a lynching or two in Alabama did not make headlines. The year before, the South had made sixty-one attempts and scored twenty-one successes. And those were only the cases reported. Taken together, they made a cause, but an isolated attempt at a rural jail was no reason to stop the presses, not when sixteen million American men could not find work; and more than a quarter of the population was trying to survive without any income at all; and two hundred thousand kids under the age of twenty-one were hoboing the country in search of an odd job, or a few scraps of food, or the little bit of fun that was supposed to be the birthright of youth. Harry Spencer, the publisher of *The New Order*, for which I wrote, was always reminding me that we had to keep our eye on the big picture, though he was waging a losing battle with his own soft spot. A few days before the arrest of the nine boys came over the wire in his office, he had seen one of his former neighbors selling apples under the Ninth Avenue Elevated around the corner from the magazine's offices, not an unusual story in those days, except that Harry lived on Park Avenue, or had until his wife tossed out him and all his May-Day-marching, slogan-shouting, parlor-pink friends.

"Spare me the sob stories about Wall Street millionaires down to their last polo pony, pal," I told him. As the only woman contributor to the magazine, I had to sound twice as cynical as the men. As a girl who still carried about her the heady scent of a small trust fund, diminished but not destroyed by the crash, I had to prove where my sympathies lay. The day the news of the lynch mob came over the wire, they were locked in an Alabama jail with nine Negro boys, listening to the mob baying for blood outside.

The details coming in were sparse, but I could piece together the story. A gang of white boys had reported being thrown from a freight train by a group of Negro youths. Fast as you could say Jim Crow, a makeshift posse formed, stopped the train at the next station, which was a small town called Paint Rock, rounded up nine Negro boys whom they found on the train, drove them to the county seat in Scottsboro, and locked them up. Then the story got really good. The posse found two white girls who had been on the freight train as well. At first the men did not realize they were girls. Both were wearing men's overalls. But once they saw what they had in their hands, the accusation was inevitable. The word *rape* seeped out from the railroad siding where they had taken the nine Negro boys and the two white girls off the train, bumped over country roads in farmers' trucks and traveling salesmen's cars and drifters' knapsacks, and hissed down the telegraph wires. By sunset, a crowd had gathered outside the rat- and vermin-infested jail that a ten-year-old with a toy gun and a little determination could have broken into, because one thing was certain, the guards did not have much interest in keeping anyone out.

I sat, shamefully safe in Harry's office, trying to imagine the terror of those boys. I pictured the mob stomping the good Alabama earth with dusty boots and respectable lace-ups. I had already learned to look at the shoes beneath the sheets, though there were no sheets that night. The men were not ashamed of what they were doing. I could hear the rabble shouting for justice, and see them twirling and lassoing the ropes they had brought to make sure it was done. In the back of the crowd, women held babies to breasts heaving with excitement, and children's eyes grew wide at the imminent thrill. If you think I'm exaggerating, take a look at some of the old picture postcards. They don't show only men in overalls, and women in housedresses, and kids without shoes either. One I will never forget features a dapper man in a straw boater, holding the hand of a well-scrubbed little girl in a starched white dress, both of them gazing up in wonder at the body of a young black man swinging from a tree. His head lolls forward like the blossom on a broken flower, and his feet dangle uselessly above the fertile earth. *Souvenir of the Confederacy*, the card says. The U.S. Postal System designated *Ulysses* pornography, but it had no problem sending postcards of black bodies hanging from southern trees through the mails. *Having a wonderful time. Wish you were here.*

As it turned out, no dead bodies hung from southern trees that night. The sheriff called in the National Guard, and between the militia and the chilly weather, the justice-seekers lost steam and drifted off.

"What's the South coming to?" Abel Newman, the magazine's book editor and theater critic, said. "Sunshine bigots, fair-weather lynch mobs?"

Abel joked, but we were relieved the story was stillborn, and not merely because of those poor boys. If the lynching of a black man by a white mob in the South did not make headlines, the rape of a white woman, two white women, by Negro men was not news many of us in the North wanted to print.

Abel turned out to be wrong about sunshine bigots and fair-weather lynchers. The crowd went home that first night, but they managed to lynch the boys in the end, a fine southern legal lynching. Everyone knew how it worked. If you put away the rope, local officials worried about outside opinion promised local citizens determined to see justice done, we guarantee a trial so fast it will make your head spin and a sentence that will warm your heart. True, the electric chair does not provide the see-it-with-your-own-eyes thrill of a lynching, but it gets the job done.

The two girls, Victoria Price and Ruby Bates, identified the boys who raped them.

"That one, yonder," Victoria repeated six times, pointing in turn to six of the defendants.

Ruby Bates turned out to be a less reliable witness. "I don't know which one of them ravished me," she told the court. "I just know an intercourse was held with me."

The statement gave rise to considerable hilarity around the offices of *The New Order*. "Hi, Alice," one or another of the men would greet me. "Was an intercourse held with you last night?"

At first, I laughed. I was, as I said, trying to be one of the boys. The morning one actually had been held with me the night before, I tried not to blush. I was also trying to be a modern woman. Unlike most of my friends, I had not even bothered to buy a dime-store wedding band when I had gone to a clinic to be fitted for a pessary. But after a week of hearing the line repeated, I almost began to sympathize with that poor benighted girl. Then I remembered the nine boys.

Orville Gilley, a.k.a. California Slim, the hobo poet, the only white boy who had not been thrown from the train, corroborated the girls' story. "I'd've knowed every one of them if I saw them at midnight in a mine. That's how close I looked them over." The hobo poet was given to vivid imagery.

The most troubling testimony, however, at least for those of us who were following the story in the North, came from the accused. Each claimed his own innocence, but several of them implicated the others.

"They all raped her, every one of them," Clarence Norris swore.

"I saw all of them have intercourse. I saw that with my own eyes," Roy Wright, the youngest of the group, insisted.

"All but them three raped them girls," Haywood Patterson testified. The three he claimed had not participated happened to be the friends he had hopped the freight with.

We told one another the boys had been tricked with promises of leniency, or intimidated with threats, or beaten.

"You know what southern jails are like," Harry said. I did not, at least not firsthand, but Harry had spent a summer trying to unionize the mills in Cherokee and Spartanburg Counties in South Carolina, an experience that had left his beautiful aquiline nose slightly flattened. He regarded the injury as a badge of honor. So did I. Nonetheless, we would have been happier if the boys had not blamed one another.

By the time we heard about the testimony of the boys, we had also learned about the two girls. That was why we were sure the boys had not raped them. The girls were common prostitutes. They had been plying their trade on that Alabama Great Southern freight train. But in the South, when a white woman is caught in bed, or in this case in a railroad gondola, with a Negro man, the first word out of her mouth is rape. Another joke began making the rounds.

"Those boys are going to burn for what they could have had for two bits," the men were saying. At least, men in the North were saying it. Southern gentlemen told a different story. Theirs was of white womanhood defiled. That was the one the jury believed.

In four days, the state of Alabama tried, convicted, and sentenced the boys to death.

8 NEGROES SENTENCED
TO CHAIR IN ALABAMA
Convicted of Attacking Two White Girls—Mistrial for Ninth, 14 Years Old

The mistrial was due to the fact that the state had asked for a life sentence for Roy Wright, who, despite the headline, turned out to be only thirteen—birth certificates were rare, and vital statistics often a matter of conjecture—but some members of the jury argued that tender years were no excuse for heinous acts and held out for the death penalty. Eugene Williams, another defendant, was only a few months older than Roy Wright, but the state chose to ignore the fact. The prosecution knew that for a conviction, older was better. When they used the term *boys*, they were referring to the defendants' social status, not their age.

By that time, I was following the story closely. My outrage grew with each new report. I told Harry I wanted to go to Alabama.

He leaned back in his swivel chair, put his long legs up on his desk, and looked unhappy. He would like to publish a series of articles on those nine young men, he said, just as he would be happy to let me write about women fighting stray dogs for spoiled produce on the city docks, and whole families living in old broken-down Fords, and babies crying out their hearts and empty stomachs in Hoovervilles, but we had to leave the sob stories to the glossies and keep our eye on the march of history.

Harry had come to his convictions through the back door. A few years earlier, he had inherited *The New Order* from a black-sheep uncle with a budding social conscience. Harry had toyed with the failing journal for a year or so, then decided to sell it, but when the market collapsed and potential buyers evaporated, he began to bone up on his political and economic philosophy. Within months, he understood the labor theory of value, could spout long passages of *Das Kapital* from memory, and believed that democratic industrialized America provided more fertile soil for a classless society than feudal Russia. Harry, whom no one except his black-sheep uncle had ever taken seriously, who had not taken himself seriously, suddenly had gravitas. He also had the passion of the convert. He was determined to save my soul. If you sympathized with the party's aims, he argued—and I did—membership was the only logical step. In those days the party was not yet a bogeyman, but a serious moral alternative, some said the only moral alternative, for anyone with a mind and a conscience.

I agreed with him, though somehow I could not make the leap. It was not fear. Half the people I knew belonged to the party, and none of them seemed to suffer any consequences, other than an occasional tendency to bore friends. I was not even worried about the mindless rigidity of party rule. We would not learn about that for a few years. Nonetheless, I remained a fellow traveler. In those days, the term was one of approval, not opprobrium.

Still, Harry kept at me. I took it as a compliment. Most of the men at the magazine were more interested in my legs. Harry was not oblivious to them. Once, when I was leaving his office, he told me my seams were crooked. But he also wanted to straighten out my mind. Bleeding heart liberals, he lectured me, did more damage to the workers' struggle than Henry Ford, John D. Rockefeller, and Andrew Mellon rolled up in one. The noxious practices of Ford and Rockefeller and Mellon, after all, would hasten the overthrow of a rotten system, and if you did not believe it was rotten, look at all those out-of-work men with starving families. The ameliorations of the do-gooders like me merely delayed the day of reckoning.

Harry was the real thing, all right, but he was no stuffed shirt. The night Abel Newman and I performed a tap dance to "The Internationale" at a party, Harry applauded as vigorously as everyone else. Nor was he a monk. Witness the comment about the seams of my stockings. But he was serious about the class struggle. He said he would think about sending me to Scottsboro.

A day or two later, the reports of foreign protests began coming in. Demonstrators smashed the windows of American consulates in Berlin and Leipzig and even dull respectable Geneva. In Havana, marchers chanted slogans against Yankee imperialism and judicial injustice. I told Harry I could be on the 11:10 to Birmingham the next morning. He said he was still thinking about it.

Americans were protesting as well. The day after Harry put me off a second time, I stood on a New York sidewalk and watched a demonstration go by. The turnout was respectable, though the numbers did not come close to the crowds that showed up each year for the May Day parade. Even if you dismissed the counts the newspapers gave for left-wing rallies as too low, and I always did, probably fewer than two thousand people marched. The crowd was not only smaller; it was different. For one thing, many of the demonstrators were Negroes. In those days, Negroes did not usually take to the streets to make their dissatisfaction known. They did not dare. For another, the parade marshals did not try to whitewash the turnout. Not that the marshals would ever admit that was what they were up to, but at most marches you could not help but notice.

If the marshals were expecting trouble, they put men at the ends of the lines. That was where spectators who did not share the marchers' ideals could make their differences of opinion known with eggs and tomatoes and spit. The men had to be tough-looking customers who would discourage others from picking fights, but sufficiently cool-headed not to resort to fisticuffs themselves. When the marshals were not expecting disruptions, however, they placed the window dressing on the outside. Those were the girls with blond hair that swung in time to the slogans they chanted, and rangy confident strides that hinted of tennis rackets and golf clubs. Deeper within the group, farther from the spectators on the sidewalk, marched the girls whose hair tended to frizz when the humidity rose, or whose noses were just a little too long or a little too hooked, or whose shoulders hunched from hours spent bending over sewing or adding machines. The names of the girls were different too. Eleanor Jackson and Grace Johnson and Prudence Fowler paraded on the outside. Esther Rabinowitz and Sarah Levy and Miriam Gold walked in the middle. The arrangement was not anti-Semitic. Most of the marshals were Jews. That was the problem. Everyone knew that Jews were left-wingers. The girls on the outside were there to persuade America that left-wingers were not necessarily Jews.

Where did I march, when I marched? My hair is dark, but a rain forest could not make it curl, let alone frizz. My nose is straight, but too long, a fine Quaker nose, my father used to call it, when he and I still joked about things. At Bryn Mawr, I was a fiercely competitive tennis player. When I marched, I marched with the window dressing, except for the one time I tried not to.

I cannot recall the cause I turned out for that day, but I blush when I remember my own personal protest. The marshal directed me to the end of the line. I pretended not to hear him and burrowed into the heart of the marchers. At least I tried to, but they closed ranks against me. Silently, seemingly without intention, they took one another's hands, and moved shoulder to shoulder, and refused even to look at me, except for one girl. She had silken red hair and a sprinkling of freckles that would have placed her on the outside, if other factors had not conspired to bury her inside. She lifted her eyes to meet mine. Hers burned with defiance and disdain. They said she knew what I was up to, and she was having none of it. She did not know what I was up to, at least not in detail, but she had my number.

No attempt was made to whitewash the crowd that turned out to protest the railroading of the boys in Alabama that April afternoon. The news reports commented on the fact that many of the whites were foreign-born. The phrase was curious, since it was a pretty safe bet reporters had not stopped the protesters to ascertain their immigration and naturalization status. Readers got the message nonetheless. Among the whites, there might be a few upper-crust types with overactive consciences, but most of them were Jews with a sprinkling of Italian anarchists thrown in for good measure.

The marchers were in fine spirits. Making a stand against injustice often cheers people up. The weather helped. Sunlight hung like bunting over the broad avenues. Birdsong mingled with the sound of marching feet and chanting voices. Daffodils rioted around the bases of trees, and geraniums cheered from window boxes. It was spring in New York, noisy, intrusive, bursting with promises sure to be broken in that busted year of 1931. The thin fabric of the girls' dresses rippled around their legs as they walked, and the strong biceps of the men bulged against their suit jackets as they hoisted their signs, and the air shimmered with hope. The marchers knew the world was falling apart, but on that lemony yellow afternoon they were alive and young and absolutely certain of how to put it together again. The despair of those years was pitiful, but looking back over the way things turned out, I find the optimism even more heartbreaking.

The marchers pumped their signs toward the cloudless sky as they walked. If I needed any more evidence that the crime against those boys was not going away, that the case was destined to become a cause, those signs provided it. Nine boys had stumbled off the train in Paint Rock and stood trial in Scottsboro. Haywood Patterson. Clarence Norris. Charlie Weems. Olen Montgomery. Ozie Powell. Willie Roberson. Eugene Williams. Andy Wright. Roy Wright. Last time there had been only two. Sacco and Vanzetti. Those two names had been short and sweet, almost musical. They went together like Marx and Engels, Gilbert and Sullivan, Lord & Taylor. But who could remember nine names? Most people did not even try. Early news accounts had not bothered to list the accused individually. I had made an effort to memorize their names, but I always forgot one or two. I had even attempted to find a mnemonic, like the one we used at school to remember the order of the stations on the Paoli Local that ran from Philadelphia out along the Main Line. Overbrook, Merion, Narberth, Wynnewood, Ardmore, Haverford, Bryn Mawr. Old Maids Never Wed And Have Babies, we used to chant. Hard as I tried, however, I could not come up with a mnemonic to help me remember the names of those nine boys. But as I stood on the sidewalk that spring afternoon, watching the crowd march by, aiming their signs at the heavens, I knew I no longer had to worry about the individual names.

FREE THE SCOTTSBORO BOYS.

JUSTICE FOR THE SCOTTSBORO BOYS.

WE SUPPORT THE SCOTTSBORO BOYS.

I did not stay until the march broke up. If I was on to something, others would be too. I could not take the chance that one of the men on the magazine would get to Harry before I did.

The offices of *The New Order* were in a down-on-its-luck brownstone that stood in the shadow of the Ninth Avenue Elevated. The building always smelled of cigarettes and garlic. The cigarettes came with the literary and journalistic territory. The garlic was more unusual. Two or three times a week, the Italian wife of the janitor, who lived in the basement, cooked lunch or dinner for editors and writers and visiting intellectuals. Her chicken cacciatore was legendary. Her pasta puttanesca was almost as famous, but that had as much to do with the origins of the recipe as its tastiness. What self-respecting left-wing journal of opinion could resist a dish dreamed up by oppressed women of the street? Whenever she served it, someone quoted Baudelaire about prostitution being essentially a matter of lack of choice. Oh, how we loved those women of easy virtue, in the abstract.

Harry's office was in the former front parlor of the brownstone. He had arranged his desk so it faced the door and placed his back to the bay of windows that curved out over the street. On bright days, visitors had to squint into the light and could not read his expression. Harry pretended to be unaware of the effect. He had a newly sharpened social conscience and the remains of a soft spot, but he was not uncanny.

I sat to the side of his desk, turned the chair so I was not facing the windows, and told him I was going to Alabama whether he sent me or not. I could always sell the pieces elsewhere, I said.

He suspected I was bluffing, but he could not be sure. Before I had begun writing for *The New Order*, I had turned down an offer to work on one of Hearst's papers. Harry thought I had acted on principle, and he was not entirely wrong. But I'd had selfish motives as well. Hearst papers were more likely than most to relegate women to the purdah of society, fashion, and gossip.

I had expected an argument, but I should have realized that if I had been following the story, Harry had too. Lawyers for the International Labor Defense, the legal arm of the Communist Party, were planning to appeal the case. Party workers were heading south to organize Negroes to stand shoulder to shoulder with their white brothers in the class struggle. *Time* magazine had devoted several breathless paragraphs to foreign demonstrations in support of the blackamoors, as it called them. Harry did not have to see the marchers' signs demanding justice for the Scottsboro boys to recognize a rallying point for the revolution when it hit him.

We talked about people to contact in Birmingham, and how much trouble I could expect in Scottsboro, and whether there was a chance that I might get in to see the boys in Kilby Prison.

"Be careful," he warned me in that deep plummy voice that had grown deeper since his wife had left for Reno and he had gone from one pack of Camels a day to two. "Joe Brodsky from the ILD went down to get a stay of execution, and some leading local citizens tried to run him out of town."

I picked up my gloves and handbag from his desk and stood. "I'll rely on their southern chivalry."

He rose and began walking me to the door. "That's another thing. Remember you're a lady." He meant woman, but his vocabulary, like his manners, had been instilled before he had begun reading political and economic theory.

I raised my eyebrows. The trick was never to stop being a woman while you were acting like one of the boys, but if one of the boys pointed out you were a woman, to feign astonishment. It was the mental equivalent of looking down at your body and throwing up your hands in surprise. Nonetheless, in this case, I knew he had a point. If southern gentlemen did not like northern men coming down to make trouble, they would be doubly furious at a northern woman questioning their judgment.

Years later, a student who was interviewing me for an oral history project cited the Supreme Court ruling, still four years in the future the day I stood in Harry's office, guaranteeing black men the right to sit on juries. She added, accusingly, that in Alabama, women, unlike blacks, had not sat on juries until 1966.

"Sat on juries," I told her, "they weren't even allowed in the courtroom. No women and no boys under twenty-one. The testimony was too racy. That was why all the men were fighting to get in. There were only two exceptions. That was at the second trial in Decatur in '33. One other reporter and I were the only women."

The student pushed the tape recorder on the coffee table between us closer to me and asked how I had felt leaving my sisters standing outside the courthouse. Only one sister, I wanted to tell her, only a half-sister, and it was not my fault. Then I realized my mistake. She was speaking politically.

"Better one than none," I'd told her.

"Two," she said.

"I beg your pardon."

"You said there was one other woman reporter and you."

"Of course, two," I'd agreed and changed the subject.

"Good luck," Harry said and flashed a lock-up-your-daughters grin that neither economic conditions nor party discipline could dim. "Grim as this is, I cannot help but see the irony."

I knew what was coming.

He did not disappoint me. "Those boys are going to burn for what they could have had for two bits. The girls are ladies of the night, women of easy virtue, *nymphes de pavé*. Like our friends across the garden."

Now he had surprised me, though I should have made the connection myself. The garden to which he referred was a small rectangle of threadbare grass, a flowering cherry tree, and a few pots of annuals Harry had the janitor put in every spring so that during the summer months he could move the lunches and dinners and parties for good causes outdoors. I had flirted with Thomas Wolfe and talked to Edmund Wilson in that garden, or perhaps it was the other way around. But the garden itself was not what Harry had in mind. He was referring to the building on the other side of it, the House of the Heavenly Rest. That was where the friends Harry referred to lived, at least temporarily. When the police arrested underage prostitutes, they took them there to await trial under the supervision of the nuns, rather than to jail. Once, as I was passing the house, I saw a slight girl break free of two policemen, who were leading her up the steps. She sprinted down the block toward the El, but the police were too fast for her. They grabbed her before she reached the flashing shadows of the train racing overhead. They did not take her back to the house. They slapped on handcuffs and bundled her into a squad car. As it pulled away, I caught a glimpse of her childish face in the rear window. Beneath a mask of cheap makeup, it was twisted with hate. Her expression haunted me for days. I found myself having fantasies about scrubbing off the cheap makeup and turning the venomous snarl into a smile.

Standing in Harry's office, remembering that girl who had not had a chance, I made up my mind. I would go to Birmingham, and to Scottsboro, and to Kilby Prison. I would also go to Huntsville. Huntsville was where Victoria Price and Ruby Bates lived.

I came out of Harry's office to find Abel Newman lurking in the hall. Abel, the critic and editor with whom I had performed a tap dance to the anthem of the CP, had given me my first assignment for the magazine, a review of a fat tome by two dour professors called *Sex in Civilization*. He had no idea how little I knew about either at the time, or maybe he did. Maybe he thought it was a joke, on the magazine, and me, and himself.

A few years before Abel had come to the magazine, he had written a play. It had bowled over both the arbiters of American taste and the theatergoing public. Critics hailed him as the new O'Neill. Hollywood beckoned. Broadway waited for the next one. But the play was never filmed, and his name never appeared in the credits of any of the other scripts he worked on during the four months he spent in California. More to the point, a second play had not materialized. People had stopped asking about it. I had never mentioned it.

He was leaning against the wall now with his hands in his pockets and a cigarette dangling from a finely modeled mouth that stopped just this side of girlish. His hair was dark and full, and his eyes, behind horn-rimmed glasses, were black and watchful. His square face would have been rugged, were it not for that mouth.

Without taking the cigarette from between his lips, he asked where the fire was.

"Alabama."

"Don't tell me, let me guess. Scottsboro."

"Can you think of a better place these days?"

"Not if you're Alice Whittier, defender of the downtrodden, champion of the dispossessed, advocate of the disenfranchised. Note the alliteration."

"You forgot Jeanne d'Arc." That was his favorite dig at me.

He grinned. His smile did not have Harry's lock-up-your-daughters flash. It was more subversive than that. "Your French governess is showing, Ace. In the circles you're trying to sink to, she's known as Joan of Arc, not Jeanne d'Arc, and definitely not Jeanne la Pucelle."

It was just like Abel to make fun of me for using Jeanne d'Arc and to know about Jeanne la Pucelle.

"Much as I'd like to wander down history's primrose path with you, pal," I said as I started down the hall, "I have a train to catch."

He stood looking after me. "Give 'em hell," he called, and for a moment I thought he was wishing me well. Then he went on. "You save them darkies," he added, and I knew he was only making fun of me, again.

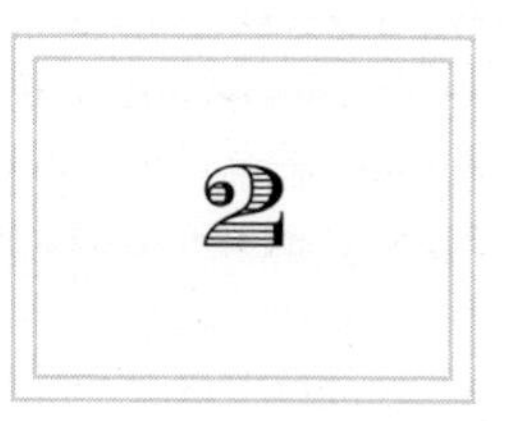

Scottsboro, the county seat of Jackson county in northern Alabama, is a charming southern village with some 2,000 inhabitants situated in the midst of pleasant, rolling hills. The cottages of the town stand back on soft lawns, shaded with handsome trees. A feeling of peace and leisure is in the air. The people on the streets have easy, kind faces, and greet strangers, as well as each other cordially. In the Courthouse Square in the center of town, the village celebrities, such as the mayor, the sheriff, the lawyers, lounge and chat democratically with the town eccentrics and plain citizens . . . They all wanted the Negroes killed as quickly as possible in a way that would not bring disrepute upon the town.

—Hollace Ransdall in a report to the ACLU, 1931

I spent a single day in Scottsboro. The town was so small, so homey, so self-sufficient—or willfully isolated; it depended on your point of view—it did not have a hotel. But I did not need to spend the night to find what I was looking for. I went there expecting bigotry and hatred and injustice. I was not disappointed. I also anticipated hypocrisy. What I discovered was worse.

I stepped down from the train into the morning mist. Greening live oaks and white clapboard buildings came shimmering out of it like a mirage. The town was prettier than I had expected, but I would not be taken in by that. I knew the smugness and boredom that could spread like mildew across the deep lawns and climb the sleepy trees. I was on intimate terms with the mean-spiritedness and duplicity that could lurk behind freshly painted facades. A few rays of sunshine were already piercing the haze. The mist would burn off as the day ripened, leaving the town standing sharp and clear in the sunlight. That was what I was waiting for.

I set out from the railway station in the direction of the courthouse. The square in front of the solid brick building dozed in the silky spring air. Towering trees promised shelter from a spring rain or refuge from a scalding summer sun. Around the perimeter, painted signs—there was not a neon light in view—offered hardware and furniture and GOOD EATS AT MODERATE PRICES. Behind the plate-glass window of a drugstore, a chrome counter and a dark wood apothecary corner pledged to quench your thirst and cure whatever ailed you. It was innocent and homey, but I saw through the facade to things as they had been the morning the trials began.

Ten thousand locals, and some who were not so local—license plates heralded from Tennessee and beyond—had crowded the two thousand residents of Scottsboro that morning a few weeks earlier, and who could blame them? There was not much to do in a small southern town, especially these days when the entire country was down on its luck. But here was entertainment for the whole family. Women opened their picnic baskets, spread their cloths, and laid out fried chicken and coleslaw and biscuits. Men compared rifles and shotguns. They did not carry them to menace, one citizen assured a reporter on the scene. It was the first Monday of the month, Fair Day in Scottsboro, when people came to gossip and buy and barter, and nothing bartered better than a firearm. Children chased one another through the crowd and around the courthouse. Dogs yelped after them. A vendor sold ice cream. Old people gossiped. Babies slept and woke and cried and giggled. If you did not know better, you would have thought you were at a revival meeting, except that here and there among the men, if you looked closely, you could see the outline in overall or jacket pocket of a bottle or a preserving jar. If you got really close, you could smell the lightning on their breath. And here, if the townspeople had anything to say about it, no one was going to be saved.

There had been a parade that morning, not like the one I had stood on the sidewalk and watched go by in New York. This was automotive, and even more jubilant. Twenty-eight shiny new Ford trucks, gassed up by the local dealer, cruised the crowded streets, horns honking, fresh paint gleaming. In Scottsboro, as elsewhere, business was bad, and the dealer was hoping the sight of southern justice in action would raise spirits and open palms that had closed against hard times. And there was music. The local hosiery mill had fielded its band. People forgot the holes in their shoes as their feet kept time to "Dixie." When word of the first conviction came whistling out of the courthouse, the band let loose with "There'll Be a Hot Time in the Old Town Tonight." The jury, which was still deliberating in the second trial, admitted they had heard the song and interpreted the good news, but Judge Alfred E. Hawkins saw no reason to declare a mistrial.

Now, a few weeks later, the hoopla was over. Men left neatly tended houses to sell feed and tend bank windows and give shaves and haircuts. Behind well-laundered curtains, women put on hats and gloves to face their neighbors. Negro servants swept shady porches. Heady aromas of baking pies and roasting meats floated from back kitchens, promising dinners and suppers that smelled as if they would be worth waiting for. A few people greeted me or tipped their hats as they passed. They did not seem unfriendly, even to an outsider. Harry had warned me to be careful. The lawyer, who had come down from New York, had been threatened. But as the morning wore on, I discovered that people were eager talk to me. They could not wait to tell me the real story. They wanted me to know the truth. They did not even seem resentful that I was a female as well as a Yankee. There are, occasionally, advantages to being a woman, especially if you have been brought up to be a lady and say please, and thank you, and hide a clinical cast of eye beneath lowered lashes and the brim of a stylish hat.

I stopped two matrons coming out of a store and asked, sweetly, if I could talk to them about the recent trial. They assured me it had been as fair as the day is long. Most towns, one of them added, would not have bothered with legal proceedings and just lynched the niggers, but that was not the Scottsboro way.

A local merchant, on the other hand, lamented the costs of the trials when so many poor white folk were on hard times, especially since thirty cents' worth of rope would have done the job just as well.

A man in spats and a stiff collar, taking the air in the town square, explained that lying, and stealing, and—he hesitated—other forbidden acts no gentleman would mention to a lady, were simply what colored folk did.

A white-haired grandmother shelling peas on her porch cited Genesis 9:20–27, the curse on Ham, and explained the boys had to go to the electric chair because God said so.

The woman who sold me a Coca-Cola, or as she called it, a dope, at a small store papered with signs for Grove's Chill Tonic and Prince Albert and Nehi, told me rape was the least of it. The papers couldn't print the rest, she explained. It wasn't fit for decent folks' eyes. "Them black brutes chewed the breast clear off the white gal."

I put the cold water-beaded bottle on the counter to write down her words. I would not quote them, but back in New York I would doubt my memory of them.

By midafternoon I had filled two small notebooks. I was sitting in the town square, flipping through the incriminating evidence, when the deputy came to find me. A few hours earlier, I would have thought it strange that he was aware of my existence. By now I knew the equivalent of smoke signals had gone up the moment I had stepped down from the train. He said Judge Hawkins and the mayor and a few other folks wanted to see me.

I followed him across the square, up the steps, and down a hall. Spittoons, each surrounded by a halo of crusty brown detritus, stood at regular intervals. I made a mental note of the local color.

The deputy opened a door at the end of the corridor. I stepped into a room with high windows and a long table. Five men stood. They were, after all, southern gentlemen. I recognized two of them from newspaper photographs, but the others were not unfamiliar. I knew their like existed in small towns all across America. Some were good at heart, and some were not so good, and most were a bit of both. They were fond of children, and liked dogs, and wanted to love their wives. Since they were southerners, they would tell you that they did not hate Negroes, and they would not be lying. Each of them harbored a lingering affection for a Negro woman whose soft breast and accommodating lap had been a shelter from life's earliest fears and miseries. Maybe that was why they continued to seek solace with the daughters and granddaughters of those women. Each of them could remember a Negro playmate, beloved and inseparable, a veritable shadow, until they were old enough to know better, or so their elders said.

The only surprise in the room was the Honorable George Huddleston. Huddleston, who represented Alabama's Ninth District in Congress, was a self-proclaimed liberal, who liked to tell the story of the time, as a boy, he had hoed cotton for two full days to make a single nickel. When he was paid, he kissed the coin and swore from that moment forward he would be a friend to the poor and oppressed. The story was corny, but Huddleston's credentials were solid. I wondered what he was doing here.

Judge Hawkins, who had presided over the trials, introduced himself and the others, and assured me they would be happy to answer any questions I might have, though he could not imagine what else I wanted to know.

"It was all in the newspapers," he explained. "The state of Alabama gave the defendants a fair trial. A jury convicted them. Justice was done. Violence was avoided." His voice, like his smile, was sincere. He was speaking from the heart, and did not understand why I could not understand.

When I started to ask about affidavits swearing that the girls had worked as prostitutes, he cut me off.

"Little lady, do you think that you know better than twelve good men and true?"

"But the affidavits—" I started again.

"Nigger affidavits," one of the others interrupted. "Not worth the two bits them bucks and wenches got paid to swear them."

The conversation went on that way for some time. The longer we talked, the less we said. I grew frustrated with their smug pride in the fact that the town had tried rather than lynched the boys. They became impatient with my refusal to see reason. Finally, the mayor reminded me that there was no hotel in Scottsboro, said he could not be responsible for my safety, and offered to have the deputy escort me to the train depot. I told him I had found my way from the station and could find my way back. That was when the Honorable George Huddleston stood. He glared down the table at me. Something about him, something besides his liberal credentials, teased at my memory.

There had been a lawsuit, an extremely foolish lawsuit, I seemed to remember. It must have been a year or two earlier. Something about an unpaid bill. That was it. Huddleston had refused to pay a bill for a fur his wife had charged without his permission. He had argued that he gave her a monthly allowance of seventy-five dollars and should not be held responsible for expenditures beyond that sum charged by her to his credit. The judge had ruled in favor of Huddleston, and conjugal happiness. There was no telling what would happen to the institution of marriage, the judge said, if wives were free to run around defying their husbands and charging expensive geegaws willy-nilly.

Every head at the table turned to Huddleston. He opened his mouth. His voice came out deep, and smooth with southern honey.

"I do not care, Miss . . . Miss . . ."

I was surprised. The lowest ward heeler knew the importance of remembering names. But then I was not a constituent, merely an interloper.

"Miss Whittier," I said.

"I do not care, Miss Whittier, about affidavits. I do not care about trials. I do not care whether those boys are innocent or guilty."

"May I quote you on that, sir?"

He ignored me and went on. "I am in favor of their being executed as quickly as possible. They were found riding on a freight train with two white women."

"Is riding a freight train a capital offense in Alabama, Congressman?"

Huddleston glared down the table at me. "I have one thing to say to you, Miss Whittier. Then I suggest you be on your way." He paused. I waited. We all waited.

"You outsiders cannot understand how we southern gentlemen feel about this question of relations between Negro men and white women."

His mouth snapped shut on the statement. That was it, his great pronouncement? But a murmur of agreement went around the table. Several of the men nodded vigorously. They knew wisdom when they heard it. They began pushing back their chairs and standing.

"One more question, Congressman," I said.

Some of the men looked incredulous, others disgusted. Clearly they had misjudged me. I was not a well-bred young lady.

Huddleston stood waiting.

"You've made it clear how southern gentlemen feel about relationships between Negro men and white women." I paused. "Would you care to make a statement about how southern gentlemen feel about relations between white men and Negro women?"

The men stopped shuffling away from their chairs, and hitching up their braces, and putting on their hats. Every face swiveled to Huddleston again. Some of them looked embarrassed, and some of them looked guilty, and all of them looked as if they were holding their breath. But Huddleston remained calm. I could not rattle him. Whether that was because of a clear conscience or a lifetime in the public eye, I had no idea.

"That is a thing of the past," he said. "It does not take place in this day and age."

Later, when I came to know Clarence Norris, the last of the Scottsboro boys to die, I would remember Huddleston's words.

I took my time making my way to the station. I did not want to give the mayor and the others the satisfaction of thinking they had run me out of town. I even made a detour down a broad street that lay napping in the shade of sheltering oaks. The trees reminded me of the local citizens, stolid, rooted, unassailable except by a force of nature. The good people—folks, as they called themselves—of Scottsboro had made up their collective mind. The kindly dowagers and the dapper man in the town square, the woman who quoted her Bible while she shelled peas, and the venerable leader who had sworn to fight for the poor and oppressed, were all in agreement. The boys had to die for the good of the community.

At least the white citizens were in agreement. I spoke to only one Negro in Scottsboro, and I did not want to talk to her. I knew from an incident I had heard about in Birmingham what could happen to a local Negro who talked to a white outsider. A bellboy in a hotel there told a reporter, in answer to the reporter's questions, that he did not know whether the boys were innocent or guilty, and did not like to venture an opinion. No one at the hotel had seen the bellboy since. I had no intention of getting anyone in Scottsboro into the same predicament, but the woman sitting on her porch, drinking iced tea and working on her needlepoint, was, like Judge Hawkins, like all the white people I spoke to that day, proud of her community. She did not want me to go away with the wrong impression.

She beckoned to me as I passed. I made my way up the path and onto the porch. She said she had heard I was going around town talking to people. "I reckon you've only been hearing from white folk."

I admitted that was true.

"Don't you think you ought to hear what nigras have to say?"

I thought of the bellboy and told her I had spoken to enough people, but she waved my words away as if she were swatting a fly, turned toward the screen door, and called, "Nettie."

A moment later a tall woman with skin like polished jet stepped onto the porch. We stood facing each other. We were the same height. We were also, I guessed, about the same age.

The white woman explained to her that I had come all the way from New York to find out how folks felt about the trial, and I wanted her opinion.

Nettie lifted her eyes to me, then looked back at the whitewashed floorboards.

"You don't have to—" I began, but the woman sitting in the rocking chair cut me off.

"Decent colored folk know those boys are no good. Isn't that true, Nettie."

"Yes, ma'am."

"Decent colored folk are as scared of those boys as decent white folk, aren't they?"

"Yes, ma'am."

"You know they got to burn sure as I do, isn't that so?"

This time Nettie hesitated a moment, but only a moment. She nodded.

"Is there anything else you want to tell the lady?"

"No, ma'am."

"Perhaps you'd like to sing one of your church songs for her."

Nettie lifted her eyes from the floorboards again. There was no hatred in them. There was nothing in them. She had made them completely blank.

"No, really . . ." I said.

"But she'd like to," the woman insisted.

"I have a train to catch," I pleaded.

The woman frowned at me. "Then maybe you'd like to give Nettie a nickel."

"What?"

"You know, a nickel for her troubles."

The last word hovered over us, as the woman went on staring at me and Nettie went back to contemplating the floorboards.

"Of course." I opened my purse, fumbled inside, and extracted a coin. I held it out to Nettie. She took it and thanked me, then glanced down at the coin. When she looked up again, she held my eyes just long enough for an emotion to break through the flat surface. Disdain flashed sudden and quick as lightning.

The woman had told me to give Nettie a nickel. I had handed her a quarter.

The railroad station was deserted. I was the only one leaving Scottsboro that evening. I made my way through the sour-smelling waiting room with its twin cuspidors out to the platform and settled on one of the benches. In the distance, a bank of clouds, their edges stained pink by the setting sun, sat low on the horizon. A breeze chased a sheet of yesterday's news down the tracks. I did not try to make out the headlines. I knew what they would say. Scottsboro had turned out to be much as I had imagined, a small-minded small town festering with fear and hatred and injustice. There had been only one surprise. I had gone to Scottsboro expecting hypocrisy. What I discovered was faith, fervent, devout, and unquestioning. Where I saw bigotry, the local citizens saw only the will of God and the laws of nature.

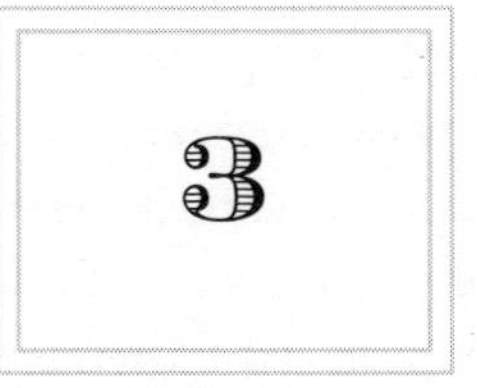

> The white girls were found in the car in a terrible condition mentally and physically, after their unspeakable experience at the hands of the black brutes.
>
> —*Jackson County* Sentinel, *1931*

> The doctor who examined the two women right after they were taken off the train testified that neither showed the slightest violence committed upon them in the actual act of sexual intercourse, though small bruises on the arm, back and a scratch on the neck were reported.
>
> —*Hollace Ransdall, Confidential Report for the ACLU, 1931*

The citizens of Scottsboro had been eager to give me the lowdown during the day I spent there, but the one man who could have told me some of the things I wanted to know was not talking, at least not to me. Years later, Dr. R. R. Bridges admitted he had gone to some lengths to avoid me. By that time, he was dying. Maybe he felt guilty. Maybe he was afraid of "going to torment," as Lester Carter would put it later. Dr. Bridges would have phrased it differently. He was an educated man from an old and respected southern family. But that did not mean he did not fear for his eternal soul.

The education and the family were two of the reasons Sheriff Wann had sent the girls to Dr. Bridges to be examined. The sheriff wanted only the best for his star witnesses, and Doc Bridges was the best. Everyone in the county said so, and Dr. Bridges did not contradict them, though he must have known, as my father who was also a physician always said, the average layman did not have an inkling of what constituted good medicine or bad. Most people judged a doctor by his bedside manner, and the money he made, and his social pedigree. According to those criteria, Doc Bridges was A-number-one. He had a degree from Vanderbilt University, and a big house on East Laurel Street, and a daddy who had been a fine man too, though not a doc. Old William P. had been a probate judge, till he got tired of the law and started the Bank of Paint Rock, the town where the boys and the two girls had been taken off the train. The old man had expected his boy to follow him into the bank, but R.R. had his heart set on doctoring. That was what made him so good at it. He wasn't a stranger to the courts, though, thanks to his daddy. He'll testify real good, they told one another. You can count on Doc Bridges.

He could have avoided involvement in the case. Precisely because he was such a good doctor, he could have told Sheriff Wann to take the girls to another physician. He had babies to deliver, and broken limbs to set, and hookworm and pellagra and the other horsemen of poverty to—to what? There was not much he could do for them, but he tried. He could have said he had his hands full with his morning office hours and his afternoon house calls, and the sheriff should take the two floozies, for that was what they were, to another physician. The girls did not need his ministrations, at least not for any injuries they had suffered on the train. Ruby required treatment for another problem, though I would not learn about that until later. But she and Victoria had no wounds or even side effects from their ordeal on the train. They did not even seem upset. Nonetheless, Dr. Bridges did not tell the sheriff to take the girls to another doctor. I sometimes wondered whether that was due to a sense of duty or an excess of vanity, but it is not the kind of question you ask. It is not even the kind of question most of us can answer.

Dr. Bridges examined the girls, and testified in court, repeatedly, and did his medical and civic duty. But he had no obligation to talk to reporters. I should not take it personally, he assured me years later as he sat dying on that wide shady porch wrapped around the big white house that was no longer a refuge from the world. He had refused to talk to the men from the local papers as well. Talking about the case outside the courtroom would only exacerbate the situation. R. R. Bridges took his Hippocratic oath seriously, in life as well as in medicine. He shrank from the idea of doing harm. Of course, that particular posture sometimes makes it impossible to do good as well. So the day I spent in Scottsboro, he told the woman in the white uniform and cap and heavy-soled shoes, who sat in his waiting room and guarded his inner office, that he was too busy with patients to see me, and he did not talk to reporters in any case.

"From hereabouts or Yankee," she said, "though I reckon the second's a heap worse. Seems to me you got a gracious plenty to tend to in your own back yard without coming down here hunting for trouble."

I did not get to speak to the doctor that day in Scottsboro, but I knew how things had gone at the trial. I had studied his testimony. I had spoken to reporters who had been there. And by the end I had his own recollections.

"How soon after the incident did you examine the girls?" Solicitor Bailey asked.

"I examined them in my office about an hour and a half after they were taken off the train. With my assistant Dr. Lynch."

"Please tell the court what you found."

Ruby Bates, the younger of the two, was a scared little rabbit. That was what he was thinking as he took her into his examining room and turned the other one, the tough one, over to Lynch. The scared little rabbit turned out to have an advanced case of syphilis. Dr. Bridges never told me that. Patient confidentiality. And Ruby did not like to talk about it. But I managed to worm the information out of her. It was nothing to be ashamed of, I assured her, merely one more example of the way she had been oppressed and exploited. I even cited the high incidence of respectable wives who contracted the disease from their husbands. That was before the second war and the widespread use of penicillin.

The other girl, Dr. Lynch reported, was not diseased. She probably had a better idea of how to take care of herself, Bridges thought. He did not say that in court. He merely described the minor abrasions and the evidence of recent sexual intercourse. A titter ran through the courtroom at that.

Children, he thought. He was testifying before a bunch of smutty-minded children.

"Could you say how recent was the sexual intercourse?" Bailey boomed the last two words. He had no choice. Outside the courtroom windows, the band from the mill had swung into "Dixie" again.

"No, sir, I could not say in time of hours or minutes."

"But you could say for sure that they had had sexual intercourse." This time Bailey drawled the words above the sound of the music, and the men in the jury box crossed and uncrossed their legs.

"I found a great amount of semen in Ruby Bates."

A chorus of snickers rose from the spectators. The judge rapped his gavel. Bailey said, "Please continue, Doctor." The solicitor was looking at his witness as he spoke, but he had one bright blue eye on the courtroom full of men who had not had this much fun since they had discovered French postcards, and the other on the state capitol.

"I made a smear to examine the spermatozoa under the microscope."

"What is the spermatozoa?" The smirk in Bailey's voice made Bridges wish he were back in his office. The books on his shelves did not think anatomy was a dirty joke. He and Dr. Lynch did not snigger like schoolboys when they conferred about bodily functions. On the rare occasion when sex reared its head in his office, he was decorous and the patient penitent.

"It is commonly called the male germ." The seriousness of Bridges's tone sobered the crowd, for a moment.

"Did you find many germs?" Bailey asked. Another wave titters ran through the courtroom.

"Yes, sir, lots of them," he answered and went on to explain that they were nonmotile.

"One last question, Dr. Bridges. Is it possible that six men, one after the other, could have had intercourse with each of these girls without their suffering lacerations?" Victoria had originally claimed that six had raped her and the rest Ruby, but for some reason—perhaps the human craving for symmetry—now each girl had been raped six times.

When I finally spoke to Bridges years later, I asked him about his answer, or rather about the mental processes that had led to it. The answer was clear. So, Bridges told me, was the question. He did not have to have sat at the knee of his daddy, the judge, to understand it. Bailey was not asking about probability or likelihood. He was asking about possibility.

"Besides," he told me, "you have to remember that three whites—the two girls and Orville Gilley—had identified the boys, and the boys had confessed. Not exactly confessed, but blamed one another. Wasn't that just like—" He stopped.

"Negroes?" I asked.

"Three of them testified against the others."

"But those statements were forced." Our early suspicions of how the sheriff had got the statements turned out to be correct. "The youngest one, Roy Wright, still has a scar on his cheek from the beating."

Odd, the things that change and the things that don't. By the time I sat on Dr. Bridges's porch, Roy Wright had been in jail for five years. He had grown four inches. But he still had the scar.

"I know nothing about that," Bridges said.

"But surely you can imagine. An illiterate Negro boy. Surrounded by white men with billy clubs and guns and heaven knows what. Threatening the worst, but telling him he'll be all right if he tells the truth. All he has to do is say that the other boys raped the girls."

Bridges, however, could not imagine. He was, he liked to say, a man of science, a physician. He dealt in observable fact.

"It is, in any event, beside the point," Bridges said. "The solicitor did not ask me to speculate about what happened on the train. He asked me if it was possible that six men, one after the other, could have had intercourse with each of those girls without the girls suffering lacerations. Girls like that—" He stopped again.

I thought of Ruby. By that time, I had come to know her.

"Girls like that," I finished for him, "could have taken on half a dozen men in succession without batting an eyelash?"

He did not like the comment. He especially did not like its coming out of the mouth of a woman who had fooled him into thinking she was a lady. He was a southerner, after all, and a gentleman, and a man.

"The solicitor asked me if it was possible. I told him, yes, it was possible."

The attorney for the defense had asked him about medical possibility too, but more diffidently. Stephen Roddy knew he was fighting, no, not fighting, surrendering a lost cause. He did not have his eye on the state house. He was not even from Alabama. He was from Chattanooga and did not know Alabama law, he told the judge and anyone else who would listen. But he was the best the boys' parents, who were also from Chattanooga and had taken up a collection, could afford. Then old Milo Moody, who people said used to know Alabama law, before he had drowned himself in a bottle, agreed to assist Roddy in the defense. Between the two attorneys, Bridges could not say who was the drunker. Rumor had it that Roddy had recently taken the Keeley Cure, but if so, he was not much of an advertisement for its efficacy. Dr. Bridges had found the incompetence of the defense team strangely reassuring. Surely the fact that no reputable member of the Jackson County bar would represent the boys said something about their guilt.

"Is it possible, Dr. Bridges," Roddy began his cross-examination, and whiskey-soaked breath rose from his mouth like swamp gas. It was hard to believe Judge Hawkins did not smell it too. "Is it possible," Roddy repeated, swaying a little on his feet, "to distinguish between the spermatozoa of a white man and that of a colored man?"

Ruby had asked him the same question. She lay on the examining table, knees apart, wide eyes fixed in terror on the ceiling, and somehow managed to squeeze out the words. "Is it different for white and nigger?"

Bridges did not answer her. The difference, or lack thereof, between white and Negro spermatozoa was none of her business.

Later, she would ask me the same question. I was ashamed to say I was not sure of the answer. But I knew where to look it up. I told her, just as Dr. Bridges had told the defense attorney, that it was not possible to distinguish between white and Negro spermatozoa. The answer gave her pause. By then she was talking a good game. She stood on stages and spouted slogans about brotherhood, and equality, and working-class solidarity. But bred-in-the-bone convictions die hard. She still believed there had to be a basic difference, deeper than color, more essential than appearance, between the races.

She was not the only one who had difficulty overcoming the beliefs of childhood. Once Eleanor Roosevelt confided to me that until she could kiss Mary Bethune in greeting without thinking, I am kissing a Negro, she would not be free of bigotry. I sometimes wonder if she ever did.

Dr. Bridges had testified under oath in a court of law. He had given scientific evidence. He had fulfilled his civic and professional duty. That was all that was required of him. And that was what he had made clear to Dr. Lynch. Marvin Lynch was young and excitable. Sometimes Bridges thought that if he had known how excitable, he might not have taken Lynch into his practice, but that was water over the dam. The younger doctor had come rushing into the private office afterward, carrying on about what he, Lynch, had said, and what the girls had done, and how if he testified to that in court, he would never be able to practice in Scottsboro again. Bridges had sat the younger man down and explained to him that they were physicians, not judges or jurors. Their job was not to determine the girls' truthfulness or draw conclusions, but to report the medical evidence as they found it. The rest was speculation for Lynch and hearsay for him, Bridges, and speculation and hearsay were not admissible in a court of law. You did not have to be the son of a judge to know that.

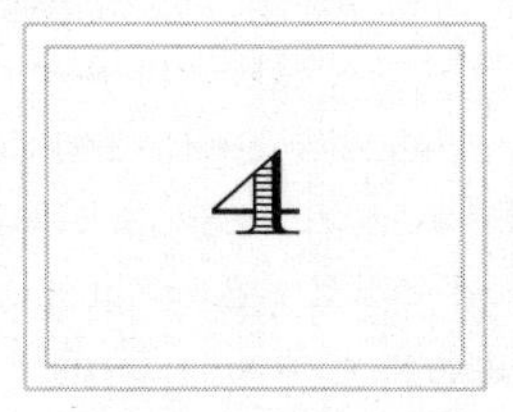

I was the only one . . . the first one who really thought it was worthwhile to ask the two women who were supposed to be the victims of this.

—Hollace Ransdall, 1974

An acquaintance of Harry's knew a man in Birmingham, who knew a social worker in Scottsboro, who was willing to take me to see Victoria Price and Ruby Bates. Mrs. Gorse, as the woman was called, had had dealings with both girls over the years. Ruby was the better behaved of the two, she told me starchily on the drive over. She wore her moral probity the way a housewife wears an apron, and for the same reason. She did not want to get soiled while on the job. Though the better of those two, she went on, was not saying good.

"These mill folk have no sense of morality. Lots of them are nothing but prostitutes." She turned left at a tilting sign that said ARMS STREET, pulled up in front of an unpainted narrow-fronted, deep shotgun house in a row of similarly dispiriting unpainted shotgun houses, and turned off the engine. "They just about have to be, I reckon. Nobody could live on the wages the mill pays, and that's the only other way they can make money. That and taking in wash, and there aren't many folks left who can pay other folks to do their wash."

She climbed out of the driver's side, and I got out of the passenger seat and looked around. I had seen photographs of similar scenes in mining villages and factory towns across the country and even witnessed a few firsthand. A layer of industrial grime lay thick on a landscape of rural decay. Wooden houses with cardboard-patched windows listed toward a muddy road. Pools of fetid water simmered in the afternoon sun. Barefoot children played cutthroat games among the slipshod shacks and stinking outhouses. Only one thing surprised me. The children chasing one another were both Negro and white. Alabama statute made the mingling of races a criminal offense, but poverty is a wily outlaw that has been known to get away with murder.

As I stood taking in the scene, a woman I recognized from photographs as Victoria Price came striding around from the back of the house. She must have heard the car pull up. She wore her brown hair close to her head in a flapper's bob. Her hooded eyes were set close together. She had a spoiled mouth, not spoiled by attention as the phrase usually signifies, but by deprivation and resentment. It made her look as if she wanted to bite the world. Her body was bottom-heavy, but she moved with assurance. No one would call it grace. Without breaking stride as she came toward us, she turned her head to one side and spat a stream of brown juice. Instinctively, I took a step back. Her grin was a slice of malice in her sallow face. I reminded myself the complexion was not her fault. I did not need Mrs. Gorse to tell me that pellagra, scurvy, rickets, and beriberi ran rampant. An argument could be made, and would have been in certain circles, that the malice was not her fault either. At least the argument would have been made were it not for those boys sitting in the Kilby death house.

Mrs. Gorse introduced us. Victoria looked me up and down. "You from the social services?" I told her I was not. "That's what I reckoned." She looked me over a second time. "You're one of them newspaper folk, right?" I admitted I was. "How much you willing to pay?"

"We don't pay for interviews."

"Some of the news fellas hereabouts bought me things. Kind of helps me recollect better."

"If you're having trouble remembering, I guess there isn't much point in my talking to you."

She looked me up and down a third time. "I ain't having no trouble. I just recollect sometimes better than others."

"Let's hope this is one of the good times."

She thought that over for a moment, said we might as well go inside and set for a spell, and led the way across a sloping porch into the house.

The room was dim, and my eyes took a moment to adjust. There was a cot, covered with a quilt of the kind that would become fashionable a few decades in the future, three mismatched straight-backed chairs, a rocking chair, a table with a hand-cranked Victrola, and another with an ancient sewing machine. Through a door, I saw a second room with a stove and table, and beyond that another door. The entire setup was grim, except for the walls. The walls made it heartbreaking. Every inch of space was covered with photographs from newspapers, and illustrations from magazines, and advertisements for products Victoria Price would never get her hands on. Women in evening dresses dabbed French perfume, and men in riding habits lounged against sleek roadsters, and people skied down mountains, and splashed in tropical waters, and danced aboard cruise ships. The only accoutrements of the good life missing were whiskey and brandy and champagne. Repeal of Prohibition was still two years in the future. Covers from the *Saturday Evening Post* and *True Confessions* and *True Detective*, and photo portraits of John Gilbert and Jean Harlow and Tallulah Bankhead hung side by side. The last, I remembered reading somewhere, was a Huntsville girl. Articles featuring photos of Victoria Price and Ruby Bates took up part of one wall. It seemed impossible that the tough customer who had tried to hold me up a moment ago spent her time clipping and pasting dreams, but these did not look like items left over from a previous tenant. Nor did I think the shriveled old woman sitting in the rocking chair in the corner had cut them out. One arm lay across her lap at an unnatural angle.

Victoria crossed the room, perched on the side of the chair, and reached an arm around the woman's shoulders. "This is my Ma. She can't work none since her accident." She lifted the woman's arm and let it fall back to her lap. "Fell downstairs fetching wash." She shook her head. "She ain't good for nothing no more. Got to do everything for her. Weren't for me, she'd've passed on by now. But I don't mind none. Course, plenty of folks don't have my good heart. Plenty of folks just forget their kin. But I reckon Ma took care of me, now she's old and lame, I got to take care of her. That's what kin's for. If they're loving kin. Ain't that right, Ma?"

Mrs. Price's eyes slid sideways to her daughter. Her lip curled.

"I suppose you want to know about how them niggers raped me," Victoria said.

"I'd like to know all kinds of things about you."

She smiled with unfeigned pleasure.

"To begin with, how old are you?"

The smile tightened. "Twenty-one."

"Twenty-four," her mother said.

On the drive over, Mrs. Gorse had told me Victoria was twenty-five, if she was a day.

"Ma ain't no good at recollecting anymore," Victoria explained.

"And you were married before?"

"Once."

"Twice," her mother said.

"Henry Pressley don't count, Ma. I wasn't with him no more than a couple of hours. I never even gone to bed with him."

"I wasn't counting Pressley neither," her mother said. "I was counting the other two. Enos and what's-his-name."

This time Victoria ignored her. "I had to leave Enos on account of he lay around on me all day drunk with canned heat. I made it eleven months, almost a whole year, but then I just couldn't take it no more. But Enos is the only man I ever knowed. Till them niggers came along and ruined me. That's why they got to burn."

"According to county records, you were convicted of adultery."

She tilted her head to one side. The gesture was almost girlish. "Won't say I was. Won't say I wasn't."

"Pardon me?"

"Don't know what it means."

I started to explain, then caught myself. "How long have you worked in the mills, Mrs.—? I'm sorry, I didn't get your husband's last name."

"I go by Mrs. Price. Same as Ma." She put an arm around her mother's shoulders again. "I been in the mills eight years."

"Twelve," her mother said.

Victoria tightened her grip around her mother's shoulders. "Now, Ma, you know you ain't no good at recollecting these days."

"Twelve," her mother insisted.

"Don't pay her no mind," Victoria said to me.

"Twelve years," her mother repeated.

"Ten," Victoria said with an air of someone who has decided to split the difference.

"Twelve," her mother said again. "She went into the mills when she was twelve. Same as me."

At twelve I was falling out of love with horses, and discovering Trollope, and accompanying my mother to my first meeting of the Women's International League for Peace and Freedom.

"Didn't have no choice when I was coming up," her mother went on. "If your ma and pa worked in the mill, you went into it soon as you turned twelve. The law said so. Only way you could get out was if the superintendent said you had something called good cause. Never did find out what good cause was, on account of nobody never got it."

"Folks don't care nothing about that, Ma." Victoria turned to me. "Nobody wants to hear about working in the mills. They ain't interested in how you can't hear yourself think on account of the screeching and hammering of them machines, and you can't breathe on account of all the lint, and you got to take care not to let your mind get to wandering, on account of next thing you know you got a hand caught or a couple of fingers missing. If folks where you come from don't know, it's only on account of they don't want to. What folks want to hear, even Yankees, I reckon, is about how them niggers raped us two white women. They want to hear about how they held us down, and beat us, and kept putting their big black things in us again and again. They want to hear how one of them pinned me down, and then one of them pulled out his privates and said, 'When I put this in you and pull it out, you will have a Negro baby.' "

William Randolph Hearst could not have phrased it better.

"All right," I said, "tell me about the rape."

"They jumped into the car where me and Ruby were setting. They had knives. Every last one of them. And then the big nigger hollered at me, 'Are you going to put out?' I didn't have no idea what the words meant, but I answered just the same. I told him, 'No, sir, I am not.' "

"Even though you didn't know what the words meant?" Only later, after I left the house, did I realize I had posed the wrong question. I should have asked why she had called a Negro sir.

"I could guess. They had them knives, and they were moving in on me and Ruby. That was when they grabbed me. Two of them held knives to my throat, and two more tore off my overalls and my step-ins, and another two held my legs. Then they went to ravishing me. All six of them. They took turns. One after the other. They wouldn't even let me up to have a spit."

"You were chewing snuff during this ordeal?"

"I said I was needful of a spit, didn't I? But they wouldn't let me. I kept fighting all the same. I kicked and screamed and fought hard as I could, but they were too big and strong."

"Dr. Bridges testified that when he examined you shortly after you were taken off the train, you had no serious bruises or wounds, and your pulse and breathing were normal. He said you didn't even seem upset."

"That ain't what he said. He said I was raped. He could tell from all the jissum."

"Which was nonmotile."

"Non what?" she said, though I was fairly sure she knew the definition of the word as well as she did *adultery*.

"Let's talk about the trip to Chattanooga. You went there to find work?"

"Ain't none 'round here. The old Margaret Mill ain't paying more than a dollar-twenty a day, half what you could get two years back."

"The Helen knitting and the Margaret spinning are the worst mills in Huntsville," Mrs. Gorse explained.

"Worst in what way?" I asked.

"Broken-down equipment, dangerous working conditions, dirt-cheap wages. Only the lowest type of mill hands work there."

"I ain't no low type," Victoria said. "Time was I ran thirteen, fourteen sides a shift, that's how low type I am, thirteen, fourteen sides at twenty-two cents apiece. Like to see you do that." She was speaking to Mrs. Gorse, but I had a feeling she included me in the challenge. I didn't blame her. I did not even know what a side was, let alone how to turn out fourteen of them in a shift. "But that was back before. Now even the best, like me, is lucky to get six sides. You know what they pay a side nowadays? Eighteen cents. Eighteen lousy cents. If they let you work. All the mills gone to short time now. Most folks can get is a couple of days every other week. Ain't no benefit in complaining neither. Ain't you heard, the bosses say, there's a Depression." She spat out the word with her snuff, and I thought how President Hoover had seized on it originally because it sounded less dire than panic or bubble or any of the usual terms for economic crises. "Pin it on them Yankees coming down here with their sacks full of money, they tell you, throwing up them new mills with fancy machines that do the drawing and spinning and carding without a single body tending. Take it or leave it, they say before they slam the door in your face. So me and Ruby decided to leave it and go looking for work in Chattanooga."

"Just you and Ruby?"

She held my eyes with a steadiness I could not help admiring. "Just me and Ruby."

"What about Jack Tiller and Lester Carter?"

The girls had spent the night before they left for Chattanooga in the North Carolina railroad yards with two men named Jack Tiller and Lester Carter. Victoria and Jack had settled at the top of a small hill, and Ruby and Lester at the bottom. Victoria must have been a card, because she kept making jokes about her and Jack rolling down on Ruby and Lester. A few times they did roll down on them. The lawyers, and the newspapers, and the humanitarians who wanted to save the boys called it promiscuous lovemaking. When it happened in a hobo camp, it was promiscuous lovemaking. When it occurred in Greenwich Village, it was free love.

"I don't know no Jack Tiller," Victoria said.

"According to the records, you went to jail for committing adultery with a man called Jack Tiller. His wife swore out the warrant."

This time she did not deny knowing the meaning of the word. She turned her face away from me and sat staring at a picture on the wall above her head. It was an illustration for a short story in the *Saturday Evening Post*. I recognized the author's name. Octavus Roy Cohen. Abel Newman had introduced me to Cohen once, though I could never understand how the two had become friends. Cohen made a fortune churning out short stories and mysteries about what he called "cullud" folk.

I gave up on Jack Tiller and moved on. "You met Orville Gilley when you arrived in Chattanooga, is that right?"

She turned from the wall back to me. The sullenness smoldered within her like damp wood. I wondered what would happen if the fire caught. "Me and Ruby come across Orville on the train coming back. I didn't know nothing about him in Chattanooga. We weren't traveling with no men."

For a woman who claimed not to know what adultery was, she seemed to have considerable knowledge of statutes about vagrancy and crossing state lines for immoral purposes.

"I thought you and Ruby spent the night before you left in the Huntsville yards with Jack Tiller and Lester Carter and the night you arrived in the Chattanooga yards with Orville Gilley and Lester Carter."

"Me and Ruby went to a boardinghouse in Chattanooga."

"Do you remember the address?"

"All I recollect is the lady who run it. Lady by name of Mrs. Callie Brochie."

"You had enough money for a boardinghouse?"

"We had a little. And Mrs. Brochie's got neighborly feelings for folks on hard times. Not like some." She stared at me. I did my best to hold her gaze.

"So you and Ruby did not spend the night in the hobo jungle with Lester Carter and Orville Gilley?"

"I already told you we didn't spend no night in no hobo jungle."

"Why did you decide to go back to Huntsville the next morning, so soon after you arrived?"

"There wasn't no work."

"You didn't give yourself much of a chance to look."

She hesitated. "Some niggers started bothering me and Ruby."

"The boys you said raped you on the train?"

"I didn't just say. Them boys raped me. But them niggers bothered us in the morning were different niggers."

"How did they bother you?"

"Me and Ruby went down to the yards—"

"From Mrs. Brochie's boardinghouse?"

"Yeah, from Mrs. Brochie's boardinghouse."

"Sorry."

The word stopped her for a moment. I realized she rarely heard it.

"A body'd be like to freeze to death in the yards that morning. So me and Ruby went looking for a fire to warm ourselves. Trouble was, only one we could find had niggers setting 'round it. I never would have set with a bunch of niggers, if I wasn't feared of freezing to death. But we asked real nice if we could set with them to get some heat, and they said yeah, then soon as we did, they started talking dirt to us."

"What kind of dirt?"

"I don't like to say."

I did not point out that she had shown no such fastidiousness when describing the rape.

"Then what happened?"

"I saw a white boy. Lester Carter. That's where I know Lester Carter from. I found him in the yards that morning. So I went up to Lester and told him them niggers were talking dirt to me and Ruby, and he put them in their place."

"But they were not the same boys who got on the train? The ones who allegedly raped you?"

"Ain't no alleged about it. And I already said they weren't the same." She looked at me, and a sly smile crept across her face. "Just on account of all niggers look alike to you Yankees don't mean we can't tell one from the other down here."

"You watch your mouth, Victoria Price," Mrs. Gorse said. "I won't have you sassing folks."

Victoria shrugged and went back to studying the *Saturday Evening Post* illustration.

"You haven't had an easy time of it, have you?"

She turned from the wall to me with a look of surprise. "I never had a break in my life. Ma neither."

"So you can understand what it's like for those Negro boys."

Her face hardened. The creases at the side of her mouth and between her eyes turned black as crayon marks. "Them boys ain't nothing like me. They're niggers."

"Nobody ever gave them a break either."

"Listen, sister, all I know is what happened. Those niggers raped me and Ruby. They held us down with guns and knives. I fought like a banshee, but they raped us over and over. They ruined me and Ruby for life. That's why I was so happy when I saw them get nabbed."

"How does that make your lot better?"

Her eyes flashed. The smoldering wood had caught fire.

"You want to know about me? Well, I'll tell you. All my life I been trash, but I ain't been so low that colored folk could treat me like trash. That's why when folks heard what them boys did to me, a bunch of ladies give me and Ruby dresses. Not castoffs some charity lady's been wearing to church every Sunday since ten years back, but brand-new store-bought dresses. And the lawyers in the courtroom called me ma'am. And they put my picture in the paper and wrote stories about me. You know what them stories said? They didn't say white trash. They said white womanhood. So don't you come 'round here talking to me about how them niggers has suffered just like me. They ain't nothing like me. They're just a bunch of no-'count niggers. I'm a defiled white woman."

> The children's bureau reports 200,000 children under twenty-one wandering through the land. These two girls [Victoria Price and Ruby Bates] are part of a great army of adventurous, venal girls who like this way of life . . . the girls semi-prostitutes, the boys sometimes living on the girls, and all of them stealing and bumming to end up with a joyous night in a boxcar.
>
> —*Mary Heaton Vorse,* The New Republic, *1933*

First thing I saw was them teeth of hern. They were white and straight as the keys on the piano they play sheet music on uptown at Kress's. Them teeth were so pretty they looked too good to eat with. One thing was for positive, they were too good to dip snuff with. But with teeth like them, you wouldn't have to dip no snuff, on account of they wouldn't give you no hurting. Just looking at them teeth made me spit the snuff out. The lady blinked, like she never saw no one spit snuff before. I wiped my mouth with the back of my hand and pressed my lips together. A body with teeth like that was bound to laugh at the mess I got in my mouth.

She was standing in the door behind Mrs. Gorse, the lady from the social services, and Mrs. Gorse was sniffing around like always, and wrinkling her nose like everything, and that meant me and Ma too, smelled bad. It made me cross-legged mad. If anyone smelled, it was

Mrs. Gorse. Not always, but sometimes when it got real hot, or when I reckon she was having her monthlies, she reeked sour. Someday I'm fixing to tell her. The house don't smell, Mrs. Gorse, you do.

"I see the young 'uns are playing with the coloreds again," Mrs. Gorse said.

"Ain't no one excepting coloreds for them to play with on Depot Street." The words were ornery, but Ma's voice sounded like she was saying she was sorry. It always did when she talked to Mrs. Gorse, and the preacher, and the church ladies who come by with hand-me-down clothes and wouldn't set in a chair for fear of catching cooties or worse.

Mrs. Gorse clicked her tongue against her teeth and studied the room real slow, like she was on the lookout for a man under the bed or a still out the back door. Lucky Maynard took off, only I'd be lying if I said I wasn't a little sorry. Maynard wasn't mean as some of Ma's boarders. He wasn't always coming after me neither. And his money sure did come in handy.

Mrs. Gorse gave up studying the room and turned to the lady with the piano-white teeth who was still hanging back in the door, like one of them church ladies who was scared to set. I didn't blame her none. If I had a dress like that, I wouldn't want to set here neither. It wasn't fancy, just plain navy blue. No ruffles nor lace nor ribbons nor nothing, just a white collar. But there was something real nice about it. Elegant, Victoria would say. Her shoes were swell too, navy blue and white. Spectators, the magazines call them. And her hose was silk. I didn't much fancy her hat, though. It didn't have nothing to it. If I had a hat like that, I'd sew on one of them veils that come down just over the eyes, specially since the lady's eyes didn't have nothing to recommend them. They were plain brown, not blue like mine. Cornflower-blue, someone called them once. Wish I could recollect who. It wasn't Shug, even though I reckon he was the sweetest-talking colored boy I ever knew. Maybe the salesman fella who come through town right after Christmas. He had a suitcase full of lip rouge and powder and perfume, and as long as he was around, it was Christmas all the time.

Mrs. Gorse was saying the lady's name was Miss Whittier, and she come all the way from New York specially to talk to me. Mrs. Gorse took one chair and told the lady to take the other one over by the window. "The nigger smell isn't so bad over there," Mrs. Gorse said.

"I scrubbed real good," Ma said in that apologizing voice.

"You can scrub till the cows come home, Miz Bates. Won't make any difference. Once niggers live in a place, it smells nigger for life."

"I don't smell anything," the lady from New York said.

Mrs. Gorse looked at her funny.

"I guess it's my northern nose."

"It must be," Mrs. Gorse said.

Ma set on the side of the cot. I took the stool.

"Now, Ruby," the lady started, then stopped. "May I call you Ruby?"

"That's my name."

"Don't you go sassing, Ruby Bates," Mrs. Gorse said.

I could have pinched Mrs. Gorse for that. I wasn't sassing no one. I just didn't understand why the lady asked if she could call me by my name.

"I don't think Ruby was sassing me," the lady said and give me a big smile that bared them pretty white teeth. "I have an idea," she went on. "It's such a nice afternoon, maybe Ruby could show me around. You could come back for me later, Mrs. Gorse."

Mrs. Gorse did not have to be asked a second time. She didn't much like setting with the nigger smell. I reckoned she didn't much like the lady from New York neither. And maybe the lady didn't like her back, on account of it wasn't such a nice afternoon, but maybe the lady said it just to get rid of Mrs. Gorse. It was funny thinking of them two not liking each other. When you're a linthead, you're so busy feeling folks looking down their noses at you, you don't notice them looking down their noses at each other.

The lady was on her feet as soon as Mrs. Gorse was out the door. "You don't mind if Ruby and I go for a walk, do you, Mrs. Bates?" she said to Ma. I knew Ma didn't care, but even if she did, she ain't likely to say so to some lady from New York who come with Mrs. Gorse, no matter there wasn't no love lost between them two.

"Is that all right with you, Ruby?" the lady asked.

She was standing in the door waiting, and there wasn't nothing I could do excepting get up and follow her outside, only I'd be lying if I said I felt partial to the idea. There was nothing wrong with her, excepting she talked funny, not just fast like every Yankee I ever heard, but like someone on the radio or in the moving pictures. Something else about her didn't set right neither. She wasn't looking down her nose, like Mrs. Gorse and them church ladies. I was wrong about her not wanting to set when she first come. But she was looking too close. She was studying me, like she was fixing to memorize me.

"I reckon there ain't no place much to walk," I said when we were outside the house.

"How about up to the Carolina yards? Isn't that where you went the night before you hopped the freight to Chattanooga?"

I didn't mind walking to the yards none, but she didn't know what she was asking for. "You going to walk to the yards in them shoes?"

"They're comfortable."

I near had to laugh. She might talk fancy, but she didn't know nothing about nothing. "Don't matter how good they fit. They ain't going to be decent to look at if you walk up to the yards in them. Nothing but mud and dirt and wet all the way from here to there."

"I'll be careful," she said and started walking, and I reckoned there wasn't nothing I could do but start in walking with her.

"All I know is if I had shoes like them on my feet, you wouldn't find me tramping up to no yards."

"There are more important things in the world than shoes, Ruby."

"Not if you ain't got them."

She stopped and turned to me. I reckoned by the look on her face I got her good.

"You're right, Ruby. I'm sorry. But I'd still like you to show me the yards. We can have a good talk on the way." She put her arm through mine like me and her was girlfriends and started walking again.

"Do you go up to the yards often?" she asked.

I shrugged.

"Everyone needs a place to get off by herself."

I didn't say nothing to that, partly on account of I didn't know what to say, partly on account of I couldn't think about nothing but them shoes. It near broke my heart to see what she was doing to them.

"But you weren't alone when you went up to the yards the night before you hopped the freight for Chattanooga, were you? It was you, and Victoria, and, let's see, who else? Lester Carter and Orville Gilley. Is that right?"

"Orville wasn't nowhere near the Carolina yards that night."

"Are you sure?"

"I was there, wasn't I? Me and Lester and Victoria and Jack Tiller went up to the yards night before we left."

"So Orville Gilley wasn't with you in Chattanooga, Jack Tiller was."

She really didn't know nothing. "You got it all wrong. Jack was in the yards with us here, but he didn't want no part of going to Chattanooga."

"Why not?"

"He was scared. Said if his wife could have him and Victoria locked up for adultering in Huntsville, just think on what she could get the law to do to them for adultering across state lines. He said Victoria shouldn't be carrying me neither, on account of I was underage, but I told him I was seventeen and plenty old enough to go where I took a fancy."

I shut my mouth real sudden, on account of I was so surprised. I never talked so much in my whole life. I reckon it ain't so hard to think of things to say when Victoria ain't around correcting and making fun. And the lady needed a heap of straightening out.

"So you wanted to go to Chattanooga? I thought it was Victoria's idea."

"I got a mind of my own."

"I'm sure you do. That's why I want to hear your side of the story. Tell me about you and Lester."

"Ain't nothing much to tell."

"He was your boyfriend?"

"I liked him good enough."

"Is he from around here?"

"He's from somewhere else, but he was laying out a sentence in jail with Victoria and Jack, and when they all got out, they brung him 'round."

"What was he in jail for?"

"Vagrancy." I recollected what Lester said and had to smile.

"What's so funny?"

"Lester. He says, know what vagrancy is? Looking for work when there ain't none."

"Lester sounds like quite a philosopher."

I cut a look at her out of the side of my eyes. Maybe I ain't so smart, but I reckon I'm smart enough to know when someone's making fun of me. Making fun of Lester too, I reckon.

The lady was quiet a minute, like she knew she been mean.

"But he sounds nice," she said after a spell.

"I reckon he was the politest boy I ever knowed."

"In what way?"

"First time he come 'round, he took his hat off soon as he stepped foot in the house. Took it off later too."

"When was that?"

"Out under the honeysuckle."

"Lester sounds like a gentleman."

I looked over to see if she was making fun again, but I couldn't make out no joke.

"I don't know about that, but there ain't nothing he wasn't polite about. On the way up to the yards, when we went walking, like me and you are now, he asked what I liked to do, and I said I liked to have a good time, and then he asked could he jazz me. Nobody never asked before. They just started in on it."

I shut my mouth again. I wasn't fixing to say that about jazzing. She was probably just like the church ladies. They thought jazzing sent you straight to hell. Unless you were married, and they looked like they wouldn't do it even then. Victoria said don't be so sure. Some ladies who talk right and dress fine and got lots of money put on a good act, but they're made same as us. Do the same things too. I looked at the lady's hand. Wasn't no ring on that finger. She walked with her back real straight and her nose in the air. I reckon she wouldn't be in too much of a hurry to mess that churchy-white collar and that old-lady hat. I reckon she'd near to faint if some fella started in to jazz her.

"And what did you say when Lester asked if he could jazz you?"

At least she wasn't afraid to say the word. The church ladies didn't even know it. Mrs. Gorse knew it, but she'd choke to death on it before she spit it out.

"I said I didn't mind if he did."

"You liked Lester right off?"

"He wasn't much to look at. His hair was making a retreat from his forehead, and sometimes his face looked like biscuit dough when it comes out of the oven before its time, but it was nice with him up in the yards that night."

"So you and Lester and Victoria and Jack Tiller spent the night there and hopped the freight to Chattanooga the next morning?"

"Like I said, me and Victoria and Lester did. Jack reckoned he'd be along in a spell."

"But he didn't show up?"

"We didn't stay long enough to find out."

I still didn't see why we had to turn tail and run back the next morning. Seems if we went all the way to Chattanooga to hustle some, we could give hustling a try, but when Victoria fixed her mind, wasn't no one could unfix it. I reckon if Jack Tiller come along, Victoria would have stayed for a spell.

"Because of the Negro boys? Not the ones on the train, the ones around the fire."

I swung around to look at her. "How'd you know about them?"

"Victoria told me."

"They didn't mean no harm."

"What happened?"

I recollected how Victoria told it. Them boys started talking dirt to me and Ruby. What if the lady asked what kind of dirt? Wasn't no way I could make it up. Besides, I wasn't fixing to tell no more lies, about coloreds nor nobody else.

"Nothing."

We walked on without talking for a spell. I kept my eyes on the tracks. You couldn't even tell the blue part on her shoes from the white no more. She couldn't say I didn't give her a warning.

"So you went to Chattanooga without Jack Tiller, but in Chattanooga you met up with Orville Gilley. Is that right?"

"Only Orville said not to call him that, no matter it was his God-given name. When he was railroading, like he was most of the time, on account of him and work didn't get along too good, he said, he called himself Carolina Slim."

"Carolina Slim?"

"It suited him pretty good. Maybe not the Carolina part, on account of he could just as easy come from Alabama or Tennessee, but the Slim part. He was scrawny as them chickens the Red Cross hands out on Thanksgiving. His big head just bobbed away on that stringy neck, and he got ears stuck out like jug handles. But once Slim got to talking, you forgot what he looked like. You couldn't even see him clear on account of all them words buzzing around him like a swarm of bees. The way he told it, he wasn't just a hobo, he was a hobo poet. He asked right off if we wanted him to recite some poems he made up, but Victoria said she wasn't interested in no poems. She was needful of the inside of a boxcar that was fit for a white woman."

I stopped. If folks could hear me now, they wouldn't be asking if the cat got my tongue. Maybe it was on account of the lady just kept asking questions. She didn't ask like the sheriff and the deputies and that man on the railroad siding, like they knew the answers and wanted to find out if I knew too, but like she didn't know and wanted me to tell her.

"So Carolina Slim helped you find a boxcar?"

"He said there wasn't no such thing as a boxcar that wasn't locked or rotted through or already taken by a heap of rats, but he knew a place up the spur with some woods and a little lake, and if we fancied that, he'd carry us there. So we hiked up the spur a ways, and turned into some woods, and sure enough there was the lake right where Slim said. It was coming on to dark, and the water was like a looking glass in the moonlight, 'cepting when a fish jumped. Lester said if he had a pole he could catch us some supper, and Slim said he didn't need no pole, his daddy learned him to catch fish with his bare hands, only he didn't like to get himself wet."

"It sounds as if you were having a good time."

"It was real fine up that spur. Slim and Lester fixed a campfire from some sticks, and me and Victoria rolled down our overalls. Then Slim said him and Lester should hit the stem before it turned late and all the shops closed up."

"Hit the stem?"

There was a gracious plenty the lady didn't know. "That's railroading talk for the main street. Victoria was fixing to go with them, but Slim wouldn't let her, on account of some folk don't take to girl hoboes, he said. Him and Victoria got to scrapping about it. She said she reckoned some folks were just plain dumb, on account of these days the world was full of hobo girls and hobo families and hobo babies. She even heard tell of hobo preachers, though she didn't have much use for them. But Slim said if she was fixing on eating supper, she better do it his way. There was a place on Rossville Boulevard, Nell Booth's Chili Parlor it was called, where he was real welcome. It wouldn't take him no longer than the time it cost to recite a couple of his poems, and him and Lester would be carrying back supper."

"Did they?"

"Slim's poems must've been good as two-bit pieces at Nell Booth's Chili Parlor. They come back carrying a onion, and a potato, and a sack of navy beans, and some coffee grounds ain't been used more than once or twice, and the prettiest piece of fatback you ever saw. We cooked the whole mess up and had a real good supper, setting around that fire by the lake."

"It sounds nice."

"It was real nice. If you lied back and looked up at the sky, you could see about every star that ever was and a big old moon just laughing down on us, and then if you set up, you could see the very same thing in the water, only there it didn't lay so quiet. In the water, the moon and the stars went to dancing. And you could smell the honeysuckle. Not just honeysuckle. You could smell all spring coming. I told that to Lester. I said I smell all spring coming, and he said that ain't nothing, I hear spring coming. We were real quiet then, and you know what, I heard it coming too."

"So you and Lester and Victoria and Carolina Slim spent the night by the lake?"

All of a sudden I recollected the way I was supposed to tell it. Me and Victoria passed the night in a boardinghouse run by a lady by the name of Mrs. Callie Brochie. Victoria picked the name, on account of it sounded so refined. I started walking faster.

The lady kept up with me. "It's all right, Ruby. Victoria isn't here now. You can tell me what really happened."

"It's getting on late. I got to go back." I turned and started walking the other way, and the lady kept up again. I looked down at our feet walking side by side along the tracks. Them pretty shoes was no better now than my ugly wore-out ones. It made me want to cry.

"What happened the next morning, Ruby?"

"The boys hit the stem again."

"While you and Victoria waited at the lake?"

The lady was coming back to the other colored boys. I could tell. I closed my mouth. Wasn't no cause to talk about them. Victoria said if you lied about one nigger, you might as well lie about a hundred. But maybe the worseness of torment you went to had to do with how many lies you told. There wasn't nothing to tell about them other boys anyway, only more about Victoria's troublemaking.

Soon as Orville and Slim were out of sight the next morning, she started in talking about how there wasn't no benefit sitting around shivering, and best we head back to the jungle and see if we could find a place to warm ourselves. I reckoned Orville and Slim wouldn't know where to find us if we did that, but I didn't say nothing, on account of I knew from the way Victoria was fixing her skirt and yanking a comb through her hair, she had her mind set to something. When that happened, wild horses couldn't unset it.

Me and her walked on down the spur and came in sight of the jungle. Three colored boys were setting on a log by a fire. Two were black as pitch, and one was molasses-brown. With his long legs sprawled out to the fire and his big hands whittling away at something, the molasses boy featured Shug.

"Wish I knew how long them fellas were fixing to be," Victoria said. "On account of if they ain't coming back for a time, we could go over there and take some money off them niggers."

Them boys didn't look to me like they had any money to take off them, but Victoria had that narrow-eyed figuring look, so I didn't say nothing.

Victoria ran her tongue over her lips. "The longer we go on standing here, the less time we got for hustling over there," she said and started walking over to them boys in that sway-hipped way she got when she's looking for trouble. And there wasn't nothing I could do but slide into my own sway-hipped walk behind her.

"Or did you go back down to the jungle?" the lady asked and brought me back from recollecting in my head.

I didn't make no answer.

"You went down to the jungle, and that's where you ran into those Negro boys, isn't it?"

Maybe she wasn't so dumb after all.

"They were setting 'round a fire, and me and Victoria were looking for to warm ourselves. That was the only reason we set with them."

"Was Victoria solicit—hustling those boys, Ruby?"

I swung to face her. "How'd you know?"

"But you didn't want to?"

"A jungle's a fearsome place. There's hoboes rolling other hoboes, and man hoboes putting themselves on girl hoboes, and on little boy hoboes too, and white hoboes looking for trouble with nigger hoboes, and nigger hoboes hunting the same with whites. I didn't like to take a chance. Besides, them boys didn't look like they had nothing to hustle off them." I stopped. That was the kind of trouble talking could land you in. "I wouldn't do no hustling anyway. Specially not niggers."

"Victoria said the boys started bothering you."

"She just said that on account of Lester come back and saw us setting with them."

You would have thought that log was hell burning the way Victoria jumped up and took off for Lester. I followed pretty quick myself. We weren't doing no sway-hipped strut then.

Lester said folks weren't so free and easy with handouts this morning, so Slim was still working the stem, but all the time he was talking, he was staring at them colored boys.

"What're you doing with them niggers, anyway?" he asked finally. "You were supposed to be waiting on me and Slim back at the lake."

"We near froze to death back there," Victoria said. Lester was still studying them colored boys. "We came on down looking for a fire.

Only reason we were setting with them niggers is the fire. Weren't for that, you sure wouldn't catch me and Ruby setting with a bunch of niggers."

Lester pushed his hat back on his head, like some fellas do when they're trying to show they're thinking. He was still studying the coloreds.

"It's lucky you come back now," Victoria said.

"Why's that?" Lester asked.

"On account of them niggers started talking dirt to me and Ruby."

Lester went on studying the colored boys, while his face turned that pasty uncooked biscuit color. Finally, he reached into his pocket real slow and took something out. It was a little pearl-handed knife he showed me that first night in the yards. He went on standing there, studying the boys through the slits he was making of his eyes, and turning the knife over, in and out of his fingers, like he was doing a magic trick.

"Well, what're you going to do about it?" Victoria said.

"I'm thinking on it."

"You're thinking on it!"

"I mean, I'm thinking whether I should whup 'em now or just give 'em a warning."

Before Victoria could make up his mind for him, and maybe he knew she could, he started walking over to the colored boys. He was moving real slow, flipping the knife in and out of his fingers. It was just a itty-bitty thing, not nothing to scare a colored boy, unless a white boy was playing with it.

Lester was standing right up close to them coloreds now. He was looking down at them, but they weren't looking up at him. They had their eyes fixed to the ground, like maybe if they didn't look up at him, he'd get wore out looking at them and go away. Only any colored who ever been stared at by a white man knows that ain't going to happen.

"What'd you say to them girls?" Lester growled.

"I didn't say nothing to them nor nobody else," the boy on the end of the log said without looking up.

"Boy!" Lester said, and I almost jumped, because now he sounded like he meant business. "You look at me when I'm talking to you, boy!"

I knew them words. Sometimes I reckon they're the sweetest words in a white man's mouth, when he's shouting them at a colored. They were specially sweet in Lester's mouth, on account of something he told me. The guard on the chain gang used to yell them words to him. Didn't matter that he was white as the guard. You look at me when I'm talking to you, boy, the guard used to holler, and it darn near broke Lester's heart being talked to like a nigger. But now he was saying them to the nigger, and he was a white man again.

Me and the lady were back on Depot Street, and Mrs. Gorse was setting in her auto in front of the house, and for the first time in my life I was glad to see her. I had a gracious plenty of talking. Then the lady asked if she could come back to visit again tomorrow, and I couldn't think of nothing to say against it.

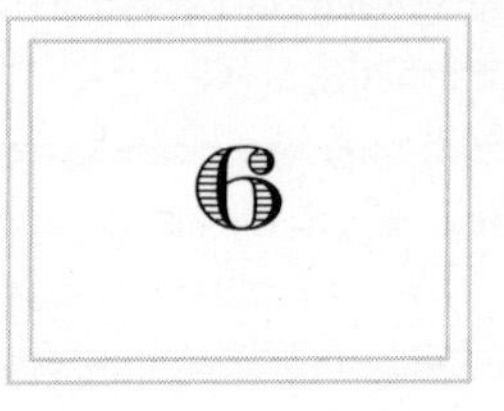

This was an education. More education than I ever got in all my eight years in college.

—Hollace Ransdall, 1974

After I left Ruby that evening with a promise to return the following morning, Mrs. Gorse drove me to the hotel. Unlike Scottsboro, Huntsville had not only a hotel, but one complete with electricity and indoor plumbing, not as ordinary an occurrence as one might think in those days before the Tennessee Valley Authority dammed the river and brought electrically powered lights and refrigerators and radios and all sorts newfangled amenities to the area. According to the desk clerk, many of the local citizens would have preferred to keep things as they were.

"Some folks hold it ain't healthy," he told me, as he turned the register toward me to sign. "They say setting over running water gives phlegm to innards. But I don't hold with that. We got indoor toilets ever since I come to work here, and I ain't seen no one get sick from them yet."

I spent most of the evening in my room writing up what Ruby had told me. When I was finished, I walked the half block from the hotel to the Western Union office. It was a small dusty place, a far cry from some of the big bustling offices in New York, but all Western Union offices were alike. The staccato clatter of the teletype machine was the same, and the aroma of pulpy yellow paper and stale tobacco, and the faint aura of anticipation that stirred the customers, and the self-importance that rose from the employees. Or maybe Western Union offices were not all alike. Maybe my memories just cast them all in the same light. I never could enter one without thinking of my father.

I do not know if my father sent more telegrams than other men of his era. I do not suppose a lapsed Quaker—if there is such a thing—physician would have had to. But one of the treats of my childhood was walking into the Western Union office, my hand secure in his, and standing at his side as he wrote out the message, and counted the words, and slid the paper to me before he gave it to the clerk, so I could check his arithmetic and make sure that he did not pay for more words than he had. Sometimes he made a mistake intentionally so I could correct him. Perhaps I would have been less angry at him if he had been a lesser father, but that is another story.

That night in Huntsville, I elbowed his ghost aside and reached for a piece of paper to write out a telegram to Harry. I had spent some time in my room figuring out how to phrase the message. I could not tell him I was on the verge of getting Ruby to admit there had been no rape in that Great Southern Railroad gondola, only sex. The news would be all over town before I got back to the hotel. I printed the words I had settled on. I was relying on Harry to remember Ruby's name.

FOUND A GEM STOP AM MINING THE DIRT

I arrived at Ruby's house early the next morning. She was out back, bent over a tin washtub. A pile of dirty garments lay on the ground on one side, several wrung-out pieces sat on a sheet of newspaper on the other. Those were more clothes, I guessed, than the Bates family owned. Apparently Huntsville still had some families who could afford to send out their washing.

I pulled my skirt close around my legs and sat on the step. Ruby glanced at my ruined shoes.

"I should have listened to you," I said.

She did not answer.

A bunch of children were chasing one another around the outhouse. She shouted at them to stop. If they heard, they gave no sign.

"They shouldn't be playing with the coloreds," she said.

"Why not?"

She shot me a suspicious look, then lifted a scrub board from the tub of soapy water and began working a piece of fabric against it.

I asked how she was this morning. She shrugged. I had got her talking yesterday, but now she had clammed up again. I wondered if Victoria had been here in the interval.

"I was thinking about those Negro boys around the fire in the Chattanooga yards. You're sure they weren't the same ones who were on the train with you?"

"They were different. You think I don't know which niggers raped me and which didn't?"

"You did have some trouble identifying them in court."

She looked up from the washing. Her mouth was a mean slit in her broad face. "That was on account of all them folks staring at me. I know which ones held intercourse with me."

The words did not sound as hilarious here as they had in the offices of *The New Order*.

"They held a knife to my throat, and tore off my overalls and step-ins, and ravished me." She put a soapy hand over the side of her mouth, spit a stream of snuff on the ground, ducked her head to wipe her mouth on her sleeve, and returned to her washing.

"Tell me about what happened after they took you off the train."

"There was a whole bunch of menfolk, pushing and shoving and asking me and Victoria if them niggers on the train interfered with us."

"Why would they ask that?"

She looked up from the tub again. She was no longer angry, merely confused.

"I mean, why would they think you'd been raped? The doctor said there were no bruises or other signs of a struggle."

"I fought hard as I could. But one had my legs real tight, and another put a knife to my throat, and then one of them pulled out his privates and says, 'When I put this in you and pull it out you will have a Negro baby.' "

"He said that to you too?"

"What?"

"Victoria told me that was what one of the boys said to her. She used the same words."

"On account of that's what he said. To me and her both." She had forgotten the laundry. She was sitting back on her haunches, angry again. "I was raped bad as Victoria. Ain't nobody can say I wasn't."

I leaned forward to hold her eyes with mine. "Ruby, do you know what's going to happen to those boys?"

She looked down at the tub again. "They're going to burn. They got to. Else there'll be a lynching for positive. For what they done to two white women."

"Ruby, look at me," I said quietly. She raised her eyes to meet mine. "Did those boys rape you?"

She went on staring at me with those big beautiful unintelligent eyes. Her mouth moved, but no words came out.

"Did they rape you?" I repeated softly.

She still did not speak. That was when I realized what the problem was. No one had ever asked her the question without letting her know what the answer was supposed to be.

I pressed the advantage. "Because if they didn't rape you, you're doing a terrible thing."

She turned to stare off in the distance. Her mouth worked the wad of snuff while she tried to sort it out. The safety of white women versus the sin of lying. The people who would not even look at her before but felt so sorry for her now they gave her new store-bought dresses, against saving a bunch of Negroes. The sheriff talking about perjury, which was just another word for lying, but this time you got punished with jail in this world instead of hell in the next, as opposed to not having to remember which Negroes were hers and which were Victoria's, because how could you remember what never happened?

She turned back to me. I waited. She lifted a hand to cover her mouth. I watched the brown juice hit the dirt. She stood. "I got to go in now."

I rose. I was not exactly blocking her way, but she would have to squeeze around me to get to the door.

"I'm sorry, Ruby. I know you must be tired to death of talking about this."

"I don't mind none. Except when Victoria makes out like I don't know how things went and she does. I could say plenty, if she just give me a chance."

"I bet you could. I bet you could tell a better story than Victoria."

I was standing one step above her. She lifted her eyes to me.

"All you have to do is tell the truth, Ruby. Then everyone will be talking about how brave you are to do the right thing, and what a terrible liar Victoria Price is."

She was still looking up at me. "You think so?"

"I'm sure of it. I'll help you. You tell me your story, and I'll write it up. But I'll put it in your words. It will sound like you."

"You mean so folks can laugh at how I talk."

"The way you talk is wonderful, Ruby. It's vivid. What I mean is so people can understand how you came to be who you are and why you did what you did."

"You think folks ain't got nothing better to do than take up for a Alabama linthead?"

"They've taken up for nine poor Negro boys."

"I ain't no nigger."

"You don't have it much better than Negroes, do you?"

"I'm white."

"Does white put food on the table? Does white give you a job, or a decent place to live, or pretty clothes? All white gives you is the right to feel you're better than Negroes."

"I am."

"How?"

"On account of I'm white," she said stubbornly.

"Those boys are not your enemies, Ruby. That's what the mill bosses, and the owners, and the people who have all the things you don't, want you to think. They want you to accuse those boys of rape, because as long as poor white people are crying rape against poor Negroes, no one is carrying on about low wages, or complaining about bad working conditions, or trying to unionize. But if you tell the truth, if you admit those boys didn't rape you, people will stop screaming for blood and start demanding their fair share. It's up to you, Ruby. You can be a hero." I paused. "Or you can go on telling the lies Victoria made up."

Now she knew what the answer was supposed to be.

"Be a hero, Ruby. Admit those boys didn't rape you."

She opened her mouth. I waited for the words. I could practically hear them. But no sound came out.

"There's nothing to be ashamed of," I said, though we both knew I was lying. Free love in a Greenwich Village apartment was, after all, different from sex in a hobo jungle. In my apartment on Tenth Street, I was making a political and social and philosophical statement. In a gravel-filled railroad gondola, she was committing a furtive economic act. Perhaps if I had kept that in mind, I would not have botched things so badly.

"It wasn't a case of rape," I insisted, "only sexual intercourse, right? You had intercourse with those boys in exchange for money. Money you needed desperately and could not make any other way."

She stepped back as if I had slapped her.

"You think I'd jazz a nigger? You think I'm a nigger-lover? I was raped. Six of them raped me, and six raped Victoria. They held me down and tore off my step-ins and told me when he put it in and took it out I was going to have a Negro baby."

"Ruby—"

"I ain't no nigger-lover," she shouted. "And ain't nobody going to say I am. Specially nobody who don't have the sense God gave them not to go walking out to the yards in shoes most folks never seen the likes of, and ain't never going to."

A few years later, I bought Ruby a pair of shoes like the ones I ruined that day in Huntsville. She was crazy about them, but I always regretted the gift. By then I was beginning to resent many of the things I gave her, but the navy-and-white spectator pumps were a special case. They always reminded me of my misstep that morning in her yard. I had gone too far. If I was determined to get her to admit the boys had not raped her, I should have avoided the question of whether she'd had sex with them of her own free will, if an impoverished, uneducated seventeen-year-old who has spent most of her life working in a southern mill could be said to have free will.

I wasn't fixing to holler at the lady, but she had it coming to her. I reckon I jazzed some niggers in my time, but I ain't what folks call a nigger-lover. The lady said she was sorry, but she didn't look sorry. She looked vexed. Then she did something funny. She took a little white piece of paper from her pocketbook and handed it to me.

"If you change your mind, I'll be at the hotel tonight."

"Ain't nothing to change my mind on," I told her.

"After that, you can reach me at this address in New York."

"I ain't fixing to be up that way."

"Write to the address on that card. Or better yet wire. You can send a telegram collect. That means I'll pay for it. Just go down to the Western Union office and tell them you want to send a wire collect. I'll be on the next train down here, I promise."

I could just feature it, going up to the Western Union office, telling the man I don't have no money but I'm fixing to send a wire all the way to New York. He'd laugh near to die. But the lady kept holding the card out to me, so I reckoned I might as well take it. I put it in the pocket of my dress, but soon as she left, I took it out and tore it to pieces. I ain't no nigger-lover, and I wasn't fixing to keep a card from anyone who said I was. I tore it to pieces and threw the pieces in the air just to show her. But she wasn't around no more to see. Only ones who saw were Sis and Bud and all them colored kids. They came running at the sight. Snow, they shouted, snow, and I near had to cry. All them poor kids had was make-believe. Just like me.

Wasn't an hour passed before Victoria come storming into the house like a tornado, hollering if I told the lady anything I shouldn't, I'd be sorry.

"I didn't tell her nothing."

"Then why'd she set so long? She come yesterday, and she come again today, and she set for a spell. She didn't set with me for more than a hour altogether."

"I told it like you told it."

Victoria raised her right hand. "You swear on a Bible?"

I raised my hand. "I swear on a Bible."

She dropped her hand and started to laugh. "Not that you got a Bible. You're a sinner, Ruby Bates, and you're going to burn in hell right along with me."

I reckoned she was funning, but I didn't think it was nothing to laugh at.

She pulled out a chair and set. "What she want to know?"

"Nothing special."

"Nothing special," she said in a squeaky little-girl voice that was supposed to feature me, but didn't sound nothing like me. "Did you tell about how they tore my step-ins?" she asked in her real voice.

"I told how they tore my step-ins."

"They were my step-ins."

"I told it like you told it."

"That's not the way you tell it like me. If I say they tore my step-ins, then you got to say they tore Victoria's step-ins. Not they tore your step-ins."

"They could've tore both our step-ins."

She thought on that for a spell. "I reckon they could."

"And I told about saying he's going to put it in and take it out, and I'm going to have a Negro baby."

"Lordy, Ruby, you are the dumbest white woman I ever saw. I'm the one going to have a Negro baby when he puts it in and takes it out. The step-ins are mine, and the Negro baby too."

"I don't see why you get all the good parts."

"On account of I thought them first."

I could feel the tears rising like a creek in spring. First the lady got me all mixed up, now Victoria was hollering at me for getting all mixed up. "It's not fair," I yelled at her. "I was raped too!"

She set studying me for a minute. Then she threw back her head, and opened her mouth that was greasy red with a brand-new lipstick she bought with money some folks collected for us on account of we were defiled, and the laughter came rolling out so loud it near to made the room shake.

"And don't you forget it, Ruby Bates. Don't you forget it for a minute."

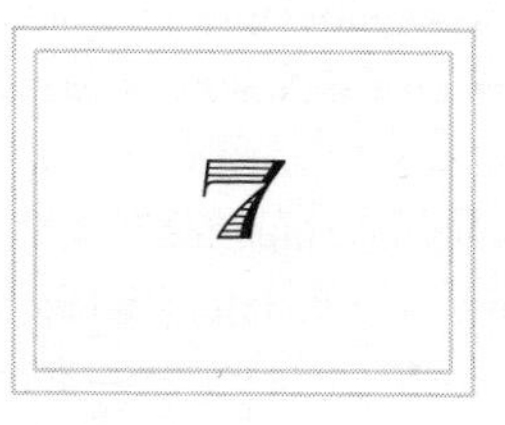

The densest and dumbest animals it has yet been my privilege to meet.

—William Pickens, field secretary of the NAACP, describing the parents of the Scottsboro boys in a letter to Walter White, secretary of the NAACP, 1931

I studied their [the Scottsboro boys'] faces carefully. They are beautiful. Their chins are up, their eyes bright with confidence, defiance, vigor . . . They are militant and unafraid . . . The boys should be sent The Daily Worker.

—Report by a representative of the International Labor Defense, 1933

It is now clear that these darkies do not mean a tinker's dam to the organizations which have supposedly been moving heaven and earth in their behalf.

—Birmingham Age-Herald, 1932

Where were the Scottsboro boys during all this? What were they up to, while Ruby and Victoria were strutting around town in their new store-bought dresses, and a handful of Alabama politicians were eyeing the governor's mansion, and Dr. Bridges was parsing the niceties of the law, and I was having the time of my life trying to save the world, though I would never have admitted it, even to myself? Eight of them were sitting on death row in Kilby Prison. Kilby was the pride of the state, a brand-new red brick compound that boasted a dairy farm, cotton mill, slaughterhouse, and hospital, among other up-to-date niceties. There was nothing that prison did not have, including a fancy new electric chair, built by a former prisoner, who was an expert cabinetmaker.

I managed to get in to see the boys. It took several attempts and, thanks to Harry, the help of Joseph Brodsky, the attorney for the ILD. Joe wanted all the good press he could get for the boys, and he knew I would be sympathetic. Most of the northern writers who covered the case were. In those days, disinterest in the face of injustice was not regarded as a journalistic virtue. Joe gave me a letter saying I was his secretary and should be let in to see the boys. The warden did not like the idea of letting a white woman in to see his Negro prisoners, but then he did not like anything about the Scottsboro boys, except having them behind bars. He sent me away twice, but on the third day he relented. "Might as well let the white whore in," he told the guards, as if the color mattered, which, of course, it did.

I had thought getting past the warden would be the hard part. It was child's play compared to getting through to those boys. Looking back at it now, I realize the situation was hopeless, but my behavior did not help. I cringe when I remember that piece of paper in my pocket. But then I was not alone in my naïveté. Witness those copies of *The Daily Worker* that were at that time winging their way to a bunch of boys who could not read.

Things went wrong from the moment the guard opened the door and I stepped into the cell block. Five of the boys stood. The other three did not even glance up from their bunks. The guard, who was young and sweet-faced with rosy cheeks and a soft mouth, shouted at them to get up off them bunks on account of there was a white woman come to see them. I took the bait and said the boys did not have to get up if they did not want to. The guard and his two sidekicks snickered.

I had made up my mind to shake hands with each of the boys. I introduced myself and held out my hand. That put the ones who were standing in a pretty bind. If they dared take my hand, the guards would be on them in a minute. If they did not, they would be insulting me.

The boys murmured, Ma'am, and kept their eyes on their shoes. They did not want to risk seeing that pale outstretched hand. There was no part of a white woman's body that could not get them in trouble.

I dropped my hand and rubbed my damp palm against my skirt. The piece of paper crackled in my pocket.

The five boys who were standing went on looking at their feet. The three in the bunks went on staring at the ceiling. Behind me, the guards snickered again.

I told the boys I was a reporter. I would deceive the warden, but not them. I figured the information made no difference to the guards. They had been ordered to admit me, and they had, but like the warden, they had my number.

I explained to the boys that I wanted to tell their story to the world. I added that there were a lot of people working on their behalf, not only up North, but in Switzerland and France and Germany and Russia, and the more people who knew about them, and the more those people knew, who they were and what their lives had been like, the better it would be for their cause.

The boys said nothing, but Haywood Patterson looked up for a split second. He always was the most reckless of the group. Over the years, I met Haywood repeatedly and saw scores of photographs of him. In some of them, he is a well-built young man with a rugged face and an air of dangerous but irresistible arrogance. The photo essay *Life* magazine ran a few years later shows a jaunty, almost debonair young man in a white shirt and dark tie, sitting on the edge of a prison bunk with a cigarette in one hand and a book in the other. He had taught himself to read by then. The man in that photograph would not be out of place in one of the tonier Harlem nightclubs. But that day on death row, when I first saw him, his hair was wild on top and greased down at the sides, his mouth was sullen, and his body vibrated like a tuning fork pitched to rage. He looked up at me, and something flashed in his eyes. It was the same disdain I had seen in the eyes of the woman on the porch in Scottsboro, but there was one difference.

The woman's look had shamed me. Haywood's frightened me, and the fear made me even more guilty.

I turned to call the guards, but they were already there. They had never left. The one with the keys stood staring into the gloom of the cell block. His smile was wide and innocently mischievous. I could imagine him teasing a sister or girlfriend until she squirmed with delight. He took a step forward and rattled the bars, but made no effort to open the cell block.

"How many times I got to tell you? You niggers get off them bunks and stand up proper. Can't you see there's a white woman among you?"

This time I did not protest. We waited, the guards on one side of the bars, the five boys and I on the other, while the three took their time climbing out of their bunks. Only then did the guard unlock the door and let me out.

The boys did not talk to me on my first visit to Kilby Prison, but as time passed and I paid visits to different jails and prisons, I was able to piece together something of what it had been like for them during those early months on death row. I got to know Clarence Norris and Haywood Patterson best. They were the ones who wrote books. When they were taken off the train in Paint Rock, neither of them could read or write, so you see what I mean about the incident's having unexpected consequences.

I was not the only one who had trouble making inroads with the boys. The International Labor Defense and the National Association for the Advancement of Colored People were waging a bitter battle for the right to represent the defendants in their appeal. The ILD had a leg up from the beginning. They did not look down on the boys. I am not suggesting they did not want to use them for recruiting purposes. You would have to be pretty naive about the workings of political groups in general and the CP in particular to be surprised by that. But the ILD was never ashamed to be associated with the boys. The men from the NAACP did not mean to be condescending, but they could not help themselves. Most of them had worked so hard to get where they were, you could not blame them for wanting to keep their distance from a bunch of semiliterate alleged rapists from the world they had left behind. But they could not keep their distance and their credibility. Since they had to defend those poor boys or yield any claim to being champions of the Negro cause, they tried to make the boys over in their own respectable image. They were fighting a losing battle.

The letter Olen Montgomery wrote asking for five dollars, which was a new guard's going rate for letting a prisoner have a woman in his cell for the night, gave the NAACP apoplexy. The ILD just sent the money, and went on publicizing the boys' innate goodness and moral beauty. They also made payments to the boys' families. The sums were not large, perhaps four or five dollars a month, and they were not bribes, merely contributions to help them get by. They also saw to it that the boys got packages of shoes and shirts and toothpaste and, as I said, copies of *The Daily Worker*. That was one of the reasons, Clarence told me years later, he was glad he was in a cell with Olen Montgomery. Olen could read and write, and did not mind doing both for Clarence.

But the ILD had more going for it than money and handouts. They knew how to talk to the boys. That was something Clarence noticed right off. The two lawyers introduced themselves by their full names. I had done the same thing, but I was a woman. Joe Brodsky and Allan Taub, the men said, as if they expected the boys to call them Joe and Al. The boys didn't. Joe and Al might not mind, but the guards and wardens had other ideas about a Negro calling a white man by his first name. A year later, Clarence's mother would tell me a story about just how dangerous that could be.

Clarence noticed something else about the lawyers' names. They were Jew names. He said he did not know anything about Jews, except that in Sunday school he had learned they were Christ-killers, but Haywood told him not to worry about that. He had worked for Jews in Chattanooga, and they had treated him all right.

The first thing the lawyers did, after they shook hands with all the boys—shaking hands with a white man was not as dangerous as shaking hands with a white woman, though none of them had ever done it before—was demand that a doctor be sent in to examine the boys. The guard did not like the sound of that. He said there was a prison doctor and any medicine you could name right there in the Kilby Prison hospital, and the boys did not need medical attention anyway. Haywood piped up then and said he needed some medicine. The guard bit. He asked Haywood what he needed medicine for. Haywood answered that he needed it for the lice, because the one that got him the night before had walked off with his cap.

Joe Brodsky laughed so hard his belly shook, which let you know right off he did not live on prison food, and even the guard had to crack a smile, but later after the lawyers left, the guard returned and stood outside Haywood's cell. Clarence could tell from looking at the guard's back how mad he was. His body was so tight it was almost twitching. The only thing that eased that kind of rage was a good down-home beating, the kind where two guards hold a boy down, while a third teaches him a lesson. The guard did not give Haywood a good down-home beating that night. The lawyers had said they would be back the next day. But he kept it in mind.

The ILD lawyers stood up to the guards, and the boys remembered it. The NAACP crackers—they were colored men, Clarence said, but they were crackers just the same—held their hats in their hands, and shuffled their feet, and tried not to make trouble. They introduced themselves to the boys as Mr. This and Reverend That, and told the boys to pray, and said there never had been a time when thinking whites regarded Negroes as highly as they did these days, and the boys should be careful not to do anything to rock the boat. They also said the boys' parents were too ignorant to know what was best for them. They did not say that to the boys, but they whispered it among themselves, and somehow word got out. The ILD saw to that.

The NAACP did have one argument on its side, however. Nothing would rile an Alabama jury more than a bunch of New York lawyers, New York Jew lawyers, coming down to tell locals how to do things. A southern lawyer who dared to defend the boys would vex folks. A northern lawyer would make them take the law into their own hands. First they would run the lawyer out of town. Then they would break the boys out of prison, head for the nearest tree, and see that justice was done.

The boys turned to their parents for advice. Since the ILD had been wooing them as well as their sons, the NAACP was not pleased. Superior age does not always mean superior wisdom, Walter White, the head of the NAACP, reminded the boys. Skilled and admirable as White was, he could not seem to strike the right note. "If you can't trust your mother, Mr. White," Andy Wright said, "who can you trust?"

The boys switched sides and switched again. They began to fight among themselves. Some of them wanted to go their separate ways, but the attorneys would not permit that. Both the ILD and the NAACP said they had to represent all the boys or they would not represent any of them. From a legal point of view, the tactic made sense, because the cases were intertwined, but those poor boys locked in the death house did not see the problem in legalistic terms.

The state had set the boys' executions for July 10, 1931, barely three and a half months after the posse had taken them off the freight train. Alabama liked its justice swift. But the ILD managed to get a stay, pending an appeal to the state supreme court, and as a result, Clarence and Haywood and Harry and Olen and Ozie and Willie and Eugene and Andy did not take the long walk down the hall to the green steel door that night. But Clarence would always remember the date, because that night Willie Stokes, not one of the Scottsboro boys, but a less celebrated black son of the South, went down the hall to the green door.

Clarence was in the last cell next to the door, and he would never forget Willie Stokes walking past on July 10, 1931, or the guard coming out later. By that time, Clarence had heard the current sizzle several times. *Zzz, zzz, zzz.*

Stokes died hard, the guard told Clarence and the other boys when it was over. He hung on to life with both fists and finally they had to stick a needle through his head to make sure he was finished. Death-house duty was grim, and the guards liked to have their bit of fun.

Stokes was Clarence's first execution, but he did not suppose he would forget any of the eighteen he lived through. He certainly would never forget February 9, 1934, the night five men walked down the hall in succession. Earnest Waller, Solomon Roper, Harie White, John Thompson, and Bennie Foster. Years later Clarence could still toll them off, as if he were reading a roll of honor. The rest of the world paid less attention. Those men did not have northern lawyers fighting to represent them, and Russians and Germans and French and Swiss rioting to save them, and Albert Einstein and Thomas Mann writing letters in their behalf, and Nancy Cunard and Kay Boyle and people all over the world sending them money and words of hope. Clarence found himself thinking about the difference between them and him the night he watched them walk past his cell, one behind the other, like hogs to the slaughter, he said. All his adult life he was one of the Scottsboro boys. That was his curse. It was also his salvation. A monumental miscarriage of justice captures the white imagination. Minor travesties rarely do the trick.

The first sign that an execution was on the way would be the quiet. Most of the time the noise in the death house was deafening. It was bad enough during the day, but worse at night. Daytime was taunts and jeers and mouthing off. Night was moans and screams and threats and prayers. The cacophony was like a big jazz band with everyone playing off-key, and all the instruments out of tune, and the whole bunch of them trying to drown out one another with different riffs on the same misery. Except when there was an execution on the way. You could tell someone's time was coming by the way the silence began to build. Before an execution, you could hear a pin drop in the death house at Kilby, or the state chaplain coming down the hall singing. "Swing low, sweet chariot, coming for to carry me home . . ." Every time a man went to the electric chair, that damn preacher came down death row singing. He went on singing while they strapped the man in. "Two white horses, coming in line, coming for to carry me home."

Clarence said the preacher was the only black man he ever hated. "What kind of a black man sings to another black man on his way to the chair about two white horses coming to carry him home?"

Eighteen times Clarence sat in his cramped cell that was barely bigger than a closet, and listened to the preacher coming down the hall, and watched the condemned man go by. Sometimes the man would hesitate in front of Clarence's cell. Sometimes the poor bastard would try to break away. He knew he didn't have a hope of pulling free, but his body could not help trying. The struggle was a reflex. When that happened, Clarence turned away. He tried not to when they walked on by. He thought he owed the men that, a last look into another black face before they died, a real black face, not that Uncle Tom preacher. So he forced himself to stand on his side of the bars, his side for the moment, and watch them walk by, until the reflex got them, if it did. Then he turned away and stood with his head down and his hands hanging at his sides until he heard the green steel door clang shut. After that, he could not see anything, but he could hear and he could smell, and maybe that was worse. The human imagination is a fearsome thing.

First the warden would ask the man if he had anything to say before he went. Clarence stood in his coffin of a cell and listened to the answers. He heard grown men crying for their mamas, and convicted killers screaming they were innocent, and sometimes nothing but silence. A little later the damn preacher would start up again, but this time there would be no white horses. This time he would be praying, and you could tell from his voice what a good time he was having. Maybe he wasn't gloating because the man was dying, but he sure as hell was rejoicing because he was staying alive.

Clarence did not rejoice. He was too busy wondering when his luck, such as it was, would run out. The lawyers kept telling him everything was going to be all right, and that was good to hear, even when he did not believe them, but then the other lawyers would start telling him not to believe the first bunch. The boys would have laughed, if they had not been so scared. All their lives nobody had given a damn about them. Now that they were on death row, white lawyers and colored big shots and all kinds of strangers were fighting to get them to sign on the dotted line.

The boys were getting a lot of attention, but the days were still too empty and the nights too long, especially the nights of the executions. The nights of the executions, Clarence said, were endless.

After the man went through the green steel door, and the warden asked his question, and the poor bastard cried or cursed or did not say anything at all, and the preacher finished singing about those damn white horses and saying his prayers, you heard the sizzle of the current once, twice, then a third and fourth time just to make sure. Clarence would try to hold his breath after that, because he knew what was coming. Little by little, the smell of burnt flesh would fill the death house, strong as a pig roasting when the fall butchering was done, only not so sweet. Clarence's stomach would heave with the stench, and all up and down the hall he would hear the sound of men vomiting, and finally when his belly quieted and the toilets stopped flushing, because this was a modern prison with running water after all, he would lie on his bunk, and close his eyes, and try to think of something besides walking through that door himself.

Some nights he would think of his mama, standing at the stove in the morning, singing to herself quietly, because the day had not quite started and things did not look as bad as they were likely to later on. But before he knew it, he would stop remembering his mama standing at the stove, singing in the morning, and see her there one afternoon when the old white man his daddy sharecropped with came in. His daddy was out in the fields, and only he and his mama and his three sisters were in the house. The man walked in, sat down at the table like he belonged there, and started talking and joking, but he was talking and joking to himself, because Clarence and his sisters were too scared to look at his big white face with the purple veins running all over it and the nose red and pulpy as a rotten apple. His mama wasn't saying anything either, but that did not seem to put the man off, because one minute he was sitting at the table talking, and the next he was up behind Clarence's mama, hugging her and kissing her and trying to push her to the bed, and his mama was twisting and hitting, and Clarence and his sisters were screaming and crying, and before Clarence knew it, he would be moving around the cell cursing and swinging and punching the putrid flesh-singed air until he finally collapsed on the bunk in exhaustion. He would be worn out from the fight then, but not tired enough to sleep, so he would try to get his mind on something else, something that had nothing to do with his mama.

He would recall driving in the buggy with the rubber tires that his daddy bought the year the crop came in good. Setting up there next to his daddy was like setting on top of the world, but thinking about that always made him remember another ride. He tried not to think of it as the last ride, but that was the name that beat in his head on the nights of the executions. That was the name for the ride from the Gadsden jail to Kilby Prison. Sometimes the recollection of that ride sent him swinging and punching around his cell just as the memory of that old white man and his mama did, but other times he played that ride in his head like a moving picture and cried like a girl for the sad parts. Even Haywood, the meanest, or at least the toughest of them all, cried on that ride.

The guard banged on the cell doors early and shouted up and down the cell block. "All you niggers better rise and shine on account of today's the day they're carrying you over to Kilby. They got a fine new death house in Kilby. Real fine." He drew out the last words. "You niggers are going out in style."

The guards began opening the cells then, one by one. They would not take a chance of letting more than two boys out at a time. Haywood was the first. He always was. Somehow they had got it into their heads that Haywood was the leader of the Scottsboro boys. No matter how often the boys told them that they did not have a leader, that most of them had not even known one another until they were taken off the train and tied together and driven to Scottsboro, the guards and the sheriffs and the prosecutors and the state of Alabama knew better. Haywood Patterson was a troublemaker. Therefore Haywood Patterson was the leader. That was why Haywood Patterson had to be taught a lesson.

They took Haywood out first, then his cellmate Willie Roberson, and handcuffed them together. The guard who had shouted at them about Kilby Prison being so fine was still talking. He was mouthing off about the new death house in the new prison, and the new electric chair in the new death house, and what a show Haywood was going to put on for them state bigwigs, and them newspaper fellas, and them two white gals he raped, because they were going to be there to see him burn too.

"Hey, Patterson," he shouted so all of them could hear, "you know what part of a nigger fries first in that new chair over in Kilby?"

Haywood did not answer.

"I'm asking you a question, nigger."

Haywood still did not answer.

"Okay, I'll tell you what part of a nigger fries first in that new chair over in Kilby. His black dick. Just sizzles right off."

The guard erupted in an explosion of laughter, and the boys looked at the floor or the walls or anywhere but the white man, because they knew he was on to something. He had hit on the secret no one would admit, the measuring stick of competition, the wellspring of unconfidence, the source of fear, the cause of the lynchings that the Commission on Interracial Cooperation kept authorizing studies to investigate. The black penis was at the heart of it all, or so the white man believed.

Clarence's turn came next. The guards handcuffed him and Ozie together, marched them out to cars waiting in front of the jail, pushed them into the back seat of one with the butts of their rifles, and climbed in the front. The driver took off as if they were going to a fire. Why not? It was a beautiful day for a drive, and the guard was glad to be out of the jail and happy to be alive.

The sun climbed higher as they drove, and the air warmed, and pretty soon the guards rolled down the windows in front, and the wind came rushing in and took Clarence's breath away. He had forgotten what outside air smelled like. All his senses knew were the sweat and piss and shit and rot of the jail, and the sweat and spit and tobacco of the courtroom, and the sweat and hate of one damn guard after another.

The ride from Gadsden to Kilby was a long one, even with a foot heavy on the gas pedal, which was the way the guard had it, and Clarence did not waste a minute of it. He kept breathing the air through his nose, and gulping it with his mouth, and turning his head back and forth because he did not want to miss anything, not the sun making the fields rise and fall like water in the midday heat, or the pollen that hung in the shafts of light like specks of gold dust, or the trees dancing in the wind the car kicked up as it sped by, or the occasional black face watching them come, then whipping around to see them go. It was so much that he thought his heart would explode with taking it all in. That was how beautiful the world was on the way to the Kilby death house.

Years later, when Clarence told me about the ride to Kilby, I remembered the first time I had gone to see the boys and the piece of paper I had taken with me. I had not intended to show it to the boys. That would have been too cruel. I had carried it as solace for me. The paper was a copy of Nicola Sacco's letter. You know the one I mean. Or perhaps you don't. It is not as well known now, but in those days everyone knew it, at least everyone in certain circles. Nicola Sacco, half of that operatic-sounding duo who were executed, not for murders they did not commit, but for who they were, poor Italian immigrants, and what they espoused, a more just society, composed it on death row. He was an uneducated man, and he wrote in broken, and therefore heartbreaking, English. Was that what I had in mind when I told Ruby I would tell her story in her own words?

Nicola Sacco wrote of how if it had not been for this thing, he might have lived out his life among scorning men, unmarked, unknown, a failure. He wrote that never in his full life could he hope to do such work for tolerance, for justice, for man's understanding of man, as now he did by accident. It is a beautiful letter, full of honor, and hope, and faith in mankind, all the things for which there was no room in the car on the way to the Kilby death house.

There was no intimidation of the court and the jury from Jackson County people. The only attempt at intimidation came from New York, where Dreiser's idiotic committee is headquartered.

—*The Montgomery* Advertiser, *1931*

Some of the committees and individuals from outside the State are honestly convinced, no doubt, that Alabama is determined to execute these eight Negroes simply because they are Negroes and without regard to their guilt. Many Alabamians are just as honestly convinced that the outside committees and individuals are determined to save the accused men simply because they are Negroes and with an equal disregard of their guilt.

—New York Times, *1931*

I returned to New York and wrote a series of articles about the Scottsboro boys. I was not the only one. Though the northern newspapers were still relegating the case to the back pages, the smaller magazines and journals of opinion were taking notice. I had plenty of competition, but I also had one advantage. I was the only one who wrote about the Scottsboro girls as well. At least, I was the only one who went further than a summary of their sordid pasts. Maybe that was because I was the only woman covering the story. I had not persuaded Ruby to tell the truth, but I had got more out of her than anyone else.

Harry admired the pieces so much he featured them on the cover of the magazine. The ILD asked if they could reprint them for fund-raising purposes. Even Abel came as close to a compliment as he ever got.

"Have to hand it to you, Ace. No one else thought of taking the tarts seriously. Ruby's 'melancholy eyes' damn near broke my heart, which, before you say it, the doctors did not take out with my tonsils and appendix. Beat you to it. Damn white of you to let the ILD use the pieces to rake in the cash."

"It's for the defense fund."

He let out a hoot of laughter. "It's for the party coffers, but that's beside the point. You really believe the party wants to get those boys off?"

"Why else would they be defending them?"

He pushed his glasses back up to the bridge of his nose and stood staring at me with those watchful eyes. "Tell me something, Ace. If you were a party recruiter, which would you rather have, nine new Negro members or nine dead Negro martyrs?"

Abel had a point, but I would not admit it. When Harry tried to convert me to the party, I shrank from committing myself. When Abel mocked the party, I defended it.

I sent Ruby copies of my articles. She did not acknowledge them, but I had not expected her to. Still, I could not help hoping. Abel, of course, guessed my disappointment, though I had been careful not to tell him I had sent her the pieces.

"What did the lovely Miss Bates think of your portrait of her?" he asked one evening when we were having a drink at a speakeasy around the corner from the office.

"How do you know I sent it to her?"

He just grinned.

"No response."

"You mean she didn't write to tell you she was so moved by your sympathy for her lousy life, so impressed by your fine sociological insight into the rotten conditions that made her what she is, she was ready to fess up, in an exclusive of course, and admit she'd lied about the rape and taken on the boys, one after the other, in the age-old pursuit of a good time and a little hard cash?"

"I never expected her to answer," I lied and could not help thinking the only thing worse than a cynic is a cynic with a gimlet eye.

Other readers were less skeptical. The articles generated a lot of letters to the editor, almost all of them admiring. They also won me an invitation to Theodore Dreiser's studio.

Dreiser had called a meeting of leftist writers and artists and publishers to discuss the appalling state of current affairs. I had heard about the meeting from Harry. He had even invited me to accompany him. I was dying to go to the meeting. I would have loved to go to it with Harry. I was more than a little susceptible to his damaged good looks and tortured conscience. I admired the fact that he had what is generally called the courage of his convictions. When his wife threw him and all his pinko friends out of the Park Avenue apartment, he took a single room in a crumbling building on Eighth Street. The place was grim, but he did not seem to mind it. Abel insisted he took an atavistic pleasure in its awfulness. The trek down the hall to the dank communal bathroom reminded him of his boarding school days, the happiest time of his life. I laughed at Abel's comment, but I admired Harry's principles. When he served tea in his office, he eschewed the cream and butter of the capitalist bosses in favor of proletarian condensed milk and oleomargarine. Harry Spencer put a new twist on the old butter-and-egg man. But I was determined not to succumb to him. The problem was not that I worked with him. Who better to take up with than people who share your interests and pastimes and passions? The problem was that he was the boss. I was damned if I would let people think I had slept my way to wherever I had got, or was going. I was damned if I would suspect it myself.

Then the second Scottsboro article appeared, and I received my own invitation to Dreiser's meeting. That was even better than going on Harry's arm. The night I made my way up to West Fifty-seventh

Street, I was in debt to no one, except those boys on death row and Ruby Bates.

The studio sat high in an ornate bastion of bourgeois respectability. A grille elevator carried me slowly upward. A butler opened the door to a soaring duplex with a wall of windows facing north. The lights of the city mingled with the galaxy of stars hanging over Central Park. The state of current affairs did not look nearly so appalling from this vantage point.

A waiter approached holding a silver tray with crystal glasses. I took one.

"Real scotch," a voice behind me said, and I turned to face Abel Newman. I was not surprised to see him there. He did not occupy Harry's position in left-wing intellectual circles. He was, in fact, deeply suspect in left-wing circles. But Dreiser had been one of those who had prophesied great things for Abel when his play opened. The admiration was as close to mutual as Abel ever got. The year before, he had been incensed when Sinclair Lewis, rather than Dreiser, became the first American to win the Nobel Prize for literature. Dreiser was the superior writer, Abel insisted, though something of a crank, he admitted.

"Not the bathtub gin," Abel went on, "that our leader Harry, that aristocratic sheep in proletarian wolf's clothing, serves. He's inside." He nodded toward a large room already crowded with people, and we moved into the crush.

I knew many of the guests and recognized others from photographs on the backs of book jackets, in the catalogues of art shows, and on the review pages of newspapers. Several of the men sported leather jackets over plaid or denim work shirts. They wore them like sandwich boards advertising that they had been to the Soviet Union. A handful of the women were dressed like peasants from Russia or Mexico or Klein's basement, though most were more smartly turned out. Everyone seemed to be talking at once. Thick ribbons of smoke curled from rouged lips and moving mouths. Ice rattled in glasses like dice in a shill's cup, encouraging comers to take a chance on the evening. The air whirred with the vibration of all those agile minds and appetite-driven bodies.

I spotted Harry across the room. He was tall enough to loom over the crowd. I also noticed the girl with him. It was the dewy Vassar graduate he had hired as a secretary a few months earlier. She was extremely pretty, but then Harry always hired lookers. The only problem, which he did not regard as a problem, was that they rarely lasted more than four or five months. That was how long they took to discover that Daddy was right. A magazine of opinion was no place for a nice girl, although by then they were rarely what Mother and Daddy would call, strictly speaking, nice girls.

Harry nodded and raised his glass to me. I saluted back with my own. The dewy girl tugged on his arm and went up on her toes to murmur something in his ear.

People were still shouldering their way into the room. Presently, Dreiser moved to the fireplace and rapped his knuckles on the mantel for attention. The hubbub died slowly with a burst of laughter here, a hiccup of conversation there, a gradual turning of heads to the big gray-haired man who had summoned us. He had improbably rosy cheeks and a series of chins that rippled down to his neck. Something about him, maybe the ponderousness of his movements, gave him a pachydermal air. He certainly did not look like the ladies' man he was reputed to be. He seemed more the poor over-the-hill soul who, when arrested for fornication by a backwoods Kentucky sheriff who did not like his politics, pleaded in court that he was too old and impotent to be guilty as charged. As I stood there remembering the gossip about the incident, which for all I knew was apocryphal, and trying not to look at Harry and the dewy secretary, I could not help seeing the irony of the situation. We were so eager to tar Ruby and Victoria, whom under other circumstances we would be trying to unionize, for doing for desperately needed money what most of us in that room were doing, with as much forethought and compunction as rabbits, for pleasure. That was what I had tried to explain to Ruby on her back steps.

Dreiser took a large white linen handkerchief from his pocket with one hand and began drawing it through the fingers of the other. For a great man, he seemed oddly ill at ease. Then he began to speak.

"The world is in a fearful state," he started. "Everywhere we look, we see men without work, women without homes, children with empty bellies. Everywhere we turn, we see political persecution, industrial persecution, racial persecution. In Harlan County, desperate men struck dozens of small mines. You all know what happened. Bosses brought in strikebreakers. Sheriffs, bought by the bosses, hounded and beat the workers. Even as we stand here, dynamitings and gun battles and old-fashioned mountain wars rage.

"In Alabama, eight Negro boys sit on death row and a ninth is in prison for a crime they did not commit. For a crime that never occurred. There was no rape on that Alabama Great Southern freight train. There were only nine Negro boys defending themselves against a gang of white boys, who could not bear to share a freight train, the lowest means of transportation, their only means of transportation, with their Negro brothers. There were only white men turning their frustration and impotence and hatred, not against the capitalist bosses, where it belongs, but against those who are even more exploited, more downtrodden, more sinned against than they. There were only two white girls, women of the most disreputable kind, women of the street, plying their trade among black and white alike. But when the white posse and the white deputies and the white sheriff caught the girls, those two white women, not of easy virtue, but of no virtue, cried rape in order to save their own skins.

"The arrest of those nine Negro youths is an affront to every decent human being. The trial of the Scottsboro boys is a miscarriage of justice the likes of which has not been seen since those two poor uneducated Italian workers Nicola Sacco and Bartolomeo Vanzetti were sent to their deaths for a crime they did not commit. We must not let history repeat itself. We must not let the Scottsboro boys pay with their lives, as Sacco and Vanzetti paid with theirs, for racism and injustice and the sins of capitalism. We must stop these executions! We must save the Scottsboro boys!"

The Harlan County miners had warmed up the room; the Scottsboro boys took it to a fever pitch. With each mention of the words *Negro* and *racism* and *capitalism*, with each repetition of the names Sacco and Vanzetti and Scottsboro, heads nodded more vigorously and yes's rang more loudly. One or two women had tears in their eyes. Harry's Vassar graduate, her face lifted to the heavens above the skylight, her firm young breasts heaving with excitement, looked like Marianne in one of those academic paintings of the French Revolution. The publisher of a small avant-garde press pawed the expensive Turkish rug with his scuffed brown shoe. A sculptor who made works from farm implements smacked the fist of one hand into the palm of the other. If those nine boys had somehow miraculously appeared among us, they would not have known whether we wanted to save them or lynch them.

"The question," Dreiser went on, "is what are we, the thinking men"—not a woman in the room batted an eyelash, not even me—"going to do about it?"

He might as well have thrown a firecracker as ask that question of that crowd, even if they had not been worked to a high pitch. The answers came fast and thick. People interrupted one another. Voices shouted each other down. A cartoonist known for the improbably buxom women in his drawings made an impassioned plea for cooperating with the International Labor Defense. A magazine writer shouted that the ILD was nothing but a communist front. A well-known playwright suggested a blitz of letters and telegrams to the governor of Alabama. A best-selling novelist recommended collaboration with the NAACP. A social-realist painter warned against working with that bourgeois gang of Uncle Toms. Everyone had a plan. The arguments raged for almost two hours. By the time the meeting broke up, Harry had formed a steering committee, two old friends were not speaking, and the best-selling novelist's wife was leaving with the social-realist painter.

I was standing beside them, waiting for the elevator, when Dreiser approached. I assumed he was coming over to speak to them, but he stopped in front of me and took one of my hands in both of his.

"Miss Whittier," he said, "I asked Harry Spencer to point you out. I wanted to tell you how much I admired your pieces on Scottsboro. An interesting approach. 'If racial hatred threatens death to those boys,'" he quoted me, "'class oppression stole every hope of a decent life from those girls.' Good," he said, "quite good."

The elevator arrived as I was thanking him, and I followed the novelist's wife and the social-realist painter into it. Abel slipped in behind me just as the door was about to close.

Outside the grillwork of the open cab, the floors swam past. Inside, I turned to Abel and did my best to avert my eyes from the couple, who were going at each other like animals in heat. We hung back to let them out of the elevator before us.

"I'll lay you ten to one they don't make it to bed in time," Abel said.

"I don't take sucker bets."

We came out of the building in time to see Harry hailing a cab. He was so busy watching the Vassar graduate fold her fine long legs into the back seat that he did not even notice us. I remembered the comment about my crooked seams, but the pang was slight.

"I know what you're thinking," Abel said, as we began walking.

"I'll lay you ten to one you don't."

"You're thinking of what Dreiser said to you."

I did not answer.

"And," he went on, "you're thinking the kick of a new affair can't hold a candle to the cause of a lifetime."

I turned to look at him. His grin was wide with satisfaction.

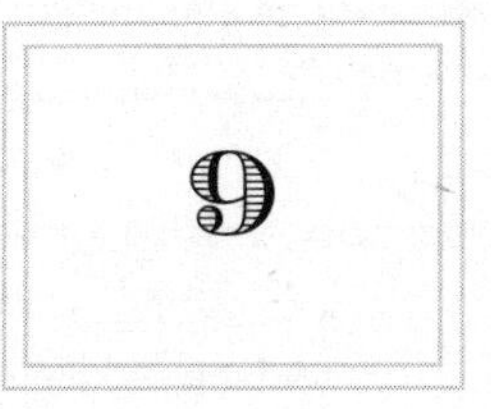

It was just one battle to find work and keep living in Huntsville . . . me and my mother went down to the Southern Railroad and boarded a train . . . I couldn't help thinking . . . about my first ride on a freight train and what came of it. And I began to worry about the lies I had told on them Scottsboro boys.

—Ruby Bates, 1933

After a spell the reporters stopped coming 'round, and the money I got for being a defiled white woman run out, and things went back to the way they were before, only worse, on account of now I couldn't get no work no matter how hard I looked. Victoria said she reckoned it was on account of how bad I testified, mixing up words and not even knowing which niggers were mine and which hers. She didn't have no such trouble, just set up there in the witness box, and pointed her finger, and said in a voice loud enough to call hogs, There he sets yonder, one after the other. Victoria said it was lucky them lawyers had her, on account of she was the only one who knew how to tell the story right. Without her, them boys would have walked out of the courthouse free as birds. I reckoned she was right. She whipped up the courtroom like a preacher whips up a revival, shouting and crying and carrying on about how them boys ruined me and her forever. Sometimes it scared me how she kept saying that. She kept saying it even when me and her were alone and there wasn't no one else to hear. Course, I done the same thing when she come 'round after the lady from New York City left. Sometimes it was hard to keep things straight.

So I wasn't sorry when Ma said me and her ought to take the young ones and hop a freight to Sheffield. That was where Ma's sister lived. But that didn't work out neither, on account of Auntie had five young ones of her own and nothing to eat in the house 'cepting a couple of Red Cross handouts. If that wasn't a heap of misery, the doc just told her she got TB. She was carrying on something awful about it. I felt sorry for her, but I didn't see what all the carrying on was for. Even an eejit knows you work in them mills long enough, you just got to come down with TB. So the next morning me and Ma said goodbye, and took the young ones, and moved on to Russellville. Folks said the mill in Russellville was hiring.

For once it wasn't a rumor told to break your heart. Ma got a job in the mill, and for a day or two you'd almost think the sun was shining again, but then I turned feverish, and Ma decided she best carry us all back to Huntsville, on account of in Huntsville the social services folks knew us.

I mended after a spell, but the mill bosses still looked the other way when I come 'round. They did the same with Ma. The Red Cross folks gave us a handout now and then, but we couldn't get our two dollars regular every week, on account the Red Cross was still checking to make sure me and Ma didn't have nothing left to sell and no kinfolk to borrow from. So me and Ma had to take care of the four of us on what we took in washing. I didn't have no heart to hustle. I never was much good at it without Victoria anyway. Victoria used to say, if it wasn't for her, I'd be giving it away. I couldn't recollect when I been so blue. That's why I was so glad to see Lester Carter come walking up the road that day.

His face didn't look like uncooked biscuits now. It was red as a

Indian's from the sun, no matter the weather hereabouts was already going to winter. When he took off his hat, the top of his head where his hair wasn't anymore was burnt too. I asked where he been keeping himself, and he said knocking along here and hoboing there. He said he got all the way out West to California and almost all the way up North to New York City. He reckoned he been all over the country, but he didn't say it like he was bragging on it. He said it like he was wore out. I told him I been around some too, but I didn't go telling him where, on account of where I been was just more of the same.

Me and him set on the step for a spell, and he told about picking raspberries in Arkansas, and doing any old kind of job in California, and hoboing through Washington and Oregon and Idaho and Nebraska and Iowa and Illinois, a heap of places I couldn't hardly keep straight in my head, and then back to Arkansas, where he come across a preacher in a hobo camp. Then he fell to quiet, and I did too, on account of no cat got my tongue faster than somebody else's not talking.

After a while Lester asked if I fancied going up to the North Carolina yards, and I said I didn't hold nothing against it. Me and him started out, and I was recollecting last time we walked up the yards. I didn't have no heart to hustle these days, but I wouldn't mind jazzing Lester. I was feeling mighty blue.

Only Lester was walking with his hat pulled low, and his hands in his pockets, and his head down studying his shoes. It ain't the way a fella walks when he got jazzing on his mind, lest maybe he ain't jazzed you before, and he's trying to figure how he can. Only thing was, I couldn't say what he did have on his mind, on account of he closed his lips tight as a social services lady's pocketbook. Me and him walked all the way up to the yards and all the way back, and I could count the words went between us on the fingers of both hands and still have a couple left over.

When me and him got back, I said I reckoned I better go on in. That was when I found out what was on his mind. I should've guessed, on account of it was on my mind too.

"Do you reckon . . ." he started, then stopped.

"Reckon what?"

"About them boys."

I didn't like to think about them boys. I specially didn't like to think about them laying out time in jail waiting to burn. I couldn't've stood it no way. But then I ain't a nigger. I reckon niggers don't feel things the way white folk do.

"Do you reckon we'll go to torment for it?" Lester asked.

I didn't say nothing to that, but it put enough fear in me to make me set down on the step again. Lester set down too, and started in to tell about the hobo camp over in Winn, Arkansas, where he come across the hobo preacher. A bunch of hobos was setting around a fire, talking about this and that, and one hobo started in on a case he heard about over in Scottsboro. Lester just couldn't keep from saying he reckoned he knew a thing or two about that. One word led to another, way words do around a jungle fire, and before Lester knew it, he pretty much owned up to the whole story.

When he finished talking, no one said nothing. The only sound in the night was the fire crackling and snapping like hell coming after him. Then the preacher spoke up. He leaned across that fire to Lester, and the light in his eyes pricked Lester sharp as the devil's pitchfork.

"You know what you got to do, boy," the preacher said, not in a setting-'round-a-campfire voice, but in a hellfire-and-brimstone kind of way. "You know, and I know, and every man around this fire knows."

Way Lester told it, even setting in the chill, he could feel the flames licking at him.

"You got to step forward and tell the Lord's truth."

Lester said he done plenty of thinking on that, but from what he seen, folks 'round these parts didn't want no truth-tellers, least not about this.

"The world is not just these parts," the preacher said. "You must go where the Lord sends you, until His truth is heard. Otherways, you will burn in hellfire for positive."

After Lester went away, I couldn't empty the preacher's words out of my head. If Lester was going to torment for not saying what he knew was right, then I was going to burn twice as bad for saying what I knew was wrong.

I waited till I was alone in the house, then I set down on the bed, took my precious box out from under it, and took off the lid. There wasn't much there to tell of. Two almost-used-up lipsticks from the salesman with the suitcase full of samples. Some ribbon me and Victoria pinched at Kress's. A ring with a colored stone me and her found in the rail yards and she let me keep for myself. And one other thing. The card the lady up in New York give me. After I tore it up that time, I picked up the pieces and put them in the box. Now I took them out and put them in my pocket.

I left the box on the bed, there in plain sight. Bud and Sis could have it to play with. I reckoned I wasn't going to need a pile of sad old trash no more.

I never was inside the Western Union office. The lady said send a wire collect, but she didn't say how a body did that. Did you step right up and order a telegram same way you did bread or pop or snuff at the company store? Victoria would know. At least, Victoria would figure it out. I wished Victoria was alongside me, only I didn't, on account of when she was, nobody paid me no mind. And Victoria wouldn't have no part of what I was fixing to do.

I crossed the road and stood outside the big window looking in. A man was setting behind a table. There was a telegraph machine on it, and turned to the side of that, on another, smaller table was a typewriting machine. A boy with a cap that said WESTERN UNION over the brim was setting in a chair near the door. All of a sudden, the man turned to the typewriting machine and began hitting on it with his two front fingers. He pulled a piece of yellow paper out and handed it to the boy. The boy folded the paper and put it in an envelope. He come out the door so fast he near knocked me over.

"Watch where you're standing," he said.

Watch where you're going, I was fixing to answer, only I didn't.

The man looked up from the desk, studied me for a spell, then swiveled his chair till he was half turned away from the window. He reached down and come up with a mason jar. Wasn't but a drop in it, and he had to tip his head way back to drink. His Adam's apple bounced like a stone skipping on water. He wiped his mouth with the back of his hand, closed the jar, put it where I couldn't see no more, and turned back to the window. He looked surprised I was still standing there. I reckoned I had to go in or go away, one or the other. I pulled open the door and stepped foot inside.

He went on studying me. I reckon he didn't think much of what he saw, a girl in a home-sewed dress and raggedy sweater with a hole in one elbow. I twisted the sweater arm so he couldn't see the hole, but the look on his face didn't change none. He was studying me same as the men in the courtroom done, when I couldn't recollect which niggers were mine and which were Victoria's.

"You want something, sister, or you just come in to get out of the night, on account of this ain't no waiting room."

"I want to send a telegram." The words sounded right enough once I got them out.

"You got money?"

I took a step forward. "I want to send it collect."

He narrowed his eyes to study me better. "Okay, give it here," he said after he finished studying.

I took the pieces of card out of my pocket and put them together on the table.

"You got to write it down." He pushed a piece of paper across the table at me, then shot a pencil after it. "Put down who it's going to and what you want it to say."

I didn't know what I wanted to say. I been so busy working up to stepping foot into the Western Union office, I forgot I was going to have to say something once I got myself inside. I couldn't just write, *I do not want to go to torment.*

"What can I say?"

"Anything you want, providing it ain't blasphemous or dirty, and whoever you're sending it to got the money to pay for it. You let me know when you're ready." He turned away from me, walked to the window, and stood looking out.

I picked up the pencil. I couldn't think of nothing to say. Worse than that, whatever I thought to say, I knew I would say wrong. I'd spell wrong too. And the lady who pretended to be nice would laugh at the dumb linthead who didn't know how to write nothing, nor spell it neither.

I looked up and saw the man staring at me.

"Ain't I seen you before?"

I didn't make no answer.

His eyes were still on me. He snapped his fingers. They sounded like a gunshot in the quiet.

"You're the gal got raped by them niggers over in Scottsboro."

I bent to the paper again. I got myself into the office, and I wasn't going to let no one run me out.

"Now, I wonder who you'd be sending a telegram to collect."

I was still trying to figure what to write, but I couldn't come up with nothing with him standing there making fun of me.

"One of them Yankees, I reckon."

I wetted the end of the pencil with my tongue, like I was fixing to write, but I still couldn't think of nothing.

"One of them Yankees I hear tell come down here to stir up more trouble."

I put down the pencil.

"What's the matter, can't fix on what to say to them Yankees?"

I turned and walked to the door. I always knew I wasn't going to send no wire. It wasn't just the money. It was all the other things I didn't know how to do.

10

> Dear Earl,
> I want to make a statement too you Mary Sanders is a goddam lie about those Negroes jassing me those policemen made me tell a lie that is my statement because I want to clear myself . . . those Negroes did not touch me or those white boys . . . i love you better than Mary does or anybody else in the world that is why I am telling you this thing.
>
> —*Letter from Ruby Bates to Earl Streetman, January 5, 1932*

In September, the NAACP announced that Clarence Darrow had agreed to represent the Scottsboro boys in their appeal to the Alabama Supreme Court. The lawyer's name was a household word. Even the boys knew it. It seemed to give them hope, despite the fact that Darrow had not had much success when he defended a young Tennessee schoolteacher whose only crime was the teaching of science. But better-informed individuals than those poor boys on death row did not seem to notice that Darrow's most stirring courtroom eloquence often led to his clients' convictions. Darrow ultimately decided not to represent the boys, but he did take on another case that pitted dark skin against light around the same time. He defended Mrs. Granville Fortescue, who was accused of shooting to death a young Hawaiian boy. The boy, who was not white, had been acquitted of attacking Mrs. Fortescue's daughter, Thalia Massie, who was. Thalia was the wife of a Navy officer and had more education, and pretenses, than Ruby or Victoria, but the story she told of being raped by a group of young men with darker skins was no more persuasive than theirs, though her physical state did indicate that something had happened. The Hawaiian jurors, however, unlike those in Alabama, demanded more evidence against the boys than the girl's condition. When the jury refused to convict the boys, Thalia's mother, Mrs. Fortescue, took justice into her own well-manicured hands and shot one of them. I mention the case not only because it was similar to and concurrent with Scottsboro, but for another curious coincidence as well. Mr. Fortescue, the estranged husband of the accused woman, was the illegitimate son of Eleanor Roosevelt's great-uncle, Robert Roosevelt. The men in Mrs. Roosevelt's family, as I would later learn, gave her a lot to live down.

The Massie case crowded the Scottsboro boys out of the news for a while. The Hawaiian trial had not only race and sex, it also had palm trees and a victim with whom the better class of newspaper and magazine readers, or at least those who could afford to buy the products advertised in their pages, could sympathize. I thought of the girls I had gone to school with. They never could have conceived of Ruby's life. But Thalia Massie spoke their language, and lived in their world of coming-out parties and church weddings and promising young husbands, and probably even knew some of the same people they did. No one wanted to read about an Alabama girl so sordid and shabby she barely seemed human, when she could look at pictures of a blond debutante and shiver there-but-for-the-grace-of-God-go-I.

Then Ruby wrote her letter, and overnight, she was back in the headlines.

GIRL'S LETTER TO BOYFRIEND
SAYS SHE LIED ABOUT
YOUTHS AT SCOTTSBORO

Ruby was in love. Later she would tell me that Earl Streetman was the only good thing that happened to her since she had hopped that freight train nine months earlier. He was the finest-looking fella she ever laid eyes on, not pale and sickly like the boys in the mill, but strong and healthy-skinned, with shoulders so wide he had to go through a door sideways. He was free with two bits too, if he had it, and the only time he ever hit her was when he had too much lightning, and that was probably her fault, on account of if Earl had lightning, he made sure she got some too. As she said, generosity was one of his attractions.

However, alcohol did not come between Earl and Ruby, though it would have some bearing on the letter Ruby wrote to get Earl back. At least, that was the way the police told it. Mary Sanders drove Earl and Ruby apart, Mary Sanders and the terrible lies she spread. Ruby was not certain exactly what Mary told Earl about her—that she had jazzed those Negroes on the train? that she had syphilis?—because Earl was not saying, but whatever it was, it did the trick. Earl stopped coming around to see Ruby and started talking sweet and sharing his moonshine with Mary. Ruby did not take it lying down. I had to hand it to her. I almost envied her. I could not imagine going to the mat for a man. She wrote a letter. She told Earl that she loved him, and that the boys on the train had not raped her, that they had not even jazzed her.

When I read the letter in the newspaper—it was printed in every southern paper and in many northern ones—I was sure she was lying, again. If she would not admit to me that she'd had intercourse with Negroes, she certainly would not come clean to a good southern boy like Earl Streetman. I was not alone in my skepticism. Just as everyone in the South was certain that where there was a white woman, there had to be Negro lust, everyone in the North knew that where there was a girl of easy virtue, there had to be promiscuous sex.

I ain't much for letter writing, and I reckon I found out why when I sent that letter to Earl. I didn't have no trouble doing the writing. Not like the time I went up to the Western Union office fixing to send a telegram. I knew for positive what to say to Earl. The words been going around in my head so much since Mary Sanders, they came out easy as water comes out of one of them indoor hydrants. I didn't have to worry none about spelling neither, on account of Earl ain't no better at spelling than me. Only thing I had to think on was getting Earl back.

I gave the letter to Earl's friend Danny Dundee. That ain't his real name. Marion Pearlman was what he was born with, but he took up Dundee for prizefighting, just like Orville did Carolina Slim for railroading. I told Danny, Don't you go giving this letter to nobody but Earl. You put it right in his hand. Just saying that made me almost start up crying again, on account of Earl had real nice hands with the cleanest nails you ever did see. Danny crossed his heart, swore he wouldn't give it to nobody but Earl, and lit out to find him.

I reckoned Earl would come 'round that night, soon as he read the letter, but he didn't come that night, so I started thinking on the next morning. And sure enough, first thing in the morning, someone comes banging on the door so loud Ma near jumped out of her skin. My heart was pounding loud as the knocking on the door, on account of I knew Earl seen the light and come back to me. Then the door flew open, and instead of Earl coming through like he was supposed to, a fella in a deputy's uniform was pushing in, and without so much as a by-your-leave, he says he's carrying me up to the police station, on account of the chief wants to see me. I didn't recollect nothing I done wrong lately, but that didn't keep me from being a heap scared.

Soon as I got there, I knew from the way the chief was studying me from behind his desk that I wasn't ma'am or lady or southern white womanhood no more. The deputy gave me a shove so's I was standing right up at the desk. Then the chief picked up a piece of paper and started waving it around like it was a flag and he was expecting me to pledge allegiance, like we done in school. I couldn't read the words, but I reckon I know my own writing when I see it. Only thing I didn't know was how the chief got it. Danny swore he wouldn't give it to nobody but Earl.

"You write this?" the chief asked.

I shook my head yes.

"You give me an answer when I talk to you."

"Yes."

"You were drunk, right?"

"I wasn't neither. I ain't never had a drink of lightning in my life. That Mary Sanders is carrying tales." Right away I wished I didn't say that. More lying would just land me in more trouble.

"Unless you're fixing to lay out the next hundred days"—he drawled out the number till I reckoned it would go on forever—"on the chain gang, you better sign this paper says you were drunk."

I was scared, as scared as when them men chased me and Victoria down in Paint Rock and started asking if the colored boys interfered with us. One thing was for positive. I was too scared to read. I took the pen the chief was pointing at me like a gun and wrote *Ruby Bates* real careful at the bottom of the paper.

I didn't get to read the paper I put my name to till the next day when Victoria come over. I was surprised. She didn't come 'round much no more. She was waving a copy of the Huntsville *Times* just like the chief waved the letter the day before, and laughing and hooting and telling me I was the dumbest white woman ever lived. She shoved the newspaper under my nose.

I didn't understand a lot of the words. Of my own free will and accord. Without any threats, promises, or inducements of any kind. But I got the sense of it. The paper I fixed my name to said I was drunk when I wrote to Earl. It said I been raped by six colored boys on the train, too. Now I wouldn't never get Earl back. And I'd go to torment for positive.

Ruby's recantation of her recantation of the rape charges continued to make news. Apparently the Huntsville police had picked up Danny Dundee for drinking, or fighting, or bootlegging, or some illicit endeavor, about which no one, including the police, seemed too sure. The police naturally searched the suspect. They found Ruby's letter. Though Dundee was charged with nothing, he managed to come up with a confession. He swore a man called George Chamlee had paid him ten dollars and a round-trip ticket from Chattanooga to Huntsville to get Ruby drunk and have her write the letter. George Chamlee was one of the attorneys for the ILD. The next thing anyone knew, the chief of police came up with a telephone call he had monitored between Dundee and Chamlee. Chamlee countercharged that Dundee had approached him with the idea of the letter. Finally, the Tennessee Bar Association stepped in and cleared Chamlee. With all those powerful men blaming one another, it was only natural that Ruby, just like the boys, should get lost in the shuffle.

Over the years, I have given Ruby's letter to Earl Streetman a great deal of thought. She always said she wrote it because she wanted to get Earl back and because she was afraid of burning in hell, and both those explanations were valid. But I think there was another motive as well. Once, when the hate mail, and the death threats, and the letter from her brother telling her to go as far away as she could and stay there had her as low as I had ever seen her, I told her that. I said there might be another reason, a fine altruistic reason, that she was not aware of at the time, like wanting to save the lives of nine innocent boys, that had prompted her to write the letter.

She said she did not see how that could be. You could tell lies to other folks and maybe get away with it, but how could you not know when you were fibbing to yourself? I told her there was something called the unconscious. By that time she was living in New York, and making appearances on behalf of the Scottsboro boys, and trying to improve herself. Everyone had an unconscious, I explained, and it made you do things for reasons you did not know, but if you were curious you could go to a doctor to find out.

"You mean the doctor tells you?" Ruby asked.

"You discover it together."

Ruby did not buy it. She knew her own mind, even if I did not.

Outside we were hobos; inside the prison we had some respect.

—Haywood Patterson, 1950

Life is funny, we would laugh about it. We had the death sentence hanging over our heads, but we were eating and dressing better than a lot of men on the outside, including our guards. Good people all over the world were making our lives a lot easier. The letters and money was still coming in from everywhere . . . But I would much rather have been on the outside looking in.

—Clarence Norris, 1979

A year to the day after a white foot came down on a black hand, the Alabama Supreme Court affirmed the convictions of the Scottsboro boys. "Some things may happen to one worse than death," the southern gentlemen justices wrote in their opinion, "and one of these things happened to this defenseless woman, Victoria Price, on that ill-fated journey."

The court set a new date for the executions. The eight boys would go to the electric chair, like hogs to the slaughter, as Clarence said of the five other men who went through the green door in a single night, on May 13, 1932.

The boys started counting the time until the silence in the Kilby death house would mount for them. Forty-nine days. Not enough time to gestate a baby or bring in some crops. Eleven hundred and seventy-six hours, Haywood calculated. During his year in jail, he had been learning to figure as well as read.

I told Harry I wanted to pay another visit to Kilby Prison. He said the sooner I left, the better.

The warden at Kilby Prison was still surly, but he did not make me return a second and third time before letting me in. He had learned the kind of fuss outside agitators could kick up. This time the guards were more bored than sadistic. The boys had changed too. They all got off their bunks to greet me. They were still wary of me. They were still terrified of what lay ahead of them. But thanks to all those letters filled with support and money and offers of friendship, they had begun to appreciate their own value.

They had a list of requests waiting for me. Andy Wright wanted a chicken cooked the way his mother made it, a bag of peanuts, and some paper and stamps. Haywood Patterson was running low on cigarettes and magazines. Olen Montgomery needed a six-string guitar, a pair of Friendly Five shoes, size seven and a half, in a light tan with a plain cap across the toe, and another five dollars for a woman, because if he did not have one soon, he confided, he would go crazy for certain.

But the barrage of requests could not disguise the terror. It pressed its face against the bars of the windows like the lynch mob that had gathered their first night in jail. It scuttled across the cells like the roaches and rats and beleaguered their bodies like the lice and bedbugs. It was inescapable, and in their desperation, they became irritable and erratic and a little mad. One of them would say it would be better if they were already dead, and another would howl at him to shut his dirt-talking mouth, because Joe Brodsky said they were going to get off, and Joe Brodsky was a smart Jew lawyer and not some scared-running colored boy who couldn't even read or write. One minute Olen was talking about how he was going to be a famous musician when he got out; the next the tears would be running out of his nearly blind eyes. Haywood could go in a flash from consoling shy quiet Ozie Powell, who had a single year of schooling and an IQ somewhere around sixty-four, as tenderly as a mother soothing a toddler, to threatening to cut his throat.

They had lost their equilibrium, the fragile balance based on their mothers' warnings and their fathers' lessons and their own body-bruising, spirit-crushing experience. That was my fault, and Harry's, and Joe Brodsky's, and Theodore Dreiser's, and Albert Einstein's, and the thousands of others', some famous, some unknown, who insisted on giving them hope. On the land they had sharecropped, in the towns where they had hunted for work, from the men who had cheated them out of money for their crops and wages for their toil, they had never expected a fair deal. But we had led them to believe that there was a larger world beyond that land and those towns and the men who tormented them, where truth would prevail and justice would be done. That was why they fought among themselves. That was why they kept repeating their stories to me. Willie Roberson confided he'd had such a case of bad blood that past March, he could hardly walk let alone put himself on a woman. Olen insisted he was so near blind he could not have seen the two girls even if he had been in the same railroad car with them, which he was not. None of them had been. Their voices piled on top of one another as they competed to make that clear. Not one of them had seen Ruby or Victoria on the train. The first glimpse they'd had of them was in the Scottsboro jail.

"Then the girls didn't hustle you?" I asked.

"That's what we been saying all along," Haywood shouted.

"But who's going to take a colored man's word agin a white gal's?" Clarence said.

I had refused to believe Ruby when she insisted she had not had sexual intercourse with the boys on the train. But I took the boys' assurance as gospel.

I wrote the story about my second visit to Kilby Prison on a portable typewriter in the Molton Hotel in Birmingham. The hotel stationery boasted of the largest and best ventilated rooms in the South. Before I sat down to work, I opened the two windows onto the spring evening.

The air was sweet with promise. It made me think of Clarence's ride to the death house. I took the typewriter out of its case and got down to work.

The piece was not hard to write. My fingers flew over the keys, describing the boys' calculation of the number of hours until May 13, and Andy's longing for chicken like his mother made, and Haywood's desire for reading material. I even included Olen's request for a six-string guitar and high-stepping shoes, though I left out his need of a woman to save his sanity. I also made clear that none of them had seen either of the girls until they were arrested, tied together, and driven to the jail in Scottsboro.

When I finished, I tore the last sheet from the typewriter, carried the pages and a sharpened pencil past the curtains rising and falling in the spring breeze, and settled in the easy chair in the corner. I began to read, editing as I went. When I came to the part about Olen's shoes, I crossed it out. I was not trying to make him out as more high-minded than he was, only to cut words. The piece was too long, and a six-string guitar, home cooking, and reading material struck me as more pertinent, or at least more affecting.

I stopped for a minute and thought about the deletion. Olen's demand for shoes reminded me of something. I heard Ruby shouting at me that no one was going to call her a nigger-lover, especially someone who did not have enough sense not to go walking to the railroad yards in shoes most people had never seen the likes of, and were never going to. I stetted the phrase about Olen's snazzy tan oxfords, stood, and went to the telephone on the nightstand. I dialed the desk and asked when the first train left for Huntsville the next morning. Ruby had not lied when she denied having sexual intercourse with the boys on the train. She had told me the partial truth about what had not happened. I was sure that, since she had tried to tell the whole truth once in the letter, I could persuade her to tell it a second time to me.

Ruby was not at her old address, but Mrs. Gorse knew where I could find her. This time, however, she did not offer to drive me there. She'd had enough of me and the Scottsboro case. That was fine with me.

The house was another bleak shotgun affair. If it were not for the street name and number, I would have sworn Ruby had not moved. I knocked on the door. I was about to knock again, when it opened a crack. Ruby's face hung in the narrow space. Her skin was pale and waxy with a sickly indoor pallor. Her big blue eyes glittered with suspicion, or perhaps a fever.

I asked if I could come in. She hesitated, then shrugged and opened the door wider. I stepped inside. The interior was like the old house, too. There was only one difference. The wormy walls were bare. Her old house, like Victoria's, had been covered with clippings, but here she had not put up a single ad or illustration or magazine cover.

I asked how she had been, and about her mother and sister and brother, and whether she was working. She answered with shrugs and monosyllables. I would have to start from the beginning again, but that was all right. I had got through to her once. I could do it again.

"Did you get the article I sent you? The one about you?"

"There wasn't no picture in it."

"*The New Order* doesn't run photos."

"Who'd want to look at a magazine that don't have no pictures?"

"Some people seem to."

"Wouldn't catch me reading it."

"But you read the piece about you?"

"Some of it."

"What did you think?"

"It was all right, I reckon." She was silent for a moment. "What does *melancholy* mean?"

At first I did not understand why she was asking, then I remembered the line about her eyes, the one Abel had made fun of.

"Sad."

"You'd look sad too, if you been through what I been through."

"That was my point."

She said nothing to that.

"A lot of people liked the article, Ruby."

"Who?"

"Readers. People I know. They said it made them understand you."

She thought about that for a moment.

"I still reckon it was needful of a picture."

"I think the article painted a more accurate picture of you than any photograph."

"I don't figure that."

"The newspapers carried your photograph when they ran the letter you wrote to Earl Streetman and the paper you signed afterward, and that didn't show what you were really like."

"I can't say nothing about that letter."

"It took a lot of courage to write it."

"I can't talk about them things. The sheriff said so."

"Did the sheriff make you sign the paper saying you were drunk when you wrote the letter?"

She pressed her lips together.

"That's what I think happened. I think you told the truth in the letter, but then the sheriff threatened you."

"I told you not to keep talking about them things." Her voice was shrill. She was a hair's breadth from losing control and spilling everything. I was sure of it.

"You don't have to be afraid of the sheriff, Ruby. Any more than you had to be scared of Victoria. You have other people on your side. I want to help you get the truth out, not cover it up."

"I told you I won't say nothing about it," she shouted.

"Just tell the truth, Ruby. You have nothing to be afraid of if you tell the truth."

She stood. Her big blue eyes were bright and hard as a neon sign. Her cheeks burned an unhealthy febrile red. "You don't know nothing about what I got to be afraid of! You nor all them men coming out here from Birmingham and down from New York. Men with funny names and big promises. Just like you. Tell the truth, Ruby. Sign the paper, Ruby. You can count on us, Ruby. You know what happens if I do that? Before you and them men see the back of the railroad depot, the sheriff got me laying out ninety days, and the mills ain't got no work for me never again, nor Ma neither, and the church and the Red Cross ladies are saying we ain't entitled to no charity. If you don't think that's something to be afraid of, you're dumber than I reckoned when you ruined them nice shoes. You ruined them shoes, and you ruined me with all that talk about telling the truth. You ruined me bad as them niggers did when they raped me. Worse. They got to burn for it. You're still walking around, free, white, and twenty-one."

I took the first train back to Birmingham and caught the next one to New York. I read, and worked, and stared out the window at the incomprehensible southern landscape, until darkness fell and all I could see was my own foolish face in the window. I had not ruined Ruby. It was not my fault that the world she lived in had turned against her. But an image of myself standing on a porch in Scottsboro, slipping a Negro maid a quarter, flashed through my mind. No one could accuse me of bigotry. I was equally stupid about black and white.

Then it came to me. I had not got the story I was after from Ruby, but I had got one that was almost as good. I had shown the scared girl with the melancholy eyes. Now I would write about the enraged woman with the burgeoning sense of injustice. It did not matter that she had turned her anger on me. I was glad that she had. Her rage at me would give the piece personal immediacy. The story of Ruby trapped by circumstance would make a perfect companion piece to the article about the boys imprisoned in the Kilby death house.

She too was serving time without hope of parole or pardon, simply because she had been born poor.

I did not send Ruby the second piece I wrote about her, though some people said it was even better than the first. Harry featured the two latest articles on the cover again, and the letters to the editor continued to come in. My father sent me a congratulatory wire. I had not answered the one he had sent after the first pieces appeared, and I did not reply now, but I could not help wondering if when he had gone down to the Western Union office he had remembered how he used to slide the paper to me to count the words for him.

A week later my mother came to town for a meeting of the Women's International League for Peace and Freedom, and managed to get away for dinner one night. We went to the Brevoort on Fifth Avenue and Ninth Street. She had a sentimental attachment to the restaurant, because in her youth she had seen an aged Mark Twain dining there, but she always struck me as out of place in that faintly bohemian atmosphere. She sat bolt upright, as she had been trained to as a girl, her spine never touching the back of the chair. Her long upper lip gave her an air of aristocratic, and entirely deceptive, disapproval. She was a forgiving woman, to a fault.

My mother, who had spent her life fighting for women's rights, belonged to a more naive generation. She believed women were politically and socially oppressed, but morally superior. She was in favor of equality of the sexes, but I always had the feeling she was more ambivalent about sex. She reminded me of an illustration of the human body in my old biology textbook. Above the waist, the organs and veins and arteries were beautifully detailed in vivid reds and blues; below, the figure was an undifferentiated expanse of white. When my father had found me studying the diagram one night, he had been so outraged he'd marched into his study and returned with his old medical school anatomy book.

Over dinner, I told her about my trip to Scottsboro, and my visit to Kilby Prison, and my expedition to Huntsville.

"Ruby Bates would have broken your heart," I said. "When you see what her life has been like, you can understand why she did what she did. All she's known is poverty and misery and deprivation."

My mother sat looking across the table at me. Even in old age, even with that long censorious upper lip, she was a handsome woman, but her gray eyes looked troubled.

"And now you're going to save her from all that." Unlike Abel, she did not sound as if she were making fun of me. She sounded worried.

A month later, the U.S. Supreme Court announced it would review the convictions of the Scottsboro boys. The ILD and the CP and Harry were practically taking bows. They deserved them. If they had not stepped in, the boys would have gone through that green door months ago. The rest of us were pretty euphoric too.

The court would not hear the case until the fall. In the meantime, I went to Washington to cover the Bonus Army of veterans, fifteen thousand strong, who had converged on the city, many with their wives and children, to set up makeshift camps and demand the bonus they were supposed to receive in 1945, because if things kept on this way, they and their families would have starved to death by 1945. Unlike the real army in which the men had served during the war, the Bonus Army did not segregate itself by color. Perhaps that was one more reason things turned out as they did. President Hoover was a Quaker with a good record of social responsibility before the Depression, nothing like his predecessor Harding, who had been sworn into the Ku Klux Klan in the Green Room of the White House, but he was a man of his time and place, who believed in social convention and public order. He commanded the army to clear the Bonus Marchers out of the city. Taking time only to dispatch his orderly to his home for his uniform because the presidential directive had caught him in mufti, General MacArthur sent in infantry, tanks, and the cavalry, led by Major George Patton. The troops teargassed the crowd, routed the Bonus Army, and managed to kill a baby in the process.

I also wrote an article about a plan to turn the top floors of New York skyscrapers, which remained empty because of the failure of so many businesses, into light airy apartments for impoverished slum dwellers. Needless to say, the plan never came to fruition. And I went to Chicago to cover the Democratic convention that nominated Franklin Delano Roosevelt for president.

In those days, I was not a Roosevelt supporter, though I had no intention of voting for William Z. Foster, the Communist candidate, or even Norman Thomas, the socialist. Harry and I argued the point often. I said a vote for Foster was a wasted vote. He said it was not only a protest, but a gesture of solidarity. Foster's running mate was James W. Ford, the first Negro to be nominated for high office by any national political party. Harry also insisted that Roosevelt was a pleasant fellow—he knew him socially—who wanted to be president, but had no special accomplishments to recommend him for the job. I admitted Harry had a point, though I did admire Roosevelt's willingness to break with tradition. Instead of sitting home in Albany, waiting to be informed of his nomination a week or two or three after the convention, as was the custom in those days, he, his wife, and several of his children boarded a plane and flew to Chicago immediately. I was on the airfield when they landed. Most of the press was. That was my first view of Eleanor Roosevelt in person. I wish I could say that as I stood watching her wave to the crowd and hide her unhappiness, because she did not want to be first lady, only her own woman, behind a brilliant smile that was already being cruelly mocked, some spark of recognition flared between us. I wish I could say my rapport with Mrs. Roosevelt predated my success with Ruby Bates, but that was not the case.

Son, white lightning struck us, that's all.

—Janie Patterson, 1931

If it had not been for the reds, and the mass protests of the workers, our boys would have died July 10.

—Ada Wright, n.d.

I was not keen on the idea at first. I had written about the Scottsboro boys, and was the first to pay serious attention to the Scottsboro girls, but the Scottsboro mothers had been touring the country for more than a year. There was nothing left to say about them. The ILD had sent so many of them out to so many cities and towns across the country that people were getting skeptical. Abel joked that when the party ran short of mothers, they brought in a local ringer. Then the NAACP made the charge in earnest. That was why Harry wanted me to write the piece, to save face for the party.

"If you can make those tramps sympathetic—" he said.

"Tramps?" I interrupted.

"You know what I mean."

I did.

"If you can make them sympathetic, and you did, Ida Norris will be a piece of cake."

An ILD chaperone brought Clarence Norris's mother to the old brownstone in the shadow of the El. If she harbored any resentment about being dragged into town to talk to some strange white woman about her private sorrows, she did not show it. Ida Norris had spent her life sharecropping on other people's land and cleaning and washing and cooking in other people's houses. She was accustomed to being ordered around, though the good intentions behind the ordering were new.

I stood at the top of the stairs watching her climb. Her back was straight and her step brisk, but something about the way she moved made me think of the wounded soldiers who had been patched up after the war. No matter how successful the surgery, they always seemed to be holding themselves together by sheer force of will.

When she reached the top of the stairs, I held out my hand. Unlike her son the first time I met him, she took it. By that time, she had been on the road, speaking before crowds, asking for money, begging for her son's life, for some time.

She was a tall woman with broad cheekbones and a wide unhappy mouth. The shadow cast by the brim of her hat hid her eyes. I doubted I would have been able to read them even if I had seen them. In those days, Negro women who had lived all their lives in the South, who had borne and raised children in the South, did not wear their emotions on their sleeves or in their eyes. I don't suppose they did in the North either.

We went into the back parlor, and I led her to two chairs in front of the window overlooking the garden. It was an incandescent late October day, and the hard yellow light slanted across her lap and turned her work-worn hands into gnarled stumps. She folded them neatly over her handbag, looked at me, and waited. I had the feeling she could have gone on waiting forever, if that had been necessary.

It took me a while to get her talking, or at least to get her to say anything beyond the slogans about the ILD's saving the boys that she had been mouthing for the past year. I am not suggesting she did not believe them, or that I did not agree with them. The party line was all well and good. But I was after the pain. We did not have to dig deep to find it. It was always there, just beneath the surface of a joke or a prayer or a pleasantry, just beneath the skin.

She had given birth to eleven children, four boys and seven girls. All but two had lived, she said, and I knew from the way she tacked on a praise-the-Lord, that she regarded the ratio as extraordinary. A boy was born dead, and a little girl had died in her arms. I asked what the girl had died of. As soon as the words were out, I realized their fatuousness. Ida Norris lived in a world without diagnoses as well as cures.

She told me about sharecropping in Georgia, moving from farm to farm in Warm Springs and Molena and Neal. The white man gave them a house and so many acres of land to grow crops, mostly cotton. At the end of the year the white man sold the crops and took out what he said they owed for seed and fertilizer and everything else he recollected giving them. Somehow there was never much left.

Life was hard, but she still found cause to give thanks to the Lord. They were all eating, though it was beans and greens with no meat to be seen. Now and then, there would be a fish. She liked to fish, and if she ever had a spell of time between the hoeing and the picking and the cooking and the washing and the tending, she would carry one or another of the young ones with her down to the creek. Wasn't nothing happier than setting on the side of the creek with Willie or Inez or Clarence and feeling a tug on that old fishing pole. Maybe she didn't get to do it more than a couple of times a year, but that did not mean she wasn't grateful. It did not seem fair to the Lord to recollect only the misery. But sometimes she just could not help herself from studying the misery. Like the day each of her children put on the white sack.

I asked what the white sack was. I could not be sure, but it seemed to me her unhappy mouth turned up at the corners for a moment, and she shook her head back and forth at the wonder of it, a grown woman who had lived as long as I had, and did not know what the white sack was. Now, that was being saved right here on earth.

The white sack, she explained, was the bag you put the cotton in when you went up and down the rows picking. One by one, her young ones put it on at five, or six, or a little younger for the big boys. Willie, Clarence, Lucille, Blanche, Inez, Port, Ina Mae, Ida Belle, and Ebeneezer slipped it around their necks like a noose.

As I listened to her talk, I realized that was something else a woman like me did not understand. We recorded the numbers—Mrs. Norris had eleven children, Mrs. Powell nine, Mrs. Weems seven—as if they were litters. But to the women who bore them, the children were individuals, who asked different questions, and harbored distinctive fears, and laughed and cried and dreamed in unique ways.

When those young ones, who were all separate blessings and diverse worries in her eyes, started out with the white sack at dawn, it did not drag them down too much, and all they had to worry about was tripping over it, because it was three or four times as long as the littlest ones. But as the sun climbed higher over the fields, and the air began to boil, and their small hands bled from the picking, the sack filled up. A body would not think something light as cotton could weigh so heavy. More than once, the littlest ones stumbled and fell.

But they learned, and if her heart broke watching them learn, she knew there were worse things. Even when the old white man with the pulpy red nose like a rotten apple came into the house while her husband was out in the fields and started in to bother her, she knew there were worse things. At least he fixed on her and didn't start in troubling the girls. Inez and Ida Mae were crying and screaming for their mama, but that was better than their mama crying and screaming for them. They couldn't have been older than six or seven, but that didn't make no difference to some white men, colored neither.

She knew she was not beating the white man's game. There was no way a body could do that. But maybe if you were real careful, if you prayed hard, and did as the white man, and the white woman too, said, if you didn't complain about the things the white man made you pay for that you never saw a shadow of, and didn't answer back when the white woman took out of your pay for something you never broke, you could pass down the white man's road, which was the only road in this life, without too much misery. That was what she used to think. That was what she taught the young ones, because they were her first fear. There wasn't a morning she did not send one of them off afraid he would not come home that night. There wasn't a white man passed, she did not wish she had some magic she could throw over the girls to fool his eyes into not seeing them. And if one of the girls did catch a white man's eyes, because she had no magic, she prayed with a hot shame that her girl would lie down for the white man instead of standing up to him, on account of once, when she was a young one herself, trailing her own white sack behind her, she had seen a white man try to jump a girl in the field. The girl was big and strapping and fought off the white man, who was a puny little thing. But a white man is bigger than his size. The law and the rules and the other white men see to that. The puny white man picked up a hoe and split that big strapping girl's skull right there where she was standing.

So you taught the girls to keep out of sight in the fields, and the boys not to be uppity, and you prayed. Her husband was not a God-fearing man, but she prayed hard enough for both of them. And she was just beginning to think that maybe they would make it down the white man's road, when she learned the truth. The white man would not let you pass down his road unless you paid in full, and he did not mean the money from sharecropping.

The neighbor's boy was named Ebeneezer, just like her youngest. He was about fourteen or fifteen, a dangerous age, especially if the boy was tall and well made. Big boys got too big for their britches. They started feeling their strength around men and their sex around women. Ebeneezer was big, but not too big for his britches. His mama taught him good. He took off his cap and bowed his head to the white man. You would not catch him on the same side of the road with a white woman. He said sir and ma'am and mister. That was the trouble. One morning he walked into the store where they went to get cheated and said, "Good morning, Mr. Jack, sir," real polite the way his mama taught him to. But Mr. Jack did not like a big strapping colored boy playing fast and loose with his Christian name. He took the gun he kept behind the counter and shot Ebeneezer dead.

When they carried the body of that hat-doffing, careful-talking boy home, Ida Norris knew that someday she would be here, begging for one of her boys' lives. If she was lucky enough to have a chance to beg. If she was lucky enough to have to beg for only one. Poor Ada Wright was begging for two of her boys.

After Ida Norris left, I sat alone in the small parlor at the back of the house, staring out the window at the waning autumn afternoon. The garden was in shadows now. The article would not be hard to write. Several pages of notes sat on the table next to me. I could hear the cadences of her speech in my head. I told myself the sooner I got down to work, the better. I did not want to lose her voice. But I went on sitting there, staring out into the darkening garden, thinking about Ida Norris. Unlike Ruby, unlike her son and the other boys, Ida Norris had told her life story almost entirely in terms of other people. I could not decide whether I pitied or envied her.

I love him [Samuel Leibowitz] more than life itself.

—*Haywood Patterson, 1933*

I owe more than I can ever pay to Mr. Leibowitz.

—*Vincent "Mad Dog" Coll, n.d.*

On the Sunday before Franklin Delano Roosevelt was elected the thirty-second president of the United States by a landslide, Harry Spencer and I took the night train down to Washington. The Supreme Court had agreed to hear the case, the executions had been stayed, and now word had spread that the Court would hand down its decision the following day.

We were both too keyed up about the decision to sleep, and we sat up late in the club car, talking about the boys, speculating about the ruling, and arguing about the party. I liked the fact that Harry was still trying to persuade me to join. I did not mind the attention he paid to my legs every time I crossed and recrossed them either.

We said goodnight beside the lower berth the porter had made up for me. Harry's was in the next sleeping car. The dewy Vassar graduate had made the reservations for us. He stood looking down at me, and I knew what he was thinking, because I was thinking the same thing.

"Goodnight," he said.

"Goodnight," I answered.

The train careened around a curve, and he reached over my shoulder to steady himself against the upper berth.

"Will you be all right?" The question was preposterous, especially posed to a woman who had gone looking for trouble in Scottsboro and Huntsville and Kilby prison.

I laughed. "Will you?"

His grin was wicked. "Lonely as a cloud."

A moment passed. He was still leaning over me, his arms braced on both sides of my head. I was hanging on to the railing behind him. A bend in the road, a lurch of the train, a change of heart, and we would be in an embrace. It would have been so easy. Even the logistics would not have been difficult. In those days porters, as well desk clerks in hotels and even ushers in movie theaters, were supposed to be guardians of public morals, but a dollar or two could persuade them to look the other way. The tracks curved and the train lurched, but I managed to fall away from Harry rather than toward him. He still ran the magazine, and I still did not want to be known as the girl who had slept her way to wherever she was going.

I said goodnight again. He shook his head, told me to sleep well, then turned and made his way down the aisle between the sleeping passengers.

The next morning I raised the window shade to a sooty dawn. The weather matched my mood. I felt let down after the previous night and apprehensive about the coming day. If the court did not reverse the convictions, the boys would walk down the corridor and through the green door in weeks, if not days.

Harry and I said little as we made our way through Union Station and took a taxi to the Capitol. In those days, the court still convened in the Old Senate Chamber. Chief Justice Hughes had laid the cornerstone of the new building a month earlier, but three years would pass before the Supreme Court of the United States had its own home.

A crowd had already gathered in the plaza at the east front. They circled the area with a quiet hush, holding their signs high, like beacons of hope in the steel-gray morning. EQUAL RIGHTS FOR NEGROES and JOIN THE ILD and SCOTTSBORO BOYS SHALL NOT DIE. I had heard they had asked for police protection, but the District of Columbia's law enforcement officers had no more affection for communist demonstrators than did their brothers in New York. Metropolitan officers and Capitol cops and what looked like plainclothes detectives milled about with billy clubs and tear gas, but no one knew whether they were there to protect the demonstrators or rout them.

We made our way past the police and the marchers, up the steps, and down the marble halls to the chamber. The vast space was almost full, but despite the crowd, a portentous silence hung from the high ceiling inside just as it did among the protesters outside. I remembered Clarence's account of the silence mounting in Kilby Prison as an execution neared.

We had barely settled in our seats when the justices, somber as a dirge in their black robes, filed in and took their places behind the high bench that ran along one side of the room in front of a row of columns crested by a soaring eagle. Their robes were identical, but they were a motley lot. Several were balding, but Justice Cardozo's shock of gray hair made him look boyish, and Justice Brandeis's unruly mop hinted at a radical bent. Seven of them were clean-shaven, but Chief Justice Hughes and Justice Sutherland sported white whiskers. Their expressions, however, were uniformly dour. I wondered if that was merely judicial demeanor or a harbinger of things to come.

Chief Justice Hughes nodded to Justice Sutherland. Beside me, I felt Harry tense. Sutherland was one of the most conservative justices on the bench. His reading of the opinion was not a good sign.

The court had restricted itself to one question, Sutherland began. "Whether the defendants were in substance denied the right of counsel, and if so, whether such denial infringes the due process clause of the Fourteenth Amendment."

Beside me, Harry was taut as a stretched bow. I held my breath.

"The defendants were young, ignorant, illiterate," Sutherland read, "surrounded by hostile sentiment, hauled back and forth under guard of soldiers, charged with an atrocious crime regarded with special horror in the community where they were to be tried."

I could not believe the words were coming from Sutherland's mouth. They were not the words of one of the most conservative members of the court. He went on for some time, but the opinion was clear long before he finished. The defendants had not had adequate representation. The cases were reversed and remanded to the lower court.

When he finished reading, there was not a sound in the Old Senate Chamber, but I could hear the cheering in my head. Not even the shouts of the demonstrators outside, who were now being rounded up and arrested, could drown it out. The boys would get a new trial.

Harry and I took the four o'clock back to New York. As soon as the porter stowed our bags in the overhead rack, we headed for the club car. Joe Brodsky, the attorney for the ILD, and several of his assistants were already there. He beckoned us over. Flasks appeared. We drank to the Supreme Court's decision. The mood was celebratory, but by the time the train reached Baltimore, I could feel the tension building again. When the ILD had first taken on the case, they'd had nothing to lose and everything to gain. The party had never attracted many southern Negroes, and anything they could do for the boys was bound to increase membership. But now that the ILD had saved the boys from the electric chair once, they had more at stake. They would need a star attorney for the next round of trials.

"What about Clarence Darrow?" a young man, who wore a Phi Beta Kappa key on a gold watch chain across his vest, suggested.

"The NAACP approached him the first time around," Joe Brodsky said, "and he wasn't interested. Besides, he's talking about retiring."

"He's been talking about retiring for years," the man with the Phi Beta Kappa key said, "but maybe he wants to redeem himself after he defended that society dame for shooting the Hawaiian kid."

Brodsky shook his head. His big fleshy face, which had seemed so happy a few minutes earlier, was set in a frown. He and his team were competent, but he needed more than competence. He needed brilliance, and dazzle, and a household name.

"What about Sam Leibowitz?" Harry suggested. "They call him the next Clarence Darrow."

"The guy who represented Al Capone and Mad Dog Coll?" The man with the key sounded incredulous.

"He got Capone and Coll off," I pointed out. By virtue of a piece I had written for another magazine, I was something of an authority on Sam Leibowitz.

"Tell them about the Eskimo Pie defense," Harry said to me. Until then, I'd had no idea he had read my article.

"There was a gangland shootout in Harlem," I began. "A four-year-old baby was caught in the crossfire. The police found a supposed witness, who testified he had seen Coll fire the machine gun that killed the baby. Leibowitz took one look and smelled prison all over him. He insists he's had so many ex-cons as clients he can spot one by the way he carries himself. He says sometimes he can even tell which prison the man served time in. He was sure the witness had made a deal with the police."

"Are you suggesting the New York police force would frame an innocent man?" the Phi Beta Kappa key asked in mock outrage.

"Let her finish," Harry said.

"Leibowitz went at the witness every way from the sun, but he couldn't shake his story. Then he came up with the Eskimo Pies. The witness had testified he made his living by peddling Eskimo Pies. That was what he was doing when he saw the murder. Leibowitz brought fourteen ice-cream pies into court and handed them out to the jurors, and the judge, and the prosecutor. While they ate, he proceeded to question the witness. The man couldn't describe the label, had no idea how the pies were made, and had never heard of dry ice. He said he carried the pies around in a pasteboard box, even in the heat of summer, and their temperature kept them from melting."

"Cheap theatrics."

I wanted to tell him that a man who does not have the sense to leave a Phi Beta Kappa key in his cufflink box where it belongs should not talk about cheap theatrics. "Mad Dog Coll went free," I said instead.

Joe Brodsky was watching me carefully. He must have heard about the Eskimo Pie defense, but I had the feeling he wanted to be persuaded. Harry must have had the same feeling, because he urged me on again.

"Tell them about the Christian fish defense." We were working as a team now.

"The defendant had shot a policeman," I began. "He had actually gone gunning for his wife, but the policeman happened to get in his way. He claimed he was at his job in a fish market at the time of the murder. The prosecutor brought a basket with twenty different kinds of fish into court and asked the defendant to identify them. He couldn't name a single fish. Then Leibowitz moved in for the cross. He pointed out that the fish market in question was in a Jewish neighborhood and accused the prosecutor of not showing the defendant a single fish that went into gefilte fish."

Brodsky laughed. "It's pronounced *ge-fil-te* fish, Miss Whittier. Three syllables."

"*Ge-fil-te* fish," I repeated, and Harry, who had no more idea how to pronounce it than I did, nodded in approval.

"Leibowitz told the jury that the state was trying to convict his client on 'Christian fish,'" I went on, "and won another acquittal."

"It's an interesting idea," Brodsky said.

"There's one more point in its favor," Harry added. "Leibowitz has won acquittals in seventy-seven of seventy-eight first-degree murder cases, with one hung jury. You don't retain an attorney with a record like that unless you're serious about getting the defendants off. In other words, hiring Leibowitz would scotch the rumors about the party preferring nine dead Negro martyrs to nine new Negro members."

Not even the Phi Beta Kappa key could argue with that.

On the way back to the Pullman car to get our suitcases, Harry put his arm around my shoulders to steady me as the train took a curve and told me we made quite a team.

We went straight from Pennsylvania Station to the brownstone in the shadow of the Ninth Avenue El. The book closed the next day, and Harry wanted to get an editorial on the Supreme Court decision in the issue. He said that since the story was my baby, we should collaborate on the piece.

After the janitor's wife brought us the pot of coffee he requested, he closed the door and we got down to work. The going was slow, but it was not dull. I liked the way he tossed out ideas and let me run with them. I loved the way he ran with mine. By the time we agreed on a final draft, it was after midnight. I was feeling pleased with him and proud of myself.

He pulled open the bottom drawer of his desk, produced a bottle of real scotch whiskey, and poured two drinks. I took the one he handed me and kicked off my shoes. He leaned back in his swivel chair, put his feet up on the paper-littered desk, and sat watching me in the circle of light cast by the green-shaded lamp.

"I was just wondering," he said after a moment.

"Wondering what?"

"How I'm going to feel after you move on. Or should I say onward and upward."

I tried not to show how much the comment delighted me. "Am I going somewhere?"

"The one thing you've never been is coy. Don't start now."

"At least, I'm not going anywhere in the immediate future."

He went on staring at me in the dim light cast by the desk lamp. "I'm glad to hear it."

A moment passed, then another. I put the glass down on his desk and stood. "Now that we've put the book to bed, I might as well go home and get some sleep."

He took his feet off the desk and unfolded his tall frame from the chair. "Now that we've put the book to bed," he repeated, as he started around the desk to me, "what do you say we do the same to us?"

Harry and I never did make it to bed that night. We did not even make it out of the office. I suppose we had been leading up to this for too long. The papers on the desk sparked and crackled beneath us.

Looking back at it now, I see that I fell for, perhaps even fell in love with, Harry for many reasons—the nose flattened in the cause of social justice, the tortured conscience that wrecked his marriage and changed his life, the easy seductive smile that belied it. I have no idea whether the same thing would have happened under other circumstances. Perhaps if we had met earlier, in a different world, at a polite dinner party or debutante dance, no sparks would have flown, and we would not have risked setting fire to the offices of *The New Order*. But a noble cause is a heady aphrodisiac. The Saccos and Vanzettis and Tom Mooneys of the world have been responsible for more affairs than anyone is willing to admit.

It isn't Charlie Weems on trial in this case. It's a Jew lawyer.

—Samuel Leibowitz, 1937

Both of us—you and I—are in the same boat together.

—Samuel Leibowitz, to a convention of the Negro Improved Benevolent Protective Order of Elks, 1939

Two months after Harry and I regaled Joe Brodsky with tales of Samuel Leibowitz's expertise, and set metaphorical fire to the offices of *The New Order*, Sam Leibowitz agreed to defend the Scottsboro boys. Abel stopped me in the hall the day the ILD made the announcement.

"Good news for the boys," he said. "Good news for the ILD. And good news for Alice Whittier."

"Where do I come into it?"

"That piece you wrote about him gives you a leg up."

"Don't be ridiculous."

"Tell me you aren't thinking of calling him."

"I already have. We're having lunch tomorrow."

Sam Leibowitz was waiting on the steps of the General Sessions Court in lower Manhattan. As soon as he saw me, he started down them with a long stride. He was a solidly built man with wide shoulders, an impressive balding head, and a dapper air. I could have applied lip rouge in the reflection of the well-shined shoes that glinted in the winter sun.

He shook my hand and said it was good to see me. He said it as if he had spent the interval since we had last met worrying about my well-being. He looked like a banker or a lawyer or a businessman, but he had the sympathetic imagination and scheming soul of an actor. I saw again why juries acquitted for him.

He took my arm and began steering me down the steps. He did not have much time, he explained, so he hoped I would not mind a nearby legal watering hole. As we walked, he told me again that he had liked my article on him.

"But you didn't use the anecdote about my name," he said.

The story he was referring to concerned not Mr. Leibowitz, but his father, who had arrived in New York from Romania with his wife and children in the last years of the last century. Leibowitz's father, Isaac Lebeau by name, had sold dry goods, notions, and just about anything else he could get his hands on from a pushcart on Orchard Street on the Lower East Side. Though he found America an improvement over the old country, life was not getting as good as he had hoped as fast as he had expected, and one day he complained about the matter to a friend. The problem, the friend explained, was that Isaac had not Americanized himself sufficiently. Take his name. It sounded foreign. If Isaac wanted to get ahead in America, he had to sound like a real American. Isaac thought about the real Americans he knew. Remember, he had not ventured far from the Lower East Side of Manhattan. The next day Isaac Lebeau hired a lawyer to add a *witz* to his name.

The anecdote was amusing, but there was no reason I should have included it in the article. I found it odd, however, that Sam Leibowitz had noticed its omission.

"Space limitations," I explained. I was not lying. I had cut the piece several times, but the anecdote had not been in the first draft.

He stopped in front of a restaurant, but did not open the door immediately. "That's not the reason you didn't use it."

"I guess I just didn't think it was that significant."

"Not that significant for me, perhaps, but too significant for you."

"What do you mean?"

"You thought if you used it, you'd be making fun of my father. You thought the anecdote would be anti-Semitic."

Without giving me a chance to answer, he pulled open the door and stepped aside to let me go in before him.

The large tin-ceilinged room was raucous with men who were dressed conservatively but gave off an aura of theatricality, as if they were addressing a jury rather than chatting with a companion or two. The maître d' cut through the crowd around the door, greeted Sam Leibowitz deferentially, and showed us to a table in a corner that was not quiet, but a little less noisy than those in the center of the room. Heads turned as we passed. Many of the men greeted Leibowitz. Others followed him with their eyes.

We ordered lunch quickly and turned to the case. He talked about the boys, and the previous trials, and the Supreme Court decision. He said the first order of business would be to get a change of venue. "Birmingham would best, but I don't think there's much chance of that."

He asked me about Victoria and Ruby, and I gave him my impressions.

As the waiter served coffee, I brought up the question that had been bothering me since I had heard he'd taken the case. Why had he agreed to work with the Communist Party, which he deplored, forgoing any fee, and even paying his own expenses, on the kind of case he had never taken before?

He gave me the conventional answers. The ILD had promised not to interfere with his conduct of the trial, and the case touched on no controversial matters of economy or government. He was defending the boys because he wanted to see justice done. He was forgoing a fee and paying his own expenses because, thanks to hard work and good luck, he could afford to.

I did not doubt anything he said, but I could not help thinking there was more to it than that. I am not suggesting that I subscribed to Abel Newman's theory of human behavior. Show me an altruist, Abel likes to say, and I'll show you a man, or woman, with ulterior motives. But I did think I was missing something about Sam Leibowitz.

I discovered what it was as the waiter was refilling our coffee cups. Leibowitz was assuring me again that the ILD had agreed not to use the case for propaganda purposes. Suddenly he stopped speaking, seemingly distracted by two men rising from the next table. They did not look like trial attorneys. If they were judges, they had nothing to do with Tammany. They reminded me of the Philadelphia lawyer who administered my trust fund. Their lean faces might have been carved from Plymouth Rock. Their backs were stiff with the conviction of their own probity. Their unseeing eyes and oblivious expressions made it clear there was nothing in life they wanted that they did not already have. I looked from them back to Sam Leibowitz. He had been watchful before. Now he seem acutely attuned. His mouth opened, as if he were about to say something. The two men moved off before he could.

He turned back to me. "The law stipulates the right of the accused to a competent defense," he repeated. We were still talking about the boys, only he was not. He glanced at the receding backs of the two men, then returned to me.

"I'll tell you another anecdote, Miss Whittier, though you won't be any more comfortable with this than you were with the one about my father's changing his name. I did very well in law school. Cornell, as you know. Had I not been a Jew, I would have gone into real estate law, or railroad law, or some respectable specialty. But firms that specialized in those fields were not open to boys like me, even boys like me who did well enough for the dean of the law school to take an interest in their futures. Do you know what he said when I told him my plans? 'Oh, no, Sam. Not criminal law. Anything but that.'" He laughed. "The law says every defendant is entitled to a competent defense. But the profession looks down its nose at those who do the defending."

After I left him, I kept thinking about the story and the two attorneys or judges who had not greeted him. In the lexicon of ulterior motives, the desire for respectability struck me as scarcely worth the trouble.

A month later, four weeks before the new trials were to begin, the sheriff of Huntsville reported that Ruby Bates had disappeared. Alabama Attorney General Thomas E. Knight, Jr., told the press he was not worried. The authorities would find her in time. Just to be sure, he alerted all state and local officials to take Ruby Bates into custody on sight.

Book Two

She [Ruby Bates] was greatly in love with Shug Moore, a young Negro man.

—Affidavit of McKinley Pitts, 1931

Somehow I began to think that it just wasn't right. Sure them boys is "niggers." But "niggers" got feelings just like white folks.

—Ruby Bates, 1933

Ruby Bates came to me for a private confessional conference concerning her testimony.

—The Reverend Dr. Henry Emerson Fosdick, 1933

The fella was dark, not dark like a colored, but dark like a foreigner. One thing I knew for positive, he wasn't from nowhere 'round here. I took notice of him soon as I come out of the house. He was standing there almost like he was waiting on me. He let me pass by, but when I got a fair way along, I looked back, and there he was following behind. After a spell, I looked back again, and he was still following, so's I slowed down to let him catch me up.

He started in talking right off. He talked funny, real fast with a lot of hard sounds that hurt on my ears almost as bad as the machines in the mill, but he didn't act hard, nor mean neither. He started in saying it was a real pretty day, and before I knew it, he wanted to know my name, and did I live hereabouts, and was I working in the mill. I reckon I know when I'm being hustled.

I was studying him, looking for his salesman's case, but he didn't seem to have none. What he did have was a Ford auto, and when I told him I was fixing to leave town, on account of no work and no charity and no nothing, he said he'd carry me to Birmingham, where he knew some folks who would let me stay.

"No strings attached," he said, snapping the words hard as a slingshot. Truth to tell, I didn't have nothing against strings, on account of he wasn't a bad-looking fellow. I reckoned he had a couple of dimes to rub together too. One way or another, I figured I didn't have nothing to lose. I told him that, and he said fine and dandy, and his name was Reuben, and what were we waiting for.

The next thing I knew, I was in a house in Birmingham with two other fellas beside Reuben and a lady. It wasn't no chippy house neither, just some folks who knew a gracious plenty about me. First, I reckoned Reuben told them, on account of I told him on the drive over. But they said they read about me in the newspapers. I ain't the smartest gal in the world, but I reckoned it wasn't no accident Reuben happened on me in Huntsville and carried me to Birmingham. I didn't mind none. They were treating me real good.

I passed two days in the house in Birmingham, and the whole time they never stopped saying how we were all workers and had to stick together, and how the enemy wasn't the coloreds—they said I wasn't to call them niggers no more—who were our brothers and sisters under the skin, but the white bosses who oppressed us all together. I didn't know nothing about that, but the more they talked about coloreds and whites being the same, the worse I got to feeling about them boys on the train, and the more I kept recollecting Shug. If Shug wasn't a colored, I would've loved him. I would've loved him a lot better than Earl Streetman, that's for positive. You wouldn't find Shug going off with no Mary Sanders. So when the folks in the house started in talking about carrying me up to New York City, where I could tell what really happened on the train, and there wouldn't be no police chief nor nobody else saying I had to lay out a sentence in jail for it, I didn't see nothing against it. The way I reckoned, I could keep from going to torment, and if whites and coloreds were all the same under the skin, after a spell they could carry Shug north too, and me and him could be together. Besides, they said they'd make it worth my while.

They didn't carry me to New York City, like they said, they carried me to a place called Brooklyn. I didn't mind none, on account of the folks in that house were real neighborly too. Only they kept asking me to tell what happened on the train from Chattanooga. Every time I turned around, a body was coming through wanting to hear about the white foot on the black hand. After a spell, I was getting wore out with telling it. All that telling didn't seem to be doing much good neither. Far as I knew, them boys were still in jail down home, and if they were still there, I reckoned I was still going to torment. One day I couldn't stand worrying about it no more, so's I asked Reuben what he thought. Now that I told the truth to so many folks, was I saved, or was I still bound to go to torment, on account of them boys were still in jail?

He set studying me with them sad dark eyes of his and an upside-down smile that made me think he was about to go to crying any minute, and I reckoned I knew the answer before he opened his mouth. I was bound to burn in hell. Then he started talking. I tried to make out the words, but he talked so fast, and made his sounds so hard, and used a bunch of words that didn't make no sense to me. I reckoned I knew religion all right, and masses was what they called folks they didn't know, but there was something in between I couldn't make hide nor hair of. It sounded like O P 8. Since I come north, I heard a gracious plenty about the ILD, and some about the NAACP, and I already knew about the YMCA, but I ain't never heard nothing about a O P 8. I didn't like to ask neither, on account of from the way he said it, I reckoned he didn't hold it highly. I was pretty blue.

Then Reverend Fosdick come over the radio. Minute I heard his voice, I knew if anyone could tell about being saved, it was him. At the end of the program, the radio announcer said Reverend Fosdick was up in New York City. I asked Reuben how far a distance we were from New York City, and he said we were in it, on account of Brooklyn was in New York City. So I asked if he would carry me to where Reverend Fosdick was preaching. He got that same sad look he put on when he talked about religion and O P 8 and masses, and I reckoned he didn't fancy the idea, and I'd just have to find Reverend Fosdick on my own, but then the folks in the house called a meeting on it. I never did see folks so partial to calling meetings. One of the fellas said how did they know Reverend Fosdick wouldn't go to the newspapers or the law and tell them where I was. Someone else said you couldn't trust a man who let John D. Rockefeller, Jr., build a church for him. But then a girl by the name of Gladys started talking about a reporter who come sniffing around the day before, and the best thing would be to get me out of there to someplace no one would think to go looking for me. So's that's how Reuben and Gladys carried me to Reverend Fosdick.

It wasn't nothing like back home, where all you got to do is walk into the church or the tent and the preacher stretches out his arms and tells you right off you're welcome in the Lord's house, sister. This was a Lord's house, all right, bigger than any church I ever seen, bigger than any revival tent even, with a tower that climbed all the way to heaven, but we didn't venture in there. Instead Reuben and Gladys carried me into a tall building with a heap of elevators, like in the moving pictures, and a long row of closed doors with names and other words on them in gold letters, and folks scurrying back and forth fast as ants, like folks did up North. Reuben and Gladys went up to one lady, then another, and they must've spoke to half a dozen folks before they come back and say the Reverend Fosdick is fixing to go on the radio for his Sunday night service in a spell, and don't have but a minute to see me. He didn't even have that, they said, until they pleaded real hard. So they carried me into one of them elevators, and it shot up so fast I reckoned my stomach was still waiting down below, and before I knew it, Reuben and the girl weren't nowhere to be seen, and I'm standing in a big office. There was carpet on the floor, and more windows than I ever seen in my life, with the sky going to dark right outside them, and setting behind a desk, a man with kinky hair, almost like a colored's but not so dark, and little round glasses with wire frames, and a prim preacher mouth. He told me to set, and I did. Then he took a gold watch from his weskit pocket, popped it open, then snapped it closed so sharp I near jumped out of my chair. He told me he didn't have but a minute and asked what he could do for me. If that cat didn't take away my tongue, I don't know what did.

"I understand it has something to do with the Scottsboro boys," he said.

I nodded.

"You are one of the accusers?"

"Me and Victoria had to set in court and say we were raped."

"Were you?"

I shook my head no.

"You were not?"

I couldn't look at him no more, but I managed to get out a no.

He pushed himself back from the desk. I still wasn't looking up, but I reckoned he was standing, on account of out of the corner of my eye I couldn't make out his face no more, just a black suit.

"You must go back," he said. "You must go back and tell the truth. Not only for those boys, but for your own spiritual well-being."

I didn't know what he meant about spiritual well-being, but soon as he said it, I knew he was right. Only chance I had of not going to torment was going back and untelling the lie down home.

Reuben and the girl were waiting on me outside Reverend Fosdick's office. Soon as I come up to them, they started in to fighting about carrying me back to the house in Brooklyn or finding me someplace different. I told them Reverend Fosdick said I had to go back down home to Alabama, but they weren't having none of that. They said I had to stay here till the trial started. Then they'd carry me down home, and I could untell my lie. They said didn't I recollect we made a deal.

I could have set down and cried. Here I finally made up my mind to go back, and they're telling me I can't. Minute they said that, I reckoned I wanted to go back more than I'd knowed. I'd had my fill of Reuben and Gladys and all them folk. Only thing they did day and night was talk a blue streak. The fellas didn't want no fun, least not with me, and the girls didn't care nothing about clothes nor lipstick nor pretty things. When it come to dressing up and looking good, them ILD folks were the sorriest bunch I ever seen. Then I recollected the card. It was right there in the tan pocketbook they bought me to go with the tan suit and coat and hat. That's another thing. If I knew when they started in promising things I was going to end up with a bunch of no-color clothes, I wouldn't've been in such a hurry. At least the lady who give me the card didn't look like she was one step away from a burlap sack. From the way she kept telling me to send her a wire and she'd pay to get it, I reckoned she'd be real happy to see me. And she wouldn't make me wear no no-color clothes neither, not if I recollected them shoes she ruined, and I surely did.

I told them I knew a lady in New York, and they could carry me to her till it was time for me to go back home.

While Ruby was making her way north, though I did not know that was what she was doing, I was heading down to Washington to cover FDR's first inauguration, the last in history that would be held in March. Of course, we did not call it his first at the time. No one dreamed there would be four before he finished.

I stood in the wind-chilled crowd that Saturday afternoon, watching in amazement as a crippled nation placed its trust and hope in a crippled man. That was something else the public did not know at the time, and the press conspired to keep the secret. I will never forget the time that a rookie newspaper photographer, who had not learned the rules, took a picture of FDR struggling on his crutches. The shutter had barely clicked when a more seasoned reporter jostled the rookie, knocking his camera to the ground and exposing the film that would have let the cat out of the bag before the American public.

I stayed on in Washington after the inauguration. On Monday, the first lady was going to break precedent and hold a press conference of her own. It would be for women only. I was wary when Harry suggested I cover it. I had no intention of being relegated to the position of woman reporter writing on women's issues. But the second round of Scottsboro trials would not begin for another two weeks, and I was curious to see the new first lady in action.

I still have the photograph of that initial unprecedented all-girl press conference, which, needless to say, our male colleagues found a hoot. Thirty-five women stand and sit and kneel on the floor—the White House had underestimated the turnout and not set up enough chairs—around a somber first lady who is still an unknown quantity. Many of the faces are familiar, Bess Furman and Emma Bugbee and May Craig, and most look pleased at where they are, but a few of us seem disgruntled at how far we have yet to go.

When I look at the photograph now, I recognize another face, though it was not familiar at the time. The name did not ring a bell either. Ward is a common surname, and Georgina did not use the Whittier her mother had christened her with as a middle name.

I remained in Washington for a few days to interview several other officials in the new administration and returned to New York at the end of the week. Sometimes I wonder what would have happened if I had stayed through the weekend, as friends had asked me to. If I had not been there to answer the phone when Sam Leibowitz called, would someone else have ended up in my shoes?

He asked if I could come down to his office.

"Now?" It was late on a Sunday afternoon.

"It's rather urgent." He hesitated. "It has to do with Ruby Bates."

I told him I would be there as soon as I could get a taxi.

In those days, many people still worked half a day on Saturday, but Sunday was sacred. The doors to the office building at the address Leibowitz had given me were locked. I had to ring several times before a watchman appeared on the other side of the glass. I followed him to the elevator, my heels striking the marble floor like gunshots. The sound reminded me of Leibowitz's usual clients.

As soon as the elevator door opened on the seventh floor, I heard the voice from down the hall. It did not belong to Sam Leibowitz, though it was as deep and rich and dramatic as he could make his when necessary. As I started toward it, I made out static and realized the voice was coming from a radio.

A door with a frosted glass window, lettered with Samuel Leibowitz's name, stood open, as did another to an inner office. Through the two doors, I saw Leibowitz sitting behind his desk, poring over a pile of papers, seemingly immune to the radio program he had turned loud enough to carry halfway down the hall.

I hesitated in the entrance to the inner office. He looked up, saw me, and stood. As he did, he reached over to the radio on the table behind him and turned the knob. The voice fell to a whisper.

"Powerful instrument," he said, gesturing toward the radio. "Think of it, Miss Whittier. The president can talk to millions of Americans, as he's scheduled to do tomorrow night, face to face, as it were, with no one in the middle to distort his words, or subvert his message, or twist the news. Just as if he really were having a fireside chat with the entire nation. It's a great step forward for democracy. It might not be too much to say that it marks the end of tyranny throughout the world."

Strange as it seems now, in those days we really did dare to believe, or at least hope, such things. An extraordinary new instrument that spread the unvarnished word would transform the world into a just and peaceful place. We should have known better. Hitler had already taken to the airwaves in Germany, Mussolini in Italy, and here at home we had

Father Coughlin. A year later, we would have Sam Leibowitz as well, though I do not mean to suggest the man was a demagogue, only that by then he would be so well known, thanks to the Scottsboro boys, that he would be sought after to comment on other crimes of the century. The twentieth turned out to have more than its share, or perhaps I think that only because the twentieth was the century I inhabited.

Sam Leibowitz gestured to one of the chairs on the other side of his desk, waited for me to take it, then sat again. The voice on the radio was still murmuring. I was surprised to hear the set was tuned to a church service. My reaction must have shown on my face.

"You're not a believer, are you, Miss Whittier?"

"Is it that obvious?"

"Probably not to most people, but it's my job to notice things. I am a believer, though I'm sorry to say I don't go to synagogue as often as I might. That's why I was listening to the Reverend Dr. Henry Emerson Fosdick just now."

I knew who Fosdick was. Most people did in those days. His face had been on the cover of *Time* magazine. His books had won him tens of thousands of ardent followers, or so his publisher claimed in the ads. John D. Rockefeller, Jr., had built him a vast church on Riverside Heights. And Station WJZ carried his sermons.

"It doesn't seem like quite the same thing, as going to synagogue, I mean."

He smiled at that. "I was trying to understand Dr. Fosdick's appeal."

"I don't understand it either," I said. "Not that I spend a great deal of time thinking about it." I was getting impatient. Next we'd be on to Aimee Semple McPherson and how she put her hands on the transmitter and healed through the radio waves, or so she and her followers claimed.

"You may give it more thought after I tell you why I asked you to come down here."

I waited.

"Ruby Bates is in New York."

"Where?"

"Close by."

I glanced around the office. "Not here?"

"I'm not that foolish. I wish she had not come north at all. I warned the ILD it could backfire. But they have their own ideas."

I did not remind him that he had told me at lunch that the ILD had sworn not to meddle in his handling of the case.

"The ILD brought Ruby north?"

"Let's just say the girl managed to get here somehow."

"So she changed her story again and is going to testify for the defense?"

He did not answer, but there was no other reason for his keeping her under wraps. The only thing I did not understand was why he was letting me in on the secret.

"You're not telling me this just because you liked the article I wrote about you."

"Ruby needs a place to stay."

"And you want her to stay with me?" I could barely keep the glee out of my voice.

"I can't very well take her home."

"Your wife and children?"

"Reporters. They've been following me around since I agreed to take the case." He did not seem unhappy about the fact.

"Where is she?"

"Before I tell you, you have to agree to my terms."

"Which are?"

"I'll give you Ruby Bates, exclusive interviews, first-person account, the whole kit and caboodle."

"Has she agreed to this?"

"She was the one who mentioned your name. But," he went on, "you have to wait until after the trial to run it."

I was going to say yes. He must have known that. But I wanted to get the best terms I could. "Do I have to wait for the verdict?"

"Only until she testifies. After that, she's all yours." And good riddance to bad rubbish, his tone said, though he was too prudent to speak the words.

I leaned across the desk and held out my hand. "It's a deal."

He shook my hand.

"Where is she?"

"With the Reverend Dr. Henry Fosdick. Apparently she heard him on the radio—I told you it was a powerful instrument—and decided only he could save her."

"And Dr. Fosdick called you?"

"He gave her spiritual counseling, but he does not feel he can go beyond that. He says he has little liking for the press and less for personal publicity."

"Tell that to *Time* magazine."

"Then let's just say for this kind of personal publicity. You can't blame him. It's a tawdry business. A lot of people don't want to get their hands dirty with it. Nonetheless, Ruby needs a place to stay, and she said she would like to stay with you. She had your card."

Long as I live, I ain't never going to forget the ride from Reverend Fosdick's church to Alice's house. She said to call her Alice right off, on account of me and her were going to be living together for a spell. I can see it in my head clear as if I was watching a moving picture on a screen.

It had gone to raining, more mist than rain to tell the truth, and circles of gold hung around the streetlights, pretty as halos on Christmas angels. The colored lights were like Christmas too, red and green to stop and start the autos. I never saw so many of them things in my life neither. And on both sides of the road, buildings standing tall as any mountain I ever seen. There were lights on them too, white squares that climbed up and down and right and left and every which way.

I rolled down the window of the auto that had a glass between the front and back seat, and stuck my head out into the mist to get a better look. When we stopped for a red signal, I could see folks moving back and forth in the squares of light. They looked real cozy. I pulled my head in.

"I reckon folks in New York are plenty rich."

"The city is full of poor people, Ruby. Especially these days. Men are out of work. Whole families live in cardboard shacks in the park. They call them Hoovervilles. After President Hoover. At least he's gone, though it's anybody's guess what we have in store with Roosevelt. But the Hoovervilles are heartbreaking. If we didn't have to worry about your being seen, I'd show you."

I reckoned she was funning. I seen a gracious plenty of shacks. I ain't come all the way to New York City to look at more. But I didn't like to say that to her.

The car went 'round a corner left, then after a spell it turned right, and the night flared up like somebody lit a match to it. The brightness burned through the mist, and bounced off the shiny black streets, and turned the drops on the auto windows into diamonds, not that I ever seen a diamond except in magazine pictures. Even the signs were spelled out in lights. POOL, and HARDWARE, and EATS, and MABEL'S HOUSE OF BEAUTY, and CAL'S BAR AND GRILL, and GORGEOUS GIRLS burned up the night. Alice called the signs neon. I didn't know nothing about that. All I knew, they were the prettiest thing I seen for a spell. Them lights were so pretty they took my breath away.

I heard Ruby's intake of breath, and watched her turning her head back and forth from one side of upper Broadway to another, and did not have the heart to tell her the lights were only a carnival huckster's call to movie and vaudeville houses, and dance joints, and billiard parlors. But as the taxi lurched on south, the lights grew more law-abiding, and even brighter. This was the real thing, and it pried Ruby's eyes open into big blue saucers of amazement. Planters Peanuts, and the Astor Hotel, and Wrigley's Spearmint, and F. W. Woolworth, and the International Casino, and Whelan's Drug Store, and Alfred Lunt and Lynn Fontaine blinded her with promises. It was more, Ruby said softly, than a girl could take in all at once.

We pulled up in front of my building, and she came down to earth. I had always found a raffish charm in the ivy-covered brownstone with the slanting stoop and painted red window boxes, but I could tell by the way she stood staring up at the facade that its allure escaped her.

"This where you live?"

"I'm afraid so." I picked up her suitcase and started up the steps to the heavy wooden door with the frosted glass inset. We entered the hall, and I saw the interior of the house with her eyes. The flocked wallpaper was dark with soot. The faded runner on the narrow stairs, which, like the stoop, listed to one side, had been worn bare by generations of tenants on their way somewhere else. A damp musty aroma clung to the walls. I knew I was being ridiculous. She had spent her life in crumbling broken-windowed shacks without benefit of electricity or plumbing, and I was worrying that my apartment was too bohemian for her.

"You don't have no elevator?"

"It's only the third floor."

I switched her suitcase to my left hand to hold the banister with my right and led the way up the stairs.

"Don't go mistaking me," she said as we climbed. "I'm much obliged to you for taking me in." She stopped on the first landing and turned to me. "Lots of folks don't want nothing to do with me."

There was a catch in her voice as she spoke. At the time I was sure it was emotion. Later I would learn that years in the mill had already begun to take a toll on her lungs.

The place wasn't nothing like what I expected. She didn't have no curtains, just some old slatted blinds on the windows, and a crazy-shaped sofa and a couple of chairs even a cat wouldn't fancy curling up on. The old fireplace wasn't nothing to look at neither, with blue and white tiles that were going to yellow, and some cracked too. Wasn't much on the walls neither, not like we done back home, and what there was no one with a lick of sense would want to look at. Paintings of foreign folks with black hair and mustaches, that didn't look like any real bodies I ever seen, more like fat red and blue and yellow dolls, farming and hammering and working over machines; and pictures of big flowers with petals spread all crazy wide; and photos of folks, not dressed-up nice like me and Victoria used to cut from magazines, but all ragged, doing things a body wouldn't want to think about let alone look at. There was a lady on a stoop with a baby in her lap and two more young ones sleeping on the sidewalk, one wearing nothing but a shirt, so his privates was showing; and a bunch of white men with faces black as coal leaning on shovels; and one with no folks in it at all, just a mess of furniture piled in front of a closed door that hollered eviction loud as if there was a sign on it. I didn't like to stare too long at them pictures, on account of they were so ugly. On account of one other thing too. I didn't like to shame her. All you had to do was take one look to know that girl was bound and determined to make herself as sad and sorry as a body could be.

The meanest picture of all was hanging over a desk. It showed a heap of black hands reaching up through a grate in the floor from one of them underground cells. It reminded me of them boys back home in jail. I wondered if that was why she put it there. Like I said, that girl was just hunting for misery.

One wall had shelves with more books than a body could read, and on a table over in a corner set the sweetest little radio you ever seen. It looked just like the one I cut out of a magazine down home. A Majestic Duo-Chief, it was called. I asked if I could listen to it.

"Anytime you like," she said.

"Ain't no time like the present."

I walked right over to it then, turned the knob, and waited a spell for it to warm up, but when it finally did, all that come out was a man's voice talking real serious. I should've knowed she'd have it tuned to something like that. I bent over and started turning the dial real slow, on account of I didn't want her to think I was going to break it, and before I knew it, the whole room was full of dance music. I couldn't hardly keep my foot from tapping and my shoulders from shaking. Then I recollected myself.

"It ain't the first time I seen one. Folks in the house I stayed a spell before this had a radio. And when me and Victoria went to Chattanooga, not the time with all the trouble, but back before, we lived in a real nice house. We had electric lights on all the time, so it didn't make no difference if it was day nor night, and a radio playing, and a gramophone too, and folks dancing, and—" I stopped. Talking to her had a way of getting me to say things I never was fixing to. "It wasn't no chippy house nor nothing like that."

"Let's get one thing straight, Ruby."

I never heard her talk that way before. She sounded like a schoolteacher or a social services lady.

"You don't have to tell me anything you don't want to. But please don't lie to me. I know about prosti—hustling."

"What do you know about it?"

"I know that if you were working in a chippy house, it was society's fault, not yours."

It was the kind of thing these folks were always saying. At least when the church ladies talked about sin, and the social services folks lectured on getting by on what they give you, you know what they're talking about, but these folks up North didn't make no sense.

"Well, I wasn't working in no chippy house, so it don't matter whose fault it lies to."

She stood there studying me for a spell, then she turned around and carried the sack she called a suitcase through a door into another room. I reckoned I was meant to follow her, so's I did.

"You can sleep here," she said.

The bed looked real nice with lots of pillows, and yonder there was a chest of drawers; and a chair with real cushions, not like them hard-looking ones in the other room; and more shelves that looked like they were about to fall down from holding up all them books.

"You fixing to let me have that bed all to myself?" I slept with Ma and the young ones all together in beds smaller than that, but I didn't like to say so.

"I'll stay on the sofa in the living room."

"It don't seem right to disconvenience you. It's your bed."

"I don't mind. Besides, that way I can answer the door and the telephone. The last thing we want is anyone finding out you're here."

"On account of you're ashamed?"

"On account . . . because Mr. Leibowitz doesn't want anyone to know where you are until you testify. The bathroom's in there." She pointed to another door, then walked into the other room, opened a chest, and came back with a big towel. She handed it to me. It was white as a church lily and smelled twice as good. I recollected the side of burlap bag used to hang beside the wash bucket at home and reckoned this wasn't so bad after all.

"Just let me know if you need anything else," she said and went back into the other room.

I returned to the living room. Five minutes passed, then ten. I remembered the clerk in the hotel in Huntsville, who had reassured me that there was no danger to the innards from sitting over running water, and wondered if I should show Ruby how the toilet worked. Then I realized I was being ridiculous. She must have come in contact with indoor plumbing during her trip north. And she had been living in a house in Brooklyn.

"You live here all alone?" she asked when she came back into the living room. "No ma or pa?"

"They're in Philadelphia. Pennsylvania, not Mississippi."

"And you just up and come here to live without them?"

"I came here to work."

She glanced around the living room. "That magazine pay you enough wages to live here all by yourself?"

The New Order did not pay me enough to live here all by myself, nor did any of the other journals I occasionally wrote for, but I was not going to try to explain a trust fund to her. I certainly did not want to try to explain that I used only part of the income from it and gave the rest to good causes. I shrugged.

"You ain't married?"

"No."

"You ever been married?"

"No."

"You got a fella?"

"More or less."

"He don't want to marry you?"

"I don't know. I'm not sure I want to marry him."

"You ain't getting no younger."

I laughed.

"Last fella I had, Earl Streetman, he was nice as can be, but Mary Sanders started in talking dirt about me, so he up and left. There was another fella too. A spell back."

She sounded more sorry about him than about Earl Streetman.

"Did he up and leave too?"

She thought about that for a moment. "We was just . . . different." Her mouth snapped shut on the word.

I knew I was walking into a minefield. I had not forgotten her tirade on the back steps of her house. But I decided to take the chance.

"Was this other boy a Negro, Ruby?"

"What if he was?"

"But that's wonderful."

"I don't see nothing wonderful about it."

"It means you're better than you think, more broad-minded than you give yourself credit for."

She shook her head. "What it means is I ain't seen him for near on two years. Couldn't, lest I wanted to get him killed and me in a heap of trouble. Besides, Shug was different. Just 'cause I take to him don't mean I'm a nig—"

"Don't say it, Ruby."

" . . . take to all coloreds." She sat looking at me for a moment with those wide blue eyes. "I bet you ain't never been with no colored fella."

The statement caught me off guard. "I never had the opportunity."

It was, I think, the first time I heard Ruby laugh out loud.

Half literate and intensely shy, she [Ruby Bates] gave monosyllabic answers at first, but gradually talked of . . . a curiously dawning class consciousness.

—*New York* World-Telegram, *1933*

If the people would all work together instead of against each other it would help everybody. Well, I guess it wouldn't help the bosses, but it would help all the workers.

—*Ruby Bates, 1933*

Ruby stayed with me for six nights, more than enough time to hear the story of her life. It was a doozy. We talked in the morning, I wrote in the afternoon, and each evening I delivered an installment to the magazine.

I was working well, but sleeping badly. My insomnia had nothing to do with the sofa. Ruby kept me awake, or what I imagined to be Ruby. I was never sure whether the disturbances were real or in my head. Did I dream her footsteps and come awake with the echo of them in my ears, or was she really padding around my bedroom? And if she was, why shouldn't she be? She was my guest, not an inmate. Was that creaking the sound of the old brownstone in the night or the stealthy opening of a drawer? And hadn't she every right to open the drawer I had emptied for her at whatever hour she chose? In the paranoia of three A.M., I imagined her snooping and, I admit it, pilfering. When the morning light delivered rationality as predictably as the bottles the milkman left on the stoop, I recognized the terrible bigotry at the root of my distrust. My only solace was that I never did anything about my suspicions. I do not count the single lapse the morning she left.

Sam Leibowitz and I had agreed that Ruby should not leave my apartment. The chance of someone's recognizing her from the pictures in the newspapers was too great. But after she had been with me for two days, I called him and explained the problem. He agreed to make an appointment with a doctor he said could be trusted.

Ruby was not happy about the plan. She was dying to go out, but a visit to a doctor's office was not her idea of a lark. She did not much care for the reason for the doctor's visit either.

She did not want eyeglasses, but when she put them on, her eyes, behind the thick lenses, grew wide with wonder. For the first time in her life she could see the world clearly. The real surprise, as far as I was concerned, was that the poor kid should be so thrilled by what she saw.

I went out rarely while Ruby was staying with me, and allowed only three people in the apartment. One evening Harry came by to meet her. I had never seen Ruby blush, but she blushed that night when he told her what a fine thing she was doing and how proud he was of her.

"That your fella?" she asked after he left.

"He's the one."

"He's a peach. He your boss too?"

"He's the publisher of the magazine I write for most of the time."

"That mean yes or no?"

"Yes, in a way."

"Victoria took up with a boss at the mill one time. She worked steady for a spell."

"I was writing for the magazine before I knew Harry."

"Same as Victoria. How else you going to catch his eye? I reckon you get treated real good."

"One thing has nothing to do with the other."

It was the second time I heard her laugh out loud.

"It doesn't," I insisted.

"Okay," she said "Ain't no cause to get cross-legged on account of it."

The second person who set foot in the apartment during Ruby's stay was Viola White. Viola came down from Harlem every Wednesday to clean my apartment and wash and iron my clothes. I was not worried about Viola's recognizing Ruby. She had heard about the Scottsboro boys. Anyone who lived in Harlem in those days had. She wanted them freed, because she knew they were nine more victims of an ancient injustice, but she had no interest in the latest twist two white girls had made in the old tale. When Viola had first come to work for me, we had made a pact. I would not try to educate her about politics, if she would not try to convert me to religion. Nonetheless, just to be safe, I decided not to tell her Ruby's real name.

One morning, out of nowhere, Alice says she's fixing to give me a new name. Me and her were setting at the little table in front of the window in the kitchen eating breakfast. One thing you could say about living at Alice's, I surely did eat good. Every morning she squeezed oranges. I ain't tasted a orange since more than two years back, and I'd be lying if I said that juice didn't go down sweet as sugar. She always asked how I wanted my eggs, and fried up bacon, and put out real cream for coffee and butter, not oleo, for bread. Only thing missing was biscuits. That girl didn't know the first thing about making biscuits. Bread neither. I reckon she didn't have to, on account of there was a store not two steps away where she could buy whatever she fancied. She never did eat much herself. You have some more, she just kept saying, and I reckoned I might as well. Ain't no telling how long a spell before anybody hands me three squares a day again.

She was heaping the last of the eggs on my plate and telling me about the lady who come down from Harlem to clean and wash and iron, and how discretion being the better part of valor—she was always saying funny words I couldn't make head nor tail of—she was going to introduce me to the lady by another name in place of Ruby.

"May," I said. "Or maybe June."

"What?"

"I always hankered after a name on a calendar. Like them pictures of flowers and trees and fields."

"But you're named after a precious stone."

I near had to laugh at that. "Ain't nobody never going to mix me up with a ruby. But you don't have to be rich or smart or fancy to feature a month. I fancy June. May's nicer, on account of things ain't too hot yet, but I reckon I'm partial to June. It sounds real pretty."

"All right, June. June Robbins, like the bird."

So when the colored girl come, Alice told her I was Miss Robbins and kept calling me June."

I didn't mind none having Viola around. She sung church hymns to herself all the while she was there. I didn't know how sick for home I was till I heard Viola singing them songs. I never did fancy churchy songs, but they sounded mighty good to me setting up there in Alice's apartment in New York City. Maybe that was why I started worrying the problem, on account of I was fixing to get my mind off home. I asked Alice about it when we set down to supper, only Alice called it dinner, just like she called dinner lunch.

"I been trying to figure something."

She stopped eating and set to studying me, like she always did when I talked. Made me feel funny, but kind of important too.

"Me and you call each other Ruby and Alice."

"Yes?"

"And you call Viola Viola."

She put down her fork.

"So how come Viola calls you Miss Whittier and you told her I was Miss Robbins?"

She was studying me so hard now I reckoned she was mad at me.

"Forget it. It ain't important."

"No," she said real fast, "it is. The reason I call her Viola and she calls me Miss Whittier has nothing to do with the fact that she's Negro and I'm white."

"I didn't reckon it did, on account of us all being in the same boat, like you and them folks who carried me north say."

"Viola works for me."

"So you're a boss?"

"I'm not a boss. I pay Viola an honest wage for an honest day's work."

"That's the same words them folks who carried me up here say, but I ain't never heard of dishonest wages for a dishonest day's work."

Now she was wearing the same face as the social services ladies when they tell you not to sass.

"It's a phrase, Ruby. I pay Viola for her labor."

"Ain't that what a boss does? Pay somebody else to do the work they got enough money not to do?"

She crossed her arms on the table and leaned toward me. "Listen, Ruby, isn't it better for Viola to work for me than not to have a job?"

"Anybody would favor getting work over not getting none. Even the mill don't look so bad when your stomach's empty and the rent man's coming 'round."

"Then you see."

"I reckon."

The third person who came to the apartment while Ruby was staying with me was my mother. She telephoned one afternoon to say she was in town on league business, and if I was going to be home later that afternoon, she would stop by.

"I have someone staying with me," I said.

A moment of silence hung between us. She was wondering if the guest was a man, though she would never ask.

"Would you rather I not come?" she said instead.

"No, I'd like you to meet her."

I could hear the relief in her voice as she told me she would be there a little after five.

My mother was gracious to Ruby, but Ruby was still terrified of her. The ramrod posture and aristocratic upper lip had cowed more worldly women, and men, than Ruby Bates. But the visit was brief, and nothing untoward occurred, until I walked my mother downstairs to put her in a taxi.

"I suppose you know what you're doing," she began as I closed the door behind us.

"I'm trying to save the boys and to help her."

"You could do that without taking her to live with you," she said as we came out onto the street.

I raised my arm to hail a cab. "She needed a place to stay until the trial."

"I'm sure there are others, some more closely connected to the case, who have apartments."

"And thank heavens I got to her before they did." A taxi pulled up to the curb. "I'm getting a terrific story out of this."

She turned to me. "You're looking for more than a story," she said, then kissed me on the cheek and climbed into the cab before I could answer.

I stood looking after her as the car pulled away. I knew what she meant, but she was wrong. I was not trying to compensate for the past. And even if I were, what was wrong with that?

Ruby was waiting when I returned to the apartment. "I reckon your ma wasn't none too happy to find me here."

"What makes you say that?"

"Way she looked at me. Just like my ma did one time when I carried home a stray cat."

"You're not a stray cat, Ruby."

She shrugged. "She's a fine-looking lady all the same. Your pa looks nice too."

I was surprised. "How do you know what my father looks like?"

"You got them pictures on the table yonder." She crossed the room and picked up one of the silver-framed photographs. "I reckoned that was your ma even before she come here, on account of you feature her some. So's I reckon the man with her got to be your pa. He's real fine-looking. I don't mean just handsome. You can tell from his face he wouldn't up and sell a house out from under kin."

The line about selling a house from under kin was a reference to her own father. Harry had wanted me to tone down the portrait of Mr. Bates in Ruby's life story. The party liked its proletariat high-minded and hardworking. But I had dug in my heels and written the man Ruby had described.

Mr. Bates had the usual weakness for moonshine and women and uninterrupted leisure. As Ruby had remarked, he had once sold the family house without mentioning the fact to her mother, though what he did with the proceeds was anybody's guess, since he was broke by the time he turned up again. Her mother somehow scraped together enough money working in the mills, and taking in laundry, and pursuing other professions into which I did not inquire too closely to buy another shack. Her father, who knew an easy mark when he laid eyes on one, returned home just long enough to sell the second house to finance another bender. After that, the family rented a place and began sharecropping. The physical demands of farming being what they are, however, Mr. Bates disappeared again. As Ruby said, her father was nothing like mine.

I crossed the room, took the picture from her, and put it back on the table.

"You don't have to grab it away like that."

"I was merely putting it back on the table."

Now she was staring at me rather than the photograph. "What're you holding against him anyhow?"

"I have nothing against my father. He's a great humanitarian."

"Don't know about that. Don't know what the word means. But

I reckon you got something against him. I can tell. He trouble you when you were coming up?"

At first I did not understand what she meant, perhaps because she said it so casually.

"Of course not."

"Then why're you so mad at him?"

"I'm not mad at him. I just don't want to discuss him."

"He must've done something bad to you."

"He never did anything to me."

"Well, he must've done something bad to someone, get you so cross-legged."

"I have work to do." I started toward my desk.

"It ain't fair. I been telling you everything, and you don't say nothing. I don't call that neighborly."

I turned back to her. "It's not an interesting story."

"Can't say till I heard it."

"All right. I wasn't kidding. My father is a humanitarian. It means someone who helps other people. He's a doctor, and he runs a clinic for poor people in Philadelphia."

"He don't sound like a bad pa to me."

"Not bad at all. Extremely good." So good that every other Sunday, and Christmas, and Easter, he would leave his family for a few hours and go down to the area around Eighth and Christian Streets, where the clinic was located, to look in on some of his more seriously ill patients. When I was small, I used to cling to him and beg him not to leave. I did not want him to abandon me to visit strange children, who, as my mother always pointed out as she pried me away from him, did not have my advantages. As I grew older, I began to take pride in his dedication. I even asked to go with him, but he and my mother agreed it was too dangerous. They would not risk my picking up a contagious disease or infection. The peril only made me admire my father more. He left a lot of room for disillusionment.

"So what're you holding against him? You say he didn't trouble you none, and you ain't got no sisters nor brothers. What'd he do to make you so cross-legged about him?"

"Nothing."

"You're the one's always talking about truth-telling."

I stood staring at her.

"Well, ain't you?"

"This is different."

"I don't see how, unless maybe you reckon some linthead ain't good enough to know your secrets."

"Don't call yourself a linthead, Ruby."

"Don't matter what I call myself. That's the way it looks from where I set. If you was really my friend, like you're always saying, you'd tell me what's troubling you."

I sat on the other end of the sofa and tried to put the jumbled memories in some kind of order.

My aunt had come to dinner that Sunday. She often came to dinner when her husband was in the sanitarium drying out. But this particular Sunday dinner stands out. After my father left to see his ailing patients, my mother went out to the kitchen for a moment to speak to the maid. Not Brigit, by that time Brigit had left service. She had a daughter to raise, and, thanks to my father, she could stay home to raise her. My father never shirked his responsibilities.

When we were left alone at the table, my aunt leaned her resentful careworn face toward me confidentially and said she was tired of all this hypocrisy. It was time I knew the truth. The words excited me. What sixteen-year-old girl, guilty with her own burgeoning prurience, sure of an older generation's prudishness, does not want the key to the closet where the family skeletons are locked? By the time she finished her story, I wanted no more secret glimpses into the family's past. I had fallen from the grace of innocence.

I sat on the other end of the sofa from Ruby. "We had a maid."

"You mean a girl who come in to work for you, like Viola?"

"She lived with us. And she wasn't a Negro. She was Irish. Her name was Brigit Ward."

I had no idea why I was telling her this. I had never told anyone.

"He put himself on her?"

I weighed the phrase. My father had not had to force himself on Brigit Ward. He was not like the white man who came into Clarence's mother's kitchen while his father was out in the fields. Brigit Ward had fallen in love with my father, the little fool. She had fallen in love with his beautiful medically proficient hands, so unlike her own, which were red and raw from lovingly washing and ironing his shirts and handkerchiefs and underclothes; and his innate good manners, so unlike the men of the family she had worked for previously, who would as soon slap her on the fanny as utter the words *please* and *thank you*; and the way he held a sick baby, which she had once seen him do in the clinic; and his imagined loneliness, because surely a man whose wife spent so much time ministering to the world rather than her husband, even when she was pregnant and could not be a real wife to him, especially when she was pregnant and could not be a real wife to him, must be lonely.

"He slept with her."

Ruby snickered. "I don't guess they did much sleeping. What'd your ma do about it?"

"Nothing."

"So what're you getting so worked up about? Ain't no skin off your nose."

"It's not that simple."

"You mean he left you and your ma and run off with her?"

"No, he stayed. They left."

"Who's they?"

I did not answer. I had not meant to say this much.

Ruby sat watching me. "She had a young one."

Again I did not reply.

"Boy or girl?"

"Girl."

"That's what's got you all cross-legged."

"What the hell does cross-legged mean?"

"What you are now. Mad enough to bite. You ever go looking for her?"

"Who?"

"You know who. Your sister."

"Half-sister."

"Did you?"

"No," I said, and did not add that I would not have had to look far. I would only have had to follow my father some Sunday or holiday when he went to visit his daughter and namesake, Georgina Whittier Ward, who was born only seven months after me. Brigit refused to abort what she called her love child—what did that make me?—and my father would not force or even encourage her to.

"It don't make no sense. You go traipsing all over the place trying to save a bunch of coloreds you never laid eyes on, but you don't go hunting for your own kin. Know what I reckon? I reckon you were fixing to go looking someday, but now you ain't got to."

"Why not?"

"On account of now you got me."

Standing on the street half an hour earlier, my mother had made the same connection. They were both wrong.

As the day Ruby was to leave for Alabama neared, she began to fret about her return. I did not blame her. People had been angry when she testified badly for the state. They would be enraged when she testified for the defense.

"I can't recollect proper once I'm setting up there in front of folks," she said.

"But this time you don't have to worry about remembering what didn't happen. All you have to do is tell what did."

"Victoria's going to be fit to be tied." The thought brought a smile to her face. She covered her mouth with her hand to hide her uneven teeth. These days she did that occasionally. Then she frowned. "Wish I had a new dress to wear. A real fine store-bought dress. That would make her set up and take notice."

"You have your new suit."

"I been wearing that since I come north. It don't even look new no more. Besides, it's real plain."

"It's supposed to be plain. You don't want to go into court looking as if you've been on a shopping spree."

"Why not?"

"We want the jury to trust you."

"I'd sooner trust a girl in nice clothes than some linthead who don't have a decent dress to cover herself with."

"What I meant was you don't want the jury to think you changed your story because the defense bribed you with money or clothes or gifts."

She did not say anything to that, and I thought the conversation was finished, but a little while later she returned to the subject.

"What if I had a new dress that wasn't bought?"

"You mean you want to make yourself a new dress?"

She shook her head. "I ain't going up against Victoria in no home-sewed dress."

"Then what did you have in mind?"

She lowered her face and looked up at me from under her lashes with those big blue eyes. "You could give me one of your dresses. You got a heap. More than any one body needs. You ain't going to miss one. Specially one you don't fancy no more. Like that long one that got beads all over it." So I had not been imagining her rummaging around in my closet. "I ain't never seen you wear that."

"It's an evening dress, Ruby. I haven't been out in the evening while you've been here. Anyway, you can't wear an evening dress to court."

"It would make Victoria set up and take notice for positive."

"That's the last thing you want," I said again.

"I ain't afraid of Victoria."

"I'm not thinking of Victoria. I told you, I'm worried about the jury."

"What do a bunch of menfolk know about it?"

"Enough to smell the big city on you."

She was no longer listening to me. Her thin lips were set in a sulk. "It ain't fair. All folks been doing is preaching at me to tell the truth. You're always saying it. 'Just tell the truth, Ruby. Just tell the truth.' Well, now I'm fixing to tell the truth, and I reckon I ought to get more—"

She stopped suddenly.

"More?"

"More than that old suit don't even have no trim nor nothing on it."

The statement was pure extortion, but I could not blame her. In a world short of money, the only world she knew, everything has a price. I told her after the trial I would take her shopping. That wiped the sulk off her face.

The next morning a man and a woman came to get Ruby for the drive south. I did not know them, but they looked like party members in good standing to me. As soon as she left, I headed up to the magazine to deliver the final installment of her life. I was taking the train to Alabama the next afternoon and would stay as long as the trials lasted.

When I came out of Harry's office, I found Abel waiting in the hall.

"I take it your guest has left."

"Safely on her way."

"Have you checked your jewelry?"

"That's not funny."

"It wasn't meant to be."

"Ruby would never steal anything from me."

"I don't know. Those pearls of yours are pretty swell. And with everyone preaching revolutionary theory at her day and night, I wouldn't put it past her to take one look at them, decide Proudhon was right, property is theft, and hightail it back to Alabama with them in her hot little hands."

"Ruby did not take the pearls, or anything else."

"You're sure?"

"Absolutely."

He grinned.

"What's so funny?"

"That means you checked."

The people here impress me as being honest, God fearing people who want to see justice done.

—*Samuel Leibowitz, 1933*

You will be a sadder but wiser man when you are finished.

—*Joseph Brodsky to Samuel Leibowitz, 1933*

I took the 11:10 to Birmingham the next morning. The club car was crowded with reporters, a familiar scene, but this time I sensed a difference. The men, and they were all men, wanted to hear what I had to say. They usually talked over me. I sometimes managed to start a sentence, but rarely got to finish one without an interruption. I joked that they had hearing problems. A voice in a higher pitch did not register. But on the train to Birmingham, on the eve of the second round of trials of the Scottsboro boys, they were suddenly attuned. No one knew Ruby had stayed with me, but everyone knew I had gone to Huntsville.

"Come on, Alice, give us the skinny. Is she is or is she ain't going to show up to testify?" they said as they passed the flask around, though it damn near killed them to ask me.

"Beats me," I answered, though keeping my mouth shut after being talked over and shouted down and ignored for so long damn near killed me as well.

Most of them bought my answer. The fact that I did not know any more than they did restored their faith in an orderly universe. But once or twice, I noticed Raymond Daniell of *The New York Times* watching me closely. Ray was a seasoned newspaperman with uncanny instincts, and I usually gravitated to him, but on this trip I kept my distance. I did not want him guessing how much I knew.

The trip to Birmingham took twenty-eight hours. We passed the time moving from club car to dining car to various staterooms and parlor cars and back, arguing about Sam Leibowitz's showmanship, and Judge Horton's reputation for fairness, and the unbridled political ambition that had made General Tom Knight, as the attorney general of Alabama was always called, step in to try the case rather than leave it to the county solicitor. We also debated Ruby Bates's disappearance and Victoria Price's moxie. But we rarely mentioned the boys.

In Birmingham, we boarded a train for Decatur, where the trials would be held. The attorneys for the defense had won a change of venue, but they were not happy about it. Decatur was a town of sixteen thousand whites and twenty-five hundred Negroes situated on the Tennessee River, fifty miles west of Scottsboro and the same distance south of Pulaski, the birthplace, during Reconstruction, of the Ku Klux Klan. The fact that the town was down on its luck did not help. In the past two years, seven of its eight banks and two of its three largest businesses had failed. Unemployment was rife. Citizens were disgruntled. I had done my homework, but I was still unprepared for the strength of local sentiment.

"Get a load of that," one of the men said as the train, nearing a station, chugged slowly past a sign. I turned to follow his gaze. The billboard stood on the side of a road that ran parallel to the railroad tracks.

NIGGER, DON'T LET THE SUN GO DOWN ON YOUR HEAD.

The local citizens also resented the attention, and expense, and influx of outside agitators. They were, however, hoping for some benefits in the form of the cold cash the outside agitators would bring with them. Western Union and Postal Telegraph had rented space in buildings near the courthouse. The Cornelian Court was turning single rooms into doubles and anything larger than a closet into a single. The prosecution, the defense, and the entire press corps, except for two Negro reporters, moved into the hotel. The arrangement was cozy, though the desk clerk did not give me much of a welcome when I checked in. He looked me up and down with an expression that made clear what a sorry sight he found me, and told the bellhop in a sour voice to take me to my room. I followed the boy across the lobby, up a flight of stairs, and down a long hall. He opened the door and stood aside for me to step in. A step was all that was necessary to be standing in the middle of the room, or at least beside the bed, which took up most of it. A single window overlooked an alley. The closet must have been meant for brooms at one time. Another door led to an adjoining room. I turned the knob. It was locked. Perhaps this had been the maid's room of a suite.

I tipped the bellboy and was about to close the door when I saw some of the reporters from the train coming down the hall. They were headed for the nearest store, one of them said. "Who the hell knew it was summer down here?" He indicated his heavy tweed suit. We were already beefing up the local economy.

When I finished hanging my suit and dress and blouses in the closet and putting my other things in drawers that stuck badly in a warped dresser, I decided to take a walk through town. I wanted to get a sense of the place. It had struck me, on the ride from the station, as bigger than Scottsboro, but not unlike it.

I came out of the hotel and started toward the center of town. Neat houses crouched in the shade of old oaks and elms and cedars. In the courthouse square, a statue of a Confederate soldier, streaked white by the local birds, stood guard. Beneath him a brass plaque held an inscription.

> Lest we forget. This monument was erected to
> the memory of those who offered their lives for
> a just cause, the defense of states' rights.

I stood looking at the words. If slavery had anything to do with the matter, no one in Decatur was going to let on.

As I made my way across the square, I could not help noticing one difference from Scottsboro. Here men did not tip their hats to me, and women did not stop to pass the time of day. They looked wary and loaded for bear.

I kept going toward a restaurant half a block from the square. Behind a plate-glass window, diners sat at a long counter and around a handful of tables, drinking coffee and eating and talking. A strip of flypaper twisted lazily in the pass-through to the kitchen. Even from this distance, the place looked homey, conducive, I hoped, to striking up a casual conversation with another diner or a waitress.

I pushed open the door and stepped into the smell of frying meat and coffee, the din of dishes, and a man teasing the waitress. The room fell silent before I closed the door behind me.

I crossed to the counter and slid onto an upholstered stool. The man next to me swiveled and stared. "Good afternoon," I said. He stood, picked up his plate and cup, and made his way down the counter to a place at the other end.

A waitress in a checked uniform with a starched white apron asked what I'd have. I told her coffee and inquired which pie she recommended. I was not hungry, but the relative qualities of pies struck me as an uncontroversial ice-breaker. She shrugged. I told her to skip the pie.

She brought my coffee. The sound of heavy china hitting the

counter rattled the silence. A knife scraped against a plate. Someone coughed. The room was holding its breath, waiting for me to leave.

I put a nickel on the counter, stood, and started out. As I pulled open the door, the man who had got up to change his seat boomed to no on in particular, "Want to know how to save the county money? Get a hank of rope. Hang the niggers. Then hang the commie Jew lawyers. Then hang the commie Jewgirl reporters. Cheaper than a trial any day of the week."

The roar of laughter followed me out of the restaurant. I hated the sound, and the people who made it, and the man who had given rise to it. But it thrilled me too. For the first time in my life, I was marching on the inside.

Back at the hotel, the desk clerk told me grudgingly, in answer to my question, where I could find someone with a car to drive me the fifteen miles to Athens. Athens was the town where James E. Horton, the judge who would preside over the trials, lived with his wife and three children in, according to several newspaper accounts I had read, a fine antebellum house built by his wife's great-great-uncle. During the Civil War, Union officers billeted there had carved an inscription in a door. THREE CHEERS FOR LINCOLN—NOV. 7, 1864. I did not see the Yankee writing on the wall until years later. That day I went to Athens for the first time, the judge received me in his office on the second floor of the Limestone County Courthouse, a block away. That was where he had directed me when I had wired asking for an interview.

A secretary showed me into the office, and the judge stood up behind a desk piled with papers. The effect was startling, especially under the circumstances. The resemblance began with his height and extended to his whole rumpled appearance. His face was long, with deep-set eyes under heavy brows. His nose was prominent, his mouth thin. Take off his horn-rimmed glasses and paste on a beard, and he would have been a dead ringer for Abraham Lincoln. The resemblance could not have been easy for a southern judge.

He had explained, when he had agreed to see me, that he could not talk about the trial, and I had reassured him I had no intention of asking about it. I wanted to write about him. I knew from my research that he was a large landowner, a planter, and a successful politician, who had been a circuit court judge for the past ten years. He was also, people said, scrupulously fair. But if I wanted my article to stand out from the others about him, I needed more.

Judge Horton told me he believed the separation of whites and Negroes was the only feasible system of social organization. He deemed it the responsibility of whites to care for Negroes, who obviously did not have the mental or moral wherewithal to care for themselves. He was, he assured me, particular in his terminology. He never used the word *nigger* about upstanding members of the race, only about those who, had they been white, would be called white trash, or worse. He said he was determined to preside over a just trial that would clear the name of the state of Alabama before the nation and the world. He said nothing about clearing the names of the boys.

When I asked about influences on his life, he confided that he had been especially close to his mother, who had instilled in him a respect for decency, duty, and truth. Like many educated southern gentlemen, he was an unnerving combination of Roman senatorial virtues and antebellum delusions. He lived in a world where the Enlightenment had never happened.

On the way back to Decatur, I rolled down the windows in the back seat, took off my hat, and let the wind blow through my hair, while I thought about decency, duty, and truth. I did not doubt the judge revered those virtues. I certainly never dreamed he would let them go down the drain in a secret meeting in the men's room of the Morgan County Courthouse two weeks later.

The car pulled up in front of the hotel, and I paid the driver, put on my hat, and made my way into the lobby. As I approached the desk to get my key, a short wiry man with dark wavy hair parted in the middle and slicked to his head was checking in. I recognized the face, though the high color was not visible in black-and-white newspaper photos. He was wearing a tight-fitting suit, severely nipped at the waist. Thomas E. Knight, Jr., the attorney general of Alabama, was a dapper fellow.

He executed a small bow in my direction and, flashing a wide vote-getting smile, told the clerk to take care of the little lady first. He did not mind waiting.

The clerk would have preferred to keep the little lady waiting, but while he searched for my key, I introduced myself to General Knight and told him I was there for the trial. He was known to court the press, even the hostile northern press, especially the hostile northern press, shamelessly.

"Whittier," he repeated my name. "Don't believe I know your husband. Which paper's he with?"

"I'm with *The New Order*."

His cheeks flamed. Later I would discover that he blushed easily, a peculiar trait in a grown man hell-bent on climbing to the governor's office on the backs of nine young Negro men.

"That's one on me," he said and apologized for his mistake. "Hope you won't hold it against me."

I assured him I would not.

"Just to prove it, ma'am, when the boys come by of an evening to hash things over, I'd be mighty pleased if you'd come with them."

The invitation was sincere. Knight was banking on this trial. It was, in a way, his birthright. Though he masqueraded as a man of the people, or at least one of the boys, his father was a justice on the Alabama Supreme Court. Knight, Sr., had written the opinion upholding the convictions and death sentences of the Scottsboro boys, the same opinion which his son had defended, unsuccessfully, before the United States Supreme Court a few months ago. The connection went back further than that. Knight's grandfather had been a captain in the Confederate Army and, after the Civil War, a delegate to the constitutional convention that had enshrined white supremacy into state law. Knight was determined to carry on the family tradition, and he wanted plenty of press coverage while he did it. He would have invited the devil himself to his rooms, if he thought the devil would write about him.

The next day, I paid a visit to the Morgan County Jail. Since two years earlier the county had declared the jail unfit for habitation by whites, local officials had decided to incarcerate the boys there. The only problem, as the officials saw it, was that the building was in such disrepair that jailbreaks entailed simply strolling off the premises. Extra guards stood duty around the clock to keep the boys in, and the locals out.

The sanitary conditions were even worse than the security. Perhaps that was one of the reasons the guard in charge let me in to see the boys. He looked like a man who enjoyed a good practical joke.

The stomach-turning mix of sweat and urine and feces and rotting animal carcasses almost knocked me over.

"Watch where you step," the guard barked.

I looked down. A dead rat lay at my feet.

The guard laughed and told me I'd find the boys in a cell halfway down the hall.

"They're all in the same cell?"

He spit tobacco juice. It landed on the dead rat. "Only one we got with a lock."

"What about the other prisoners?"

"Ain't no other prisoners. Lest you count the roaches and rats and now and then a cottonmouth." He stopped at the head of the corridor. "You're on your own from here on in, sister. I don't go no deeper than I got to. Stink gets so bad nobody but a nigger could breathe it and live."

I started down the hall. He had not lied about the smell getting worse. I tried to close my nose and breathe through my mouth. My father had learned the trick in medical school and attempted to teach me, but I had never managed to pull it off. My stomach heaved.

The boys might have been the only inmates, but they were making enough noise for an entire prison. As I made my way down the hall, I could not see them. The one cell that wasn't empty had mattresses propped against the bars. But I could hear them shouting and threatening and cursing. Someone must have caught a glimpse of me, because a voice shouted to mind their language on account of the lady reporter who came to visit in Kilby and sent packages from New York City was here. They began taking the mattresses away from the bars and piling them in the center of the cell. Clarence Norris apologized for the ruckus and explained they were trying to get rid of the bedbugs.

"The roaches and rats is bad," Andy Wright said, "but the bedbugs is the worst. And it ain't just the mattresses. They get in our clothes, and we got no change, just them prison suits."

"I'll get you some powder," I promised.

They started to laugh, but Clarence told them to hush. "They don't mean no disrespect, ma'am," he said, "but we already tried powder."

"Yeah," Andy said, "and them bedbugs ate up every bit and came back for more. They's mean. Meaner than Haywood."

Haywood rewarded him with a punch in the arm.

The boys were no longer afraid to talk to me, but there was only one topic on their minds that afternoon. Was Sam Leibowitz going to get them off?

"Mr. Leibowitz got that letter from the Bates girl saying wasn't no rape at all," Clarence pointed out.

"Yeah, but the other lawyer got a different paper says the letter don't matter none on account of she was drunk," Haywood answered.

"What you think, Miz Whittier?" they asked one after another.

I thought of the seventy-eight defendants charged with murder one, surely as dire as rape even in the black-and-white South, who, thanks to Sam Leibowitz, were walking the streets free men and women, and told them they were in good hands.

As I was about to leave, Haywood moved to the bars at the side of the cell and beckoned me over.

"Maybe you're right, Miz Whittier. Maybe Mr. Leibowitz going to get some of the boys off. But I don't got much hope."

I was surprised. "Your trial is the first. Mr. Leibowitz is putting all his efforts into it. Why would you think you don't stand as good a chance as the others?"

"On account of my black skin, that's why. He maybe get off Roy or a lighter boy. But he ain't going to get off skin like this." He held out his arm. "Anybody with eyes know that."

I could have told him that from what I had seen, the local citizens did not make such subtle distinctions, but I did not think the observation would cheer him.

When I returned from the jail, Tom Knight was standing in front of the Cornelian Court telling a gaggle of reporters that he had ordered still another statewide search for Ruby Bates. He smiled into the hot still afternoon, wiped his flushed face with a big white handkerchief, and assured us that every sheriff in every county in Alabama was looking for her. There was no place on the Lord's green earth that she could hide.

A few hours later, he was back, informing reporters that he had spoken to Ruby's father, who had given him several addresses where Ruby might be found. I thought of the stories Ruby had told me about her father. Mr. Bates would be the last person to know his daughter's whereabouts. Knight was getting desperate.

The following morning, word went out that a large crate had arrived at the railroad depot for Samuel Leibowitz, Esquire. By the time the baggage man delivered it to the hotel, every reporter on the premises and various local curiosity-seekers had gathered in the dining room, which Leibowitz had commandeered. We crowded around while two of his assistants pried open the crate. Leibowitz pushed aside some packing straw and lifted out a miniature train engine. He nodded to his assistants, and they began unpacking the rest. Car by car, gondola by tank car by flatcar by boxcar, a long freight train took shape across the floor of the Cornelian's dining room. When it was assembled, Leibowitz walked the length of it and back again.

"This, gentlemen"—his eye moved to me—"and lady of the press, is an exact replica of the Alabama Great Southern freight train on which a rape is alleged to have taken place on March twenty-fifth, 1931. It has been made by the Lionel Company to exacting specifications, complete in every detail, including a locomotive with brass fittings and all thirty cars, arranged in"—he hesitated—"the precise order they were that day."

We walked up and down admiring various features and calling attention to finer points. Who does not delight in a model train?

"She's a beaut," one of the reporters said above the murmured admiration. "But what are you going to do with her, Mr. Leibowitz?"

"We're going to take it to court," Leibowitz replied.

"Will it fit?" someone else asked.

"It's thirty-two feet long, half the width of the courtroom inside the railing. It will fit. We made sure of that."

"Okay, so once you get it inside, then what are you going to do with it?"

Leibowitz only smiled.

18

The air is acrid with the smell of unwashed men.

—*Mary Heaton Vorse,* The New Republic, *1933*

The courtroom was one big smiling white face.

—*Haywood Patterson, 1950*

What did I feel like down there [in Alabama]? I felt like a Jew in Nazi Germany.

—*Morris Shapiro, assistant to Samuel Leibowitz, 1982*

I felt the town smoldering before I even opened my eyes that morning. It was not only that the weather was unseasonably warm for the end of March, and promising to get worse as the sun steamed its way up the sky. The mounting tension had stripped nerves raw and set tempers on hair triggers. Walking the town the day before, I had recognized the mood in the sneering glances of the white locals, and the condescending expressions of the out-of-town reporters, and the averted eyes of the Negro residents. I had heard it in the silence that fell as I approached a knot of men on the street, and the epithets muttered in my wake. Even the children, schooled in their parents' fear and fury, stopped skipping rope and chanting ready-or-not-here-I-come to stand and stare, their eyes wide with precocious hatred. Word went out that Judge Horton, a peace-loving man, had decided to carry a loaded pistol on his drive to and from

Decatur each day. The town was about to boil over, and the trial had not even begun.

I bathed and dressed quickly and hurried down to breakfast. Neither the prosecution nor the defense teams were in the dining room, but the reporters were out in force. As I made my way to join a group, I overheard snatches of conversation. Everyone was talking about the trial, but this morning no one was making predictions. They were not even cracking jokes. A consciousness of something out of the ordinary stopped them. It was the sense of history being made. In Chicago and St. Louis and both Portlands, people were picking newspapers up off their front stoops and staring at the headlines.

DECATUR PROMISES NEGROES FAIR PLAY

and

STATE DEMANDS THE CHAIR FOR NINE NEGROES

and

WITNESS STILL MISSING

In Paris and Berlin and Moscow, where it was already afternoon and evening, concerned citizens were forgetting for a moment Premier Daladier and Chancellor Hitler and Comrade Stalin, and wondering at the magnificent hypocrisy of a nation founded on liberty for all. Closer to home, in the White House, President Roosevelt, battered by demands to intervene and warnings to stay out, was weighing moral niceties against national realities—he had been in office for fewer than three weeks, and without his southern base he would not be able to get a single bill through Congress—throwing in political calculations, and turning the whole mess over to his secretary Louis Howe, who had no compunctions about saying no to any request that was not in the best interests of his boss. And in the decaying local jail, the boys, some of whom were still semiliterate, others who were reading everything they could get their hands on, were agonizing not about national developments, or world events, or even racial injustice, but only whether each of them stood a chance in heaven, or hell, of being saved.

I left the dining room with several other reporters and made my way across the square to the two-story yellow brick courthouse. It stood solid and unimposing in the hot spring morning, the ungainly spawn of civic good intentions and aesthetic overreach. The columns flanking the front entrance overpowered the too-small portico. The narrow steps invited a mincing approach to justice. Nothing hinted at the majesty of the law, except perhaps the statue of justice standing in front, matched, or foiled, depending on your point of view, by the Confederate soldier who had given his life for the cause of states' rights.

A crowd was already milling about, though word had gone out that there would be a half day's delay and proceedings would not begin until the afternoon. Men lining up to get into the courtroom kept taking out handkerchiefs and bandannas and mopping brows drenched from heat and anticipation. Women, who would have to wait outside for secondhand reports, warned them not to forget a word. Even the children knew something smutty was afoot.

I spotted Sam Leibowitz in the crowd and began making my way toward him. He was shaking hands with people, telling them how glad he was to be there, and assuring them he had not come down to tell them how to run their state. All he wanted to do was save innocent boys from the electric chair. A reporter asked if he thought he could find a fair jury in Decatur.

"North or South, East or West, juries are alike. I have never known a bad jury, gentlemen. I have never encountered a willfully malicious one. I do not expect to in the fine state of Alabama."

Some of the reporters were taking it down, but I kept my eyes on the faces of the locals. They were not buying it. Leibowitz said he had not come down to tell them how to run their state, but then why else was he here?

As the morning wore on, impatience mounted. Both whites and

Negroes milled about the square anxiously. They sat on the benches and grass, and stood, and sat again, and kept eagle eyes on the courthouse, separately.

Suddenly the line of men waiting to enter surged forward, then back. Cries of they're opening the doors, and 'bout time, and watch you don't push flew among them. Women and children hung on to male arms until the last moment, then, as the men reached the door, peeled away to settle in for the wait.

I joined the line of men making their way into the courthouse. The scent of unwashed bodies closed in around me. When I reached the door, I presented my press pass. The guard motioned me through. Somewhere behind me, a deep voice muttered about womenfolk who don't know their place and how it would suit him fine to learn them a thing or two. A soldier standing with a fixed bayonet could not help smirking in complicity.

Then something happened that made the men forget the uppity woman reporter. Judge Horton came striding up the steps. The crowd separated to let him through. Some of the men tipped their hats. Others stared. The judge nodded back, but did not stop to speak to anyone. As he was about to start up the stairs to the second-floor courtroom, two Negroes approached him. Though they were not staying at the hotel with the rest of us, I recognized them as the reporters for the Norfolk *Journal and Guide* and the Baltimore *Afro-American*. Judge Horton had arranged for them to cover the trial and even ordered a special press table to accommodate them.

The men introduced themselves and thanked the judge for his consideration. They spoke quietly, but their voices carried. So did Horton's as he said he was happy to be of help. He started to turn away, hesitated, then turned back. The man in front of me nudged another in front of him and jerked his head toward the judge. He need not have bothered. Every eye in the place was on Horton. He held out his hand. The two reporters were quick on the uptake. Each in turn took Horton's hand and shook it. A man behind me muttered something under his breath. I could not make out the words, but the tone was ugly. Another man hawked tobacco juice. He did not even aim for the spittoon. Judge Horton started up the stairs, the two reporters withdrew to the Negro area, and I made my way up the steps among the angry sour-smelling men, suddenly full of hope.

Inside the courtroom, rows of long windows ran along two walls. They were closed against the noise of the square, and the yellow shades were drawn, but midday light filtered through, cooking the air. An American flag and another for the state of Alabama hung limp on either side of the judge's bench. The tables for the state and the defense were still empty, but reporters were milling around a longer one for the press. Instead of a jury box, two rows of chairs that swiveled and tipped to allow the jurors to make themselves comfortable were bolted to the floor. In front of each row, a brass pipe, also attached to the floor, served as a footrest. Spittoons stood at regular intervals, each surrounded by the familiar corona of hardened tobacco juice and saliva.

I made my way to the press table. A couple of hundred eyes, hot with fury, followed me as I went. In the absence of the Negro boys and the Jew lawyer from New York, I would do.

I took my seat, organized my pencils and pad, and looked around. The white spectators were still filing in. There would be a full house and then some. Men straggled into the last rows, telling others to move down, shouldering their way into tight spaces, pushing and shifting until they were jammed like cattle in a freight car. When there was not a single space left in the white section, the guards began to let in the Negroes. One after another, in overalls and suit jackets and patched and mended shirts, black and brown and coffee and molasses and whiter than some of the whites, they made their way down the gauntlet of armed uniformed soldiers in silence, their eyes focused straight ahead or on the floor, their faces impassive. They knew what an errant gaze or uppity demeanor could bring down on them. There was less pushing and shouldering, but in the end they were packed in just as tightly as the white men.

Then, with everything primed to begin, nothing happened. Four hundred and twenty-five spectators sat sweating and waiting, the white men sprawling as best they could on the worn wooden benches, ready for a good time; the Negroes sitting with heads bowed, waiting for the ax to fall. The white men smoked and chewed and spat and passed bottles of soda pop from hand to hand. The Negroes sweated in silence, a twitching muscle, a hand raised to swat a fly the only signs of life. Outside, the voices of another two hundred men, waiting to get in, pressed against the closed windows.

Steps sounded in the hall outside the courtroom, and Tom Knight came swaggering through the door, his team trotting after him. He smiled and waved and raised his hand, index finger and thumb cocked like a gun, to fire greetings at acquaintances in the white section.

A moment later Sam Leibowitz and his associates entered. Leibowitz looked around at the spectators, both black and white, and smiled. But the whites were not buying, and the Negroes were afraid to.

The teams of attorneys arranged themselves around their respective tables, and still the proceedings did not begin. The temperature continued to rise. So did the noise level. Spectators called good wishes and advice to Knight, and talked among themselves, in voices meant to carry, about Leibowitz. The eyes of the guards, stationed with fixed bayonets, darted around the room. Trouble was in the air, thick as the smoke swirling around the ceiling fans.

Then, just when it seemed that if something legal did not happen soon, something illegal would, a guard standing at the windows whispered something to another guard, who passed it on, and the room fell silent. A minute went by, then another. Slowly, from a distance, we heard the sound of feet shuffling up the stairs. As the noise grew steadily louder and closer, heads began to turn.

Haywood Patterson appeared in the door. He held his hands, cuffed in steel rings, in front of him, as if in supplication. His chest strained against the bib of the too-small prison-issue overalls. His ankles, pockmarked with angry red bites, stuck out of the too-short pants legs.

An armed deputy walked on either side of him. As they guided him down the aisle between two sections reserved for whites, every pair of eyes followed him. Perhaps decent human beings were present in that courtroom, men who had consciences, and treated the Negroes they employed fairly, and belonged to the Association for the Prevention of Lynching, but all I saw was a sea of hate-slicked faces and bloodthirsty grins.

One by one, and flanked by two, the other boys followed, their hands shackled, their prison overalls either hanging loose on their frames or binding them like shrouds. Sam Leibowitz must have been in heaven. He had warned the boys not to try to slick up. The locals would not like it. Only Roy Wright, who had escaped conviction at the first set of trials and had been brought over from the Birmingham jail, was not in prison-issue clothing. He wore store-bought dark trousers and a white shirt with a big soft collar. I could tell from his walk that, frightened as he was, he was proud of the outfit. But Sam Leibowitz had been right. The crowd was incensed. They growled and snarled as he went by, like dogs about to pounce. Some of the press took notice as well. The next day the Birmingham *News* would report that Roy Wright had sashayed into court looking like a Georgia gigolo. Whether the reference to Georgia was a result of state rivalry or merely an attempt at alliteration was anyone's guess.

The deputies steered the boys to a line of chairs against the wall behind the defense team. Two of the officers went down the line removing the handcuffs, while the others stood guard. A deputy ordered the boys to sit. They did. Haywood glanced around the courtroom. Clarence and Andy kept their eyes on Sam Leibowitz. The other boys did not look up.

A voice boomed out over the courtroom, snapping us to our feet. Judge Horton entered.

"Holy Toledo," one of the reporters at the table whispered. "It's the Great Emancipator in the flesh."

The judge called the court to order. Men shifted position to get comfortable. Some spit out tobacco juice; others dipped more snuff. The fun was finally going to begin.

Wade Wright, the Morgan County solicitor, lumbered out from behind the prosecution's table. He was a big man with a round face and several chins but no neck. His head sat directly on his meaty shoulders. As he began to read the indictments, his voice grew deep and rich, transforming the dusty legal language into music. He was known throughout the county as an "all-day singer" and had made his reputation whipping souls into ecstasies of repentance and redemption. Wade Wright had crooned and harmonized more than his share of sinners into heaven. Some of the spectators began to nod and sway in rhythm with his words.

The moment he finished, Sam Leibowitz was on his feet, making a motion that the indictments be quashed. Unlike Wright, he made no attempt to sway bodies or set toes tapping. He spoke of systematic exclusion of Negroes from grand jury rolls, and the violation of defendants' rights, and the Fourteenth Amendment. You could feel the excitement hissing out of the courtroom like air out of a punctured tire. They had come to hear details saucy enough to sear a grown man's ears. This stuff was drier than a temperance meeting and twice as hard to understand.

Matters grew worse. Sam Leibowitz called to the stand several local officials, who explained Negroes did not sit on juries because they did not have sound judgment. Same as women, one witness said. Even, Leibowitz asked, if the Negroes, unlike many of the whites who served on juries, had college degrees? Schooling had nothing to do with it, the man answered, and anyway, nigras stole.

Leibowitz kept at it all afternoon. He found a dozen ways to ask the same question, one to which everyone in the courtroom already knew the answer. Negroes did not serve on juries in the South because in the South Negroes did not serve on juries. The spectators coughed and shifted and griped in murmurs that grew steadily louder.

The next morning, Leibowitz started in again. He called nine local

Negroes to the stand to show that they were educated men, pillars of the community, unquestionably qualified for jury duty. Then, just when it seemed from the groans and yawns and angry shuffling feet that the spectators had had enough, Judge Horton announced he would hear no more testimony.

"The motion to quash is overruled."

The spectators sat up. Maybe the good part was finally going to start.

Only it didn't. Leibowitz had been trying to prove the indictments were illegal because Jackson County, in which Scottsboro was situated, did not include Negroes on grand juries. Now he turned his sights on the Morgan County petit jury system. When he had the county's leather-bound jury book brought into court, spectators began to whisper about leaving. When he again called Negro doctors and ministers and businessmen to testify and addressed them as mister, the boredom turned to anger. When he asked a jury commissioner, who claimed not to know if all the names in the book were white, if he meant that for an honest answer, the angry murmurs turned to snarls. The Jew lawyer from New York was calling one of them a liar. To listen to him, you'd think they were on trial instead of those damn niggers.

The sun was low in the sky by the time the judge adjourned the court on the second day. The spectators streamed out into the sultry spring evening sullen with disappointment. They milled around, complaining about the trial, and the expense, and the Jewlawyer-fromNewYork. It had become one word. By the time Sam Leibowitz emerged from the courthouse, they were itching for action.

Captain Burleson, the commander of the National Guard unit, cut through the crowd to the lawyer's side. "My men will escort you back to the hotel, sir," he said.

Leibowitz thanked the captain, but told him he preferred to walk with his associates.

The next morning in court, Leibowitz stated his intention to call hundreds of witnesses, if that was what it would take to prove that

Morgan County kept Negroes off the jury roll simply because they were Negroes. Groans and curses and threats ran through the white spectators. The Negroes made no sound. Judge Horton banged his gavel. He cleared his throat. He said he had heard enough testimony. He denied the motion.

The white outrage turned to murmurs of approval. The Negroes remained silent.

Judge Horton went on. The defense, he admitted, had made a prima facie case that Morgan County had excluded Negroes from the jury rolls.

Most of the spectators were relieved that the judge had put an end to the farce, but here and there among them, the legally sophisticated took note. So did the attorneys and the press. Reporters scribbled. Knight frowned. Leibowitz's face was impassive. But we knew. Sam Leibowitz had challenged the Alabama jury system.

The court turned to the matter of jury selection. The defense used most of its challenges to get rid of the men in overalls from outlying rural districts. The state, which was allowed only half as many strikes, tried to weed out younger men from the larger towns. At the press table, we followed the proceedings and made notes, but we were really thinking about Sam Leibowitz's coup. So much for his assurances of not wanting to put the southern way of life on trial.

The moment Leibowitz stepped out of the courthouse that evening, reporters surged around him shouting questions. They wanted to know about the appeal. He pointed out he had not yet lost the case. They asked if he feared for the safety of the Negroes who had testified. He said they had shown great courage and added that the sheriff had arranged for their protection. Two weeks later, the house of one of the witnesses would go up in flames. It would be only the beginning.

Once again, Captain Burleson approached and offered Leibowitz an escort back to the hotel. Once again, Leibowitz declined. But this evening, the captain was not taking no for an answer. When we arrived back at the hotel, we found a reinforcement of National Guardsmen patrolling the grounds with fixed bayonets. I was making my way past them to the entrance when I noticed three people standing at the back of the hotel. There was nothing unusual about that. I had seen the Negro staff congregating there on and off since I had arrived. But something was different now. The two men were Negroes, though they did not work at the hotel. They were the reporters Judge Horton had shaken hands with the first morning of the trial. But the woman—girl, really—was white. The cut of her suit and the wave of her dark hair under a fashionable brimless hat would have told me she was not a local, if the fact that she was talking to the Negro men had not already given her away.

I started toward the three of them. To this day, I cannot tell you whether I intended to join the group or break it up before she got the men run out of town, or worse. I managed neither. Four deputies were approaching from the other direction. I reached the group a moment before they did. Perhaps that was why they assumed I was part of it. Or maybe they just saw the chance to finally get something on the commie Jewgirl reporter from New York.

Two of the deputies came up behind the reporters, pulled them away from the girl and me, and clamped cuffs around their wrists. The reporters did not struggle. They did not even utter a word of protest. They knew better.

I felt a big hand closing around my upper arm and another in the small of my back pushing me forward. The force made me stumble, but I caught my balance and tried to keep going. I had no idea what charge they were going to trump up, but I did not want to give them grounds for disorderly conduct. He pushed again. I did not need much imagination to know he was dying to teach me a good black-and-blue lesson.

Beside me, the second deputy was shoving the other girl along. They pushed her into the back seat of a waiting auto, hustled me in after, and slammed the door on us.

"Are they arresting us?" the girl asked me.

"It looks that way."

"For what?"

"What makes you think they need a reason?"

One of the deputies leaned down, stuck his face in the window, and told us to shut up. He climbed in behind the wheel. The other got in on the passenger side. The driver threw the gearshift into drive. The auto lurched forward. In seconds, we had left Decatur in the rearview mirror.

Muriel Rukeyser and I were never charged with any crime or even misdemeanor that night. I did not know she was Muriel Rukeyser at the time. Or rather I knew her name, but it meant nothing to me. In those days, it meant nothing to anyone except her family, and friends at the ILD, and a handful of Vassar teachers and students who had read her poems. But in the years ahead, the world, or at least that segment of it that cared about poetry, would come to know it. Muriel was one of the few people involved in the Scottsboro case who owed none of their later success to it.

But that was all in the future the night the deputies took us to the Huntsville jail and held us there for several hours. They wanted to teach us a lesson. Unfortunately, neither of us learned it. Muriel returned to New York the next morning, not because she was any wiser, but because Sam Leibowitz made her departure a condition of his continuing as counsel. He told the ILD he would brook no idealistic young girls making political capital out of the case. A few days later, Muriel came down with typhus.

I was more fortunate, on both counts. I never contracted the disease, though we had shared the same cell. And Leibowitz let me stay. He said he was honoring my press credentials, and that was part of it, but there was another, more important reason. The night I returned from the Huntsville jail, I remembered something I had seen during my visits to Ruby and Victoria.

Professional pride forces me to conclude that cold type per se is less effective than the personification and dramatization of news which the stage makes possible.

—*Raymond Daniell on* They Shall Not Die, *a play about the Scottsboro boys, 1934*

Mornings and evenings, the lobby of the Cornelian Court was filled with sweating, smoking males, hiding their heat-flushed faces behind arm-wide expanses of white pulp turned black with bad news. Farm problems. Factory problems. Foreigners-from-across-the-Atlantic-and-above-the-Mason-Dixon-Line problems. But when I returned from jail after eleven that night, the lobby was empty, except for one man sitting behind a copy of the Montgomery *Advertiser*. He lowered the paper as I came through the door. Abel Newman peered at me from behind his horn-rimmed glasses. I could not imagine what he was doing there. Scottsboro was my baby, and neither politics nor crime was his beat.

"I hear you and some Vassar kid ended up in the hoosegow. How were the accommodations?"

"I've stayed in worse."

He let out a hoot of laughter. "The hell you have, or you wouldn't be so pleased with yourself. Wipe those canary feathers off your mouth, Ace. You'll be dining out on this story for the next year. And you get to stick it to the folks back in Philadelphia at the same time."

He was wrong about the last. My being thrown into jail would not distress my parents. They would see it as carrying on the family tradition. My mother had done time for women's suffrage. My father had gone to jail with Margaret Sanger. But I was not going to explain that to Abel.

"What are you doing down here?" I asked instead. "You didn't come all this way just to help me readjust to society."

"What do you think I'm doing here? There's a trial going on, in case you haven't heard."

I was furious with Harry, and my face must have given me away, because Abel smiled. It was not a friendly smile. "Don't worry, Ace. You've still got the lock on the story as far as Harry's concerned."

"Then who sent you?"

"Not a magazine or newspaper. I'm talking high art, not pedestrian journalism."

"High art?"

"Okay, maybe middlebrow commerce. I'm writing a play about the case. What they call a well-wrought play, complete with a courtroom scene and a lot of moral heft. Not to mention sex, violence, and nine strapping darkies. I see it as kind of a left-wing minstrel show, but with the real thing, not whites in blackface."

"Are you serious?"

"About the play, not about the minstrel show. I've already got a producer interested."

"When did all this happen?"

"You mean when did inspiration strike? When I ran into my old buddy Octavus Roy Cohen. He was coming from his publisher, weighed down with his ill-gotten gains. The gold practically clanked when he moved. And I had to ask myself that age-old question about the meaning of life. Why was I wasting my time reading dull books and going to bad plays for the greater glory of *The New Order* when I could be living high off the hog like old Octavus? He's made a bundle writing about 'colluds.' Or as the ads for his books put it, 'For the audience partial to nigger stuff.'"

"You wouldn't write anything like that."

"I would, if I knew how, but I don't have his flair for comedy. No, this producer Joe is in the market for something more inspirational. Claude Rains has agreed to play Leibowitz, if he likes the script. And they've lined up Ruth Gordon for everybody's favorite ingénue, Ruby Bates. Now all we have to do is persuade Paul Robeson to play the nine boys."

"That's not funny."

"Sure it is. A year from now, I'm going to be living like a king. Or Octavus Roy Cohen. Come on, I'll tell you more about it over a drink in my room. It's right next to yours. We even have a connecting door."

I had started walking, but now I stopped.

"Don't worry, Ace. The arrangement is pure coincidence. It was the only room left, if you can call it that. Feels like a closet and costs as much as a suite. And the door is locked."

"That means you tried it."

"I knew you'd be disappointed if I didn't."

I never did have a drink in Abel's room that night. All that talk about Octavus Roy Cohen had reminded me of something. I told him I would take a rain check on the drink. It was almost midnight, but I did not think Sam Leibowitz would mind being disturbed.

Sam Leibowitz had refused offers of protection from the Alabama National Guard and the local sheriff, but he could not bring himself to turn away the two detectives Mayor La Guardia sent down from New York. They recognized me and knocked on the door to Leibowitz's rooms. Mrs. Leibowitz, who had accompanied her husband to Decatur for the trial, opened it. She was a solid maternal-looking woman, but when she smiled, the weight of her features fell away, and I caught a glimpse of the starry-eyed piano student at the Institute of Musical Art, Juilliard these days, who had knocked Sam Leibowitz for a loop when they had met on vacation in the Catskills fifteen years earlier.

I told her I was sorry to bother her at this hour, but I had just thought of something that might interest her husband. She said it was no bother. "Mr. Leibowitz is up half the night working anyway."

She went into the other room to tell him I was there, then returned and asked if I would like coffee or a cold drink or a piece of cake. I told her I did not want to put her to any trouble.

"It's no trouble. I have a kitchen full of food."

Only then did I realize I had not seen her or her husband in the dining room for the past few days. I asked if all that fine southern cooking was getting to be too much of a good thing.

She smiled and shook her head. "The food doesn't bother me. It's the letters and calls. Mr. Leibowitz tries not to let me know, but I have eyes, I have ears. I see and hear what people are up to. Maybe I can't do anything about the tarring and feathering, or the running out of town on a rail, but I can make sure nothing goes into his stomach that shouldn't. I wouldn't put poison past some of these people. I don't mean the Negro cooks and waiters. They know Mr. Leibowitz is on their side. But the others. Who knows what someone crazy with hate could do between the time the food leaves the kitchen and the time it arrives in front of him? So now I do all the cooking and serving right here. I sleep better," she said, as her husband came out of the inner room pulling on his jacket.

I told him I would not take much of his time.

"If this is about that business with the Vassar girl from the ILD—" he began.

"It's not," I interrupted. "I just remembered something about my visit to Victoria Price."

He asked me to sit down and took the chair across from me. Mrs. Leibowitz excused herself.

"The walls of Victoria's house, and Ruby's too, were covered with illustrations and photographs clipped from newspapers and magazines," I began. "I suppose it's an attempt to spruce up those awful places."

He waited. At that moment, he had little interest in the local living conditions, but he knew I would not have bothered him unless it was important.

"One of the pictures hanging on the wall in Victoria Price's house was an illustration from the *Saturday Evening Post*. For a story by a man named Octavus Roy Cohen."

"He writes humorous pieces about Negroes, doesn't he?"

"If making fun of Negroes is humorous. But this wasn't one of those. This was a story about a woman who ran a boardinghouse."

His face was impassive, but he was listening closely.

"The story was called 'Sis Callie.' The name of the woman who ran the boardinghouse was Callie Brochie."

I saw him make the connection. He managed an exhausted smile and thanked me.

The trial would resume on Monday morning. In the meantime, local citizens and visiting agitators went about their weekend business. Men mowed the lawn and fixed the porch step and read the paper. Women cooked and sewed and shopped. Some of the press wrangled invitations to rounds of golf at the Valley Country Club. Others shelled out thirty-five cents for a fishing pole and a nickel for bait and headed for the Tennessee River, still undammed by the TVA. On Saturday afternoon, Abel paid a visit to the Decatur jail. I offered to go with him. I already knew the boys, I pointed out. He said he thought he could manage on his own.

I did not see him when he returned from the jail, though I knew he was back. I heard the door open and close when he came in, then the sound of feet pacing the room. A few minutes later he began to type. The sound continued all afternoon and into the evening. He did not go down to the dining room for dinner. One of the reporters mentioned he'd had something sent up to his room.

After dinner, Tom Knight invited several of us back to his suite. As he'd promised when we had first met, he asked us in occasionally to ply us with moonshine, tell us how he thought the trial was going, and spread his unsubtle but not ineffective affability. It was hard not to like Knight, until you remembered what he was up to. Abel did not show up there either. I made it my business to, though being the only woman in a room full of men trying to outdo one another with old war stories and a tolerance for Alabama lightning was not what my mother had in mind when she fought for equal rights for women.

Five or six of us had gathered, and by the time Knight passed the jug a second time, he was well into his complaints about Judge Horton.

"I know why he's kowtowing to the defense that way," Knight said, though I had noticed no such deference. "He thinks this case is going to take him straight to the Supreme Court."

The words landed in the room like a grenade. We sat in silence wondering if it would go off. If one of us reported that the attorney general had accused the presiding judge of acting from political ambition, Knight would have found himself summoned before the bench. But the attorney general had spoken off the record, and we were professionals. The grenade was a dud.

Knight picked up the big jug and began circling the group again. When he came to me, I looked up at him in my best ingénue manner.

"I don't know about Judge Horton's ambitions," I said, "but rumor has it that this case is going to take you straight to the governor's mansion."

He let out a yelp of glee. "I've already been offered the lieutenant governorship!"

We could not use that statement either, but there was a certain pleasure in having him admit it. At least, I had thought there would be, when I had egged him on. But all I felt was discomfort. It was ridiculous. Tom Knight and I were not alike. His success necessitated the sacrifice of nine innocent boys. Mine was merely the by-product of trying to save them, and Ruby.

On Sunday morning, while most of Decatur, including Tom Knight and his team, went to church, Sam Leibowitz and his men worked. They were, with the exception of George Chamlee, an ILD attorney from Chattanooga, Jews, but they had not worshipped on Saturday either. Though none of them was particularly observant, the situation was more complicated than that. Their local coreligionists had found acceptance by aping community attitudes. The last thing they wanted was a bunch of New York Jews coming down and making trouble for them. The case had already claimed one casualty. A Montgomery congregation, whose rabbi had espoused the boys' cause, had given the rabbi an ultimatum. Keep his opinions about the case to himself or resign. The rabbi resigned, though that did not stop some of the more fervent of the flock from hounding and harassing him until he picked up stakes and moved to New York, where, a few of his former congregants observed, he belonged. Leibowitz and his team would not have been welcome in an Alabama synagogue had they chosen to enter one.

The press corps did not attend church either. Some slept off their hangovers. I went for another walk through the town. Abel worked. The sound of typewriter keys striking the roller on the other side of the wall had awakened me that morning. He was still at it when I returned after lunch. There was a silence for a while in the afternoon, then the noise started again. When your fingers are the ones dancing on the keys, the sound is pure music. When someone else's are making the noise, it's as maddening as a jackhammer.

I went down to dinner early to escape it. When I returned to my room after another session with some of the boys in Tom Knight's suite, I found Abel stretched out on my bed in his shirtsleeves.

"I thought you said the connecting door was locked."

"I keep my side locked. I can't help it if you don't do the same. A Freudian slip, no doubt."

"What did you use, a paper clip or a hairpin?"

He grinned and held a sheaf of papers out to me.

"What's that?"

"Read it. Or I should say, read it and weep."

"Gee, pal, you've got to get over that excessive modesty."

I took the pages from him without enthusiasm. It was too soon for a play about the boys.

The only chair in the room was the straight-backed one behind the desk. I pulled it out and sat.

"You'd be more comfortable over here." He patted the bed beside him.

"I thought you wanted me to read."

"I can keep my mind on my work, even if you can't." He patted the bed again.

I sat on the side. "Move over."

He did.

I kicked off my shoes, stretched out beside him, and began to read, but I was too aware of his presence. The mattress shifted as he reached over to take a pack of cigarettes from the night table. A match struck in the silence. A perfect smoke ring rose toward the mottled ceiling.

"Stop showing off," I said.

He inhaled, then exhaled a straight plume of smoke.

I tried to shut him out as I skimmed the stage directions, but it was no good. Our feet, two in black socks, two in sheer stockings, lay parallel and neat at the bottom of the bed. His khaki hip was only inches from my navy linen one. When he reached up to put his arm behind his head, his hand brushed my shoulder.

"Keep still," I snapped.

"Jeez," he answered, but did not move again.

I went back to the pages, but I was still conscious of him lying beside me. The mattress seemed to rise and fall in rhythm with his breathing. I moved a little away from him to make a place to put the pages after I read them. Then, as the boys stepped forward and began to speak, I forgot Abel. Only they were no longer the Scottsboro boys, they were individuals. I had taken weeks to memorize their names. Abel had captured their voices in a day. Charlie talked about women, the mother who had died when he was four, the girls he had known before he went to jail, and the women he thought about all day and dreamed about all night, because they were on the outside and he was on the inside and would never have them. Andy described climbing up into that big delivery truck for the first time. He had quit school at twelve, after his father died, to help his mother support the rest of the family, and had to kneel on the driver's seat to see over the steering wheel. When he turned the key in the ignition and the huge beast roared to life, he had been so terrified he'd wanted to leap out, but he had hung on, and learned to steer, and as he swooped down streets and careened around corners, he thrilled with a power and a pride he had never known with his black feet on the ground, and never would. Olen explained to the unseen audience that he wasn't much good with words, but he took out his guitar and said that if they didn't mind, he'd play them how he felt. Clarence talked about watching his mama at the sink when the white man came. Haywood told how he felt standing in the courtroom. The sun poured in the windows hard and bright, and made everything white whiter, and him, surrounded by all those white faces, blacker. The color covered him like a coat of thick poisonous paint, strangling his throat, constricting his lungs, breaking his heart.

I finished the last page of the scene, put it on the pile between us, and looked over at Abel. He moved the ashtray on his chest to the bed between us, turned on his side, and rested his head on his hand.

"Well?"

"The only thing I don't understand is how you've gone all these years without writing."

His expression gave away nothing, but a dark flush rose in his cheeks. I had finally mentioned the forbidden subject.

"I assume that means you think it's good," he said evenly.

"Good is damning with faint praise."

For the next half hour, we discussed the characters' voices, and strengths, and fears, and how he had managed to turn the collective known as the Scottsboro boys into nine individual young men in a few economical riffs. I told him I was green with envy, and he said I damn well ought to be. Then we stopped talking and lay there grinning at each other. The pages made a decorous wall between us, but our feet were almost touching, and now that I had turned on my side too, our faces were only inches apart. Somewhere in the night outside the window, a plaintive voice sang that it was bound for Canaan land. From another window came the sound of Bing Crosby asking his fellow man if he could spare a dime.

Abel took the cigarette from his mouth, ground it out in the ashtray on the bed between us, then reached over me to put the ashtray on the nightstand behind my head. He had rolled up his shirtsleeves and the dark hair on his forearm brushed my cheek. He lifted the pages from the bed between us and put them on the table. Then he removed his horn-rimmed glasses slowly, unhooking them from behind one ear and the other, before he moved toward me.

I had always loved the look of Abel's mouth, but the feel and taste of it were even better. Unlike most men, he did not seem in a hurry to progress to other things, and we went on kissing, deeply and hungrily, as we warmed our bodies against each other in the cool spring night. But gradually the urgency began to build, and he undid the buttons of my blouse, and I went to work on his tie and braces and shirt. When we had extricated each other from our clothing, I hesitated for a moment, cowed by a sudden unexpected shyness. We knew so much about each other, but not this, and the old intimacies made this ultimate one somehow embarrassing. It would have been easier with a stranger. It had been easier with Harry, whom I did not know nearly so well. Then Abel came toward me again, the familiar face and the agile unknown body, and my mind clicked off, and I began to do what I had wanted to for longer than I had realized.

We slept tangled together, turning in tandem, brushing mouths and hands and fingertips against skin in a sleep-drugged need to make sure the other was still there. When light began to trickle into the room, I swam up into consciousness to find his black eyes watching me, and we made love again. I had been shy because I had thought we knew each other too well, but now in the fullness of that ultimate knowledge, the diffidence turned to trust. At least that was the way it seemed.

I was sitting up in bed watching him move around the small room, putting on his glasses, pulling on his trousers, picking up his shoes and shirt and tie to carry through the connecting door to his own room. Somewhere in the back of my mind was the knowledge that I would have to break the news to Harry, but I would face that when the time came.

He leaned across me to reach the pages on the far nightstand. The idea of pulling him back down teased the morning, but it was well after seven, and Judge Horton called the court to order promptly at eight-thirty, and we were responsible people. I thought of Harry again. We were responsible about most things.

I picked up the pages and handed them to him. "It's a beautiful scene. It's going to be a wonderful play." I should have stopped there. But I was a little drunk, on him, and on the play. "I didn't think you had it in you."

The pain flashed behind his glasses.

"I don't mean the talent," I went on quickly. "I mean the humanity."

He groaned, sat on the side of the bed, and put his hand on my thigh. "Let me tell you about humanity, Ace. A kid would kill for a lollipop, if he had the strength. Men and women would be fornicating in the streets, if they weren't afraid of rotting in eternal hell for the momentary pleasure. Your average upright citizen would lie and cheat and steal, if he thought he could get away with it. And your girl Ruby would sell her newfound conscience for a swell hat or another pair of shoes. For all I know, that's how the ILD got her to change her story. The first time she did it for love, now for filthy lucre."

I hated it when he got this way. And I hated the idea of selling out Ruby. I did not want another girl who had not had my advantages on my conscience.

"You're too hard on her."

"Hell, I'm not blaming her. I'm just pointing out that human nature is not the pure natural spring you and Harry and the almighty party seem to think. It's a cesspool of greed and lust and murderous instincts."

"Let's leave Harry out of this."

He shrugged. "Fine with me."

Again, I should have stopped, but I didn't.

"At least he believes in something."

He sat staring at me. "What is that supposed to mean?"

"Just what it sounds like. Harry believes in something."

"Yeah, the way a five-year-old believes in Santa Claus."

He should have stopped too. Perhaps if he had, I would not have gone on.

"Harry's a credulous fool, and Ruby's a grasping bitch, and I'm a self-styled Joan of Arc. It must be hell being the last rational un-self-deluded man on earth."

"That's not what I said."

"It's what you meant. We're all fools and con artists, but you've got our number."

He sat staring at me for a long moment. "Or maybe I just got too close."

"What do you mean?"

"You know what I mean. Last night."

I looked away from him.

He took his hand from my leg and stood. "You're a left-wing cliché, Ace, the man, or in this case woman, who loves mankind, but doesn't have much use for her fellow man."

"That's a rotten thing to say."

He picked the script up off the bed. "The truth frequently is," he said as he started for the door.

After it closed, I waited for the sound of the lock turning. The silence was cold comfort.

As I moved around the room, bathing and dressing and getting my notebook and pencils together for court, I kept running the conversation in my head. I could not understand how things had come apart so quickly. As Abel said, we had been so close.

20

It is impossible to exaggerate the girl's [Victoria Price's] appalling hardness. She is more than tough. She is terrifying in her depravity.

—*Mary Heaton Vorse,* The New Republic, *1933*

Judge Horton . . . is fair according to his lights, but those lights are the lights of a "Southern gentleman," which means that he accepts and takes for granted . . . the necessity of white supremacy in the South.

—*Joseph Brodsky, 1933*

I did not stop for breakfast on my way to the courthouse. I wanted to be in time for the session. And I did not want to take the chance of running into Abel in the dining room.

During the past week, the crowds had dwindled as the proceedings had grown drier, but this morning the line of men waiting to get into the courthouse snaked down the steps and into the square again. Word had gone out that Victoria Price was going to take the stand. That girl said things would make a grown man's ears sizzle like drippings in a hot skillet, they told one another. I had no sympathy for Victoria Price, but I hated the snickering men's indictment of her more.

The men joked, and elbowed one another in the ribs, and milled about in the spring morning. I put Abel out of my mind, and threaded my way through them and up the stairs to the courtroom. It was already baking in the light streaming through the yellow-shaded windows. The aroma of unwashed bodies and sour breath and stale tobacco lingered from the week before.

A few minutes before eight-thirty, a court officer shepherded in the jury. Eugene Bailey, Jr., John J. Bryant, Eddie Edwards, William L. Grimes, Robert L. Lander, James F. Stewart, Jr., G. Forman Wallace, Irwin Craig, Cecil B. Crawford, John Davis, Eugene E. Graves, and Robert L. Kitchens. Unlike the boys after their arrest, these men had got their names in the paper right off, even their professions. The jury was made up of three farmers, two mill workers, two bookkeepers, a barber, a salesman, a bank cashier, a storekeeper, and a draftsman. After they had been selected the previous Friday, Judge Horton had told them that he was troubled by the talk of lawless behavior he had heard around town, warned them that he expected proper restraint and a fair decision according to the law and the evidence, and sent them to the Hotel Lyons for the weekend. There they had passed the time listening to the radio one member had sent home for, taking chaperoned walks, and being shaved by the barber among them, who was on a busman's holiday. On Sunday morning, they had attended services at St. John's Episcopal Church. Most of them were Methodists or Baptists, but the banker on the jury was a vestryman at St. John's, and rank has its privileges.

They shuffled down the two lines of chairs now, a respectable-looking bunch, clean-shaven, recently barbered, dark-suited and -tied. As a group, they appeared neither vicious nor sympathetic. They took their seats and put their hats in their laps. They did not look comfortable, but that might have had as much to do with the precariousness of the rocking-and-tilting chairs as the responsibility entrusted to them.

A moment later, at precisely eight-thirty, Judge Horton entered and called the court to order. In half an hour, the state had read the indictment again and the defendant, Haywood Patterson, had pled not guilty. At nine o'clock, Tom Knight called Victoria Price to the stand. It was not a moment too soon for the spectators.

Victoria took her time crossing to the witness chair. I knew from the set of her shoulders and the sway of her hips that she was having the time of her life, though her expression was somber, and her simple black dress with a white fichu at the throat prim. The straw hat was demure too. A single red feather at the crown was too tired to lend any brashness. Only the three large rings on her left hand suggested that she was anything but a clean-living churchgoing woman adrift in a world filled with marauding southern Negroes and malicious northern whites.

Knight left the questioning of Victoria to Solicitor H. G. Bailey, a tall gray-haired man who led her through the familiar story in a respectful tone that implied he understood how painful this must be for her. The only new element in her testimony was the actual appearance of the pair of step-ins, which she claimed the boys had torn off her.

Had she washed the step-ins since the rape? Bailey asked.

"Yes, sir," Victoria answered in an affronted voice that made it clear she knew cleanliness was next to godliness.

Bailey introduced the laundered step-ins as evidence.

Leibowitz was on his feet. "We object. This is the first time in two years any such step-ins have been shown in any court of justice."

Now Knight was standing too. This was too good to leave to an underling.

"They are here now," he said, and the courtroom erupted in laughter.

Bailey turned the witness over to the defense. I looked at my watch. His direct examination had taken only twelve minutes.

Sam Leibowitz stood and covered the distance to the witness stand in a few strides. "Miss Price," he began gently, almost gallantly, then stopped. "Shall I call you Miss Price or Mrs. Price?"

"Mrs. Price." The voice that had described the details of her sexual violation with undisguised relish turned sullen speaking her own name.

Leibowitz asked her age. There was a brief verbal tussle, not unlike the one I had witnessed between Victoria and her mother.

"Would you explain," Leibowitz asked finally, "how you could be twenty-one two years ago and twenty-seven now?"

"I ain't that educated that I can figure it out," she shot back.

The laughter was loud and protracted. She beamed at her audience.

Leibowitz asked his assistants to move the miniature train to the area in front of the witness stand. Necks craned to get a better view. Murmurs of begrudging admiration spread. It was a fine piece of work.

Leibowitz turned back to Victoria and began asking her about the train she had hitched a ride on in Chattanooga two years earlier. How had she boarded and where? Which way had she sat facing? Who else was in the car? She squirmed in her chair, and twisted half around, and looked at Bailey. Leibowitz took a step to one side, blocking her view of the solicitor.

Leibowitz picked up one of the model cars and handed it to her.

"Is this a good representation of the car you traveled in that day, Mrs. Price?"

"I can't say."

"In what way is it different?"

"It's not the train I was on."

"Of course you were not on this miniature train. I asked you if this is a fair representation."

"Just a little bit."

"How does it differ?"

"The one I was on was bigger, lots bigger."

The audience sniggered.

Leibowitz took a boxcar from the carefully arranged freight train and asked if it was a fair representation of the one she claimed the boys had crossed to get to the gondola in which she and Ruby were riding.

"I won't go by that one. I'm going by the boxcar the Negroes came over the top of."

"I'm asking if there is any difference between this miniature car and the one you say these Negroes came over the top of."

"Sure there's a difference."

"Would you please tell the court what it is?"

"That's only a toy."

This time the laughter was as loud as applause.

"She got him good," a man behind me muttered.

If Leibowitz felt his model train had laid an egg, he did not show it. He moved on to the events leading up to the alleged rape. Victoria had never heard of Jack Tiller. She had never spent a night in the Chattanooga jungle. She had never seen a group of Negroes sitting around a fire. She seemed insulted that Leibowitz would even suggest such things. He asked about previous charges against her for lewdness and adultery and moral turpitude.

The attorney general sprang to his feet. "I want to be sure that the witness understands what these words mean."

"Do I use words you don't understand?" Leibowitz asked her.

"You speak them too fast," Victoria shot back.

She got another laugh on that and a few amens for good measure.

Leibowitz returned to the events on the train. For the second time that morning, Victoria told the story of her sexual violation. It was full of flashing knives and menacing guns and powerful Negro men prying her legs apart.

" 'You haven't hollered none yet until I put this black thing in and pull it out,'" she quoted the rapist's words to the room full of breath-bated men.

"You are not embarrassed when you utter those words before all these men?" Leibowitz asked.

"We object," Knight shouted.

"Sustain the objection," Judge Horton said.

The men who had not already shed their jackets, tugged them off.

The handful who were wearing ties loosened them. They mopped their faces, and spit in the direction of the spittoons, and mopped again.

"They said they were going to take us girls up north and make us their women," she went on.

The reporters scribbled furiously. The line was not as juicy as the one about putting a black thing in and pulling it out, but it was printable.

"Do you see in this courtroom the men who you say attacked you?" Leibowitz asked.

Her eyes swept the crowd like a searchlight. She lifted her arm slowly and pointed at Haywood Patterson. "There yonder, there's the one that raped me first," she cried, as if her heart would break with the words.

"You're a little bit of an actress, aren't you?" Leibowitz said quietly.

"You're a pretty good actor yourself," she snapped back.

So many amens rang out, the courtroom sounded like a revival meeting.

Victoria settled back in her chair and crossed her legs, the better to show off her new silk stockings.

"Now, Mrs. Price," Leibowitz went on, "when you got to the railroad yards in Chattanooga, what did you do?"

"I walked down by the corner of the depot, and found a boy standing there, and I asked him did he know a woman by the name of Callie."

I sat up straighter.

"And he said he knew a lady by name of Callie Brochie and gave me directions down four or five houses on Seventh Street to find her."

"Did you find the house?"

"Yes, sir."

"What sort of house was it?"

"I don't recollect."

"Was it one floor or two floors?"

"I never did pay no attention to that."

"Did you stay there that night?"

Knight was on his feet, his face flushed a bright red. "I can't see the relevance of Mrs. Brochie and what the witness did in Chattanooga. The only thing we are interested in here is whether she was raped on that train."

"I am testing the witness's credibility," Leibowitz said calmly. "Did you stay there that night?" he repeated to Victoria.

"Yes, sir."

"Did you know Mrs. Brochie before, or was that the first time you met her?"

"I knew her before by the name of Callie Martin."

"You and Ruby Bates slept there that night?"

"Yes, sir."

"And got up the following morning?"

"Yes, sir."

"You are sure about that. You don't want to change your statement?"

Knight shouted his objection. Judge Horton sustained it.

"Nothing further." Leibowitz turned away from the witness chair and took a step toward the defense table, then, seeming to remember something, he turned back to the witness.

"By the way, Mrs. Price, the name of Callie Brochie you apply to this boardinghouse lady. Isn't it the name of a boardinghouse lady used by Octavus Roy Cohen in the *Saturday Evening Post* story 'Sis Callie'? Isn't that where you got the name?"

"We object," Knight shouted before she could answer.

"Sustain the objection," Judge Horton said, but Leibowitz returned to the defense table with a lighter step.

When the court reconvened after lunch, the state called Dr. R. R. Bridges to the stand. Bailey led him through the same story of examining the girls he had told two years earlier in Scottsboro. The only difference was this time when he finished answering Bailey's questions, he had to face a real cross-examination. Leibowitz spared neither the details nor the terminology. He quizzed Bridges on vaginas and clitorises and scrota and testicles and labia, both minora and majora.

"The act of intercourse brings the head of the male organ up against the mouth of the womb, is that correct?" Leibowitz asked, and the room full of men caught their breath as one.

"Semen expelled from the male organ flows into the vagina," he went on, and the courtroom exhaled in a single sigh.

The judge did not recess until early evening. I watched the spectators filing out of the courtroom. They had the glazed, spent appearance of men emerging from a burlesque house. A dictionary of dirty words echoed in their heads. A stag movie ran behind their eyes. They had complained about the cost of the trial. The Scottsboro proceedings had set the county back eight thousand dollars. This trial would come in at twice the price. But they had got their money's worth today.

The next morning, the courtroom was filled to capacity again. Men who had missed out on the previous day's proceedings had begun lining up at dawn. They sat now, shoulder to shoulder, sweating, spitting, smirking in anticipation.

Dr. Bridges took the stand again. He sat erect, his thin neck rising from his stiff white collar, his long face taut with responsibility, and distaste. Unlike the judge, he was not a dead ringer for Abe Lincoln, but he gave off a powerful whiff of probity.

Sam Leibowitz moved to the witness stand with the springy step of a prizefighter. Beside the judge and the physician, those avatars of southern chivalry, he came off as a scrappy troublemaker. I thought of the two men who had snubbed him the day we'd had lunch in New York.

He picked up the cross-examination where he had left off the day before, asking about vaginal folds and alkaline secretions and the life expectancy of semen. The men leaned forward in their seats, hanging on every word.

"In the case of a prostitute," Leibowitz began, making the word curdle like sour milk, "where a prostitute has intercourse with man after man, time after time, regularly, repeatedly, is it more likely the semen expelled by men into the vagina would flow out of it more readily than from a girl who was virtuous?" His actor's voice caressed the last word, as if he wanted to protect it from the bad company into which it had fallen.

A small voice in my head cried out objection, but Attorney General Knight did not. I sat listening to Leibowitz ask about the anatomical and biological and moral differences between nice women and whores. Sam Leibowitz might rub elbows with gangsters and hit men, and pull some flashy tricks in a courtroom, but when it came to women, he brooked no funny business.

"Suppose Ruby Bates had intercourse only a few hours before she was examined, and another act of intercourse the day before that, and she was the type of girl that did not clean herself, did not douche herself, did not wash herself out."

How? I wanted to shout. There's no running water in a hobo jungle. There isn't even a pump, for God's sake, let alone privacy.

"That would leave a deposit in the vagina, would it not?"

"Yes, sir," Bridges answered.

"But no one could say from that deposit when the intercourse took place or with how many men, is that right?"

"That is correct."

"Tell me, Doctor, are the muscles in the hips and thighs of a woman stronger than those of a man?"

"No, sir."

"But isn't it almost impossible, if a woman is lying on the ground, for one man to pull her legs apart with his hands? Isn't it next to a physical impossibility?"

Bridges twisted his head on his neck, as if his collar were too tight. "What is the question, sir?"

"If a normal healthy woman is lying on the floor, and somebody takes hold of her legs, one leg with one hand and the other leg with the other, and seeks to pull her legs apart, isn't it next to a physical impossibility?"

"No, sir."

"Wouldn't he have to have leverage?"

"No."

Leibowitz looked unhappy with the answer, but he went on. "As a physician and a man of science, you have observed women and men. Wouldn't you say that the ladies are better actors, better performers than the men?" He did not intend the statement as a compliment.

"I don't believe that addresses the witness's competence," Judge Horton interrupted, but Leibowitz kept going.

"I mean when a woman goes back to the doctor after she has had time to think about it, she can easily put on an act of hysteria."

Knight objected. Judge Horton sustained the objection.

"Have you ever seen cases, Doctor, where women, after they have had time to think things over, put on a crying act before the doctor in order to seem more modest than they are?"

Again Knight objected, and again the judge sustained the objection.

Leibowitz turned the witness over to the state.

As I sat watching him make his way back to the defense table, I knew my reaction was unreasonable. I wanted him to discredit Victoria's testimony. I prayed he would persuade the jury to acquit Haywood Patterson. So why was I quibbling with his methods?

Bailey approached the witness stand. "In extreme cases, Doctor," he began, "doesn't hysteria often come a good while after the cause of the excitement?"

"Yes, sir."

"Did you see the parties again after you examined them the first time?"

"The next morning."

"How did they appear?"

"They were both hysterical."

"Nothing further," Bailey said.

As I sat watching Dr. Bridges leave the witness chair, I felt I had gone through the looking glass. The defenders of the downtrodden were doing their best to crucify two hapless amateur hookers, while the champions of ignorance and intolerance were making a stand for two uneducated impoverished sinned-against sinners.

Tom Knight stood to call the next witness. The spectators leaned left and right to find a clear line of vision. Everyone knew Dr. Marvin Lynch, Dr. Bridges's assistant, was scheduled to take the stand. Dr. Lynch was young, and not as dry as the old doc. Now would come the really hot stuff. But instead of calling the witness, Knight asked Judge Horton if he could confer with him privately. The judge declared a recess, and he and the state's attorneys left the courtroom. A murmur of disappointment ran through the audience.

The men returned a few moments later. As Judge Horton raised his gavel to call the court to order, a sandy-haired boyish-looking man with an open face but an uneasy manner stood. He identified himself as Dr. Marvin Lynch and asked if he could have a private word with the judge. As Horton led the young doctor out of the courtroom, the buzzing of the spectators grew as insistent as a swarm of bees.

I did not learn what happened between Judge Horton and Dr. Lynch that afternoon until years later, and then I had to piece it together from the judge's account, and Dr. Lynch's equivocations and denials, and the story Dr. Bridges told me, perhaps in an attempt to clear his conscience, as he lay dying on his shady colonnaded porch.

The judge took Lynch to the same anteroom in which he had conferred with the state's attorneys a moment earlier. The doctor's face was flushed, and he was perspiring heavily. The judge could not help thinking that he looked less like a doctor than like a boy who is being hauled on the carpet for some childish infraction of the rules.

Lynch looked around the room nervously. "Is there someplace where we could talk more privately?"

Horton assured him they would not be interrupted.

The doctor was not reassured. Someone might come through the door suddenly, he insisted. Someone might be listening on the other side of the wall.

Horton did not like Lynch's cloak-and-dagger behavior, but something was troubling the younger man, and the judge believed it was his duty to find out what it was. He summoned the bailiff and led him and the doctor down the hall. When they reached the men's room, he told the bailiff to stand guard at the door and not let anyone in.

"I don't care who it is or how urgent the need. No one."

"Yes, sir," the bailiff answered.

The judge opened the door, gestured for the doctor to go in ahead of him, and closed it behind them. The doctor pushed open the door of the single stall to make sure it was empty. It swung closed with a bang. The two men, whose ages might have made them father and son, stood facing each other between the rust-streaked sinks and stone urinals. The judge waited.

"Did General Knight say, Your Honor, that he did not require my testimony, because it would be a repetition of Dr. Bridges's?"

"He did."

"I'm afraid . . ." Lynch started then stopped.

"Yes?"

"I'm afraid the general misstated my case, sir."

"In what way?"

The doctor glanced around the bathroom, then back at the older man. "My testimony would not be a repetition of Dr. Bridges's."

"How would it differ?"

This time the pause went on for longer. "Those girls were not raped," the doctor said finally.

The judge put his hand on the sink to steady himself. He had gone into this with an open mind, as any honorable man would, but he could not help thinking there had to be a fire to cause all this smoke. "Are you sure?"

"As soon as I examined them, I knew. They were not even red."

The judge was still holding on to the sink. "My God, Doctor, is this whole thing a horrible mistake?"

The boyish face grimaced, as if he were trying not to cry. "After the examination, when Dr. Bridges left the office for a moment, I looked both those girls in the eye and told them they were liars. I told them they had not been raped."

"What did they say?"

"They laughed in my face."

"My God, Doctor," the judge said again.

The two men stood staring at each other in the small urine- and antiseptic-smelling space. On the other side of the door, the bailiff was telling someone the men's room was closed until further notice.

"You must testify, Doctor."

Lynch shied like a frightened horse. "I want to, Judge. I believe it's my duty."

"Exactly," the judge said. He was relieved. Lynch might be young, but he was a southern gentleman. The boyish panic was only the prelude to acting like a man.

"But I can't. If I testify for those boys, I'll never be able to practice medicine again. Not in Alabama."

There was no need to say more. Both men understood that the idea of practicing medicine or law or any other profession anywhere else was unthinkable.

Judge Horton put his big hand with the long powerful fingers on the younger man's shoulder. If the doctor were his son, he would insist he do his duty. But the doctor was not his son, merely a frightened boy. Judge Horton would not use the word *coward*, even in the privacy of his own mind. The doctor was a frightened boy, who had not had the benefit of someone like the judge, or the judge's admirable mother, to instill in him a sense of decency, and duty, and truth. And it was too late for that now. You could shape a sapling. The only way you could mold a tree was by hacking off its parts. The judge did not want that on his conscience. He took his hand from the doctor's shoulder and told him to go on ahead. He would follow in a moment.

Lynch bolted out of the room.

The walk back to the courtroom was the longest of the judge's life. The law was sacrosanct. Individual concerns paled beside it. But the judge could not overcome his uneasiness about the young man who had just bared his soul to him. The other young man waiting in the courtroom in undersized prison overalls did not cross his mind at the moment.

Dr. Lynch was not a coward. He had not had to come forward to tell the truth, even privately. He could have permitted the attorney general's explanation of repetition to stand. Horton wished he had. No, he could not wish that. Nonetheless, the act of admitting the truth to the judge had taken courage. The judge had no appetite for ruining a courageous young man.

He was getting closer to the courtroom now.

Besides, Lynch's account was only one man's opinion. The girls had laughed at him, but they had not retracted their story. As for their not being red, as he so distastefully put it, Dr. Bridges had been over that in his testimony. The older doctor could not swear they had been raped, but he could not swear they had not.

The judge stood unseen, a little back from the door, and looked into the courtroom. The jurors sat waiting, sober, respectable, patient. He knew half of them personally. Eugene Graves had been at the bank for as long as Horton could remember. You could not find a more honest bookkeeper than Bill Grimes. Jim Stewart was a respected member of the chamber of commerce, just as his daddy had been before him. Bob Kitchens had sold the judge his auto. He did not know the mill worker or two of the three farmers or Lander, who was unemployed, but you could not hold that against a man these days. They had seemed, during the voir dire, to be honest, well-intentioned citizens. If he could not trust them to see that justice was done, he could not trust the law.

He stepped into the room, called the court to order, and told the state to call its next witness.

Solicitor Bailey called a farmer named Ory Dobbins to the stand. Dobbins, whose land abutted the railroad tracks, repeated the story he had told in Scottsboro of having come out of the house on his way to the barn when he saw a train going past. He noticed a woman trying to throw herself from a gondola.

"The girl was setting up on the end, fixing to jump off, but a Negro grabbed her and threw her down in the car."

"How far were you from the tracks when you witnessed this?" Bailey asked.

"Forty yards," Dobbins answered.

The prosecutor turned the witness over to Leibowitz.

"You say you were standing forty yards from the tracks when the train went by, Mr. Dobbins?"

"Yes, sir."

"Forty yards, you testified, not sixty or thirty?"

"Forty yards is what it is."

"Let me ask you if you didn't say this at Scottsboro two years ago. I am reading from the official record. 'Q: How far from the track? A: About one hundred yards.' That is what you said at Scottsboro. Which is it, Mr. Dobbins? Forty yards or a hundred?"

"Forty."

"And yet two years ago you were just as certain it was a hundred."

"When I found out I was to witness, I got a tape and measured."

"Mr. Dobbins, would you say you know your farm pretty well?"

"Surely do."

Leibowitz moved to the defense table, picked up several photographs, and returned to the witness stand. One by one, he handed the pictures to Dobbins. One by one, Dobbins confirmed that yes, that was his barn, his house, his view of the railroad tracks. One by one, Leibowitz showed the photographs to the jury.

"You were standing where when you saw the train go by?"

"By the woodpile."

He handed Dobbins a crayon. "Would you mark the spot on this photograph?"

Dobbins marked the spot. Judge Horton leaned over his bench to get a better view. Leibowitz took the photo from Dobbins and showed it to the jury. He returned to the witness and held the photograph so both he and the jurors could see it. "If you were standing here, and the house is here and the barn here," he said, pointing to each spot, "then you could not have seen more than fifty or sixty feet of track."

"I seen the track," Dobbins insisted.

"And if the train was traveling at a speed of at least twenty-five miles an hour, you would have been able to see the car for no longer than one and a half seconds."

"I seen the girl trying to throw herself off."

"You saw only one girl?"

"Saw one girl, and the colored that grabbed her."

"Not two girls?"

"One girl."

"He told you he saw one girl," Bailey interrupted.

Judge Horton warned the attorney that if he had anything to say, he should say it to the court.

"In Scottsboro," Leibowitz went on, "you told a different story. I'm reading from the official record. 'Q: Did you see anybody on the train? A: I seen two girls and the coloreds that tried to grab them.'"

Dobbins glanced at the prosecution's table.

"Are you even sure it was a girl?" Leibowitz pressed.

"She had on woman's clothes."

Judge Horton, who had been leaning back in his chair, sat up. "She had on woman's clothes?" he asked the witness.

"She had on woman's clothes," Dobbins repeated.

"What kind of clothes?" Leibowitz asked quietly. "Overalls?"

"No, sir, a dress."

Leibowitz did not have to remind anyone in that room that Victoria had described, time and again, how the boys had torn off her overalls.

"Do you have an auto, Mr. Dobbins?"

"Yes, sir," Dobbins answered proudly.

"Was it in working condition that day?"

"Yes, sir."

"Yet, when you saw this white woman being attacked by a Negro, you did not get in your car and drive somewhere to report it?"

Dobbins looked startled. Leibowitz did not wait for him to answer.

The state rested its case.

No unprejudiced person could have listened to the testimony unfold without being convinced of the innocence of Haywood Patterson.

—*Mary Heaton Vorse,* The New Republic, *1933*

When a nigger has expert witnesses, we have a right to ask who is paying for them.

—*Resident of Decatur, Alabama, 1933*

Kill the Jew from New York.

—*Title of a pamphlet on sale in Decatur, 1933*

Dallas Ramsay, the first witness for the defense, held his callused black hand in the air and swore to tell the truth. He lived, he said in answer to Sam Leibowitz's questions, in a four-room shack next to the hobo jungle in the Chattanooga railroad yards. On the morning of March 25, 1931, he had seen two white girls with a white boy in the jungle just before six o'clock.

Leibowitz asked the bailiff to bring Victoria Price into the courtroom. The bailiff pushed open the door, and Victoria stepped through. He took her elbow to guide her toward the witness stand, but she shook off his hand, strode across the area behind the railing, and stood center stage, bristling with defiance.

"Is that the girl you saw?" Leibowitz asked the witness.

"She seems like the same girl," Ramsay said slowly. "Only she's a little heavier now than what she was then."

Victoria's lips moved in what looked like a silent curse.

"Do you recognize her?" Judge Horton asked.

"Yes, sir, I recognize her."

Knight objected. "Your Honor, I do not see what relevance this man's testimony has."

"I'm going to show that the state's main witness is a perjurer," Leibowitz answered quietly. "That's what I'm going to show before I'm through. This is only the beginning."

Leibowitz called Beatrice Maddox. A young Negro woman with a round face and frightened eyes under a gray cloche hat took the stand. She identified herself as a longtime resident of Chattanooga. Yes, she was married, and the sister of Roy and Andy Wright. She admitted that, hard as she had tried, she had been unable to find a Callie Brochie on Seventh Street or in the telephone book. Leibowitz turned the witness over to the state.

"Are the Wright boys your half-brothers?" Bailey asked.

"They're my brothers," Mrs. Maddox answered. "Same mother, same father."

Bailey did not seem to like that. "Do you work for the city of Chattanooga?"

"No, sir."

"Are you an expert on telephone books?"

"No, sir."

"Do you have anything to do with the publication of Chattanooga's telephone book?"

"No, sir."

"Who asked you to look for Callie Brochie's address?" Bailey demanded.

"My kinfolk's in trouble. I taken it on my own self to look for it."

The simple answer caught Bailey off guard. "No further questions," he muttered.

Leibowitz's next witness was another longtime resident of Chattanooga, but there the similarity ended. George W. Chamlee, a former district attorney of Hamilton, the county in which Chattanooga was located, was an unusual man with a complicated history. He had once written a magazine article defending lynching under certain circumstances. He had subsequently defended three communists on charges of advocating the overthrow of the government by reminding the court that their grandfathers had seceded from the same government and sworn allegiance to a new nation. He was the attorney whom Danny Dundee had accused of bribing him to get Ruby drunk in order to write the letter to Earl, and whom the Tennessee Bar Association had subsequently cleared.

Leibowitz asked Chamlee how long he had lived in the South. All his life, Chamlee answered. And his father and grandfather? They too were born, raised, and lived their lives in the South.

"Your grandfather fought for the Confederacy?" Leibowitz asked.

"He helped entertain General Sherman and managed to detain him for three days."

Spectators stirred uncomfortably. They did not know whether to cheer the brave ancestor or hiss the traitorous descendant.

"Your office is located on Seventh Street in Chattanooga?"

"Yes, sir. I've lived or had my office there for twenty-five of the last forty years."

"Will you tell the gentlemen of the jury how many blocks Seventh Street consists of?"

"About eight blocks."

"And what kind of a neighborhood is it?"

"Perhaps one of the richest in the city."

"Then you would not be likely to find a house on it that took in boarders?"

"No, sir."

"You are acquainted with all the folks on that street?"

"I wouldn't say all of them, because in this Depression there is some moving in and out, but I know most everybody there."

"In all the time you have lived in the city of Chattanooga, in the twenty-five years you have lived on Seventh Street and had your office on Seventh Street, have you ever known any person by the name of Callie Brochie living there or keeping a boardinghouse there?"

"No, sir. I have examined city directories for the years 1930, 1931, and 1932 to see if I could find any such name as Callie Brochie in Chattanooga, and I went from one end of Seventh Street to the other, but I found no one by that name. For forty years, I have been over Seventh Street on an average of once or twice and sometimes ten times a day, and I don't believe there was ever a boardinghouse there. I don't believe there was ever a boardinghouse in Chattanooga owned by a woman named Callie Brochie. I don't believe such a woman has been in Chattanooga within the last three years."

"No further questions," Leibowitz said and returned to his seat. The silence in the courtroom was more menacing than all the jeers and threats and angry amens.

On the way out of the dining room that evening, Abel asked if I felt like going for a walk. I was surprised. We had eaten meals together, along with the others, and strolled back and forth to the courthouse in a group, but I had not seen him alone since the morning we had quarreled. He had spent all his free time working on the play. I knew because long into the night and early in the morning, I heard the typewriter keys.

The night was soft, but the tattoo of military boots on pavement shattered the quiet.

"Ma'am, sir," a young voice said as we made our way past. "I hope you're not fixing to go too far."

We assured him we had no intention of going far. From the hotel to the end of the block and back was the accepted route for northerners walking the Decatur streets in the dark these days.

Abel strolled out into the night, his hands in his pockets, his hat on the back of his head. For a compact man, he had a long stride. I put my hands in my pockets, matched my pace to his, and asked how the play was coming.

"Can't you hear?"

"I hear the typewriter banging. I can't hear if pages are being thrown into the wastebasket."

"You're a mean-spirited woman, Ace."

We had slipped back into the old routine. I had not thought it possible that night in my bed, but then I had not believed the morning would turn out as it did.

We walked on in silence. Neat frame houses sat behind small well-tended yards. Here and there, windows glowed in the night like fireflies. Curtains danced on the occasional breeze. From a darkened porch came the squeak of a swing and the giggle of a girl.

"Ah, young love," Abel said, but his voice was hoarse, and I think for a moment he was remembering that night too.

Looking back now, I cannot be sure when the sound began to register. Perhaps it had been there all along, and I was too busy wondering what had gone wrong between Abel and me to notice. Perhaps we'd had to get this close to hear it. At first, I could not place it. Distant thunder would have been louder, insects more musical, frogs more rhythmic. This was a dull muffled sound without a beat.

"Do you hear that?" I asked.

"What?" Abel said, but then he must have heard it too, because he stopped walking and put a hand on my arm to keep me in place beside him.

I smelled them before I saw them. Human sweat turned the spring night sour. Gradually shadows began to take shape in the darkness. They were bobbing and weaving around us. The sound I had not been able to place was the shuffle of boots. I was willing to bet they were not military-issue.

They were all around us now, but still no one spoke. The silence made the shuffling of their feet more ominous. I caught a flash of white eye, a gleam of bared teeth. A face leaned in close, then pulled back before I could put it in focus. Abel's hand on my arm was like a tourniquet.

I heard another sound, like a throat being cleared, then felt something wet and slimy on my cheek. I started to reach up to rub it off. Abel kept my arm in place, but he was too late.

"The commie Jewgirl from New York don't like tobacco juice on her commie Jew skin."

At that moment I was terrified of two things: the mob of mindless men, and the possibility that Abel would think he had to make some show of courage to protect me from the mob of mindless men.

"Evening, gentlemen." Abel's voice sounded almost normal in the darkness.

No one answered.

"Nice night, isn't it?" he persisted.

There was another hawking sound. I steeled myself, but nothing hit my skin.

A face darted forward and hung in front of me. I felt the sour breath as he spoke. "I ain't never swung a girl before."

Laughter rattled the night air.

Abel leaned between the face hanging in the darkness and me.

"Now, take it easy, Harvey," he said.

The man jumped back as if he had been bitten.

"How'd he know you?" another voice whined.

"Harvey and I are old friends," Abel said. "He sold me some of the best moonshine I ever laid hands on."

"Bad as a Jew," another voice said.

"Old Harvey'll do anything for a buck."

"Stop using his name," a voice hissed.

The shuffling of shoes ceased. The only sound was of fear, ours and theirs, inhaling and exhaling in the darkness.

"Now we got no choice," a voice hissed. "Gotta swing them commie Jew bastards."

Someone grunted yeah. The rest said nothing.

I could feel Abel beside me, shrugging elaborately, a large pantomime to be read in the dark. "Either that or just forget the whole thing."

The silence dragged on. Someone hawked and spit again. Shoes shuffled. I could not be sure, but I thought one or two of the men were beginning to back away. Some of the shadows looked down at their feet. Others gazed up at the sky. I had the feeling every man there was sorry he had got into this mess, but no one dared to be the first to try to get out.

"I wouldn't waste no rope on them two," a voice in the back of the crowd growled. "We come out for the Jew lawyer and the niggers, and I ain't settling for nothing less. Specially not a gal and little four-eyes here."

There was a chorus of curses, but they carried no conviction. The voice had given them a way out, and they were hell-bent on taking it.

"Get the hell out of here," the voice who did not want to waste rope barked at us.

We turned and began walking back. Abel still had his hand on my arm. I could see the lights of the hotel hanging in the distance. A block had never looked so long.

Abel and I were not the only ones threatened that night. More than two hundred men had met to put an end to the insults against their community and the outsiders who were making them. The gathering was anything but exclusive. Word of it had traveled by telephone and barbershop and back alley. That was how several of Captain Burleson's informers had learned of it.

When I heard about the informers, I could not help wondering if the man who had been unwilling to waste rope on Abel and me had been one of them. I could not decide whether he and Abel had skillfully defused the mob, or we had been merely lucky. Of course, there is one more alternative, that I am making too much of the incident. Perhaps we were never in danger at all. The rabble that surrounded us that night, spitting and threatening and swinging their ropes, was nothing more than a mob of ordinary men, impoverished, frustrated, emasculated by the conditions and time in which they lived. I cannot think of a more dangerous bunch.

Judge Horton must have agreed, because when the court reconvened the next morning, he ordered the jury removed from the room and sat grim-faced, watching them file out. When the door closed behind them, he turned a stern countenance on the spectators. The court would protect the prisoners and everyone involved in the proceedings, he said. He had ordered the National Guardsmen to shoot to kill.

Here and there among the spectators, men grumbled and muttered and spat. The judge was almost as bad as the commieJewlawyerfrom-NewYork.

Horton ordered the bailiff to bring the jury back, and the defense called Willie Roberson. Leibowitz knew he was taking a chance by putting Haywood on the stand. Some people said he was courting disaster to call the others as well. At Scottsboro, their testimony had been confused at best, self-incriminating at worst. But he knew that though they were being tried separately, they stood accused together. He wanted to tear holes in the whole trumped-up story.

Willie shuffled forward, a short awkward boy, more dazed, it appeared, than frightened. He repeated the bailiff's words, then took the seat and sat staring dully ahead of him, his eyes unfocused, his mouth slack. A few years later, Willie would undergo a psychiatric examination. The results would indicate a mental age of nine.

Leibowitz's questioning was gentle, but Willie's testimony was still painful to watch. He spoke slowly, groping for words and blinking into the distance. He admitted that he had been syphilitic since 1930, had had large cankers on his privates at the time he hitched the ride on the train, and had to walk with a cane because of the pain. The men in the audience squirmed, but not with pleasure. He had spent the entire trip, from the time he boarded until the posse took him off, alone in a freight car, nursing his agony. His physical condition made it impossible for him to run over the tops of freight cars, fight white boys or anyone else, rape, or have sexual intercourse.

Olen Montgomery moved hesitantly to the witness stand next. He admitted he was blind in his left eye and half blind in his right. Like Willie, he could not run or leap along the top of a moving train, and had boarded alone and remained in the same car until the posse took him off.

One after another, Ozie Powell and Andy Wright and Eugene Williams described, with the help of the Lionel model, which was finally justifying its expense, where they had been on the train. They repeated that, with the exception of Haywood Patterson, Eugene Williams, and the two Wright brothers, none of them had known the others before they were arrested. Nor had they seen any girls on the train until they were taken off it in Paint Rock.

Haywood was the last to take the stand. Unlike the others, he did not shuffle, but covered the distance with a few long strides. His face was a billboard of black rage in the flat white landscape of the courtroom. I understood why they hated him. I also realized that he had not been issued the too-small overalls by accident. They made him look ludicrous, like a carnival giant, hamstrung, hog-tied, and set up to be the butt of jokes.

He took the oath, sat, and turned to face the courtroom. The gesture was a confrontation.

Step by step, Leibowitz questioned him about his movements and actions that day on the Alabama Great Southern freight train. Step by step, Patterson described the white foot coming down on his black hand, and the fight that followed, and pulling Orville Gilley back to safety. His grammar was weak, but his words were powerful.

Leibowitz turned the witness over to the state.

Tom Knight stood and buttoned his tight-tailored jacket. He would not leave the ringleader of the boys to an underling.

"When you were in Scottsboro . . ." Knight stopped. "You were tried at Scottsboro?"

"I was framed at Scottsboro."

"Who told you to say you were framed?" Knight snapped.

"I told myself."

A rumble of anger ran through the court. "Just wait till the sun goes down on the jail tonight," someone sang out.

Judge Horton banged his gavel.

Knight asked about the fight on the train, and the boys who were thrown off, and Orville Gilley.

"You say the boy called Gilley was hanging off the side of the car?"

"Yes, sir, and some of the boys was trying to push him loose."

"What did you do?"

"I walked up to the boys and told them not to push the white boy off, on account of the train was going too fast, and I was afraid the boy would get himself killed."

"Then what did you do?"

"I pulled the white boy back on the car."

"All by yourself?"

"Andy Wright give me help."

"You pulled the white boy back in the car?" Knight repeated incredulously.

"Yes, sir, I pulled him back."

"Then what did you do?"

"I didn't do nothing."

"You didn't go to the car where the girls were?"

"I didn't see no girls."

"You did not go to the car where the girls were and rape them?"

Patterson raised his eyes to Knight's face. The whites glinted. "You think I'd pull a white boy back to be a witness if I was fixing to rape any white woman?"

"I'll ask the questions," Knight snapped, but it was too late. Haywood had made his point.

By five o'clock, the slanting rays of late afternoon sun were burning through the yellow window shades, and the air was thick as soup. Deep lines of exhaustion hewed the judge's face. Knight's dapper suit was wilted to a rag. Leibowitz, who had started the day on the balls of his feet, dragged himself from the defense table to the witness chair. He called Dr. Edward A. Reisman to the stand. While the witness approached and took the oath, the bailiff set up several oversized medical diagrams.

Leibowitz ran through a few brief questions to establish the fact that Reisman was a Chattanooga gynecologist, who, with the exception of a brief stint of training at Bellevue Hospital in New York City, had lived all his life in Tennessee. Leibowitz launched into the familiar questions, but Reisman, unlike Bridges, gave categorical answers.

"To my mind it would be inconceivable that six men would have intercourse with one woman and not leave telltale traces of their presence in considerable quantities of semen in the vagina. To my mind that would be inconceivable," he repeated.

The next morning, Thursday, Leibowitz called Lester Carter to the stand. I knew Lester only from photographs and Ruby's description, but I could tell the moment he entered the courtroom that he had undergone a makeover. His receding hair was brilliantined back from his pale forehead. The creases in the trousers of his obviously new suit were razor sharp, and there were no half-moons of perspiration at the armpits. He made his way to the witness stand, blinking against the light, as if he had been sitting in a darkened room.

Leibowitz led Lester through a detailed account of the night in the Carolina yards with Jack Tiller and the girls. That was when he delivered his memorable line about hanging his hat on a little limb and going to have intercourse with Ruby. He testified to pretending not to know the girls on the train so no one would guess they were crossing state lines for immoral purposes, and meeting Orville Gilley in Chattanooga, and more intercourses—he seemed to like the plural of the word—with Ruby. He also talked about the boys who had talked dirt to the girls in the jungle.

"I told them Negroes I'd whup them good if ever they tried that again."

Leibowitz's gaze cut to the jury. If he had heard it, they had too. Lester had not said niggers, or coloreds, or even nigras. He had said Negroes. More than his brilliantined hair or store-bought suit, the word gave him away.

He went on to describe how, in jail, Victoria had asked another boy to say he was her brother, so she would not be charged with crossing state lines with a man; and told Orville to stick to the story of the rape, because they could make some money on it; and said she didn't care if they stuck all the Negroes in Alabama in jail. If his first use of the word had not discredited him, the second would. The fact that his voice squeaked and his hands flew nervously as he spoke did not help. Leibowitz turned the witness over to the state.

Wade Wright stepped up to the witness stand and cleared his all-day singer throat.

"Did you have some communication from New York before you went there?" he asked.

"I wrote to this fellow Brodsky."

"And Brodsky wrote back and said he wanted you to come there?"

"Yes, sir."

"He paid your way?"

"No, sir."

"How long did you stay with Mr. Brodsky?"

"I never stayed with him. He got me a room."

"He paid your room rent?"

"Yes, sir."

"You say you hitchhiked up North and rode an automobile back."

"Yes, sir."

"Whose automobile?"

"I don't know."

"Who drove it?"

"Fella named Pete."

"Who paid the expenses?"

"I bought my own meals."

"Where did you get the money?"

"Mr. Brodsky would give me three or four dollars all along."

"Where did you get that suit of clothes?"

"I bought it in New York."

"How much did the suit cost?"

"About eleven dollars."

"Who paid for it?"

"I paid for it out of the money I would get."

"The money you would get from Mr. Brodsky?"

"Yes, sir."

"Amen," someone on the other side of the railing said, and Wright returned to his seat.

Sam Leibowitz stood. "The defense rests," he said.

A shocked silence fell over the room. I was as surprised as everyone else. Where was Ruby Bates? What had happened to the star witness we had been keeping under wraps? The sniggers began to build. They had not had to worry about Ruby Bates coming back down and spoiling things after all.

"With reservations," Leibowitz added.

What happens to a worker who realizes why she is as she is. Sometimes it's like the regeneration of a soul that's been lost . . . Her whole life was laid bare, why she was as she was, why she became what she had become, why she had done what she did, why she considered the Negro expendable for any member of the white race. When she finally understood, she also understood why she'll have to walk into that courtroom tomorrow and tell the truth—and she'll do it. And that will take guts, maybe the kind you and I will never know.

—Joseph Brodsky, 1933

I kept wondering how Ruby's testimony could do anything but end the case. If one of the two complainants who brought these boys to the brink of death confessed that neither she nor her companion had been raped, where was the case? There was the word of only one woman, known as a tramp and contradicted by her companion. How could twelve men, no matter how prejudiced, now find Patterson guilty?

—John Spivak, reporter, 1933

A moment later a messenger hurried down the aisle and handed Leibowitz a slip of paper. He studied it, then stood, approached the bench, and whispered to the judge. The judge announced a brief recess. People stretched, and milled around, and spit tobacco and snuff, but nobody left the courtroom. The minutes dragged by. I wondered how long Leibowitz would draw out the suspense. Finally, Judge Horton called the court to order again.

Leibowitz stood. "The defense calls Ruby Bates."

A wave of mutters and curses ran through the crowd. A nervous not-quite-sane-sounding titter rose from the back of the courtroom. Tom Knight sat behind the prosecution's table, his sweat-slicked face shining like a waxed apple. Judge Horton left the bench and came down and stood in the railed enclosure, looking toward the entrance. He nodded to two National Guardsmen. They moved to the doors and pulled them open.

The first thing I noticed was that she had persuaded someone to buy her another suit. This one was gray, and she would not have liked that, but it was stylishly cut, as was the matching, and flattering, cloche hat. The outfit was inexpensive, but it was rich enough to break Victoria's heart. That was probably what Ruby had thought when she put it on. But she did not look as if she were thinking it now. She looked terrified.

She started down the aisle. Her step was slow, and something about it was peculiar. It took me a moment to figure out what it was. She was walking with that absurd bridal gait, right foot forward, left catches up, left foot forward, right catches up. I wondered where she had got the idea.

She reached the witness stand and waited. Her face looked as if she were about to burst into tears. Her voice slid all over the register as she took the oath. Instead of returning to the bench, Judge Horton moved to a seat in front of the spectators and sat facing Ruby. I could imagine what she thought of that.

Leibowitz asked her name. His voice was gentle, his manner solicitous. He ran through a few preliminary questions, then moved on to the events of the night before she and Victoria hopped the train for Chattanooga.

"Did you have intercourse with Lester Carter?"

"I certainly did." Ruby's voice was a whisper, and Judge Horton leaned forward in his chair to hear it.

"Did Victoria Price have intercourse with Jack Tiller in your presence?"

"She certainly did."

"Bring out Victoria Price, please," Leibowitz said.

Ruby's face went white, but she tugged the jacket of her suit into place and smoothed the skirt.

The bailiff left the courtroom and returned a moment later with Victoria in tow. Her entrance was not nearly as dramatic as Ruby's. She had also miscalculated when she dressed that morning, or else Tom Knight had calculated. For her own testimony, she had worn the austere black dress. Today she was wearing a calico skirt and a rough black sweater. Compared to Ruby in her city-bought suit, Victoria looked like a hick. Knight was counting on the jury to spot the difference.

The bailiff started to lead Victoria to the witness stand, but again she shook off his hand and made her own way. The two old friends faced each other, Victoria standing, Ruby sitting, literally within spitting distance. Ruby was the first to drop her eyes. Victoria was not so cowed. She went on staring at the girl she had taken under her wing and out for good times. Even from the distance of the press table, I could see her chest heaving with short shallow breaths. Her hands were balled into fists. I had heard about a brawl Victoria had got into with the wife of one of her boyfriends. Mrs. Price, the man who swore the affidavit said, was a regular Jack Dempsey. I could believe it.

Victoria went on glowering at Ruby. I had the feeling Leibowitz would not have minded if she sprang at his witness, but Tom Knight would not let that happen. He stood, came out from behind the prosecution's table, and edged his way between the two women. Keeping his back to Ruby, he leaned toward Victoria and murmured something in her ear. Victoria's fists unclenched, but her body did not relax.

Knight returned to his seat. Leibowitz approached the witness.

"Is this woman Victoria Price?"

"Yes, sir," Ruby breathed.

"That is all," he said, and the bailiff strong-armed Victoria out of the courtroom.

Leibowitz resumed his questioning. Ruby admitted that she had spent the night in Chattanooga in a hobo jungle, that she had never heard of a Callie Brochie until Victoria borrowed the name from a magazine picture, and that she had told it like Victoria had told it.

"Did Victoria Price warn you what would happen if you did not follow her story?"

"She said we might have to lay out a sentence in jail, for going to Tennessee with men weren't our husbands."

Leibowitz moved to the defense table, poured himself a glass of water, sipped it, and returned to the witness stand.

"On the train back from Chattanooga that day, did any Negro attack you?"

"No, sir."

"Did you see any Negro attack Victoria Price that day?"

"No, sir."

"Have you told the God's honest truth?"

"Objection," Knight bellowed.

"Sustain the objection," Judge Horton said.

"Did any of those Negroes rape you?" Leibowitz repeated.

"No, sir."

Leibowitz returned to his seat.

There were no amens now, or even mutters of anger. The only sound was the scratching pens and pencils at the press table.

Judge Horton returned to the bench. Tom Knight stood and took the few steps to the witness stand with a slight swagger. His expression stopped just short of a smile.

"Where did you get that suit?" he demanded.

Ruby looked startled. "Well," she began slowly, "I bought it."

"Who gave you the money to buy it?"

"Well . . . I don't recollect."

"You don't recollect? Where did you get that hat?"

"I bought it."

"Who gave you the money to buy it?"

Ruby's mouth moved, but no sound came out.

The judge leaned down from the bench. "Do you know?"

"Dr. Fosdick of New York." The words poured out in a rush of relief.

"He gave you the money to buy the suit and hat?" Knight asked.

"He certainly did."

"Didn't you know that when I asked you the first time?"

A hoot of laughter exploded in the back of the courtroom.

"He got her now!"

"Good as a turtle on her back."

Leibowitz practically leapt from behind the defense table. "Your Honor, I ask that you bring those men"—he waved toward the back of the courtroom—"before the bar. It is discourteous to the court for them to be snickering and laughing and rooting for the blood of this Negro."

Before the judge could answer, Chamlee rose from his seat behind the defense table. "If the court please," he began, "they don't mean any harm. It's just the way of these men in the South."

Leibowitz's head swiveled to his colleague. He might have been looking at a stranger. Chamlee sat. Leibowitz remained on his feet a moment longer, then took his chair.

"How long have you had that pocketbook?" Knight's back was to Ruby as he spoke, and again the question startled her.

"I have had it for over a year," she answered finally.

Knight swung around to face her. "Did you see Haywood Patterson, that man yonder"—he raised his arm to point at Haywood—"on the train that day?"

Ruby hung her head.

"Look at him," Judge Horton said.

Ruby raised her head slowly. "I couldn't say. I saw so many."

"How many did you see?" Knight demanded.

"I won't be sure. A whole bunch."

Knight began to fire questions like gunshots.

Which railroad car had she been riding in?

Ruby could not say.

Who else was in it?

She was not sure.

Had she seen that man yonder—he pointed at Haywood Patterson again—pull Orville Gilley back onto the train?

She had seen one of the Negroes pull Orville Gilley back, but she could not be sure now which one it was.

"You're sure Dr. Fosdick gave you that hat."

Ruby shied back from the words. "He give me money to buy it with."

"When did you go to New York?"

"Three weeks ago."

Knight proceeded to trace her itinerary. Did she go by car or truck or train? Was she in Chattanooga then, and Montgomery after, and Birmingham before? Where did she get the money for fare? For food? For a place to sleep? He hung over her, raining questions down in a torrent.

"Please step back," Leibowitz said.

"I am treating the witness with all courtesy," Knight snapped, and whirled back to Ruby.

"Where did you get the money to go to New York?"

"I had some money when I left home."

"Where did you get it?"

"Working at the mill."

"How much work had you been doing at the mill?"

"One or two nights out of the week."

"What was your average earning per night?"

"All the way from a dollar and ten cents to a dollar and twenty cents."

"How much money would you say you saved from one or two nights' work a week? Ten dollars, twenty, thirty?"

"I had fifteen dollars."

"Do you know what the railroad fare to New York is?"

"Twenty-six dollars from Chattanooga," she said proudly. For once she knew the answer.

"Where did you get the rest of the money?"

She had not seen it coming. "I borrowed it," she said slowly.

"From who?"

"I can't recollect."

Knight moved to the state's table, picked up a sheaf of papers, and returned to Ruby. She glanced down at them in his hand as if they might bite.

"I will ask you if you were not asked this question at Scottsboro. 'After the white boys got off the train, what happened?' And did you answer, 'They come along down the gondola car and came over and ravished us'? Did you say that?"

"I said it, but Victoria told me to."

"You said everything Victoria told you to say?"

"Yes, sir."

"I will ask you if you made the following affidavit at Huntsville on January sixth, 1932." Knight proceeded to read the statement she had put her name to in the sheriff's office. " 'My evidence against the Negroes at Scottsboro was absolutely the truth,' " he concluded. " 'If I wrote a letter to Earl Streetman, or any other person, contradicting this testimony, I was so drunk I did not know what I was doing.' " He showed her the paper. "Is that not your signature?"

"Yes."

"Were you telling the truth?"

"No, I didn't tell the truth then."

Knight started away from the witness chair, then turned back. "When I examined you in the presence of Victoria Price and several police officers, did I not say to you that I did not want to burn any person who was not guilty?"

"I think you did. I won't say for positive."

"Did I not tell you the only thing I wanted was the truth?"

"Yes."

"I also told you I would punish anybody who made you swear falsely, did I not?"

"Yes, sir."

Knight relinquished the witness. Leibowitz said he had no further questions.

I smiled at Ruby as she went past the press table, but her head was down, and she did not see me.

They say I'm not fit to be a member of the white race in the South no more. They say it because I took up for Negroes. Well, I don't care to be that kind of a member of the white race.

—Ruby Bates, 1933

We are sitting on a mountain of TNT.

—Samuel Leibowitz, 1933

I could hear them talking downstairs. Mrs. Hickey was mad as a hornet. She was hollering she didn't want no part of me no ways. She called me linthead and white trash and worse. But Reverend Hickey was saying he wouldn't sit still for such talk, on account of I was one of God's children. That just made her holler louder about how it was past time he started thinking about his own young ones, and stopped bringing home white trash to set a bad example and get folks riled up until there was no telling what they would do. He come back at her then about how there wasn't no point in going to them meetings of Southern Women for the Prevention of Lynching, if she didn't practice what she preached. About then, one of the young ones started in crying, and I shut my ears against the whole bunch of them. Truth to tell, I was getting tired of all them reverends who said one thing and meant something else. Captain Burleson, who carried me over here, said I should be much obliged to Reverend Hickey for taking me in, on account of most folks wouldn't. Then he put some of his men around the house and hightailed it out, and the Rev put me up here in this bedroom. I never even had a chance to lay eyes on them young ones Mrs. Hickey was hollering I was going to spoil, and I reckon that wasn't no accident. Mrs. Rev acts like I got some sickness them kids is going to catch.

If things was different, I wouldn't mind being up here none, on account of the room is real pretty. I reckon some of them young ones Mrs. Rev is worried about are girls, and didn't they fall into a pot of honey, with two pink covers on two separate beds, and a little table with a pink skirt around the bottom and a looking glass to see yourself in on top, and yonder by the window a rocking chair with a big yellow-haired Raggedy Ann you could hug. Not like them corncob dolls you can't hold close without getting all scratched up.

I set in the chair, and took the Raggedy Ann on my lap, and tried not to think about what happened in court. All the time I was up North, folks kept telling me I had nothing to worry about. All I got to do was tell the truth. But it turns out the truth ain't no easier to tell than a made-up story, not with all them men boring eyes into you, and the lawyer fella with the red face hopping around from one thing to another like a jumping bean, and folks laughing and hooting and make fun. Even Alice was laughing. I saw her when I come off the chair, but I pretended like I didn't. She don't have no right to laugh at me. Not after all that talk about us being friends.

Me and Victoria were friends too. Sometimes I recollect them days when I first gone to work in the mill, and she was learning me about the machines and the bosses and all, and I reckon things were better then than I knew. We didn't have no money, but we had a heap of fun. Now the good times are gone, and so's Victoria. Me and her can't even put eyes on each other without staring knives. It made me feel blue how it worked out today. All this time I couldn't wait to show off my new store-bought suit. I reckoned she'd about to die when she found out I got two of them. But she was so cross-legged it made me forget the suit. It ain't as much fun being a heroine as folks say, not when you got so many other folks hating you so bad they got to hide you away with a bunch of soldiers outside to keep you from going to harm.

I couldn't see none of them soldiers from the window, just a barn across the way and a field yonder. A breeze was coming in off the field. It smelled real sweet, not like every place I ever lived where no matter which way the wind's blowing, you can count on breathing privy or garbage or some barnyard animal folks are fattening for the kill. At Reverend Hickey's it just smelled spring, like that night up the spur from the hobo jungles before everything come undone.

It was going on to night, and yonder over the field, the sky looked like it was on fire, all red and purple and pink, the kind of sunset that makes your heart all swollen and sore with looking at it. I set there, watching the colors flame, and all of a sudden I knew. That wasn't no sun going down like fire. It was honest-to-goodness flames.

I stood to get a better sight over the barn. It wasn't just a fire neither. It was a cross-burning. You couldn't see wood no more, just flames in the shape of a cross. I stood in that fancy bedroom watching them flames licking the coming-on night, and I knew one thing for positive. That burning cross was meant for me.

Mrs. Hickey knew it too. She was hollering *linthead*, and *tramp*, and *young ones*, and *out, out, out*, her voice getting louder all the time, as she come up the stairs, and the Rev pounding after her saying, hush, and behind the two of them, the soldiers' boots on the steps sounded loud as them machines in the mill going full speed.

They drug me down the stairs and out into the yard, and for a minute I thought they were going to give me over to the crowd yonder around the cross, but they shoved me into the back of a car, and one of them got in after me and pushed me down on the floor. The last thing I heard as we drove away was the Rev telling them he was sorry. He done his best, but he had to think of his young ones.

After a spell we stopped, but I couldn't say where, on account of they wouldn't let me set up none. The soldier who was driving climbed out, and I heard him talking to some other fellas. Then he come back, and off we went again.

"Captain says to take her to the hotel," the driver said. "That's where they're keeping all the Itskys and the Witskys. So we only got to guard that and the jail."

"So folks only got to break into that and the jail," the soldier in back with me said, and laughed.

After a spell, the car stopped, and they yanked me out, but I couldn't see nothing, on account of it was pitch-black and they drug me inside so fast. They were shoving me down a hall and up stairs, and I would have fell for positive if they weren't hanging on to me. Then a door opened, and Alice was standing there, and she yanked me inside and closed the door after me.

"Hello, Ruby," she says, like everything's regular as pie, like folks ain't burning crosses, and soldiers ain't sneaking me around in the dark, and me and her are back in her apartment, setting and talking like friends.

I was so surprised, and mad too, all I could say was, "You didn't have no cause to laugh at me."

"What?" she said.

"Today. In court. You didn't have no cause to laugh at me."

"I wasn't laughing at you. I was smiling. I was trying to show how proud I was of what you did. It wasn't easy. I know that."

Then she told me how everybody was worried about me being safe, and Captain Burleson and Mr. Leibowitz, the Jew lawyer, had figured the best place for me was in the hotel, but the hotel was full up, and they didn't want no one downstairs to know I was here besides, so they asked if I could stay with her, and she said sure.

"Ain't you scared?" I asked her.

"There'll be two guards outside the door all night. But even if there weren't, I would have been scared, but I still would have said yes."

"How come?"

"Because it's the right thing to do. Like your telling the truth today."

While she was talking, a door opened, not the one to the hall, but another one, and a man come walking into the room like he lived there. He wasn't her fella, the peach who come to visit up in New York City. This was somebody different, not so tall, and dark with black hair and big black eyes behind glasses. I reckon glasses ain't so bad on a fella.

"Not to mention that she gets your exclusive story once again," he said and come right up to me and stuck out his hand. "Hello, Ruby. I'm Abel Newman."

"Just ignore him, Ruby. He judges everyone by his own standards."

I didn't make no sense of nothing they were saying, but I knew one thing for positive. They were just pretending to talk to me. They were really saying things to each other. They talked almost like he was her fella and she was his girl. I reckon I got her wrong that first time she come to see me in that churchy white collar and old-lady hat. She was a cool customer, all right. I reckon butter wouldn't melt in her fancy-talking mouth.

He pulled up a chair for me and set down on the side of the bed, leaning at me with his elbows on his knees and them big black eyes staring into me through the glasses. He said he wanted to know all about me, and now he was talking to me instead of Alice, and right off he started in asking questions. He had a real neighborly way about him, saying did I mind telling him this and how he always wanted to know that, and listening real good to what I answered, not just with his ears but with them big black eyes too, and pretty soon I forgot about the burning cross and the ride in the back of the car, and I was talking as good as I come to talk with Alice. I told him about going into the mill, and how Victoria took me up when other folks wouldn't have nothing to do with me, and Lester and Orville and the salesman who come through town the Christmas before it all started, the one with the sack full of samples.

"He'll be the love interest," he said out of the side of his mouth, and

I reckoned he was talking to Alice again. "Only I think I'll make him into a union organizer. Like Harry that summer they broke his nose. Have you noticed, Ruby, that girls always fall for union organizers?

"Tell me more about your salesman," he said, and now he was talking to me again.

"He wasn't no union man," I answered. "Ain't no way to get yourself shut out of a mill for good better than union talk."

"You don't have to worry about that anymore," Alice said. "The ILD is going to take you north. You have work to do there to help save the boys. Besides, after today, it isn't safe for you down here."

"That's right, Ruby," he said, "you burned your bridges."

I didn't like the ring of that none. The fella made burning bridges sound more scary than burning crosses, and I was plenty scared of them.

I couldn't make out what it meant when the jury came in laughing.

—Haywood Patterson, 1950

Wade Wright moved toward the jury through the fetid air like a swimmer paddling for shore. Tom Knight would deliver the final summation for the state, but Wright would warm up the crowd.

"Gentlemen of the jury," he began, and his all-day singer's voice caressed the words, "I stand before you today because five months ago the Supreme Court of the United States," he hissed, as though he were speaking of Satan himself, "reversed the ruling of the Supreme Court of Alabama. The Supreme Court of Alabama upheld the verdict of a jury just like you. The Supreme Court of Alabama upheld the sentence of death in the electric chair to these nigras.

"Now, why did the Supreme Court of the United States overrule the finding of the supreme court of this state? Because communist sympathizers took up the cudgel. Because communist sympathizers marched in the streets, and sent letters and telegrams to the government, and did their unholy best to subvert justice and overturn the laws of this sovereign state."

An amen rose from the back of the courtroom.

"You have heard the testimony in this courtroom. The same testimony that those twelve men heard in Scottsboro two years ago. You have heard of the unspeakable ordeal suffered by Victoria Price, a white woman, at the hands of these nigras. The defense questions Mrs. Price's story. The defense questions the word of a white woman on the basis of a bunch of nigra lies and outsider propaganda. Did you ever hear of a more damnable effort to destroy and break down this girl?"

"No," came the response from the other side of the railing.

"How did they do it? They did it with money. Mr. Brodsky bought that fine suit of clothes Lester Carter wore to tell you his lies. Mr. Brodsky paid Lester Carter's rent. Mr. Brodsky gave Lester Carter spending money." His all-day singer's voice rose and fell in rhythm with the repetitions, and his body swayed in time. "That man Carterinsky—"

"Objection," Leibowitz shouted. "I move for a mistrial."

"Motion denied," Judge Horton said.

"That man Carter is a new kind of man to me. Did you watch his hands? If he had been with Brodsky another two weeks, he would have been down here with a pack on his back a-trying to sell you goods. Are you going to countenance that sort of thing?"

Several no's came back this time.

"Brodsky brought Ruby Bates down here too, Ruby Bates in her fancy New York clothes. Ruby Bates couldn't tell who paid for those fine clothes, until all of a sudden she remembered. A minister bought them for her." He paused. "She says." He got the laugh he was trolling for. "I tell you, gentlemen, Ruby Bates was guilty of perjury right here in this courtroom." He threw back his body and raised his hands heavenward. "May the Lord have mercy on the soul of Ruby Bates!"

No amens met this prayer.

He dropped his hands and lowered his eyes to the jury again. "Now, the question before you," he said, his voice building with each word, "is this. Is justice going to be bought and sold in Alabama with Jew money from New York?"

"Objection," Leibowitz shouted again. "I move for a mistrial."

"Overruled," Judge Horton answered. He turned to the jury. "Gentlemen, you will ignore the solicitor's words and put them out of your minds."

The spectators smirked. The jurors looked stern, as if they were trying to put the words *Jew* and *money* and *New York* out of their minds.

"Gentlemen of the jury," Wright went on, "a verdict of guilty in this case will resound around the world as a victory for law enforcement. Show them that Alabama justice cannot be bought and sold . . ." He hesitated long enough to let the jurors fill in the words he was not permitted to repeat, then returned to his seat.

Leibowitz stood and approached the jury slowly.

"Gentlemen of the jury," he began, "the less said in this courtroom about North and South, Negro and Jew, the better. I have no intention of assaulting your ears with ranting and raving. I appeal instead to your intelligence and reason. I address your sense of honor and duty to give even this poor scrap of colored humanity a fair, square deal."

He walked back to the table, took a sip of water, and faced the jury again.

"Now, as for the Jew money from New York, let me say this. When the hour of our country's need came, there was no question of Jew or gentile, of black or white. All together braved the smoke and flame of Flanders fields."

Two of the jurors shifted positions in their chairs. A third yawned. If Sam Leibowitz had not already lost them with talk of reason and logic and colored humanity, he would now with talk of Flanders fields. Antietam and Shiloh and Manassas were the battles seared in their memories. There, southern manhood had fought shoulder to shoulder against, not beside, the flotsam and jetsam he spoke of.

Leibowitz continued for the rest of Friday afternoon. On Saturday morning, he resumed his summation. He went over the testimony, citing the discrepancies, poking holes in the state's case. He questioned Victoria Price's character. He reminded them he was not defending Ruby Bates, who was not on trial. He assured them he was interested only in seeing justice done to that poor moronic colored boy over there.

I glanced at Haywood Patterson. He seemed to be following Leibowitz's words, but I could not be sure. He registered no emotion at the word *moronic*.

"I believe, before God," Leibowitz went on, "that these boys are the victims of a dastardly frame-up. Two years ago the defendant stood trial for the same crime at Scottsboro. The verdict was nothing more than a judicial lynching, a mockery of justice, and an insult to God himself. Do not let that mockery repeat itself. Do not insult the Almighty again. I ask you to consider the evidence, and if you do, you must acquit this poor piece of humanity."

He stood for a moment, as if stupefied that he had finished his summation, then walked slowly to the defense table and sat as if every bone in his body ached.

Tom Knight pushed back his chair and strode briskly to the jury.

"Gentlemen, I will not repeat my colleague's appeal to racial prejudice. Such emotions have no place here. I ask instead for a verdict of guilty with a sentence of death in the electric chair based solely on the evidence."

He proceeded to go through the evidence step by step. He cited every hole Leibowitz had torn in the state's case and tried to mend it. He arrived at Ruby's testimony.

"The attorney for the defense asks you to take the word of one southern woman against another. But the woman he asks you to believe is a known liar. She has changed her story again and again. She has admitted to lying in the past. She has sold her soul for a New York suit and a fancy hat."

Heads nodded to every accusation.

"On the evidence, gentlemen, there can be but one verdict, and that verdict is death, death in the electric chair for raping Victoria Price. Nothing else is possible. If you do not do that, if you shirk your duty and acquit this Negro, this thing"—his voice vibrated with disgust—"you might as well put a garland of roses around his neck, give him a supper, and send him to New York City in a high hat and morning coat, gray-striped trousers and spats. For that is what you will be doing."

Knight flashed his affable vote-getting smile at the twelve jurors and made his way to his seat.

Back at the hotel, we settled down for the wait. Some predicted it would not be long. At Scottsboro, the first jury had returned a verdict in less than an hour. Others were not so sure. At Scottsboro, the boys had not had Samuel Leibowitz defending them. Now and then word of the jurors' deliberations drifted back to the hotel. They had sent a messenger to Judge Horton to ask about certain evidence. No one knew what it was. They had taken a recess for dinner. They had returned from dinner. We scrutinized the shards of information like primitives casting animal bones for intimations of fate.

No one dared leave the hotel. We were afraid of missing something. We were also afraid. Rumors of lynch mobs and death threats and armed men wandering the streets swooped through the night air like bats. The sound of National Guard boots patrolling the grounds of the hotel was less reassuring than it should have been. I was glad the ILD, with the help of the sheriff, had smuggled Ruby out of town the morning after she spent the night in my room.

Late in the evening, I stopped by Tom Knight's rooms. The level of liquid in the big glass jug was low. Knight was holding forth, as usual, but his heartiness seemed forced and his laugh hollow. Meanness hung in the air. For the first time, he scented the possibility of defeat, and it poisoned his cordiality. We sensed it too, and it made us bloodthirsty.

At eleven-thirty, one of Knight's men arrived with the news that Judge Horton had ordered the jury sequestered for the night.

"One more for the road," Knight cried. His voice was too loud, and his hands, as he lifted the jug to refill glasses, shook. Moonshine slopped over the sides and onto the floor. We smiled and exchanged furtive glances. Most of us in that room believed the boys were innocent and wanted them acquitted. We also would not mind witnessing Knight's downfall. We were principled and right-thinking, but we were not nice.

On my way through the lobby, I ran into Abel. "You missed Knight's party," I said.

"I was at the jail."

"You walked to the jail!"

"With military escort. A couple of guardsmen were going down there, so I tagged along. It was quite a party."

"The mob outside?"

"The boys inside. They were singing spirituals. You should hear the pipes on Olen and Ozie They were so good the guards started making requests, and backed them up with cigarettes and some smuggled moonshine."

"I'm sorry I missed it."

His laugh was not kind. "I bet you are."

The sound of his laughter followed me into my room. In all the speculation about the verdict, Abel had been the only one who remembered the boys.

The next morning I awakened to church bells. It was Palm Sunday. As Sam Leibowitz observed, I am not a believer, but there was something chilling about the jury deliberations spilling into Holy Week.

I was sitting at my desk going over my notes from the previous day's proceedings when I heard the noise in the hall outside my room. Voices were calling to one another that the jury was in. I glanced at my watch. It was ten o'clock. They had been out for twenty-two hours. Surely that was a good sign. Bigotry is impatient. Reason takes its time. I grabbed my hat and handbag.

I don't think I will ever forget the walk to the courthouse. We moved like a small army. Leibowitz and Brodsky and Knight and his team led the way, and the rest of us fell in step behind them. I was sorry Ruby was not there. She deserved to be. She had risked more than any of us.

The courtroom was half empty. Perhaps word had not reached the churches. The only Negro present was the janitor. He stood in a corner, turning his cap in his hands, looking as if he wished he were somewhere else.

The lawyers and the press and the spectators milled about impatiently. We were waiting for Judge Horton, who had to drive over from Athens. People smoked and chewed and spat. The press doodled on pads we had at the ready. One reporter was writing alternate leads:

Haywood Patterson, 19, was found guilty of rape again today and sentenced to death by a Morgan County Jury.

A Morgan County jury found Haywood Patterson, 19, not guilty today of the rape he was convicted of two years ago at Scottsboro.

Captain Burleson entered the courtroom, followed by a detail of more than two dozen of his men. There were so many of them that at first I did not see Haywood. He was still wearing the too-small overalls. The guns of the two guards behind him were pressed into his back. They used the weapons to nudge him into his chair at the defense table, then took seats directly behind him. His face was impassive. He managed to take a cigarette from his pocket and light it with his manacled hands. Sam Leibowitz, cheeks hollow, eyes black-rimmed with sleeplessness, leaned over and whispered something. Haywood's face remained expressionless. A few feet away, at the state's table, Tom Knight sat erect, the muscles of his face twitching beneath sweat-slicked flushed skin.

A burst of laughter exploded from the jury room. Knight's face turned wine-dark. Leibowitz leaned over to Haywood and murmured again. This time Haywood nodded. Surely a jury who had just condemned a man to death would not be laughing.

The clock on the wall of the courtroom said ten-thirty. Had Horton insisted on finishing his breakfast before starting for Decatur?

"He's here," one of the reporters standing near the window said. A moment later, Judge Horton entered the courtroom and took his place on the bench. Below him, the stenographer opened his notebook to a fresh page.

"Let the jury come in," Judge Horton said.

A bailiff opened the door to the anteroom. The men filed in. They too looked exhausted, but some of them were grinning. The next-to-the-last man said something to the one behind him. They both laughed. Beside me at the press table, the reporter drew a circle around his acquittal lead.

The laughter died. The only sound in the courtroom was the shuffle of the jurors' shoes as they gathered before the bench. They had done the same thing ten days earlier, when they had raised their hands and sworn to render a true verdict. Eugene Bailey, the draftsman whom they had elected foreman, stood among them, folding and unfolding a slip of paper. Every eye was on him.

I glanced over at Haywood. He was still sitting behind the defense table. No one had thought to tell him to stand.

"Have you agreed upon a verdict?" Judge Horton asked.

Bailey went on folding and unfolding the slip of paper. The juror next to him gave him a nudge. "We have, Your Honor."

"Let me have it, then," the judge said.

Bailey stepped forward and handed the judge the slip of paper. Horton took it from him, opened it, and read. Not a muscle in his face moved. He raised his eyes to the courtroom. He did not look at Haywood. No one was looking at Haywood. Every eye was on the judge and that slip of paper.

" 'We find the defendant guilty as charged,'" he read, " 'and fix the punishment at death in the electric chair.'"

Leibowitz passed a hand over his face. Brodsky slumped in his chair. For once, Tom Knight remained quiet. Even Wright, the all-day singer, was silent. Not a sound broke the hush. The jury had condemned one man, but sentenced nine to death. The trials of the other boys would be carbon copies.

Then, as if at a signal, everything started to happen at once. The judge was on his feet thanking the jurors. Reporters were crowding around the two teams of attorneys. Tom Knight, his old ebullient self, was crowing about justice being done. Sam Leibowitz, reeling from exhaustion and his first loss to the electric chair, was railing against judicial lynchings and swearing to appeal. People were shouting and shoving and racing out of the courtroom. And in the midst of it all, Haywood Patterson sat smoking a cigarette. His face was a mask. His eyes were as impenetrable as the shiny dark glasses of the deputies. He was not merely alone in that courtroom. He was nonexistent. The world had forgotten him. Even the guards had stopped paying attention to him now that they did not have to protect him from the violence an acquittal would have brought on. And as I stood thinking that, I knew I was writing the lead to my article.

I started toward the defense table where he sat smoking. "I'm so sorry," I said quietly. He looked up at me, but his face remained unreadable and his eyes blank. They did not change as a guard approached to take him away.

"It's your own fault, boy," he said as he prodded Haywood to his feet. "If you got yourself a good God-fearing Christian lawyer from hereabouts instead of that JewlawyerfromNewYork, you could've got off easy with life."

A spark flashed in Haywood's eyes. I could not tell if it was anger or merely the reflection of our unforgivable whiteness.

"I'd sooner die in the electric chair," he said, "than go to jail for something I ain't done."

Haywood Patterson had written the last line of my story.

Book Three

If you ever saw those creatures, those bigots whose mouths are slits in their faces, whose eyes popped out at you like frogs, whose chins dripped tobacco juice, bewhiskered and filthy, you would not ask how they could do it.

—*Samuel Leibowitz, 1933*

She [Ruby Bates] has become Harlem's darling, set foot in the White House and addressed the speakers of Congress.

—*Huntsville* Times, *1933*

If you had been in the Pennsylvania Station at 4:23 the following afternoon when the train from Birmingham pulled in, you would never have guessed that a jury had found Haywood Patterson guilty and sentenced him to death a second time. Men and women and children, black and white, old and young, tall and short, suited and overalled, fashionably hatted and pedestrianly capped, bare-faced and rouged, laughing and crying, crowded several thousand strong into the vast concourse and spilled down the stairs to the platform. As Sam Leibowitz stepped off the train, they swarmed around him and spirited him up the stairs. For a moment I lost sight of him. Then he reappeared, fighting to keep his balance and hold on to his hat, as he bobbed above the group of men who had hoisted him to their shoulders. He sailed across the concourse, an unsteady figure suspended between the mob of humanity below and the light-filled space above, buoyed up by two words, shouted and chanted and cheered over and over again. One was the name of the man who had become synonymous, in these circles at least, with heroism. The other was the name of the town that was a cry of shame.

Leibowitz, they sang.

Scottsboro, they howled.

Leibowitz!

Scottsboro!

They carried him down the concourse and up the broad marble stairs past the newsstands and the florist shop and the big Savarin Restaurant and out to Seventh Avenue, where another group of men had commandeered a cab. The last I saw of Sam Leibowitz that afternoon was the back of a man's head beneath a knocked-askew homburg in the rear window of a taxi pulling away from the curb.

For a moment the crowd disintegrated into a collection of individuals. Men wondered if they should return to their offices. Women debated stopping at Child's for a cup of tea or going home to start dinner. The lackluster possibilities dimmed the afternoon sun and sapped spirits. Then someone started to chant, Free the Scottsboro boys, and the individual bodies coalesced into a single organism again. It marched east along Thirty-fourth Street, turned north on Broadway, and kept going until it splintered against several squads of extra police blocking Forty-sixth Street, but it fought through and fused again to head north to Columbus Circle and on up Broadway to Eighty-sixth Street, where a phalanx of mounted police and radio cars and a paddy wagon finally broke the mob down to its parts. Miraculously, only one injury occurred and one arrest resulted. The arrest was of a man who allegedly kicked a police officer in the mouth. The injury was to the police officer who was allegedly kicked in the mouth.

A few days later Sam Leibowitz went to the Salem Methodist Episcopal Church in Harlem and told a crowd of four thousand supporters that he would not give up his battle to free the boys if he had to sell his house and home. The writer in me heard the redundancy, but the reporter noted the cheering crowd.

"I promise you, citizens of Harlem, that I will fight with every drop of blood in my body and with the help of God that those Scottsboro boys shall be free."

As the audience rose, chanting and cheering and amening, the Reverend Frederick A. Cullen stepped to the lectern. The pastor was the father of the poet Countee Cullen. Perhaps that explained his vivid imagery. He took Leibowitz's hand in his and raised their clasped fists above their heads.

"We hail a new Moses," he thundered to the crowd. "A new Moses."

The man I'd had lunch with three months earlier had wanted respectability. The man who returned from Decatur had won canonization.

Outrage against the verdict continued to build. In Harlem, the publisher of *The Amsterdam News* posted a notice asking people to sign a petition to demand justice for the Scottsboro boys. Nine hours later, twenty thousand people had put their names on the list, and more were waiting in line. Farther afield, at the Phoenix Theater on Charing Cross Road in London, the Black Flashes, the Eight Black Streaks, the Mississippi Page Boys, the Hot Shots, and Black Bottom Johnny, not to mention several lesser lights, performed in a gala benefit to raise money for the cause. But those stars had nothing on the main attraction here at home.

Ruby was almost as famous as a moving picture star. Her life story, as told to me, had begun appearing in *The New Order* as soon as she testified. Since coming north again, she had granted interviews to several major newspapers. She did not even mind the headline in the New York *World-Telegram*.

RUBY BATES, "POOR WHITE
TRASH," TO SPEAK HERE

The ILD arranged for her and Mother Patterson, as the party had christened Haywood's mother, to lead a march on Washington. People had stopped talking about the ILD's preferring ten dead martyrs to ten new members. They had lost the most recent round, but they were keeping the boys alive.

Alice took me shopping, just like she promised, and I got a swell new outfit for going down to Washington. The coat had a belt that tied real tight around the waist and fancy sleeves that flared out like bells over the elbows with another set of long tight sleeves coming out from under them. I made her get me a hat too, with a brim that went down on one side and up on the other. I looked as good as any of them folks, even the fancy white ladies, only not so many of them as coloreds turned out for the trip. I don't hold nothing against that. Mother Patterson and I got real friendly since I come up North again, specially since the folks at the ILD got us living together in someone's apartment. Being with her and all them colored folk fixing to march was almost like being down home, only here folks reckoned being good to coloreds was something to brag on, not be 'shamed of.

The morning we were fixing to set out on the march, Alice come by early and carried me and Mother Patterson to a place called Union Square. That was where folks were fixing to get into buses and trucks and autos to go to Washington. There was a heap of them, and they kept walking up to me and shaking my hand, and patting me on the back, and saying they were mighty happy I done the right thing. I wished Victoria and my brother and all them other folks down home could hear the way they carried on. Then me and Alice got in one auto with some fellas from the ILD, and Mother Patterson got in another, and we set out.

It was a long ride, but I didn't mind none. The other folks did a heap of talking, and I did some sleeping, and we sang songs I never did hear before, about dumping the bosses off your back, and the starvation army, and the union maid who never was afraid of the goons and the ginks and the company finks and the deputy sheriff who made the raid. When we got to Baltimore, they carried me to a auditorium full of folks, and I stood up and told the things the ILD folks taught me.

"The Scottsboro boys are innocent," I said into a microphone, and folks started whooping and hollering and stomping.

"I lied. I lied on account of I was excited by the ruling class of the South." Now I reckoned they were fixing to tear the place down.

"We are going to Washington," I said, and I had to wait for the cheering to stop. "We are going Washington to make sure the Scottsboro boys do not die."

I never heard nothing like them folks clapping and hollering and stomping for me. I reckon Victoria ain't never going to hear nothing like it neither. When me and her set out for Chattanooga that time, she said we were going to be in high cotton. I reckon I finally was.

We drove into Washington through sheets of rain. It was coming down so hard that the wipers could not clear the windshield fast enough, and Ike, the ILD man who was driving, had to navigate with his head out the window. When Ike joked that the bosses had probably paid off God to make sure it rained on the march, I felt Ruby, beside me in the back seat, tense. All the fuss had made her forget about going to torment, but the crack about God reminded her that He had not forgotten about her.

The rain began to taper off a little before noon, and the marshals swung into action, directing people here and there. In half an hour the lines were formed, and we set out for the White House, three thousand strong, with Ruby and Mother Patterson in the lead. James Ford, a Negro Communist Party leader, William L. Patterson, Negro national secretary of the ILD, and a few others marched right behind them. I tagged along after the group. The party liked the stories I was turning out. They also believed I could handle Ruby. And Harry was vouching for me.

The rest of the marchers stopped at the gate while the guards let ten or a dozen of us at the head of the line through. We made our way beneath the dripping trees up the drive to the White House. Louis Howe, the president's official secretary and unofficial henchman, met us on the portico. He was a small man with bulging eyes and a pockmarked face—the ugliest man in New York State, he used to call himself when the president was still governor—but his manner was smooth and practiced. He shook hands with Ruby and Mother Patterson and the two Negro men. He told them how sorry the president was that he could not receive them, but he was closeted with Dr. Hjalmar Schacht. Most of us knew we stood no chance of getting in to see Roosevelt. He had been in office barely two months, just a little more than halfway through what would become known as the Hundred Days, and could not afford to alienate his southern base by receiving a group of Negroes demanding justice for the alleged black rapists of two white women. ILD strategy calculated that for publicity purposes being turned away was as effective as seeing the president, but the fact that Roosevelt had chosen to meet with an envoy from a fascist state rather than the representatives of the forgotten man, to whom he had sworn a new deal, did not sit well. We made our way back down the drive, regrouped with the other marchers outside the gates, and started along Fifteenth Street toward the Capitol. By that time, most of us looked like drowned rats, but I was proud of Ruby. She marched along at a brisk clip without a word of complaint, though I knew the soaking of her brand-new outfit must be breaking her heart.

When we reached the Capitol, the marchers stopped outside, and our small contingent climbed the steps and followed a guard down the marble halls to Speaker Rainey's office. We crowded into the room, and James Ford stepped forward and handed the speaker a petition for legislation guaranteeing enforcement of the Thirteenth and Fourteen Amendments. "We demand congressional action for the unconditional release of the Scottsboro boys," he said.

Rainey took the paper from Ford, but did not glance down at it. "The petition will be referred to the Judiciary Committee," he said. "As for the Scottsboro case, that is a matter for the courts. Congress has no authority to direct the release of men charged with a crime."

He was right, of course, but this was about public relations, not legal maneuvers. Two news photographers had followed us into the speaker's office. A moment passed. I held my breath. I knew what was supposed to happen, but Ruby seemed to have forgotten, or else her stage fright had returned. We were all staring at her, but her eyes were on her soaked feet. This is no time for worrying about shoes, I wanted to tell her. The silence dragged on. I was standing at the edge of the group, too far away to give her a nudge.

The speaker began to turn away. Perhaps one of the two men or Mother Patterson delivered the shove I wanted to. Perhaps Ruby remembered her part on her own. She stepped forward. The speaker turned back to her. She repeated the words she had been told to say.

"The Scottsboro boys are innocent."

"You testified once that they were guilty?" the speaker said.

"Yes, sir."

"Now you retract?"

"Yes, sir."

"What caused you to change your mind?"

"I didn't want to see innocent boys suffer," she said, and I heard the shutters of the news cameras click.

By the time we reached Vice President Garner's Senate office, Ruby did not need prompting.

"The Scottsboro boys are innocent," she repeated in bell-like tones I had never heard her use before. Again, the camera shutters clicked.

Over the years, Ruby would put up scores of newspaper and magazine pictures on the walls of a succession of houses, but as far as I knew she never put up any photos of her talking to the vice president of the United States. The fact that she did not or could not show off her moment of glory struck me as one more injustice against her. Abel said it was merely an irony.

The march to the White House was only the beginning. When we returned to New York, Ruby starred in a fund-raising reenactment of the trial at Madison Square Garden. Harry and his committee did not think small.

The huge auditorium at Fiftieth Street and Eighth Avenue was almost as full as it had been for the fight between the Spanish heavyweight Isidore Gastanaga and Paul Pirrone a few weeks earlier, or so people said. I am not a fight fan.

The crowd was motley and high-spirited. Some of the men and women in the front rows wore evening dress. Workers and party stalwarts, both Negro and white, who crowded the stands, were less well turned out. The mechanically cooled air—the refrigeration system, which had not functioned properly since the building opened in 1925, was finally working—throbbed with high hopes and good intentions. Actors played Judge Horton and Attorney General Knight and the defendants and the jury. Leibowitz and Brodsky and Lester Carter played themselves. At the end of Lester's testimony, the man impersonating Attorney General Knight turned to the audience and roared, "If we had Ruby Bates here, we'd show you that Lester Carter is a liar."

A voice came over the loudspeaker. "The defense calls Ruby Bates."

The words echoed through the auditorium. The lights dimmed. A spotlight swung through the crowd and came to rest on one of the entrances to the arena. The doors opened. Ruby came through it as if propelled from behind and stood blinking into the spotlight trained on her. The huge auditorium fell silent. Then the audience was on its feet, clapping and shouting and cheering.

Joe Brodsky stepped out of the shadows, gave Ruby his arm, and led her down the aisle through the riotous crowd. The audience took a few minutes to quiet sufficiently for her to take the chair representing the witness stand and repeat the testimony she had given in the courtroom, edited for dramatic purposes and delivered with a brio she had not shown in Decatur. Ruby finished telling her story and stepped aside, but her part was not over. After an actor playing Wade Wright ranted about Jew money from New York, and Leibowitz gave a stirring summation to the jury, she stepped back into a circle of light. It beat down on her like the eye of God. She lifted her face to the crowd.

"I tell you those boys never raped me," she said. "They are innocent."

The crowd, as they say, went wild.

After the program, I went around to the stage entrance to congratulate Ruby. I was not the only one. The mob was so thick I could not get near the door. Sam Leibowitz came out, and Joe Brodsky, and some of the actors. Ruby was one of the last to emerge.

A group of young women surged toward her. She took a step back, and even in the dim light from the streetlamp, I saw the fear in her face, and knew again what a mob meant to her.

Several of the girls pushed their programs toward her. She shrank farther back.

"Would you sign my program, please, Miss Bates?" There was no mistaking the awe in the girl's voice. Even Ruby heard it.

"You want me to write my name?" Ruby asked.

The girl handed Ruby the program and a pen, and even produced a book for her to lean on as she wrote. I could not be sure, because it had no dust jacket, but it looked like a battered edition of *Ten Days That Shook the World*.

"Could I have your autograph too, Miss Bates?"

"Would you sign mine, Miss Bates?" the others chimed in, one after another.

I stood on the edges watching. Unlike some of the boys she had accused, she knew how to write her name. She had never suffered the shame of the scratched X. But it was not something she was accustomed to doing. She leaned on *Ten Days That Shook the World* and began to write. Her hand moved slowly, forming the letters carefully. The tip of her tongue protruded between her teeth as she concentrated.

When she had signed all the programs and her fans had drifted off, I stepped forward and held my program out to her.

"Will you autograph this for me, Miss Bates?"

I was joking, but she took the program from me and began to write her name on it. And why, I realized with shame, should she not?

While Ruby was signing programs and giving speeches and raising money for the boys, Judge Horton was sitting in his handsome house with THREE CHEERS FOR LINCOLN carved in the door, brooding about their plight. I did not find out about that until later, when I returned to Athens to interview him.

After Haywood Patterson's conviction, he postponed the trials of the other eight boys on the grounds that local tensions were running too high. Within days, rumors that he was dissatisfied with the verdict began to circulate. He was more than dissatisfied. He was so certain the trial had been a travesty and his beloved Alabama had disgraced herself that he approached Attorney General Knight with a suggestion. He should have known better, but men who value decency, duty, and truth in themselves often see it where it does not exist in others. He proposed to Knight that the state *nol. pros.* the rest of the proceedings and pardon Haywood Patterson. Knight told Horton if they did that, they would be committing political suicide.

"What does that have to do with the case?" Horton asked.

Knight laughed.

I was not in Athens at the end of June when Judge Horton convened the court. Few people were. Even the ILD attorneys thought they were merely laying the groundwork for another appeal to the Supreme Court. Judge Horton caught them all off guard.

He began with a detailed analysis of the evidence that had convicted Haywood Patterson. Victoria did not emerge in good odor. "Her manner of testifying and demeanor on the stand militate against her," the judge read from his opinion. "Her testimony was contradictory, often evasive, and time and again she refused to answer pertinent questions. The proof tends strongly to show that she knowingly testified falsely."

When I told Ruby about Judge Horton's findings, she wanted to know why there was so much about Victoria and so little about her. I tried to explain that she should be happy she was barely mentioned, since the judge was citing only false testimony and faulty evidence. She looked pleased at that. She was coming along nicely.

Judge Horton set aside Haywood Patterson's conviction and granted a new trial, though he was hoping the state would not prosecute. Again, he should have known better. Minutes after he adjourned the court, Tom Knight announced he would retry Haywood Patterson at the earliest possible moment. Then he played a trump card. Orville Gilley, who had not testified at the second trial because he had been hoboing somewhere in California, would take the stand for the state and corroborate every detail of Victoria Price's story.

Ruby was terrified. She swore she would not go back to Alabama for the proceedings. She'd had enough of threats and vilification and burning crosses. Who could blame her? She was also having the time of her life on the road. I still have some of the programs from her tour. The cities read like stickers on an old vaudevillian's suitcase. Syracuse, Buffalo, Cleveland, Detroit, Chicago, Milawaukee, Minneapolis, Des Moines, Omaha. Lester was on some of the bills, and Mother Patterson too, but the name at the top was always Ruby Bates.

The tour was long and exhausting, but Ruby did not find it arduous. She was accustomed to hopping freights and sleeping in boxcars and hobo jungles. An old jalopy or bus ticket and someone's spare bed was going first class to her.

I followed Ruby's progress during those months, though I did not see much of her. I was busy with other stories and different people.

That summer, the Bonus Army of war veterans, who had descended on Washington a year earlier, returned to demand their money again. President Roosevelt was no more eager to give them their benefits than President Hoover had been, but instead of leaving them to their own meager resources in makeshift shantytowns, FDR had the Veterans Administration set up a camp for them at Fort Hunt in Virginia, near Mount Vernon. It boasted field kitchens, and medical facilities, and trucks to take the men back and forth to town. The marchers did not believe Roosevelt would pay them, but they were hoping that, unlike Hoover, he would not send the army to rout them. The force he sent packed a different wallop. I know, because I was there.

In the years since the day Eleanor Roosevelt paid a visit to the Bonus Army camp, stories have grown up around the incident. One was that Louis Howe, the president's secretary, tricked her into going. Another was that she had no idea where she was headed when he invited her for a drive. But Eleanor Roosevelt needed neither urging nor ruses to get her to visit a bunch of down-and-out veterans and their families. When she had seen the headlines about the troops' charge and the teargassed baby a year earlier, she had cried in desperation and anguish, she would tell me later. The difficulty would have been keeping her away from that scene of misery and desperation, not persuading her to tour it.

Four days before the visit, she informed reporters that she planned to drive out to the camp to inspect conditions. The day of the trip, rumors began to circulate among the press. She was going without a Secret Service detail and taking no reporters with her.

I was waiting at the gates when Mrs. Roosevelt pulled up in her red roadster. Actually, she swerved up and slammed on the brakes. The first lady was a fast and erratic driver. Louis Howe, the man who had turned Ruby and the rest of us away from the White House, was beside her. Mrs. Roosevelt climbed out of the roadster. Mr. Howe did not move.

"Inspect the camp," I heard him tell her as she closed the door. "Get their stories, and their gripes."

"What are you going to do?" she asked.

He pulled his hat low over his eyes, crossed his arms over his chest, and hunkered down in the passenger seat. "Take a nap.

"Don't forget to tell them that Franklin sent you," he called after her, as she started toward the gate.

I approached her before she reached the entrance, introduced myself, and reminded her that I had been at her first press conference a few months earlier. She held out her hand, gave me the smile that was a joke in the cartoons and caricatures and brilliant in real life, and said she remembered me, as well as my mother from her work with the Women's League for Peace and Freedom. She added that she had read my pieces on Scottsboro. I asked her what she had thought of them. She hesitated. The case was a political hot potato for her husband. "I found them sympathetic." She was, I would learn, a consummate politician herself.

"The men are waiting, Eleanor," Mr. Howe called from the front seat of the roadster.

"I had not planned to take along any members of the press," she said to me.

I told her I had no wish to interfere with her tour of the camp, but I had written a story on the Bonus Army the year before, when President Hoover had ordered them driven out of town and General MacArthur had routed them, and had returned now to see how they were faring under her husband's administration. She stood staring at me for a moment. I did not know whether she believed my presence was a coincidence, but I suspected she was thinking of my Scottsboro articles again.

"Then we might as well combine forces," she said and started toward the gate, past a jalopy with a sign painted on the side: WE DONE A GOOD JOB IN FRANCE, NOW YOU DO A GOOD JOB IN AMERICA. In a few steps, Mrs. Roosevelt's low-heeled oxfords and my own sturdy walking shoes were covered with mud. Ruby would have been scandalized.

I trailed her around the camp for more than two hours. She was magnificent. She did not just walk through the field kitchen. She stopped to ask what the men were being fed, then lifted pot covers to see that the officials were not trying to hoodwink her. In the infirmary, she inquired about the number of doctors and nurses and sick men, and the availability of medicines, and the protocols of treatment. She made her way up and down the lines of tents and stopped to chat with the men along the way, asking their names, and hometowns, and where they had served during the war. Her voice darted about, high and flighty as a bird, but her manner was down-to-earth and easy.

Every account of Mrs. Roosevelt's visit to the camp that afternoon ends with the same line, ascribed to an anonymous veteran. The comment is so perfect that it sounds apocryphal, but it is not. I know, because I heard the veteran utter it as we left.

"Hoover sent the army," he told the group of men waving her goodbye. "Roosevelt sent his wife."

When we reached the roadster, Mrs. Roosevelt asked where I was going. I told her I planned to catch a train back to New York. She said she and Mr. Howe would drop me at Union Station.

Strange as it seems now, Mrs. Roosevelt had no police escort or Secret Service detail that day. She often managed to get away without one. She careened through traffic talking and laughing and, it seemed to me, enjoying herself immensely. When we reached the station, I climbed out and thanked her for the lift.

"Send me your article on the Bonus Marchers, Miss Whittier," she said. "And anything else you think I should see."

I promised her I would do that.

26

RUBY BATES DYING

—New York Times, *November 25, 1933*

In October, the state of Alabama removed the Scottsboro case from Judge Horton's jurisdiction and transferred it to Judge William Washington Callahan. Callahan, who had attended neither college nor law school, only read law in a local office, told the press he planned to debunk the Scottsboro case. No one was sure what he meant, but the phrase did not imply an inordinate respect for the legal process. He refused to provide facilities for the press and banned photographers from the courtroom. "There ain't going to be no more picture-snapping around here," he announced after two photographers were brought before the bench for trying to capture the facade of the courthouse on film.

No Negroes attended this round of trials. They did not come within a several-block radius of the courthouse. They did not dare to. The town was even more of a tinderbox this time around.

Protests continued farther afield. One Saturday night, four members of the CP handcuffed themselves to a traffic light at Broadway and Forty-seventh Street and threw the keys down a sewer opening. All over the theater district, curtains went up late and playgoers stumbled to their seats halfway through first acts because of the traffic jams and confusion.

I decided not to go south for the this round of trials. They promised to be a repeat of earlier travesties and injustices. Harry agreed. Our reasoning was political, but our motives were also personal. We were spending a lot of time together. I had not told him about that night with Abel. Confession might have eased my conscience, but it would have done nothing for Harry's peace of mind or the magazine's morale, in view of the fact that he and Abel had to work together. Or perhaps I was merely letting myself off the hook.

Harry had not stopped trying to persuade me to join the party. Sometimes, lying together late at night, our bodies humming with recent sex, like the idling engines of two well-tuned cars, we would spar about it. His low voice, mingling with the purr, gave an urgency to his arguments, and I often succumbed. After all, I subscribed to the principles. And the romance of being one with all those others who shared my passions was seductive. But the next morning, when the hard surfaces and sharp edges of the world once again took shape in the light filtering through the window, I retreated from the brink.

Ruby did not want to go south for the trials either, though the ILD was putting pressure on her to. That was why, when she turned up on my doorstep one night in November when Harry was out of town, I was sure it was a ruse.

I opened the door into the dim hallway to find her leaning against the wall.

"I got awful cramps," she whimpered, "but it ain't my monthlies. And I'm burning up too."

I drew her into the apartment and closed the door behind her. As soon as I saw her in the light, I knew this was not a ploy. I felt her forehead. Her skin was on fire and clammy to the touch. I led her into the bedroom, took off her coat and shoes, and made her get into bed. After I put a cold compress on her head, I went back to the living room and began calling doctors. The ringing on the other end of the line seemed to go on forever. I was not surprised. It was after ten.

I went back into the bedroom. She was curled on her side in a fetal position, her face covered with a film of sweat, her damp hair plastered to her head. I asked her if she felt well enough to get up.

She opened her eyes. They looked glassy and febrile. "You going to throw me out?"

I sat on the side of the bed and stroked her wet hair back from her forehead. "I'm not throwing you out, Ruby. I'm taking you to the hospital."

Her glazed eyes blinked. "Hospital's where folks go to die."

"It's also where they go to get better. Can you sit up?"

I did not give her a chance to answer, but lifted her to a sitting a position. As I got down on my knees to slide her shoes on, she swooned back onto the bed. This time I lifted her more gently and held on while I struggled to get her arms into the sleeves of her coat. I buttoned it, propped her against the headboard, then put on my own.

"Hold on to me." I positioned her arm around my shoulders, slipped mine around her waist, and got her to a standing position. We made our way across the apartment, into the hall, and down the stairs with Ruby hanging on to the banister and me steadying myself against the wall. As we came out on the stoop, a taxi cruised by. Years ago, Abel had taught me a two-fingers-in-the-mouth whistle designed to stop any cabbie. I put my fingers in my mouth and blew. The driver slammed on the brakes. I got Ruby down the steps and across the sidewalk, and opened the door to the taxi.

The cabbie turned around and looked at us sourly. "I ain't taking no drunks."

"She's not drunk," I said.

I could tell from his expression that he did not believe me.

"And I'll double the fare if you get us to St. Vincent's fast."

The driver overcame his temperance scruples and shifted the gears.

Emergency rooms were not as crowded in those days. They wheeled Ruby away from me within minutes. A man in a white coat with a stethoscope around his neck returned a little while later. He introduced himself as Dr. Lacey.

I asked if she was going to be all right. He answered with a question of his own.

"Are you a relative?"

I envisioned Mrs. Bates sitting in Alabama in one more of a succession of crumbling shotgun houses. I thought of Ruby's brother, who had sent her a hundred dollars and told her to go as far away as the money would take her and stay there. "If your own kin don't want nothing to do with you," Ruby had said when she'd got the letter, "you best not expect nothing from strangers."

"She's my sister." I could hear the defiance in my voice. I was daring him to believe me. But he had more pressing matters on his mind.

"She has a pelvic inflammatory disease," he said. "As a result of gonorrhea," he added disapprovingly, and I felt a momentary regret for the sister lie, followed by a flash of shame for the regret. "It infected her tubes and spilled into her peritoneum. The result is similar to a perforated appendix. I'm having her prepared for surgery. We don't have much time."

The last I saw of Ruby that night was a white sheet on a gurney disappearing through pale green doors. The color reminded me of the trees she had described going by the gondola that afternoon two and a half years earlier. It also made me think of the darker green door to the execution chamber in the Kilby death house.

I went to a pay telephone and sent a wire to Sam Leibowitz in Decatur telling him his star witness would not be able to testify after all. Then I made my way to a bleak white room that smelled of antiseptic and stale coffee, and sat down to wait.

A few minutes later, a young nurse in a wimple came through and asked if there was anything she could do for me. I thanked her and told her I was all right.

"He should be out soon," she said.

"He?"

"Isn't that your husband with the broken arm?"

"I'm waiting for the girl they just took into surgery."

Her dimpled smile froze into a grimace as the nature of Ruby's problem registered. She turned and left without a word.

I was alone in the waiting room again. I moved from the sofa to a chair, then back to the sofa. The hard white light made my head ache. The hospital smell made me queasy. I walked to the widow, pried open two slats of the venetian blind, and peered out. I was sure the sky would be turning from black to gray. The street lay in darkness, broken only by circles of illumination falling from the streetlights. A single car cruised by. I went back to the sofa, sat, and closed my eyes. When I opened them, the doctor was standing in front of me. I did not think I had fallen asleep, but I could not be sure.

"We cleaned her up," he said, and I could not help noticing the unmedical terminology. "But we're not out of the woods yet."

"Can I see her?"

He shook his head sternly. "Go home and get some rest. Your sister has a long battle ahead of her, and she's going to need you."

The sun was coming up as I let myself into the apartment. The Western Union boy turned up a few minutes later. I tore open the envelope. The wire was from Sam Leibowitz.

JULIUS APPLEBAUM ON WAY TO BEDSIDE STOP WILL TAKE HER TESTIMONY AT ONCE AS AN ANTE-MORTEM STATEMENT UNDER LAW.

For two days Julius Applebaum sat cooling his heels in the hospital waiting room. The doctor would not let anyone except immediate family in to see Ruby. That meant me. He would certainly not permit a stranger to take a statement from her. Applebaum begged the doctor. The lives of nine young men were at stake, he pleaded. The doctor said he knew nothing about that. His responsibility was to the one young woman in his care.

"A tramp," Applebaum spat out the word. "She lied about those boys. And now she's dying because she got gonorrhea more times than I got fingers and toes."

"What's the charge, Mr. Applebaum, lying or promiscuity?" I snapped.

Two male heads swiveled to me. They had forgotten I was there. Now that they remembered, they were annoyed at my outburst. They turned back to each other.

"You want to save lives, Doc? Think of those nine innocent boys," Applebaum insisted.

"My responsibility is to my patient," the doctor repeated.

On the third day after Ruby's surgery, the doctor finally permitted Applebaum to take her statement. It was on its way to Sam Leibowitz within the hour.

That evening the doctor told me he was moving Ruby from intensive care to a ward. I told him I would pay for a private room. He must have suspected by then that we were not sisters, or if we were, we had been raised under grossly different circumstances, but as he had told Applebaum, saving his patient's life was his only interest. He said he would arrange to have her moved to a private room.

By the end of the week, she was sitting up in bed, eating the meals served to her on trays, and paging through the newspapers and magazines I brought her. As she was the first to admit, she had never had it so good.

She even had visitors. People from the ILD came to see her, and the various party members who had put her up during her days in

New York, and Haywood Patterson's mother. I was there when Mrs. Patterson visited, and I picked up again on something I had noticed on the trip to Washington. Ruby was most comfortable with the woman who had the most reason to hate her. When she was with Mrs. Patterson, she did not watch what she said or how she said it. Jane Patterson was easier too. Each of them knew how to treat the other. They were less sure about how to treat us. They did not quite trust the way we treated them either.

Even Abel paid a visit. I was as surprised to see him there as Ruby. He brought calla lilies, which made her blush with pleasure, and stayed for almost an hour. She had the time of her life.

Only when he stood up to leave did I realize why he had come. He was doing research.

I followed him into the hall. "I hope you're not planning to put this in your play."

"This?"

"Her illness."

He stood in the bright white hall grinning at me. "I didn't know you were such a prude. No, Miss Grundy, I will not put Ruby's hysterectomy due to an advanced case of gonorrhea in the play. I want the audience to root for her, not boo her off the stage."

Each morning, I read Ruby the newspaper accounts of the previous day's trial proceedings. Judge Callahan turned out to be as bad as we had feared. Leibowitz requested a twenty-four-hour postponement so the jury could hear the testimony Ruby had finally given Applebaum. The judge refused, and Ruby's evidence was never heard. That was the least of Callahan's ploys.

He objected to the defense's questions even when the prosecution did not. Charging the jury, he informed them no white woman would yield sexually to a Negro man of her own volition. He instructed the jurors on the proper form for convicting, but neglected to tell them how they were to go about acquitting, until the prosecution, fearing the appeal Leibowitz was planning, reminded him.

For the third time, a jury found Haywood Patterson guilty and sentenced him to the electric chair.

Ruby's testimony did arrive in time to be read at Clarence Norris's trial. "The nine Negroes did not commit this crime," she swore. "They are innocent boys. They did not rape Victoria Price or myself."

The jury found Clarence Norris guilty and sentenced him to death in the electric chair.

A play of terrifying and courageous bluntness of statement—thoughtfully developed, lucidly explained and played with great resolution . . . For once good works match the crusader's intentions.

—Brooks Atkinson's review of They Shall Not Die, *a play based on the Scottsboro case by John Wexley, 1934*

When the curtain fell on the third act of "They Shall Not Die," . . . I experienced a sensation the theatre never had given me before . . . I had seen reality in grease-paint.

—Raymond Daniell, 1934

Three days after Judge Callahan postponed the trials of the other boys, on the grounds that Sam Leibowitz had already begun appeals to the Alabama Supreme Court and the judge did not want to waste the county's money, the doctor said Ruby could go home from the hospital.

"I heard the good news," I said as I entered her room that evening. She was sitting up in bed wearing a blue bed jacket I had bought her because it matched her eyes, but she did not look happy. "Aren't you pleased?"

"I reckon."

I sat in the chair beside the bed. "What's wrong?"

"The doctor says I can go home, but I ain't got no home to go to."

"What about the ILD apartment?"

"That ain't no kind of home."

"Do you want to go back to Alabama?"

"Ain't no way I can do that."

"Then what would you like?"

She looked down at her lap, then up at me from under her lashes. "I was thinking I could come stay with you again. Just for a spell."

I should have seen it coming.

"There isn't any room."

"Your place get smaller since I was there back last winter? I wouldn't disconvenience you none. I could sleep on the sofa."

There were half a dozen reasons why I did not want Ruby to stay with me. "All right," I said, "but just for a few nights, until you're feeling entirely recovered."

She grinned, then remembered herself and covered her mouth with her hand.

The next day, I brought Ruby back to my apartment. Harry was annoyed. Taking in a single stray did not hasten the revolution. It merely interfered with our sex life.

Abel was amused. "Forget Joan of Arc. Now it's Lady Bountiful."

My mother was worried. "You can't undo the past," she warned me.

"I'm not trying to undo Ruby's past. I'm just trying to help her build some kind of a future."

"I wasn't talking about Ruby," she said.

Abel's play was to go into tryouts in Washington in early February. The producer had decided on Washington rather than Boston, New Haven, or Philadelphia because of the political and social significance of the play. He should have known better. Perhaps he did know better. A week before the first performance, the Theatre Guild announced a cancellation. District of Columbia laws, the guild said, prevented the three child actors from performing. Most people, however, read between the lines and understood the real reason for the change in plans. Despite the Brain Trusters from Harvard and Columbia and the bright young things with social consciences from all over the country who were flooding into town to work for the new administration, Washington remained a southern town. It would not welcome, or even abide, a play about Scottsboro.

The cancellation, as the producer had probably suspected, only piqued interest in the play.

"Banned in Boston means sold-out houses in New York," Abel told me. "I'm counting on banned in D.C. having the same effect."

The ILD brought Ruby, who was on the road again, back to town for the opening. I took her shopping for an evening dress. She chose a backless black gown. Not until we were standing side by side in the lobby of the theater did I realize how closely it resembled the evening dress she had envied in my closet. We looked like the Bobbsey Twins dressed for a night on the town.

The audience was a motley crush of black ties and leather jackets and long satin dresses and work shirts and fur wraps and Russian peasant blouses. ILD and party members, who would usually not be caught dead on Broadway, rubbed elbows with the customary first-nighters. Harry, who had seen a rehearsal, had persuaded the CP to endorse the play, though it did so with the caveat that it did not usually approve of bourgeois dramas written by philosophically incorrect playwrights, but it would make an exception in this case due to the subject matter.

Ruby and Harry and I made our way down the aisle to our seats. The usher gave us playbills. I paged through mine to find the cast list and pointed it out to Ruby.

Ruby Bates. . . . . .Ruth Gordon

She let out a sigh of wonder.

I ain't never seen nothing like it. The lights outside on something Alice called the marquee were so bright they turned night into daytime. Inside was all lit up too, and crowded with folks dressed to kill.

I was dressed to kill too in a slinky new dress I got Alice to buy me, just like the one in her closet I tried on once, but she wouldn't let me borrow. Folks kept coming over and saying hello to Alice and her fella, the peachy tall one, not the dark one with glasses, and telling me to keep up the good work. Then we went inside to a big hall with fancy plush seats and a thick velvet curtain hanging yonder, and walked all the way down to the front and set. Alice opened a little book a lady in a uniform give us and showed me my name printed right there. I couldn't hardly believe my eyes. A linthead like me getting her name wrote in a book. I wished Ma and Victoria and folks down home could of seen it.

After a spell, the room went to dark, and the big velvet curtain went up until you couldn't see it no more, and there right in front of us was a bunch of boys, colored and white both, and two girls in overalls, and I knew right off the girls were supposed to be me and Victoria, and I'd be lying if I said it didn't feel funny to set down there in the audience watching someone who was supposed to be me up on the stage. The girl was real pretty, and she talked better than me, even though she was trying not to, but you could tell she did, and she was doing all them things I did. She got carried to jail, and testified in the courtroom, and gave Danny Dundee the letter to give to Earl. It was all just like it happened, except for the salesman who come through town around Christmas. Up there on the stage, the salesman didn't have no sack of samples, on account of he ain't selling nothing but the Union. I didn't take much to that, but I liked the rest, specially the part when the salesman tells the girl who's supposed to be me how pretty she is, and how good at heart, and how he's fixing to marry her. I reckon I liked them things that never did happen in real life better than them things that did.

Afterward, there was a party in a Park Avenue apartment where the Depression had never happened. While the champagne flowed and the canapés circulated, a photographer got the idea of taking pictures of the various real characters with the actors who played them onstage. Sam Leibowitz posed with Claude Rains, and Lester Carter stood beside an actor called Bob Ross, and Ruby and Ruth Gordon put their arms around each other's waists and smiled into an explosion of lights. The flashbulbs were still popping when I wandered out onto the terrace that ran around the building like a medieval moat twenty floors in the air.

A cutting wind blew from the west, and I was sorry I had not stopped for my coat, but I would not go back inside. As I came around the corner of the terrace, hoping to get in the lee of the building, I found Abel standing alone at the railing, looking out over the city.

"Shouldn't you be inside?" I asked. "You're the guest of honor."

He turned and put his back to the wrought-iron rail. "Either that or the scapegoat. We won't know until the reviews come in." He slipped out of his dinner jacket and held it out to me. "You'd better take this."

"I'm fine."

"Your teeth are chattering, Ace. Take the damn thing."

I put it around my shoulders and hugged it to me. It did not smell of cigarettes or aftershave or anything. I started to tease him that he had bought a new dinner jacket for the opening, then thought better of it.

Through the French doors to the living room, we could see the photographer lining up Sam Leibowitz and Lester Carter and Ruby and the three actors who played them for a group shot. A flash went off, then a second and third.

"Never underestimate the stupidity of the great unwashed public," he said.

"It's a wonderful play," I answered. "They'll love it."

"I wasn't talking about the reviews."

"Then what?"

He nodded toward the living room. "Great publicity idea, those pictures. Only no one seems to have noticed that there's no one here to take a picture with Al Stokes and Joe Scott and Eddie Hodge and . . ." He reeled off the names of the actors playing the boys.

"I should think that gives credence to your worldview."

"Exactly." The smile he flashed at me was bankrupt of pleasure.

A gofer came through the front door to the living room, carrying a stack of newspapers, and we went inside. The producer passed the papers around, and people grabbed them, and paged through to find the reviews, and began reading lines and paragraphs aloud.

"Several years ago, Abel Newman wrote a great play," the director read from one paper, and beside me I could sense Abel holding his breath. "Tonight he proved the achievement was not a fluke."

I felt him exhale.

Around the room, people were calling out words and sentences and paragraphs.

"Powerful."

"Reality in greasepaint."

"An Alabama Court comes alive on Forty-fifth Street."

The room was bubbling with excitement.

The front door opened again, and a large man with a florid face barreled in. I recognized him as one of the angels who had backed the show. He was taking off his Chesterfield and top hat and white silk scarf as he entered. He glanced around and noticed Al Stokes, the actor who played Haywood Patterson, standing nearby. The man shoved his coat and hat and silk scarf into Al's hands. "Bring me a whiskey and soda, my good man," he said.

Al hesitated, as if he were taking a beat on the stage, then carried the hat and coat and scarf across the room and dropped them on a chair. When he looked up, he found me watching him. I dropped my eyes, but it was too late. He knew I had seen.

He moved off to join a knot of actors, and I glanced around the room to see if anyone else had noticed the incident. Most of the guests were still congratulating one another. Ruby was standing with a noisy group from the ILD. Harry was talking to Ruth Gordon. Only Abel met my eyes. He gave me another bankrupt grin.

TWO NEW YORK MEN ARRESTED AT NASHVILLE ON CHARGES BY WOMAN WITNESS: SHE ALLEGES $1000 OFFER

—New York Times, *October 2, 1934*

If he [Samuel Leibowitz] told the facts about the Ruby Bates reversal of testimony, it would be plenty.

—Walter White, Secretary of the NAACP, 1934

Harry and I were on our way to the Brevoort for dinner when the words jumped out at me from the newsstand. TWO MEN ARRESTED and BRIBERY and SCOTTSBORO. He reached into his pocket and came up with a handful of pennies. We stood in the cool October night under circle of light cast by a streetlamp reading the accounts.

The Nashville police had arrested two men, both of New York, for trying to bribe Victoria Price to change her testimony. The two men had approached her several days earlier, and she had pretended to play along with them, but had immediately alerted the authorities. Victoria said they had offered her a thousand dollars, but one of the police officers reported finding fifteen hundred in single dollar bills in the car the men were driving, though the arrested men denied the money was theirs.

Harry took the papers I had been reading, folded them with his, and tucked them under his arm. We started walking toward Fifth Avenue.

"Do you think it was a frame-up by the police, like the Danny Dundee business?"

He did not answer.

"The Tennessee police could have planted the money."

He kept walking.

"Frame-up or not, it certainly doesn't help the boys."

"I had a feeling something was wrong when she didn't try to squeeze them for more."

I stopped walking and turned to him. "You knew about it?"

He shrugged. "It's only suborning if you persuade someone to commit perjury, not to tell the truth."

He started walking again, and I fell in step with him. "The party sent those men down there, didn't it?"

"Without the party, and its tactics, those boys would have been dead long ago."

I could not argue with him on that point.

The first thing the next morning, I called Sam Leibowitz.

"I've had a bellyful," he shouted into the phone. He was not playing with his voice for dramatic effect. The rage was genuine. "I warned them not to bring Ruby Bates up here in the first place. Before we went to trial in Decatur, I sat in this office and spent two hours talking myself blue in the face with Joe Brodsky, and he finally agreed. Next thing I know, the girl is gallivanting around New York. As if that isn't enough, they dress her up like Mrs. Astor's pet horse and take her back to Decatur for Haywood's trial. The minute I saw her walk into that courtroom in those fancy New York clothes, I knew the jury wasn't going to believe a word she said."

By the time the evening editions hit the stands, the bribery story was off the front page, though still in the news. Leibowitz had issued a statement saying he would resign as defense counsel unless every communist was immediately removed from the case. Brodsky told reporters he had never been so disappointed in anyone as he was in Mr. Leibowitz, who was obviously more interested in personal aggrandizement than in the welfare of the defendants.

After I finished reading the accounts, I put on my hat and coat and started for a grammar school on the Lower East Side. I wanted to see how Ruby was taking the story.

Several weeks earlier, I had persuaded her to enroll in the Works Projects Administration remedial education program. Five evenings a week, she and ten or a dozen other women folded themselves behind desks in a classroom and tried to keep their minds on third- and fourth-grade primers.

I arrived as a group of young and middle-aged women came streaming out of the building into the dusk, noisy and rambunctious as children released from class. When Ruby saw me, she broke away from the others. By the time she reached me, she had stopped laughing. I asked her how things were going.

"Them kids' books ain't never going to help me get work."

I told her not to be so sure. The statement was as close as I would go to the education-for-its-own-sake argument. "Come on, we'll get a cup of coffee."

She looked at me from under the brim of one of the hats I had bought her. "I wouldn't say no to something stronger."

"Neither would I." I linked my arm through hers and started down the street toward an old speakeasy gone respectable.

We found a table in a corner, and when the waiter came to take our order, Ruby surprised me. On her last road trip, someone had taught her to drink Manhattans.

"Dry," she added to the waiter. "What's tickling your funny bone?" she said to me.

"Absolutely nothing," I answered and tried to look serious.

"I reckon you heard about Victoria and all that money they were fixing to give her," she said after our drinks arrived.

I told her I had.

"It ain't right."

I knew her outrage was more materialistic than moral, but I still felt sorry for her.

"I suppose they thought they were helping the boys."

She did not say anything to that. I asked her about school. She answered in morose monosyllables. I did not blame her. In the light of her experience, Dick and Jane could hardly have been instructive. We sat in silence for a while. The drink did not seem to be cheering her up.

"It ain't right," she said again. She did not have to explain what *it* was.

"Just be glad you're not mixed up in it."

"I don't hold with that. I'd be plenty glad to get mixed up with a thousand dollars."

"It's not the money."

"That's what you're always saying, but if you ain't got money, it's always the money."

"You did the right thing, Ruby, for the right reasons. You should be proud no one had to bribe you not to send nine innocent boys to the electric chair."

She thought about the implications of that for a moment. At least, I thought she was thinking about the implications, but when she spoke, I knew I was wrong.

"You reckon they were really fixing to give her a thousand dollars?" Her voice was a keen of anguish in the murmur of conversation that rose and fell around us. It reminded me of mothers mourning dead children, and women lost loves. That was when I knew. I sat staring across the table. In the dim light, her face hung like a pale unhappy moon, or a mirror, because as I looked into it, I saw the reflection of my own stupidity.

"Maybe more," I added to punish her. I was angry now, at her, and at myself. "They found fifteen hundred in the car."

"Fifteen hundred!" The keen rose to a wail. Around us, a few heads turned, but I did not care. Ruby was my only concern. I was trying to figure out how she had played me so well. I thought of asking how much they had paid her, but I did not want to know. I just wanted to get away from her, and my own blindness. But I did not have to ask.

"They were fixing to give her three times what they give me."

She had finally found a use for the lessons she was learning in those dog-eared schoolbooks.

A week later, I received a wire from Mrs. Roosevelt. She said she had read the pieces I had been sending her since that day at the Bonus Army camp and had a project she wanted to discuss with me. Would I come to lunch at the White House? It would be informal, with only four of us at table.

The usher showed me to a sunny alcove on the second floor. Mrs. Roosevelt was waiting with her secretary, Malvina Thompson, whom I remembered from the first all-woman press conference, and a man with a lean midwestern face and morose eyes, whom I recognized instantly. Harry Hopkins, a former social worker, ran the Federal Emergency Relief Administration.

We sat down at a small table, and a steward wheeled in a cart with four plates on it. As he removed the covers on the dishes and placed them in front of us, Mr. Hopkins's face grew longer. I looked down at my plate and understood why. Mrs. Roosevelt was determined to teach the country to eat nutritional meals for a few cents per person. Today we were lunching on hot stuffed eggs with tomato sauce and mashed potatoes.

We did not waste much time on small talk. Mrs. Roosevelt never did. She explained that Mr. Hopkins was not satisfied with the reports he was getting back from the field on the emergency relief program.

"We're up to our ears in statistics and social worker pieties," he said, "but we don't know what effect we're really having. We have no idea what it's like for the people on the other end of the operation. How does it feel to lose your job and your home and your self-respect? When does a man turn to drink and become dangerous? When does a woman give up hope and stop taking care of her children?"

"Or take to the streets to take care of her children?" I suggested.

There was a second of silence.

"Exactly the kind of thing we're looking for," Mr. Hopkins said, and his unhappy eyes lit up at the connection.

"One of the other writers we sent out, Martha Gellhorn, reported a shockingly high incidence of syphilis," Mrs. Roosevelt added. Pronounced in her high flutey voice, the word took on an incongruous innocence.

"Only when we know these things will we be able to judge if the relief problem is actually helping people or merely handing out money," Mr. Hopkins said. "We've been sending out reporters and writers to go where they choose, within a certain district, talk to whomever they wish, and report back to us in unofficial letters. We thought you could cover Alabama and Tennessee."

"In view of your experience in the area," Mrs. Roosevelt explained.

"We want you to speak to Negroes as well as whites," Mr. Hopkins went on. "They're not getting nearly their share of the pie, and when they do get anything, whites manage to steal it from them. Of the six thousand cotton checks we issued in Tuscaloosa County, only one hundred and fifteen were made out to Negroes, and every one of those ended up endorsed over to a white man."

"It's unconscionable," Mrs. Roosevelt said.

"The pay is thirty-five dollars a week," Mr. Hopkins continued. "You get train vouchers for the trip south, and five dollars a day for food, hotels, and local travel. You won't be living high off the hog on that."

"Miss Whittier has visited the Kilby death house and the Decatur jail, which was worse," Mrs. Roosevelt broke in. "She even spent some time incarcerated in Huntsville. I doubt she feels the need to live high off the hog, Harry."

"What do you say?" Mr. Hopkins asked.

I did not have to think about it for long. Harry was right. Trying to save the life of one misguided young woman was sentimental sob stuff. Changing the system was what mattered.

I said yes.

Every night I wrote to Mr. Hopkins. When I finished my report, I wrote in my journal. The material was too good to waste. Someday I would do something with it. I wrote to Harry too, or wired him, but as the weeks passed, he responded less regularly, and I wrote less often. I had thought Harry would be pleased with me for trying to change the world rather than save an individual, but he was merely disappointed in me for going to work for Mr. Hopkins. The new administration reinforced his conviction that do-gooders delayed the overthrow of the bad old system, and he did not approve of my contributing to their efforts. That may not sound like sufficient cause for the cooling of an affair, but in those days friendships and romances and even marriages often foundered on political passions. I knew a Trotskyite and a Stalinist who not only divorced, but divided their four children along ideological lines. Or perhaps without the glue of the Scottsboro boys, Harry and I simply did not have enough to hold us together.

The case, however, was far from closed. In January, the Supreme Court agreed to review the most recent convictions of Haywood Patterson and Clarence Norris. I celebrated the news alone in a grim room in the mill town of Guntersville. When Mr. Hopkins had listed the hardships of the job, he had neglected to mention loneliness.

A few days later, I paid another visit to Haywood Patterson and Clarence Norris in the Kilby death house. The other boys were still in the Birmingham jail.

The last time I had seen Haywood had been in the courtroom in Decatur, when he had sworn he would rather go to the electric chair than spend his life behind bars for a crime he did not commit. I wondered if he still felt that way, but the question was too terrible to ask.

He struck me as more subdued than he had been in Decatur. When he had first arrived back in the death house, he told me, the warden had taken one look his hair, which he wore long and slicked back, pronounced it too much like a white man's, and ordered the barber to cut it all off in what Haywood called a Kilby 'do. A year earlier, he would have laughed as he told me the story. Now he did not even smile. The warden had been as effective as Delilah.

The death house was full up that winter. The crowded living conditions were bad, but other aspects of the arrangement were worse.

"Back in the Birmingham jail we still got us some good times," Haywood said. "But out here, everyone's wrapped up in the Holy Spirit. All anybody ever talks about is what it's like in heaven. Only ain't nobody here likely to find out. They say if you burn in that chair, you go on burning eternal."

I told them I doubted that was true, but my words provided no solace. I might know something about newspapering and the law, but both men perceived that when it came to heaven and hell, I was a babe in the woods.

The crowding took another toll. It meant that Haywood and Clarence spent more nights watching more men take the walk. A week earlier a man called Isaac Mimms had gone through the green steel door.

"Know what he told me on the way past?" Haywood said. " 'You boys ain't never going to go through that green door. You got too many folk working for you.' You reckon he's right, Miz Whittier?"

I told him he was, and tried my best to believe it.

I wrote to Sam Leibowitz and told him about my visit to Kilby. He wrote back about his preparations for the appeal to the Supreme

Court, though I knew he had his mind on other matters as well. That winter, Sam Leibowitz was riding higher on the Scottsboro boys than any of us. All through January and half of February, he stood in the chill night outside a Flemington, New Jersey, courthouse and broadcast a summation of the day's proceedings in the trial of Bruno Richard Hauptmann for the kidnapping and murder of the Lindbergh baby. Leibowitz's work for the Scottsboro boys had burnished his reputation so highly that Hauptmann even welcomed him into his cell for a heart-to-heart talk. The accused kidnapper believed the man who was fighting for nine wrongly accused Negroes would believe one innocent, he proclaimed, white man. Leibowitz was even more certain he could persuade Hauptmann to confess his guilt and name his accomplices.

Nonetheless, Leibowitz was not neglecting the Scottsboro appeal. He had never argued before the Supreme Court before, and knew all his courtroom tricks and impassioned appeals to justice and goodness and right would be worthless before that august body. The highest court in the land concerned itself with constitutional law. The justices had probably never heard a criminal lawyer argue, Leibowitz wrote me, and I remembered the two men at the next table who had snubbed him the day he and I had lunched in New York.

I managed to get up to Washington for the arguments. There were no demonstrations outside the Capitol this time, but inside, the old Senate chamber was full again. As I slid into a seat, I remembered the last time I had been there. I had not heard from Harry for several weeks.

Chief Justice Hughes nodded to Leibowitz to begin, and the attorney stepped before the high bench. I had always thought of Leibowitz as a big man, more than six feet tall and broad of shoulders, but standing before the justices in that vast room with the tall columns and soaring eagle, he looked somehow diminished. He began in a low dispassionate voice, his face bland, his gestures small. The justices sat gazing down at him with equally impassive expressions as he argued that though the state of Alabama did not specifically exclude Negroes from serving on juries, the administration of jury selection did, in fact, exclude them, and this exclusion was unconstitutional. His words were precise. They spoke not of right and wrong, or justice and injustice, only of the law of the land.

The justices began interrupting him with questions. He confined his answers to the narrow issue, but I could tell he was chafing under the constraint. His body cantilevered toward the bench. His gestures grew larger. His voice began to rise. He was still policing himself, but straining against the task. To those of us who had seen him in action before, he looked like a trussed animal.

Finally, the injustice was too much for him. This was a crime, he said, his voice mounting with anger, perpetrated by the state of Alabama against nine ignorant wretched young men. Worse than that, he breathed, and I could almost feel the fire coming out of his nostrils, it was a fraud, not only against the defendants but against this very court. Yes, the names of Negroes appeared in the jury book, but they had been forged, entered after the trials. Examination by an expert under a microscope had revealed that the black ink in which the names were written was above the surface, not below, of the red ink line drawn to separate prospective jurors listed at one time from those listed later.

The accusation was too much for the chief justice. "Can you prove this forgery?" he asked gravely.

"I can, Your Honor. I have the jury rolls with me."

There was a moment's silence. Although Leibowitz had not argued before the high court before, he knew that exhibits were not introduced into these proceedings. Later, Justice Brandeis would tell him that during his career as a Supreme Court justice, he had never seen such a thing permitted until now.

"Let the court see them," Chief Justice Hughes said.

The only sound in the room was the squeaking of the floorboards as the court attendant walked to the counsel table, picked up the heavy red book, and carried it to the bench. Leibowitz followed and handed up a large magnifying glass.

Hughes took the glass, bent his head over the book, and studied it. When he looked up, his face was dark as an Old Testament prophet's. Without a word, he slid the book to Justice Van Devanter on his right. Van Devanter studied it, then passed it on to Justice Brandeis, who looked at it, then gave it to Justice Butler, who took a few minutes before passing it to Justice Roberts. Roberts took a look, then handed it back to the page, who carried it down to Justice Cardozo at the other end of the bench. Cardozo lifted the magnifying glass to the page, then slid the book to Justice Stone, who had to make a longer pass to Justice Sutherland, because Justice McReynolds's chair was empty. Justice Sutherland looked down at the book, then passed it back to the chief justice. None of them had spoken a word, but their faces made it clear. They had seen the falsification. Nonetheless, forgery was not a matter of constitutional law.

Three months would pass before the court handed down its verdict. The boys paced their cells. The ILD continued to raise money on their behalf. I went back to wandering city streets and country roads; talking to the unemployed—as conditions had grown worse, the adjective had become a noun—and the hungry, and the hopeless; and sending my impressions back to Mr. Hopkins in Washington. Finally, on April first, the court read its opinion. Forgery might not be a matter of constitutional law, but denying federal rights was. The justices overturned the convictions on the grounds that no Negroes had sat on the juries.

In the Kilby death house, in the Birmingham jail, on the streets of New York and Berlin and Paris and Moscow, people rejoiced. In Alabama, the mood was less celebratory and more determined. Tom Knight announced the state would seek new indictments to prosecute the Scottsboro case to its conclusion in, he trusted, the death chamber.

A few weeks later, I resigned my job with Mr. Hopkins. He was not surprised. None of us lasted on the road for more than several months. The heels of my sensible shoes were worn down, my hats were dusty and sun-bleached and rain-stained, and I had lost twelve pounds. My body ached from sleeping in lumpy beds, alone. But I was not sorry I had taken the assignment. I had seen poverty and misery and despair and even hope. I had marveled at the resilience and goodness and selflessness of the human heart, and the venality and greed and pettiness. I even stopped thinking the two sides were mutually exclusive. Mrs. Roosevelt had something to do with that.

When I came through Washington to tie matters up with Mr. Hopkins, she invited me to stay the night at the White House. After dinner and a screening of *Mutiny on the Bounty* with Clark Gable in the second-floor hallway across from the president's suite, she invited me to her rooms for a talk. The conversation turned out to be the most intimate I would ever have with her.

She said she had seen my mother a few weeks earlier, when a delegation of the Women's League for Peace and Freedom had come to tea. "I was surprised to find that she did not know about our friendship. She said she gets to see you only when she goes up to New York."

We were sitting in the large study off her small bedroom, two women adrift in a sea of history. Abraham Lincoln had inhabited the suite during his days in the White House. Andrew Jackson had planted the towering magnolia tree outside the tall windows. The breathtaking view stretched down to the Washington Monument. But now the curtains were drawn against the night, and a fire burned in the brick fireplace, and Mrs. Roosevelt was determined to straighten out my life, as she was constantly straightening out the lives of so many others whom she befriended.

"I'm afraid I haven't been in touch a great deal lately, with all the traveling for Mr. Hopkins." My voice trailed off.

"I got the impression there was more to it than that."

The flames licked at the logs in the fireplace. Perhaps if the setting had been less cozy, or the lateness of the hour had not worn down my guard, or I had not known about Mrs. Roosevelt's father, I would not have spoken. But the room was snug against the chill rainy night, and it was after eleven, and by then I had heard the story of Elliott Roosevelt. Most of us in the press had, though no one would print it. In those days, public figures were permitted to have personal heartaches as well as private lives.

Shortly after the president and the first lady moved into the White House, she received a letter from a man called Elliott Roosevelt Mann. You did not have to go far back to discover that Elliott Roosevelt Mann was the illegitimate son of Mrs. Roosevelt's father, Elliott Roosevelt, and a maid on their Long Island estate called Katy Mann. The girl had named her illegitimate son after his father, just as Brigit Ward had christened her daughter Georgina Whittier Ward after my father, George Whittier. Nothing ever became of Mr. Mann's overture to his half-sister, or the story, but it had stayed with me, and now it gave me the courage to tell her my own version of it. The only other person I had confided in about my father was Ruby Bates. Strangely enough, Mrs. Roosevelt's response was not unlike hers. Ruby had not understood what the fuss was about. No skin off my nose, she had said. That was just the way men were. Mrs. Roosevelt was less cavalier. She found my father's behavior unconscionable, but then men often were, she added.

We sat in silence for a moment, staring into the fire in that history-filled room, and when she spoke again, I was surprised.

"If you cannot forgive, Alice, you cannot love."

When the train pulled into the Thirtieth Street Station in Philadelphia the next afternoon, I still had not made up my mind. I watched the last passenger step down from the car. Others began to board. They climbed the steps, and made their way down the aisle, and waited while the redcaps heaved their luggage into the overhead racks. The porters began filing off the train. On the platform outside the window, a conductor shouted all aboard. I stood and grabbed my suitcase down from the rack. The train had started to move by the time my feet hit the platform.

I told the cabdriver to take me to Rittenhouse Square, then realized it was the middle of the day. No one would be home. Strange that I still thought of it as home. I gave him the address of the clinic. His eyes cut to the rearview mirror to get a better look at me. A woman who first directs him to Rittenhouse Square, then decides to go to Eighth and Christian, must be up to no good.

The waiting room was packed with women speaking in a babel of tongues, and children crying, and a nurse in a white uniform trying to keep everyone under control, and, towering above them all, my father. He had not yet seen me, and as I stood watching, he bent, took a screaming infant from a mother's arms, and cradled it against his chest. The screaming subsided to a mewl, the mewl descended to a few hiccups, then silence. He looked up from the child. His face was beatific as a saint's. But he was not a saint, any more than he was the devil. He was merely human.

He bent to hand the baby back to its mother, and when he straightened again, he saw me. The saintliness slid from his face. He hesitated a moment, then started toward me. I met him halfway.

The idea was mine, but my father encouraged me. He even told me where I could find her. Georgina Whittier Ward was working for the Albany *Times Union*.

"She's a reporter!" I said.

"It must be in the blood," he answered.

I sent a telegram saying I was coming to Albany to do a piece on WPA projects in the area and would like to meet her. She wired back with a date and time and the address of her apartment.

I recognized her as soon as she opened the door. I am not suggesting I would have picked her out in a crowd. I hadn't when we had both attended Mrs. Roosevelt's first all-women press conference. But she had my father's wide-set blue eyes and his full mouth. The snub nose and freckles must have come from Brigit.

She closed the door behind me, and we stood facing each other for an awkward moment. I wondered if we should embrace. She held out her hand. I shook it.

She led the way into a small sitting room. A tea tray sat on a table. It was laid out as beautifully as if an excellent housemaid had arranged it. I hated myself for the observation.

She saw me looking at it. "My mother taught me well," she said. "Your mother taught her."

We sat across from each other, and she poured tea, and we got down to the prickly business of getting to know each other. I had thought the difficulty would be in getting past our mothers. Surely she bore a grudge against mine, just as I resented hers. But our father was the real minefield. When the man she spoke of bore no resemblance to the man I knew, I was annoyed. When he was the familiar figure who took his daughter along to Western Union offices, and showed an interest in her schoolbooks, and tried to teach her the difference between right and wrong, I was furious. I had always called him Pa. He was Da to her. Somewhere in the conversation, we began referring to him as George.

I asked if he was the one who had steered her into journalism.

"My mother," she said. "She wanted me to be you."

"Your mother wanted you to be like me?" I was surprised.

"I didn't say my mother wanted me to be like you. I said she wanted me to be you."

I thought about that for a moment. "I'm sorry."

She shrugged. "It's not your fault."

I stayed at Georgina Ward's for more than an hour that afternoon, and when I left, I told her that next time she was in New York, she must be sure to let me know. But I did not mean it, and she was too smart not to sense my insincerity.

I had planned to spend the night in Albany. I was sure that once Georgina and I met, we would want more time together. But when I left her apartment, I went straight to the station and caught the first train back to New York. Outside the windows of the Pullman car, the Hudson lay like a wide black ribbon curling through the bare countryside. I had left a greening Alabama, but here spring was still far away.

My meeting with my half-sister had not gone as I had expected. I had been prepared for resentment. I had plotted means to overcome it. I had imagined the things I could teach her, the ways I could help her, the doors I could open for her. But Georgina Ward needed nothing from me. She was doing perfectly well on her own. And I did not want a sister at this late date, no matter what Ruby said.

I reckoned I couldn't lose nothing by writing. Them folks at the ILD chewed me up and spit me out, and I reckoned Alice wouldn't do no different, but then maybe she would too. I still recollect them pictures she put on her walls to make herself miserable as a body can be.

I set down and wrote how I couldn't get no more work than a couple of days every other week, and how a body couldn't hardly live on that. I told her how sometimes even when the boss was fixing to let me work, I couldn't, on account of I was coughing so bad with the TB. I told her I missed the good times we used to have, and I hoped she was still my friend, on account of she was the only friend I got these days. And I asked if she could spare some money. It didn't have to be much. Any little thing would help, but I reckoned fifty dollars would see me through till my cough got better and I could work again.

Wouldn't you know a week later I got a letter back. She said she was sorry I wasn't feeling good, and told me to go see a doc, and even gave me directions to a government clinic hereabouts. I reckon she went to some little trouble to find that. And she put in a money order. I reckoned if she took the trouble to write, she'd do that too. Them pictures on the wall again. It was for a hundred dollars. I was sorry I didn't ask for a hundred, on account of then she'd of sent two.

I saw Harry a few times when I returned to New York, but we did not resume our affair. We did not argue. We had simply come to the realization that whatever had been between us had run its course.

Two weeks after my return, he sailed for Europe. He was not taking a holiday, he was setting out on a mission. In Germany, Hitler was sending communists and Jews, who were not necessarily the same people, no matter what Americans thought, to work camps. In Italy, Mussolini was trumping up a war against Ethiopia. In Spain, the right and left were fighting in the streets. If we did not stop the fascists now, he insisted, we would have to fight a bigger and bloodier war against them later.

I went to the boat to see Harry off. So did several dozen other people. Afterward, Abel and I stood on the pier watching the *Normandie* grow smaller as the tugs nudged it out to sea.

"I had a letter from an old friend of yours," he said, as we turned to go.

"Ruby?"

"Give the little lady a great big hand. She's working in some mill town in upstate New York. I forget the name."

"Cohoes," I told him.

"Yeah, I figured if I'd heard from her, you had too. Our girl Ruby has a long list of correspondents. She wasn't the sweetheart of the ILD for nothing. Only the ILD has stopped sending money, so now all she has is old friends like us."

"You think she's all right?"

"You know a mill worker who is?"

"Did you send her money?"

"Less than you did, I bet." He raised his arm to hail a cab. "But then I never set out to save her, so I don't have to salve my conscience for dropping her."

The farcical finale . . . left the state in the anomalous position of providing only 50 per cent protection for the "flower of Southern womanhood."

—The Nation, *1937*

In January 1936, Haywood Patterson went on trial for the fourth time. The proceedings did not cause the same stir. People were getting tired of the case. There was a sense of déjà vu. Judge Callahan presided. Lieutenant Governor Knight was the head prosecutor. Sam Leibowitz led the defense team. Victoria told her story again, as did Lester Carter. Ruby did not make an appearance. She was too scared to return, and the defense team did not seem to think she had done much good last time around. Orville Gilley, the hobo poet, was missing too. A week earlier, he had been convicted of assaulting and robbing two women in Tennessee. The only other difference was the contingent of twelve Negroes among the one hundred veniremen. Seven asked to be disqualified because their employers could not do without them, or they were too old to serve, or they opposed capital punishment. Haywood was not sorry to see them go. "I don't want no scared Negroes judging me," he told Sam Leibowitz. The state rejected the other five.

I did not attend the trial. I had written a book about my travels for Mr. Hopkins, and I could not miss the party celebrating its publication.

The trial lasted only two and a half days. The jury deliberated eight hours, longer than anyone expected. They found Haywood Patterson guilty. There was, however, one new wrinkle. John Burleson, the foreman of the jury, was a farmer and devout Methodist who had never smoked, chewed tobacco, or tasted a drop of alcohol in his life, though he did religiously read the *Saturday Evening Post*, *Colliers*, *Liberty*, *Time*, *Country Gentleman*, and the *National Geographic*. Burleson believed that Victoria Price was lying and Haywood Patterson was innocent. He made the case to the other jurors, but they argued that if they came in with an acquittal, they would not be able to return home to their communities. After considerable discussion, the twelve men reached a compromise. Burleson was not happy with it, but he feared a mistrial would lead to still another trial and death sentence. The jury found Patterson guilty, but this time they sentenced him to seventy-five years in prison.

Sam Leibowitz was pleased, and promised that he would not give up until he had got Patterson out of jail. Haywood was less happy.

"I'd rather die than spend another day in jail for something I didn't do," he told reporters, as he had the guard and me almost three years earlier.

Victoria was disgruntled too. "It ain't fair," she informed the press. "They should of all got the chair. Justice wasn't done."

Leibowitz had promised he would continue to fight for the boys. The ILD was still raising money for them. A new group called the Scottsboro Defense Committee had formed. After more than five years, Alabama was in a fix. It could kill neither the boys nor the case.

The situation was not only making the state look ridiculous, it was also costing it money, and not only for the trials. When, almost a year after Haywood Patterson's fourth conviction, Governor Bibb Graves came to New York to negotiate loans for Alabama, he found that none of the bankers he had dealt with in the past would pony up a penny. The story got around pretty quickly.

A month after Bibb went home empty-handed, the week between Christmas and New Year's, I got a call from Sam Leibowitz suggesting lunch. I suspected something was up. I even had an inkling it might have to do with the bankers' snub of the governor. The only thing I did not understand, once I heard the story, was why Sam Leibowitz went out of his way to tell me about it. Then I realized. He had to crow to someone, but Mrs. Leibowitz already knew he was a hero, and I could be trusted.

"I got a call from Tom Knight the other day," he began as soon as the maitre d' had shown us to Leibowitz's table in the restaurant near General Sessions Court. "He said he was in town with Alabama's new attorney general, Albert Carmichael. I naturally invited them to dinner. He was kind to Mrs. Leibowitz in Decatur, and he's not so bad out of the courtroom. I even promised him I wouldn't say a word about the case."

"And he told you he had come up to talk about the case."

"You heard about the loans?"

I nodded.

"He also said if anyone found out we were meeting, it would be prejudicial to what he had in mind. So he declined my invitation to dinner and asked if I would come to his room at the New Yorker Hotel the next morning."

"How early did you get there?"

"The beds hadn't even been made up, but he and Carmichael were ready. As soon as Knight started talking, I knew what was up."

"Oh, come, now, it didn't take you that long."

He smiled. "He went on for a while about how much money the

trials were costing Alabama's taxpayers, and what a nuisance the case had become to the state, and wasn't it time we laid it to rest. I just let him talk. Finally, he got around to the offer. He said if I would plead three or four of the boys guilty of rape, the state would make a deal on the others. Three *or* four, can you imagine? As if one dead or imprisoned innocent boy more or less makes no difference. I don't understand those people."

"What did you say?"

"I let him run on for a while longer. Dig his own grave, as it were. Then I stood and walked to the window."

I could see him replaying the scene in his head as he recounted it. He was a consummate director as well as actor.

"I called him over. 'You see down there, Tom?' I said and pointed out the window. 'Just three blocks in that direction is the Fourteenth Precinct Police Station.' I paused. He had no idea where I was going. 'The sergeant behind the desk there probably gets a dozen complaints a day. A lot of the complaints come from crackpots, publicity seekers, and liars. Now, the sergeant is no genius, but years of listening have given him some ability to tell whether or not a complainant is telling the truth.' He still didn't get it. 'What's your point, Sam?' he asked. 'If Victoria Price and Ruby Bates had walked into that station house and told the sergeant nine Negro boys had raped them, the sergeant would not have had to question them for five minutes to know they were lying. He would have tossed them out on the spot. And that would have been the end of it.' 'But they didn't walk into that precinct,' he said. 'Precisely,' I told him, 'and that's the shame of it, because even the dumbest cop on the force would have spotted those two tramps as liars.'"

I said nothing. I wanted to hear the end of the story more than I wanted to defend Ruby.

"I told him he knew damn well they lied that day at the Paint Rock station, and the Price girl has been lying ever since. And now he wants me to plead three or four of the boys guilty of something they never did. 'The state of Alabama finally realizes it's made a horrible mistake,' I told him, 'and you want me to pull your chestnuts out of the fire so you can save face.'"

"What did he say to that?"

"By that time the face that needed saving was so red I was afraid he was going to have an attack right on the spot. It didn't help that it was cold as the dickens outside, so the hotel was pumping up heat like nobody's business. He decided to take another tack. He said at least some of the boys were guilty of assault, and if I pleaded Patterson, Norris, Weems, and Andy Wright guilty of that charge, he might release the others."

"Did you agree?"

"I asked him if Judge Callahan had agreed. He said he was waiting to get my answer before he asked Callahan. I told him to get Callahan's answer, then he and I would talk."

"Do you think Callahan will go for the idea?"

"It's hard to say. All I know for certain is that Knight and his new attorney general are running scared, and that's good for the boys."

After we said goodbye outside the restaurant, I thought of one more reason, other than his need to exult in the good news, that Sam Leibowitz had told me about the meeting. He could not tell the boys. To raise their hopes again would have been unconscionable.

A few weeks later Callahan gave his answer. It was pungent. "There will be no fifty-dollar fines for the heinous crime of rape in my courtroom."

When Sam Leibowitz told me that Tom Knight's color had run so high in that overheated hotel room that he had worried for the attorney general's health, I thought he was joking, and perhaps he was, but four months later, Tom Knight was dead at the age of thirty-nine. The papers ascribed his demise to complications from liver and kidney ailments, but I could not help thinking his obsession with the Scottsboro boys had helped do him in.

The night the news of his death came over the wires, a bunch of us who had covered the first Decatur trial met in a bar in the West Twenties to toast the memory of the man whose beliefs we abhorred and whose charm we had, on occasion, found hard to resist.

"It's almost enough to make me a believer," Abel said. "The guy spent the last four years of his life trying to send nine innocent men to the electric chair. Instead, they sent him to the great courtroom in the sky. And they're all still here."

The comment made me uneasy. Judge Callahan had announced he would try the remaining Scottsboro defendants again. New juries might easily impose new death sentences. It never occurred to me to worry that Abel might be jinxing anyone other than the boys, but then I am not a superstitious woman.

In July, another jury convicted Clarence Norris of rape and sentenced him to the electric chair. Andy Wright got ninety-nine years, Charlie Weems seventy-five. The sentences made no sense. All three of them had been charged with the same crime and tried on the same evidence.

Then the illogical spiraled into the ludicrous. At least, the situation would have been ludicrous if it were not so tragic. The state of Alabama dropped charges against Olen Montgomery, Willie Roberson, Eugene Williams, and Roy Wright.

Within hours, Sam Leibowitz and some of the reporters still covering the trial lined up two cars, hustled the boys into them, sped across the state line to Tennessee, and caught a train from Nashville to Cincinnati. At 9:25 the next morning, they arrived in Pennsylvania Station in New York. Two thousand people met them. Women wept. Men reached out to touch them. Sam Leibowitz punched out the crown of his straw boater and sent it sailing toward the latticework steel and glass roof of the vast concourse. He said he was getting rid of the Alabama dirt, but I could not help thinking he was throwing his hat in the ring.

Papers across the country carried the story. "We will permit no exploitation of the boys," Leibowitz told reporters. "No barnstorming, no theatricals of any kind. In a day or two, we're going to put them in charge of a responsible agency with a view to giving them a chance to resurrect lives almost crushed by the relentless persecution of the state of Alabama."

A month later the boys opened at the Apollo Theater in Harlem. I still have the handbill.

THE SCOTTSBORO BOYS

In person

With

AN ALL-GIRL REVIEW

FIFTY FASCINATING FEMALES

The show did not run for long. Shortly after it closed, the boys accused Sam Leibowitz of making millions off them. He had not made money off them, but he had made hay. Thanks to them, he was the country's best-known defense attorney. No one could begrudge him that.

I was not doing badly either. Assignments rolled in from *Life* and *Collier's* and all the glossy magazines Harry and I used to sneer at. I visited the White House often and corresponded with the first lady regularly. That was why the Scottsboro Defense Committee approached me.

The committee had been negotiating for the pardons of the five boys who remained in jail, but Governor Graves was slippery. He held out hope, then snatched it away. The committee asked me if I would ask Mrs. Roosevelt to speak to the president about speaking to the governor about the matter. Graves was a longtime supporter of FDR.

I told the committee I did not think it would do much good. Nonetheless, I wrote to Mrs. Roosevelt. Her reply surprised me. The president had refused to see us the day we marched in Washington, but he had been sufficiently distressed by the case to ask for a detailed memorandum on it. The report had appalled him. Mrs. Roosevelt thought there was an excellent chance her husband would intervene.

A week later she wrote to tell me that he had invited Governor Graves to the Little White House in Warm Springs, Georgia, to discuss the matter. My first reaction was to telephone Sam Leibowitz. Then I read the rest of the letter. The governor had declined the invitation.

I don't care whether they are Reds, Greens, or Blues, they are the only ones who put up a fight to save these boys and I am with them to the end.

—Janie Patterson, 1933

Most of us who live long enough keep a file of private film clips in our heads. They document where we were and what we were doing when momentous events occurred, or more to the point, when we heard that momentous events had occurred. I was in Harry Spencer's office when I learned of the arrest of the Scottsboro boys. I was giving a speech to raise money for Dutch war orphans when a messenger brought a note to the podium saying the Japanese had bombed Pearl Harbor. I was in London on an assignment for *Collier's* when I found out FDR had died. And early in 1939, I was at a party in the Village when I heard about Harry Spencer.

The gathering was large and noisy, a cacophony of rattling ice, and mounting laughter, and arguments about the Supreme Court ruling that sit-down strikes were illegal, and Prime Minister Chamberlain's pronouncement that the situation in Europe was serious but not hopeless, and the civil war in Spain. Then I heard the words.

"Harry Spencer," someone said. "Barcelona," he added.

"Damn shame," someone else commented.

The room went silent. People were still talking. I could see their mouths moving. Faces contorted with laughter. Glasses clinked. I heard nothing. The room began to spin. I reached out to steady myself on the back of a chair, but the world did not stop going around. I put down my drink and made my way out of the apartment.

When I awakened the next morning, I could not remember the end of the evening, but I had a vague sense that something was wrong. I was not a stranger to that particular morning-after sensation, but this morning I could not account for it. My head and body did not ache from too much alcohol. I could not recall saying anything untoward to anyone. I was in my own apartment, alone. Then I remembered. Harry was dead.

That was all I knew. I needed more details. Harry Spencer died in Barcelona is an inadequate epitaph. I wrote to men he had fought with in Spain, and traveled with in France and Germany, and worked with in the party. No one knew any more than I did. At least, no one was willing to tell me any more.

Abel pleaded with me to let it go. "What difference do the details make?"

I answered that if he did not understand, I could not explain. What I meant was that I did not understand myself. I merely felt I had to know.

Abel was the one who told me. He broke the news one Sunday morning. He and his new girl occasionally invited me over for Sunday breakfast. Sally was an expressionist painter, and not a very good one, but she was lovely to look at, and she adored Abel. He seemed happy. Sally must have thought so too, or she would not have been so willing to put up with me.

"What's in the *Herald*?" I asked Abel as we exchanged papers across the table.

"The usual malevolence, malfeasance, and mendacity."

"Don't you just hate him when he gets like that?" Sally asked.

"Absolutely." I always agreed with Sally about Abel, even when I didn't.

"That's right, girls, gang up on me," Abel said.

I took the paper from him and glanced at the headline. England and France had recognized Franco's Spain.

"Did you see this?" I turned the paper so Abel could read the headline, though he must have noticed it.

He nodded.

"So Harry died for nothing."

"You thought there was a meaning to his death?"

"You know what I mean. He died fighting the fascists, and now England and France have recognized the fascist regime. Which means Harry gave his life for nothing."

"In other words, if the fascists had lost, Harry would have given his life for something."

"Please, Abel," Sally said, "it's Sunday morning."

"I forgot. On the Sabbath, the world's misery and cruelty rest."

Abel went back to reading the paper. Sally escaped to the kitchen to make a fresh pot of coffee. But I could not let it go.

"The lousy fascists," I said.

Abel did not look up, but I had a feeling he was not paying attention to the paper.

"The lousy fascists killed Harry." My voice was looking for a fight, though I knew it was not Abel's fault. Maybe I could not forgive him for standing on the sidelines while Harry had risked everything. Maybe I could not forgive myself.

Abel looked up. "The lousy fascists did not kill Harry."

"Of course they did."

"The lousy communists killed Harry."

"What are you talking about?"

"It was a witch hunt. Barcelona was swarming with Stalin's police. First they did in the anarchists, then the Marxist Workers' Party, then anybody they could get their hands on. Just be glad they didn't torture him first. Some of the bodies they found—" he stopped. "I'm sorry."

"I don't believe it," I said.

He looked at me from behind the horn-rimmed glasses. "Sure you do. That's why you had all those arguments with Harry. That's why you never got around to joining the party. Harry may be a martyr, but I'll be damned if I know to what."

The three of us had planned to go to a movie that afternoon, but when I begged off, neither of them tried to persuade me to change my mind. I thanked Sally for breakfast and went out into the February afternoon. A taxi cruised past. I let it go. I was in no hurry to get back to my empty apartment.

I made my way slowly, thinking about Harry and our past, and after a while, about my future. Recently Sally had started making references to marriage and babies. As I walked through the watery winter sunshine, I saw the years spool forward. I would bring the babies gifts, I would take the children to museums, I would become not the old maid aunt exactly, I was damned if I'd turn spinsterish, but an outsider, chiseling pieces of other people's happiness. I knew the image was melodramatic and self-pitying. I loved my work. I had an address book full of friends. I rarely spent an evening alone. I was doing just fine.

Everywhere I go, it seems like Scottsboro is throwed up in my face . . . I don't believe I'll ever live it down.

—*Andy Wright, 1952*

As the years rocked around, the letters slowed down to a trickle . . . So much time passed, I guess people forgot about us or went on to other things.

—*Clarence Norris, 1979*

Even as people lost interest in the cause, the boys remained famous. At the 1939 World's Fair in New York, crowds waited in line to gawk at wax statues of them in Madame Tussaud's pavilion. Two years later, America went to war, and one by one the men won parole, all except Haywood Patterson, the toughest, the meanest, the ringleader, or so Alabama officials continued to insist.

Freedom did not improve their lives appreciably. Many of their friends forgot them. Their enemies had better memories. Employers refused to hire them when they found out they were the infamous Scottsboro boys or fired them when they discovered the fact. Parole boards hounded them and sent them back to prison for the least infraction. After nine months of freedom, Clarence Norris went to his parole officer to complain about discrimination against him at the lumber mill where the prison officials insisted he work. The parole officer made a phone call to the deputy warden of Kilby Prison, and before Clarence knew it, he was back behind bars. He remained there for two years, the hardest and most spirit-crushing of all the years he spent in prison. "I am sick to my soul," he wrote me. "I could kill every cracker in Alabama and be joyful doing it."

Out on parole again, the men tried desperately to leave Alabama, but other states refused to take them. After deliberating briefly, Michigan slammed the door on Clarence, and Charlie Weems, and Andy Wright. Reeling from the Detroit race riots of 1943, the state decided it had no room for another Negro, let alone three who were down on their luck. Ohio held out hope to Clarence, until the Cleveland parole board pronounced his mother, the stoic woman who had taught me about being a Negro mother in the South, a low type. More than one girlfriend cried rape to settle a score, and the trumped-up accusations fell on credulous ears. After all, the public had been associating the boys with the act for some time.

Their health had been broken by a combined total of more than a hundred years in some of Alabama's worst prisons and jails. When their physical conditions did not do them in, their psychological wounds did. Brutalized by a lifetime of suffering at the hands of America's judicial and penal systems, they were, if not their own worst enemies—the rest of the world saw to that—then a pretty close second.

Early in 1943, I got a letter from Roy Wright. He was still known as the youngest of the Scottsboro boys, though he had grown to manhood. He wrote that he had joined the merchant marine and married. "I reckon maybe the world ain't such a bum place after all," the letter said. "I reckon maybe Kathleen is the reward the Lord give me for all them years the white man took away."

I wrote back immediately, congratulating him, and wishing them luck, and including a check for their new life together. I even dared to think that perhaps one of the Scottsboro boys might live happily ever after.

The next time I heard about Roy and his wife, I was on an air base in England. *Collier's* had sent me over to write a series on how the hundreds of thousands of American GIs staging for the invasion were faring. I came across the paragraph in a dog-eared newspaper someone had left in the officers' club. Roy Wright, the youngest of the infamous Scottsboro boys, had returned home from a transport to find his wife with another man. He shot her to death, then, overcome by remorse, turned the gun on himself.

The next morning I went down to London. I told myself there was no reason to stay on at the base. I had more than enough material for the *Collier's* article. But I had another motive as well. Abel Newman was in London.

Abel was in the army now, attached to the Special Services Information Division, writing films intended to raise morale both in the services and among the public. He had originally been posted to an air base in Georgia to make a movie about Negro GIs, but the script he wrote was not likely to raise anyone's morale. The air base he had been on had an all-Negro squadron of flyers, all Negro except for the white colonel in charge. The locals did not like the idea of Negro flyboys, so every now and then the Klan dropped by to teach those uppity officers a lesson. Abel had put one particularly nasty incident in the script. He had also shown Negro GIs squatting on their haunches in a field eating table scraps, while German POWs dined on roast beef in the mess. "What we fight for," a voice-over intoned. The brass took one look at the screenplay and decided Abel could do more for morale writing about how well the RAF and the AAF were cooperating in England.

I tracked him down at Claridge's, where a lot of British and American movie people were staying. It was after nine by the time I reached the hotel, and I was afraid he might be out to dinner, but he was in his room. When he opened the door and found me standing in the hall, he showed no surprise. These days strange people were always popping up in unlikely places.

He invited me in, and produced a bottle of whiskey, and we sat around comparing notes on which friends were stationed where, and what writers had wrangled cushy jobs and were strutting around in swanky custom-tailored uniforms, and who was sleeping with whom in London and New York and California. This was not what I had come for, or perhaps it was.

I asked him about Sally, and he told me she had married a major two months earlier.

"I'm sorry," I said. "I always liked her."

"The hell you did."

I let it go. I had not disliked Sally, but I liked Abel better without her.

We talked some more about the war, and the script he was working on, and the piece I was writing for *Collier's*. I was putting off giving him the bad news, though why I thought of it as particularly terrible, I could not understand. I had been traveling from base to base for the past two weeks. This was not even my initial tour. I had been one of the first women posted to the European Theater of Operations, thanks once again to Mrs. Roosevelt, and the Scottsboro boys, and Ruby Bates. I knew that planes did not return from missions, and men went up in flames and down into the sea, and factories were working around the clock to turn out not only equipment and munitions, but coffins for the invasion everyone knew was coming, though no one knew when or where. All around me, the world was snuffing out bright young men with brilliant futures as easily and unremarkably as candles. Roy Wright had not been a bright young man. Despite his release and marriage, not even the wildest optimist would have predicted a brilliant future for him. I suppose that was the point. Roy Wright had never had a chance. None of the Scottsboro boys had.

Finally, I told Abel the news I had come to London to report. He did not speak when I finished, but went on sitting on the side of the bed watching me.

I stood and crossed the room to him.

"I wish you'd hold me," I said.

He looked surprised. I did not blame him. I was surprised myself. I'd had plenty of experience with sex, but when it came to affection or solace, I was a virgin.

He stood and put his arms around me. Only then did I begin to cry.

That night Abel and I made love again. I suppose that was what I had tracked him down in London for. Afterward, I dozed off and on, but a semiconscious mind is a fertile landscape for hallucinations. Roy Wright wandered through my half sleep, a thirteen-year-old child who left home for the first time in his life to hop a freight and ended up in a Scottsboro jail, a sixteen-year-old boy sporting a scar on his cheek from one more jailhouse interrogation, a nineteen-year-old youth strutting across the Apollo stage, the grown man who wrote me saying maybe the world wasn't such a bum place after all. When I finally awakened, light was beginning to filter in around the black-out curtains, and Abel's wide myopic gaze was only inches away. We moved toward each other beneath the rough government-issue blanket he had thrown over the satin bedspread. Roy Wright had been wrong. The world was a bum place, all right. But in that frigid room in the death-infested city, Abel and I beat back the bum world with the only force that could give it a run for its money.

The men came home from the war, and the women left the factories and offices and disappeared into suburban tract houses, and Americans concentrated on making up for lost time. They had babies and cars and back yard barbecues. They forgot the Scottsboro boys.

In 1950, with the encouragement of I. F. Stone, Haywood Patterson published the story of his life. It was not pretty. He had spent almost two decades in some of the worst prisons in Alabama. When they put him in a cell crawling with snakes, he overcame his fear by wearing the reptiles around his neck and in his shirt. When other prisoners tried to make a gal-boy out of him, he turned into a wolf and broke in his own gal-boy. When a guard paid another prisoner to kill him, he suffered twenty stab wounds, including one to his lung, but survived. Unlike the other boys, he never won parole, though he escaped twice. The first time, he was caught, and the prison guards made him pay for the attempt. The second flight was worthy of a Hollywood movie. He made his way through snake-infested cornfields and creeks, drowned two bloodhounds and fought off a third, and managed to reach his sister in Detroit. He lived underground for a few years, but shortly after the publication of his book, the FBI arrested him. Alabama requested extradition, but the governor of Michigan refused. For a while, things looked good for Haywood Patterson, as they had for Roy Wright. Then he got into a barroom brawl and killed a man, in self-defense, he swore. The jury convicted him of manslaughter and sentenced him to six to fifteen years. Within months, he was dead of cancer. His death, like more than half of his thirty-nine-year life, took place behind bars.

Abel saw the paragraph in the paper before I did. The date was January 26, 1961. I remember it because the night before, we had watched the newly elected JFK in the first live telecast of a presidential press conference. As radio had thirty years earlier, television was transforming public discourse, though not necessarily for the better.

Abel handed me the newspaper across the breakfast table. After the war, we too had married, though we had not moved to the suburbs or had a baby or bought a barbecue. In a world adrift in a glutinous substance called togetherness, we were often and stubbornly separate.

He had folded the paper open to an inside page and was pointing to an article, a few lines really, at the bottom. I took it from him and read. One of the two women who had accused nine young black men of rape in the infamous Scottsboro case, then changed her story and toured with the ILD on behalf of the boys, was dead.

I sat staring at the brief announcement for more time than it warranted.

"It seems there ought to be more," I said.

"She had her day in the sun."

"I wonder what she died of," I went on, though I was really wondering how she had lived.

I looked up and found Abel watching me. His head of thick dark hair was now nothing more than a close-cropped fringe of white, like a tonsure, or a halo. It gave him a misleadingly cherubic look. But his eyes, behind bifocals, were still watchful.

"You're not going into a teary mea culpa about this?"

I assured him I was not. I even kept my word. But I could not help doing a little research. I told myself I owed Ruby that much. In view of the books and articles I had written, and the places I had gone, and the people I had known, perhaps I owed her a great deal more, but I did not like to think about that.

I tracked down Ruby's brother and wrote to him, though I did not expect an answer. Ruby's siblings had turned their collective back on her a long time ago. The family had not had much affection for me either. So I was surprised when I got an answer from her sister.

"You won't be bothered with hearing from Ruby anymore," she wrote. "She's dead, like you heard."

The letter gave me confirmation. I was looking for explanation.

I tried to track down a death certificate with a series of polite but ineffectual southern voices. Finally, I called the Scottsboro *Daily Sentinel*. The first few people I spoke to were no help. Then I reached an older-sounding voice.

"Now, why does that name ring a bell?" he mused to himself.

I waited.

"Oh, yeah, now I remember. The tramp who accused those nine nig—those nine nigras of raping her. Well, you don't have to worry about her anymore. She's dead."

"I know that, but was there an obit?"

He laughed. "The gal wasn't exactly Scottsboro's favorite daughter. She wasn't even from hereabouts."

"The city clerk doesn't have a death certificate."

"Didn't die here either. But everybody knows she's dead. Her folks, everybody. It's a generally accepted fact. Ruby Bates is dead. She isn't going to be making no more trouble, nowhere, nohow."

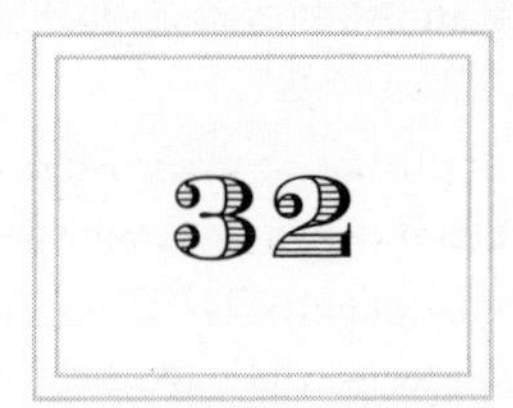

I received a telephone call from an Alabama newspaper reporter. He had learned, he said, that Birmingham attorney Arthur Hanes planned to file a multimillion-dollar suit on behalf of Ruby Bates against NBC for libel, slander, and invasion of privacy. In addition, he continued, there were rumors that a woman in southeast Tennessee claimed to be Victoria Price, and she was also planning to file a suit.

—*Dan T. Carter, in* Scottsboro: A Tragedy of the American South, *1976*

In pardoning Clarence Norris, 64 years old, Governor Wallace in effect acknowledged that Mr. Norris had never committed a crime.

—New York Times, *1976*

I'm not mad because the girl lied about me. If she's still living, I feel sorry for her because I don't guess she sleeps much at night.

—*Andy Wright, 1950*

1976

I seldom watch the morning news. I still prefer the crackle of paper, the smudge of newsprint, and the heft of the whole story with my coffee and toast. But I had turned on the television that morning while I dressed. Abel had already left the apartment. He had an early meeting with a woman who wanted to stage a revival of his first play. We tried not to live in the past, though the other night we had watched a program on television called *Judge Horton and the Scottsboro Boys*, based on an excellent book by a young history professor. Both the book and the program had struck us as remarkably accurate.

The name emanating from the television set stopped me on my way from dresser to closet. As the announcer went on to give a brief, though sufficiently eye-opening for the sleepy early-morning audience, report, I stood staring at the screen. I did not recognize her, but neither did I doubt her identity. Despite all reports to the contrary, Ruby Bates was alive, though not well, judging from the appearance of the woman beside the announcer. Her large cornflower-blue eyes were hidden behind Coke-bottle-thick, black-rimmed glasses. The small thin mouth she used to paint fat and red had shriveled to a pathetic hole in her lumpy face. Wattles swung from her chin. She looked ancient. I did the calculations. She was sixty-two, younger than I by nine years. She was also a walking advertisement for our society's failure to deliver decent health care, and eliminate enduring poverty, and redress unconscionable injustices, and for my complicity in that failure.

The camera moved from Ruby to the mountainous woman standing beside her. Her neck was thick, her arms massive, her face doughy. I did not recognize her either, but as soon as she opened her mouth, I knew who she was.

"They ruined my good name." The eyes stared directly into the camera. The voice was loud and spoiling for a fight. "They ruined my good name, and now they got to pay."

You could say one thing for Victoria Price. Unlike Ruby, she ran true to form.

The camera panned to Ruby again, and the reporter shoved the microphone in front of her face. She shied back. The fear in her eyes was wild enough to flash through the thick glasses. It was the first sign I had seen of the old Ruby.

"You were the first to file a multimillion-dollar suit against the National Broadcasting Company, Miss Bates. Does that mean you stand by your accusation that you were raped by the nine boys?"

She went on staring, wide-eyed and terrified, into the camera.

My God, Ruby, I wanted to shout at the screen, don't you remember anything I taught you? Don't just stand there. Answer the question. But she had slipped back into the old Ruby. Beneath the layers of flesh and age and illness, she was the girl the gang of angry, starved-for-excitement men had taken off the freight train that March afternoon forty-five years earlier. Now, it's a easy question, the leader of the posse had said. All you got to say is yes or no. Did them niggers rape you like they done to your friend or didn't they?

Yes, the terrified girl on the railroad siding had murmured.

"Yes," the old woman on the screen repeated.

Any guilt I might have felt for my treatment of Ruby over the years evaporated with that single affirmative word. Or was I merely looking for an excuse?

The forces whom Ruby and Victoria were determined to make pay for ruining their good names this time were NBC and Professor Dan T. Carter. Ruby and Victoria were claiming damages of several million dollars for libel, slander, and breach of privacy. I had not thought the program or the book it was based on libeled, slandered, or invaded their privacy, but then I am not a legal expert.

I telephoned Sam Leibowitz. We had kept in touch over the years.

"Last time it was the Jew lawyer from New York who was besmirching the honor of two southern women," he shouted into the phone. He was a justice of the New York Supreme Court now—one more Scottsboro success story—and had a reputation for stormy clashes with attorneys and other judges, and for harsh sentences. "This time around, it's the big New York, and you know that still means Jew, conglomerate that's taking advantage of two sick impoverished old women. You think things have changed? Think again. I saw an interview the other night with an Alabama writer. You know what he said? 'Nine black boys on a train with two white girls? It was the most logical thing in the world.' This is 1976, and they still think black men just can't help themselves! The only thing that surprises me is that the network didn't make sure those two tramps were dead."

I told him about the report of Ruby's death, and another a few years later of Victoria's. He dismissed them as hearsay, and I knew he was right. He never would have taken casual assurances on the matter. He would have done his homework. My first mistake, I realized now, was looking for Ruby Bates. She would have married.

I spent the day on the telephone. That was not much in exchange for forty years of neglect. I finally pieced together the outlines of the story.

After I had lost touch with Ruby, she had returned to Huntsville to live with her mother. Her family was not happy, but as one relative told the Birmingham *News*, it's not easy to turn your back on your children, regardless of what they've done. Despite her illness, she hung on doing odd jobs for a few years, then moved to the Yakima Valley in Washington State. She was finally taking her brother's advice and getting as far away from Scottsboro as she could. For two years, she worked as a migrant farmworker. The mills began to look good by comparison. She met a carpenter named Elmer Schut, a lanky man with a thin mouth, jug ears, and devilishly arched eyebrows. Ruby fell for the eyebrows. When they were married, she naturally took his name. Unlike me, she had no professional persona. Or rather the one she had was not one she wanted to hang on to. For good measure, she started telling people her first name was Lucille.

Victoria had a harder time finding true love. During the war, she took a third husband, or a fourth, depending on whether you believed her or her mother, but the match did not last. In the early fifties, she married a Tennessee sharecropper named Walter Dean Street. Like Ruby, she took her husband's name, and began calling herself Katherine Street.

My conviction that the Scottsboro girls were both dead was not an accident. Ruby and Victoria had done their best to bury them.

I knew she'd come. Elmer said he wouldn't lay no money on it, but I recollected them pictures she kept on the wall in her apartment back when I lived with her. A body set on suffering other folks' miseries ain't going to stay away from a dying woman. Least that's what I told her. Can't say it ain't the truth neither. My breathing ain't so good these days. And I can't get around like I used to. Me and Elmer are in a bad way. And we ain't got nothing to tide us over till we get the money from them TV folks. So I reckoned I couldn't lose nothing by calling her. Elmer said we don't have no money for no long-distance calls, but I told him I was fixing to reverse the charges.

"Ain't no way she's going to pay them," he said.

"Shows what you know," I come back at him.

I didn't even get a chance to ask for the money. She said she'd be on the next plane out to see me.

Abel thought I was crazy for going. "What difference does it make?" he asked. "They're all dead, except for Clarence Norris, and he's safe as long as he stays out of Alabama. Besides, this suit isn't about rape. It's about libel, slander, and invasion of privacy. She can cry rape as much as she likes and it won't make any difference."

"I just hate to see her do it."

He picked up the book he had been reading. He knew he could not argue with me about this.

I was watching at the window for the car. When it stopped in front of the house, I stepped back on account of I didn't want her to catch me spying. First thing I noticed when she got out was her gray hair. I reckoned with all her money she'd do something to fix that. Second was her shoes. All these years and she still ain't learned nothing. The yard was muddy. By the time she got to the steps, them shoes would be ruined for good.

I opened the door, and she come in, and stood staring at me for a spell, and I'd be lying if I said I wasn't near to crying, me and her coming face to face after all them years. Then she leaned over and kissed my cheek, like I seen folks do in movies and television. She smelled real good. I was glad I took a bath that morning.

She was trying not to look around the place, but I reckon she couldn't help herself. She probably never seen a dump like it since she come looking for me back then in Huntsville. I told her to set, and she did. I got to hand it to her. She still wasn't like them church and social services ladies, afraid she was going to catch something from setting in a chair.

"I suppose you're surprised to see me," she said.

"I reckon it ain't much of a surprise. You always turn up when you smell something cooking."

She didn't fancy that much.

"I'm here about you, Ruby, not me."

"Yeah, that's what you always say."

"Why did you lie again? Why did you say those men raped you?"

"On account of they did."

"You know that's not true. After all these years, after all the speeches you made, and they were good speeches, they were wonderful speeches, how can you turn around and tell the same old lie?"

"You set there in them nice shoes you got all muddied again and that fancy coat a body wouldn't never feel a chill in, and you ask me how I can tell a lie? I reckon you still ain't learned nothing. You ain't learned what it's like when kin turn their back on you for being a nigger-lover, and folks swear they're going stick by you and then don't give you the time of day no more, and you can't find no work, and you're too sick to do the work you can find. Now Elmer got emphysema, and I can't hardly walk no more, and the only thing worse than the doc's news is them bills the hospital keeps sending."

"Do you need money, Ruby?"

I could have laughed at that, excepting I didn't, on account of these days laughing just ends up in a coughing fit. "Take a look around. What do you think?"

She opened the fine-looking pocketbook she was holding in her lap. I never seen a alligator down home looked that pretty. "How much?"

"I reckon a thousand will tide us over for a spell."

She took out a checkbook and started writing. I reckon I could've kicked myself for not asking for two.

She handed me the check. I took it.

"Thanks," I said.

She didn't say nothing back.

"The way I see it, everybody got something out of Scottsboro excepting me. Folks say the Communist Party got a million dollars. That Jew lawyer ain't done bad for himself. You done pretty good too. Maybe you done better than any of them. Once I seen your picture in the paper with Mrs. Roosevelt. So I reckon this ain't charity. I reckon you owe me."

When I got back to New York, I told Abel about my visit to Ruby and the check I had given her.

He shook his head. "Guilt money."

I did not argue with him. The two words had always bound Ruby and me.

Ruby got her thousand dollars out of me, but she did not get her two and a half million from NBC. Six months after she brought the charges, Ruby Bates Schut was buried in a local cemetery beside her husband Elmer, who had died a week earlier. A few days later I saw her a few blocks from my apartment. I stopped to stare. The apparition was not Ruby, of course, just a woman in a thin coat and worn shoes asking passersby for money to buy a cup of coffee. I gave her five dollars.

A few days after Ruby's death, I flew to Alabama. Governor George Wallace, the man whose cry had been Segregation Forever, but who again had his eye on a presidential run and the more than four hundred thousand black Alabama voters created by the Voting Rights Act, had decided to pardon Clarence Norris, the only one of the nine young men taken off the train on March 25, 1931, who was still alive. The papers called him the last of the Scottsboro boys. He was sixty-four.

The governor's mansion was crawling with reporters, but Mr. Norris had agreed to give me an interview afterward, for old times' sake, he said. We talked in a lounge at the airport. He did not want to spend any more time in Alabama than necessary. He sat across from me, a dapper man in a gray suit and patterned tie, his blue top coat on the chair beside him, waiting for a flight to take him home to New York to his wife and two daughters.

I asked him if he thought the South had changed much.

He laughed and shook his head. "When I seen the crowd waiting for me on the tarmac out there, I told the man from the NAACP who come down with me, 'No way I'm getting off this plane. That's a lynch mob if I ever seen one.' 'Lynch mob,' he says. 'Those are your fans.' Same thing going down at the statehouse. Black and white all mixed up together. And all cheering for me, a black man." He shook his head again. "The women just couldn't stop grabbing at me. And after the governor give me my pardon, the attorney general took me out to lunch. There was a whole mess of us, whites and blacks setting down in the restaurant together. And not just any blacks. Black assistant attorney generals, and black lawyers, and a black member of the Alabama House of Representatives, and a black judge. We sure didn't see nothing like that back during the trials. And look at this."

He gazed around the antiseptic airport cocktail lounge. "Me and you setting here together, a white woman and a black man, drinking at the same table, and no one coming up to make trouble. That's one thing I never did think I'd live to see."

He also talked about how much had not changed.

"You know the first thing the governor says, when I walked into his office? 'Clarence Norris,' he says, 'how come black folk look so young when they get old?' Like that's supposed to make me feel better about all them years in prison. Like it's a compliment. Then one of the black guys in the meeting pipes up and says it's on account of we eat soul food—fried chicken and collard greens—and white folks eat beefsteak. The governor comes back and says he likes collards plenty. Used to eat them every morning for breakfast with cold coon."

He paused to let it sink in.

"Course, the North ain't much different. When I first got up to New York, I worked in sweatshops. Only jobs I could find, and I had to use my brother Willie's Social Security for that, on account of I was still a fugitive from the law in this here state of Alabama. The only thing worse than the job in them sweatshops was the way them white bosses, and they were the only whites in the place, played us blacks against them Spanish." He shook his head at the memory, then fell silent and sat staring into his drink. I could not be sure, but he looked as if he were smiling.

I asked what he was remembering.

He looked up, and under his trim mustache, his grin grew broader. He was the last surviving Scottsboro boy, but Governor Wallace was right. He did look young.

"I guess I know you long enough and times have changed enough so's I can tell you."

"Strictly off the record," I promised.

"It's pretty raw."

"I can take it," I assured him.

"When I got my first paycheck, up in Cleveland that was, for shoveling coal in a machine shop, I took it to a whorehouse." He paused. "Nothing special about that. Only this time I asked for a pretty white girl." He paused again. "I wanted to see what all the fuss was about."

"And did you?"

He shook his head. "What I seen was that the fuss was just one more white lie."

We were back to Ruby and Victoria and the men who had taken him off that train so many years ago.

Earlier in the day, a reporter had asked him if he was bitter.

"No," he said, "I'm just glad to be free."

Ruby was the one who was bitter. She had died still raging against her life, still fearing going to torment after her death, still lying. The lie had stolen freedom and manhood and years from Clarence Norris and Haywood Patterson and Charlie Weems and Olen Montgomery and Ozie Powell and Willie Roberson and Eugene Williams and Andy Wright and Roy Wright. It had snuffed out humanity in Ruby Bates and Victoria Price and all the generations who told it and all the millions who believed it. The lie was a murderous force, but the fight against the lie, that was something to live for.

Acknowledgments and Bibliographic Notes

Setting fictional characters loose among the ghosts of history is a dicey matter. I have tried to be true to the facts of the Scottsboro case and faithful to the spirit of the time and the significance of the events. For the facts, I am deeply indebted to two superb nonfiction accounts. *Scottsboro: A Tragedy of the American South*, by Dan T. Carter, is the definitive history of this unconscionable chapter in American history. *Stories of Scottsboro*, by James Goodman, is a brilliant study of the myriad voices and conflicting perceptions of the case. Three autobiographical volumes provided insight into the young men who became known as the Scottsboro boys: *Scottsboro Boy*, by Haywood Patterson and Earl Conrad; *The Last of the Scottsboro Boys*, by Clarence Norris and Sybil D. Washington; and *The Man from Scottsboro: Clarence Norris in His Own Words*, by Kwando Mbiassi Kinshasa.

The eyewitness accounts of Hollace Ransdall for the American

Civil Liberties Union and Mary Heaton Vorse for *The New Republic* proved invaluable for both understanding the events and creating the fictional character of Alice Whittier. Alice is a product of my imagination, but she could not have come into being without the writings of those two extraordinary women. Tad Bennicoff of the Seely G. Mudd Manuscript Library of Princeton University generously provided transcripts of Ransdall's reports, and the Southern Historical Collection of the University of North Carolina at Chapel Hill kindly made available an interview with Ransdall for the Southern Oral History Program.

John Wexley wrote a play about Scottsboro called *They Shall Not Die*, which inspired the play in the book, but Abel Newman, the man, is not based on John Wexley, the playwright.

Much of the trial testimony in the book is taken verbatim from the trial records. I am grateful to Nancy Moore and the Cornell Law Library, and to the Minnesota Law Library for access to the trial transcripts, and to Patrick Rayner for overcoming interlibrary loan obstacles. Karen L. Jefferson, Head of Archives & Special Collections of the Robert W. Woodruff Library of the Atlanta University Center, granted me access to a wealth of information and helped unearth particular items in the papers of the Commission on Interracial Cooperation and the Association of Southern Women for the Prevention of Lynching. The Schomburg Center for Research in Black Culture of the New York Public Library led me back to the records of the International Labor Defense. Bob Clark, archivist of the FDR Library in Hyde Park, generously helped me track down President Roosevelt's unobtrusive involvement in the case. And once again, I am especially beholden to Greg Gallagher of the Century Association library; Adrienne Fischier and James Harney of the Harvard Club of New York library; David Smith of the New York Public Library; and Mark Bartlett and the entire extraordinary staff of the New York Society Library for their enormous aid, continued support, and unfailing good humor.

I have relied heavily on Raymond Daniell's coverage of the trials for *The New York Times*, and I am grateful to Eden Ross Lipson for taking me behind the scenes at the paper to get a glimpse of the real Daniell. Many other friends helped with suggestions, insights, and sympathetic ears, and for all of that, my thanks go to Liza Bennett, Anne Eisenberg, Nimet Habachy, Joe Keiffer, Michelle Press, and Louise Shaffer. I am deeply grateful to Richard Snow and Fred Allen, superb editors, ace historians, and boon companions.

Once again, my greatest debt of gratitude is to my editor, Starling Lawrence, who makes me feel I can go out on a limb, if only to give him a good laugh when I fall off it; my agent, Emma Sweeney, whose enthusiasm, encouragement, and friendship I treasure; and my husband, Stephen Reibel, whom I owe more than I can say.

Afterword

I had a curious experience while writing *Scottsboro*. It occurred repeatedly. Like all novelists, I'm frequently asked what I'm working on, and when I answered Scottsboro, people invariably expressed their approval, even admiration. I was tackling a thorny and important issue. Then after a beat, they'd continue. "Refresh my memory. What was that about again?"

The word Scottsboro is iconic in American lore. Everyone knows it stands for a terrible racial injustice. But few, I discovered, knew the details of the horror, not merely how outrageous the crime against the boys was, but how deeply it convulsed the nation, how widely it reverberated around the world, and how it incited and exacerbated other prejudices.

The isms ran rampant. Racism was at the vicious heart of Scottsboro. Sexism, both veiled and overt, colored every aspect of it.

Anti-Semitism raged through and around it. Communism exploited it for propaganda purposes and helped save the boys' lives. Scottsboro is important not only in its own right, but also for what it tells us about America and its fault lines during a good part of the twentieth century.

The challenge for a novelist was finding an intimate way into the story. The fictional truth of Scottsboro lay at the intersection of historic events and individual lives.

Telling the tale through the eyes of the nine young men would leave no room for nuance. Their suffering was too acute, the crime committed against them too unspeakable. The reader might ache with their referred pain, but would fail to understand the forces that came together to inflict that pain. The story of Scottsboro was at once more complicated and more subtle.

I began to think about the others—lawyers, judges, journalists, social workers—who enlisted in the Scottsboro cause. Some risked their lives. Some also built their careers on the backs of those nine young men. Human motives are rarely as simple as they appear or as admirable as those who claim them would like to believe. Others, determined to railroad nine young men who were guilty of nothing more than being born black, had their own strongly held if odious beliefs. Perhaps the most intriguing character in the story was one of the two girls who cried rape, though none had occurred, then changed her mind and changed her mind again, repeatedly. Ruby Bates began whispering in my ear.

At first I resisted letting Ruby tell her story in her own southern-accented words. I dislike reading dialect; I couldn't imagine writing it. The fact that I was born and have lived all my life in the North would make getting her voice right even more difficult. And Ruby was a semi-literate part-time prostitute whose racism was matched only by her venality. She would make an excellent heavy, not an engaging narrator.

But Ruby, who was both perpetrator and victim, continued to nag at me. Her story was Scottsboro too, she insisted. Understanding her racism and venality was one of the keys to making sense of this cruel miscarriage of justice. Ruby's contradictions and uncertainties, her generous instincts and her appalling selfishness, her humanity and her inhumanity were the essential ingredients that gave rise to Scottsboro.

Ruby's story and those of the nine young Scottsboro boys and the others involved in the case met with somewhat different reactions on opposite sides of the Atlantic. Both British and American readers were outraged by the brutality and injustice. Who would not be? The British, many of whom had never heard of Scottsboro, thought it was important that the story be told. Some Americans, however, seemed more willing to let people forget. "Refresh my memory," people had said. "I know it was terrible, but do we have to keep talking about it?" one reader, the descendant of slave-owners, asked me.

ELLEN FELDMAN
2015

PICADOR CLASSIC

CHANGE YOUR MIND

PICADOR CLASSIC

On 6 October 1972, Picador published its first list of eight paperbacks. It was a list that demonstrated ambition as well as cultural breadth, and included great writing from Latin America (Jorge Luis Borges's *A Personal Anthology*), Europe (Hermann Hesse's *Rosshalde*), America (Richard Brautigan's *Trout Fishing in America*) and Britain (Angela Carter's *Heroes and Villains*). Within a few years, Picador had established itself as one of the pre-eminent publishers of contemporary fiction, non-fiction and poetry.

What defines Picador is the unique nature of each of its authors' voices. The Picador Classic series highlights some of those great voices and brings neglected classics back into print. New introductions - personal recommendations if you will - from writers and public figures illuminate these works, as well as putting them into a wider context. Many of the Picador Classic editions also include afterwords from their authors which provide insight into the background to their original publication, and how that author identifies with their work years on.

Printed on high quality paper stock and with thick cover boards, the Picador Classic series is also a celebration of the physical book.

Whether fiction, journalism, memoir or poetry, Picador Classic represents timeless quality and extraordinary writing from some of the world's greatest voices.

Discover the history of the Picador Classic series and the stories behind the books themselves at www.picador.com/classic